A LADY'S DOWNFALL

"Celia!" She heard Trevor's voice, but for a moment was incapable of answering. "That damned, bloody horse . . ." Strong arms gripped her shoulders for a moment, then began running with gentle expertise along her legs and arms.

"I—I am quite unharmed, I assure you!" Her voice came out ragged but determined. "There—there is no need to manhandle me!"

Trevor helped her stand, one hand beneath her elbow and the other firmly about her slender waist. He steadied her on her feet by the simple expedient of holding her against him.

"Thank you." She started to pull back, but his hands did not slacken their grip on her. Instead, she felt herself being drawn inexorably closer. She looked up in confusion, trying to fathom the fiery glow that lit his eyes.

Somehow, his face was all that she could see. He loomed closer to her, his eyes holding hers captive, preventing her from escaping—or even wanting to. Slowly—so slowly he seemed hardly to move—his mouth sought hers, exploring with a gentle, persuasive pressure that left her helplessly clinging to him. . . .

TANGLED WEB

2.50

TANGLED WEB

BY JANICE BENNETT

ZEBRA BOOKS
KENSINGTON PUBLISHING CORP.

ZEBRA BOOKS

are published by

Kensington Publishing Corp.
475 Park Avenue South
New York, NY 10016

First printing: February 1988

Printed in the United States of America

Oh, what a tangled web we weave,
When first we practise to deceive!
Sir Walter Scott
from *Marmion*

CHAPTER ONE

A stunned silence greeted Sir Roderick Marcombe's dramatic pronouncement. His elegant figure shifted slightly against the wine velvet upholstery of his massive desk chair, but his eyes, of a clear, piercing brown, never left his granddaughter's face.

Miss Celia Marcombe stared at him in shock, then broke into a musical peal of laughter. "You are the most complete hand, Grandfather!" she exclaimed, amusement rippling in her voice. "For a moment, I honestly believed you to be serious!"

"I am," came the calm reply.

The merriment faded from her eyes and she regarded the stern-featured countenance of the elderly man who sat opposite her across the heavy mahogany desk in the bookroom. Her last traces of lurking humor vanished. She shook her head slowly, and her pretty mouth worked twice before she gained sufficient command over her voice.

"You—you cannot mean it!" It was little more than a gasp, and she swallowed to steady herself. She turned to Miss Elizabeth Westerly, her companion cum chaperone who sat discreetly withdrawn in a corner, seeking some clue from her that this was all nothing but a jest.

The woman's plain, angular countenance mirrored Celia's own horror and revulsion at the decree which Sir Roderick Marcombe had just laid down. Her hand remained suspended in midair, her fingers still clutching a needle. This, she slowly lowered, along with her embroidery hoop, into her lap.

"Oh, Celia," Miss Westerly cried softly, dismay causing her gentle voice to quaver. Such a thing should not befall a lady of such tender years as her beloved charge. It was monstrous! Easy tears filled her gentle gray eyes.

Miss Marcombe shook her head, warning her companion to silence. This was no hoax, then. Her grandfather was in earnest. She turned back to him, her movement causing a dark ringlet to creep forward across her face. She swept it back with long, graceful fingers. "I—I won't do it, of course," she informed him on a half-laugh that sought to deny the truth.

"You will," Sir Roderick Marcombe declared calmly. He drew a small enameled box from the pocket of his smooth-fitting mulberry coat of Bath cloth and with a practiced grace, helped himself to a pinch of snuff. One hand brushed lightly across the intricate folds of his starched neckcloth to free any particles that might be clinging to its pristine crispness. He regarded the slender young girl, a touch of amusement lighting his determined eyes. "You will do as you are told, miss."

Miss Westerly drew in an audible breath. "Oh,

Cousin Roderick!" she exclaimed impetuously. "You—you cannot be in earnest!"

Sir Roderick ignored her, as he did all too frequently. His lips twisted slightly as he observed his granddaughter's mixed reaction to his last words.

Celia's fingers clenched on the arms of her chair. Part of her still wanted to laugh at the absurdity of the situation, to treat it as the joke it ought to be. Her high spirits, however, rebelled at such a high-handed and inconsiderate method of settling her future. He had not even had the courtesy of discussing the matter with her! She took a firm hold on herself, keeping her mercurial temper under tight control.

"The whole thing is ludicrous!" she informed him with a finality in which she hoped he would believe. Her defiant eyes met his firm, steady gaze, which belied her reason, warning her this was all too true. She took a deep breath. "You cannot possibly expect me to go through with anything so—so preposterous!"

His eyebrows raised in mild surprise. "I can and I do, my dear. I may dispose of my property as I choose."

"I am not your 'property'!" she declared roundly, her outrage at this statement momentarily getting the better of her. "I'm your granddaughter!"

He raised a hand, shrugging. "The same thing," he replied calmly.

Celia leaned back against the soft cushion of the wing chair in which she sat and gazed at the elderly gentleman in fascinated horror. "You honestly expect me to submit tamely to . . ." She broke off, shaking her head slowly. "Papa would never have permitted—

or even suggested—such an odious scheme!"

His thin smile was genuinely amused. "I do not suppose he would. You have been allowed far too much license, my girl. High time you were broken to bridle, and that is a task demonstrably far beyond the capabilities of our good Cousin Elizabeth. It only makes me more certain than ever that I am right in not pitchforking you into the Marriage Mart. Run off with some fortunate hunter, sure as like." He regarded her through half-lowered eyes. "No, my dear, you will do as you are told."

Celia rose from her chair, the smooth silk of her dove gray gown of half-mourning rustling slightly at her unsteady stride. The conflicting urges to scream and to laugh at her grandfather vied within her. Neither would help. To defy him would only make him more adamant, while laughter would leave him unmoved. His sense of the ridiculous tended to work only in his own favor. And at the moment, she herself was beginning to find it rather difficult to see the funny side of this. She crossed the long library to the French windows that opened onto the formal rose garden. There she paused, her slight frame trembling with her erratic emotions.

An enchanting scene stretched out before her unseeing eyes. Neatly raked gravel paths separated sections of green lawn that were bordered by carefully pruned and tended rose bushes. Blossoms of pink, yellow, and red were scattered profusely among these, and their delicate fragrance wafted through the air on the soft spring breeze.

Miss Westerly laid aside her embroidery and stood, running smoothing fingers over the wrinkles in her black bombazine round gown. She felt so inadequate, but made a valiant effort to rise to the occasion. She moved to join her charge and laid a soothing hand on her arm, striving to find something to say that might help a hopeless situation.

Celia spun around suddenly, her large brown eyes flashing with a burst of spirit. "I won't marry someone just because it's convenient for you." She stressed the last word.

"Temper, my dear." Sir Roderick continued to regard her with an infuriating amusement, as if she were a child refusing to go to bed.

"I won't!" She almost stamped her foot in frustration. She took a rapid turn about the room, stopping again to stare blindly out over the roses. Losing her temper would do her no good. Anger, as she well knew, never moved the stubborn old man. But he was kindhearted under all, with an honest affection for her, and pity might cause him to reconsider where her rantings would only stiffen his back. She bit her lip, took a very deep breath, then allowed her shoulders to droop with a despondent air.

"I won't," she repeated, but this time it was without heat, almost a whisper. "I—I cannot possibly marry a man I have never even met."

"Well, you shall meet him," said Sir Roderick, quite reasonably. "This afternoon."

"What?" Startled, Celia's feigned dejection dropped away from her in a flash. This was suddenly taking on a frightening element of immediacy.

Sir Roderick ignored the interruption, addressing himself instead to Miss Westerly. "The wedding can wait for a few months, I suppose. That should give you time enough to prepare her."

"But—but do you think . . . ?" his cousin Elizabeth began, bravely steeling herself for a confrontation with a man whose mere frown could reduce her to stammering incoherence.

"This afternoon!" Celia broke in, her mind still occupied with her grandfather's previous comment. "He is coming here?"

"I have invited him to stay for a se'nnight," Sir Roderick nodded with a complacency that penetrated Celia's shaky, tenuous control, shattering it into fragments.

"No!" she cried, trying to deny his words. "I won't see him. I—I shall have nothing to do with him!" Her voice rose on a note of panic that was not altogether assumed. "You cannot make me marry some—some stranger!"

"But I can." The amusement faded from Sir Roderick Marcombe's eyes, to be replaced by a deliberate determination. "Come now, my dear," he continued more persuasively. "I am not such an ogre as all that, you know. I would not have my only grandchild marry a man who was not honorable and good. Lord Ryde will make you an excellent husband."

"And a good manager for your estate," she threw back at him, her full lips tightening, revealing the anger that had at last taken over.

"And a good manager for my estate," he agreed. "I am growing old, child, and Trevor—Lord Ryde—has helped me before, when I have been ill. He knows the estate, he knows my people. He will keep it in trust for your children."

"If he has been here so much, why have I never met

him?" she threw back at him. "I have lived here now for nineteen months!"

Sir Roderick's brow lowered slightly. "He has had . . . other projects that have kept him away."

"Away from an estate in which he has been so involved?" she asked with feigned sweetness. "You surprise me."

"You will not sneer at him, my girl," Sir Roderick ordered. "His work has been for the government, and it has taken him into some dangerous situations, even into France. But he has come home now, at last."

France? She dismissed it from her mind, refusing to be impressed by hints of intrigue or heroism. That aspect of his life did not concern her. Service to his country did not lessen the disservice he did her.

"I thought—your godson," she said, not able to bring herself to say his name, "had just inherited an estate of his own. Why should he want yours as well? Or is he just naturally grasping?"

"Unworthy, my dear," Sir Roderick Marcombe chided her. "It is the money I am offering that he needs now, although I daresay he could manage without it. He is a man to be reckoned with."

"I suppose nearly a thousand acres and an excellent home farm have nothing to do with it."

Sir Roderick smiled again. "He is a very capable young man. He will take them, but he does not need them. What is more important is that I trust him. When I am gone, I know he will look after what is mine as I would myself, as if it were his by blood."

She focused on the earlier part of this speech. "If he is so capable, why does he need money?"

"You have yet to see his estates," he explained, a

bitter note rising in his voice. "The property has been let go to ruin, mismanaged for generations, milked for every cent it could produce, and not a groat put back into it. The house is practically tumbling about him. It will take a fortune to set all to rights."

"And this is what you wish for me?" she demanded, her indignant humor momentarily struggling to the surface.

He smiled at that, but did not rise to the fly. "He never expected to come into the title and estate, or I suppose he would have inspected it earlier. Came as quite a surprise to him."

"Honey fall, you mean," Celia interpolated.

"Not in the least. He is as careless of convention as you seem to be, and cares nothing for the barony. And as for Hastings, the estate, that can only be considered a liability. He has inherited a mountain of debt. And the tenanted farms are almost as bad. No, it will take a number of years and a great deal of money to make the place productive again—to make it what it should be."

Celia was silent for a moment as she considered the extent of the new Lord Ryde's liabilities. "Surely there must be other ways of getting money than marrying it," she said with disdain.

"Of course there are. He marries you as a favor to me."

This time she did stamp her foot. "Do you think no one would marry me for my own sake?" she demanded.

For a moment, Sir Roderick considered the vibrant little face with its dark, flashing eyes. "Oh, undoubtedly, my dear. But the fact that you are a considerable heiress tends to intrude on the mind." His voice held only apology. "It would be difficult to eliminate the fortune hunters from those who paid you court. But that is not to the point. I wish Trevor to be the one to take over my estates."

"Then let him!" she exclaimed. She took another deep breath, forcing herself to be calm, to think more rationally. "There is no reason for you to involve me in your plans for the estate."

"But there is. All that I have is tied up here in Ranleigh, and shall remain so for my descendants. I cannot provide for you outside of it." He paused, and his eyes strayed momentarily to the drab figure of Miss Westerly. "It is no pleasant thing being a penniless female. There is very little chance for marriage. A dowry, as our good cousin can tell you, is vital." He paused, allowing his words to sink in.

Elizabeth averted her face as soft color warmed her cheeks. His words were all too true, though he could not know the full extent of the drudgery and bleakness that all too often marked the life of a poverty-stricken lady of quality. She herself might be condemned to it, but Celia must not be! She would do everything in her power to prevent it!

"Trevor will take care of both you and Ranleigh for me," Sir Roderick went on to his granddaughter. "And now, I have work to do." He picked up a pen, toying idly with it for a moment. "Trevor will arrive late this afternoon, I should think. You will wear your new sprigged muslin, and be pleasant to him." He held her eyes for a moment, then turned his attention to the stack of papers that lay piled on the desk before him. "Cousin Elizabeth, see to it that she is ready. You may both go now."

Celia stood her ground, momentarily speechless. It hurt deeply, more than she would have guessed, to have her feelings and wishes held of so little account. Her grandfather now seemed oblivious to her presence as he read one of the papers with care.

"And if I refuse?" she asked at last, trying to hold her voice level.

"You won't," he replied calmly, not bothering to raise his eyes from his work. "You have not met him yet, you know. You may close the door as you leave," he added pointedly.

Elizabeth Westerly glanced at her charge's fiery expression and deemed it time to coax her out. Nothing could be accomplished at the moment except to set up the old man's back. She scurried to her corner and collected her workbag, then crossed to the door and held it open, watching Celia with an anxious eye.

With an exclamation of mingled frustration and distress, Celia spun about and ran from the room. Elizabeth followed, and the heavy bookroom door swung closed hard behind them and startled the footman who stood at attention in the Great Hall.

Celia hurried on ahead, across the marble mosaic floor to the main staircase with its dark cherrywood railings that gleamed from constant polishing. The carpeted stairs she mounted at a most unladylike gait. At the top of the second flight she took the first turning, then ran down the long picture-gallery, past the painted likenesses of generations of Marcombes long gone.

Leaving this area, she entered the original Tudor

portion of the building. Here, she headed toward the back of the sprawling house and descended the short flight of steps that brought her to her own apartment. She thrust open the door and closed it behind her with a satisfying slam.

A small brindle cat looked up from its curled position on the cushioned seat that ran the length of the mullioned bay. It blinked sleepy eyes. Celia crossed over and dropped down beside it, then scooped the furry armful onto her lap. She sighed deeply as she leaned forward slightly to rest her forehead against the paned glass and gaze out. Idly, she stroked the animal into a state of purring ecstasy.

Her window presented a charming prospect of rolling green sward, edged on the far side by a wood that bordered a stream. Usually this tranquil, sun-drenched panorama held her entranced, but today she stared out upon it as if it were a strange entity, realizing what the beloved estate was about to do to her.

A soft tap sounded on her door, which opened almost immediately. Miss Elizabeth Westerly stepped into the room, her gentle, troubled gray eyes resting on the huddled figure of her charge.

"I don't know whether to laugh, scream, or cry," Celia said without looking up. "This whole situation is ridiculous. I cannot marry someone for no other reason than to allow him to inherit the property." She turned her head to meet her chaperone's worried eyes. "I can hardly believe it! To be—to be bartered off for the estate, forced into marriage as a condition of giving Ranleigh to his godson!" She shook her head, still not able to accept that such a thing could really happen to her.

"It is like something out of *Marmion,"* Miss Westerly agreed. "Romantic tragedy is best left within the pages of a book."

Celia considered Scott's latest poem for a moment, and could not help but smile at the appropriateness of the lines to which Elizabeth referred. *"Her kinsman bade her give her hand To one who loved her for her land,"* she quoted. "It is exactly like *Marmion,* is it not? But I promise you, dear Elizabeth, I shall not retaliate by entering a nunnery, as Claire did. I shall find another way to avoid this marriage."

Miss Westerly sank down on the long bench beside her and reached across, taking Celia's hand in a comforting squeeze. "It will do you no good to openly defy your grandfather, my love."

Celia closed her eyes, her spark of liveliness yielding to the disturbing reality. Unconsciously, she cradled the unprotesting cat closer. "I know. He is not a man you can cross—easily. He has a rather disturbing habit of getting his own way. But this time he will not! He cannot. I am not his 'property', and I will not be treated that way, no matter what he says. I will not be bought or sold!"

"It would have been wiser, perhaps, for your grandfather to allow you and Lord Ryde to meet before informing you of his intention," Elizabeth said thoughtfully. "But it is useless to reflect on should-have-beens. We must deal with the actuality."

"And it is a very disturbing one, indeed," Celia informed her, sitting up and facing back into the room. "You are right. *Why* did he not allow us to meet first, and then suggest the marriage? Is there something wrong with this Lord Ryde?" She stared at her companion without seeing her, trying to fathom her grandfather's reasoning. "I suppose he knows it would make no difference to me, either way. I could never agree to such a marriage. But, oh, Elizabeth, it is the way he settled it, as a purely business arrangment, that makes me so angry! Surely even the meekest and most biddable female alive would object to being made party to a land transaction!"

Miss Westerly managed a slight smile. "You are certainly neither meek nor biddable, my dear."

Celia twisted her fingers in her silken skirts, forming deep, sharp creases and wrinkles. "I could never like—or respect—a man who would agree to such a cold-blooded marriage!" She turned the full force of her large, disturbed eyes on Miss Westerly. "What sort of paltry man would be party to such a deal?"

"Your grandfather belongs to an older generation," Elizabeth reminded her. "Arranged marriages were quite the norm when he grew up, I believe."

"Well, that is no excuse for this godson of his." She thought for a moment. "Do you suppose he is weak, and lets himself be dominated by Grandfather's stronger will? Or is he merely heartless and grasping? He is only agreeing to marry me so he can obtain control of a very valuable estate."

"You don't know his reasons," Elizabeth pointed out. "Do you not think you should reserve judgement until you have met him?"

Celia sighed. "I know. Poor Elizabeth. My unruly temper." She tried to force a smile. "I am probably being every bit as unreasonable as Grandfather. But it really is the outside of enough for him to actually expect me to accept this—this business arrangement of his! And try as I might, I cannot think of a single reason why a man should agree to marry a girl he has never met. Ranleigh, and the money, can be the sole temptation, and I can only despise him for that!"

"There are far worse fates for a female than an arranged marriage," Elizabeth said softly.

Celia turned a considering eye on her companion, and experienced a stab of guilt at her selfish preoccupation. The life of a penniless but gently bred female, forced to earn her own livelihood, could be no pleasant thing. There was no chance for love or a family, only the grim prospect of genteel servitude, caring for a more fortunate woman's offspring. She was even denied the hope of ever having children of her own.

But to submit to a marriage with a man she held in contempt . . . The thought sickened her. There could be no happiness for her in that. Perhaps she was an air-dreamer, but she longed for a man she could look up to and esteem, who would be proud and dignified, with a will and determination stronger than her own, yet reasonable, gentle—and loving.

As yet, her fate had not been sealed. And she would not surrender, not give up her dreams without a fight!

She turned back to the window, staring thoughtfully out. "This would never have happened to me while Papa was alive," she said at last. "He had the courage to defy Grandfather."

"I don't believe I ever met your parents," Elizabeth commented, encouraging any change of subject.

"We never lived at Ranleigh," Celia told her. "Papa liked town life, so we had a house in London. He was always laughing. . . ." She broke off as the remembered grief engulfed her.

Her father's jovial countenance had been his livelihood, as it was for many gamesters. Mr. Gregory Marcombe had married in defiance of his father, never expecting to be denied an income from the family fortune. But Sir Roderick, even then, had ruled with an iron hand and cut his only child off without a penny for support. Gregory had contrived quite well by his wits and determination, and with the help of his wife's meager portion had managed to establish his family creditably. His son had attended Eton and Oxford, then purchased a commission in the Navy when Napoleon's fleet had become a menace. His daughter he had provided with an excellent governess who, while instilling in her pupil every accomplishment necessary for a young lady of quality, had quite failed to teach her to govern her volatile and too-often mischievous spirits.

"My—my parents died together," Celia added, trying to fill the silence she had created.

"A carriage accident, was it not?" Elizabeth prompted gently in an attempt to divert the girl's troubled mind into a reminiscent vein.

Celia nodded, recognizing her companion's well-intentioned purpose. It would give her a chance to calm down, order her thoughts, perhaps find a new approach to her problem.

"It was nineteen months ago. They were lucky in a way, you know. They were so devoted to each other, I—I cannot imagine one trying to live on without the other. Papa was right to defy Grandfather in his choice of a spouse." She shook her head, for she was back to where she had started. "And so am I. I must defy him, too."

"It—it is one thing for a man to break from his family and manage on his own," Elizabeth said. "A female cannot easily—or safely!—free herself from her protectors and means of support. For a defenseless, penniless girl, of remarkable beauty and fiery temper, to venture forth on her own. . . ." Elizabeth shuddered at the probable outcome.

Celia firmly squelched a laugh at hearing herself so described. She rose from the seat, dislodging the indignant cat as she did so. Crossing the large, elegantly appointed chamber, she stared into the beveled glass mirror that hung above the ornately carved dressing table. Her large brown eyes gazed back at her, shadowed with worry.

"Your grandfather believes he is doing his best for you, you know." Miss Westerly gathered up the animal and proceeded to soothe it. Her eyes, filled with sympathy, rested on Celia.

"I do know," the girl agreed ruefully. "It—it is just that he does not truly know me, if he thinks I could ever find such an arrangement acceptable!"

There was a very good chance that this was true. They had met for the first time nineteen months ago, and her grief at her bereavement had left her numb and docile, not caring what became of her. He might not be aware of the strength of her character or the liveliness of her mind, for she had not, until this very day, given many signs of it.

So listless had she been, in fact, that she had suffered without complaint the chaperonage of her grandfather's eldest sister, Miss Aurelia Marcombe.

Raised by the most rigid tenets, this stern and unbending lady looked upon any form of levity as a sin and had a habit of quoting Scripture upon every opportunity in the hopes of edifying her charge. Guiltily, Celia reflected that she had not been sorry when the old woman died nine months ago—her only real regret had been that this sad event caused her to return to deep mourning. And now, with no respite, to come to this!

"Am I unreasonable to want a say in determining my future, in choosing my own husband?" Celia asked. "*Was* I allowed too much license when I was growing up?"

Elizabeth was silent. Celia returned to her seat in the bay window and gazed out across the wide expanse of lawn of several long minutes.

"No," Elizabeth said at last. "But we cannot all have life just the way we would like it. Sometimes you just have to accept what you get, then—then make the best of it."

Celia grasped Elizabeth's hand, giving it a quick squeeze. "I am so glad Grandfather found you to be my chaperone."

This last was true in every sense. Elizabeth, at nine-and-twenty, had worked as a governess for almost thirteen years. The air of gentle authority she had developed over this time worked a soothing effect on Sir Roderick, and he had at last been persuaded to relax some of the more confining restrictions that his elderly sister had placed on Celia. More than that, though, Celia had found a friend and confidant in Elizabeth.

"If only Charlie had not been killed. I—I could use

a brother to protect me now." Celia made an attempt at her usual humor.

"He died at Trafalgar, did he not?" Elizabeth asked. "A terrible battle that must have been. So many good and noble men, surrendering their lives for their country."

Celia nodded, almost smiling at her companion's dramatic statement. "My only brother lost at sea," she agreed. "They—they never even recovered his body, you know. And Jonathon wounded so badly he will limp all his life." Slowly, her head came up. "Jonathon!" she repeated softly. "I do have someone to protect me! Jonathon!"

"Captain Edelston?" Elizabeth asked, perplexed. "Would he be able to help you?"

"Yes!" Celia stood, then began to pace slowly about the room, a gleam of hope lighting her eyes. "I must think!"

Jonathon, Charlie's best friend, her self-appointed elder brother. He would help her, if she could only decide how. She had not actually seen him since just after the accident that claimed her parents, but his letters arrived periodically, full of his good humor and concern for her, brightening her days. He would never stand for her being married off in such an intolerable fashion.

Then the idea came to her, so absurdly simple yet so absolutely outrageous that it took her breath away.

"Elizabeth!" She spun back to face her companion. "What would Grandfather do if there were another suitor for my hand?"

"I—I believe he has made up his mind that you shall marry Lord Ryde."

"But if our affection is of long standing, and approved of by my parents?" Celia persisted.

"Is it? I mean, is there one?" Elizabeth asked, confused. "Who?"

"Jonathon," came the firm reply.

"But. . . ." With difficulty, Elizabeth mastered her bewilderment. "Forgive me, but is he not a great deal older than you? You are not even nineteen. I had thought him the same age as your brother."

"He is. He has just turned thirty. But I have known him all my life, and he has always loved me. He—he told me that he promised Charlie as he lay dying that he would marry me!" she extemporized swiftly, fearing her chaperone's disbelief. For this hazy, half-formed plan to work, Elizabeth must be completely convinced that it was not a hoax.

"But he—he has not come forward since you were old enough to marry, has he?"

"Yes, when my parents died, but I was only sixteen then, you know, and in mourning. We agreed we must wait. But in his last letter he said that he wished to come and see me, so I am sure he means to claim me at last!" Celia held her breath, afraid that she had become carried away, afraid that Elizabeth would suspect the unlikeliness of so lame a statement.

Mercifully, it passed over the woman's bemused head. "But . . . but your grandfather . . . Ranleigh. . . ."

"If I am already engaged, that will make everything quite different," Celia declared with a confidence she was far from feeling. "Lord Ryde can hardly press his suit in the face of my previous attachment. And Jonathon will not demand a dowry. Grandfather may leave Ranleigh where he will! I shall be quite all right without it." She could only hope this last was true.

"It would seem a most peculiar circumstance if he were to leave such a large estate to someone not of his family," Elizabeth protested. "Or if your Captain Edelston did not insist on it for your dowry. It—it may be indelicate of me to say this, but Ranleigh is a very large and profitable estate, and the house is mentioned in almost every guidebook to the historic and noble homes."

"Jonathon will ask for no dowry," Celia repeated with certainty. "And as for appearing odd in leaving all to his godson, Grandfather will not care a fig for that."

Celia turned away, her plans beginning to solidify. Jonathon would not let her down. He would come, of that she was sure. He would do whatever she asked of him. He would pretend to be her suitor, act a part to save her, get her away from her grandfather and . . . She quailed, but only for a moment. It was shocking of her to use the good-natured Jonathon so dreadfully, but her only other choice was to go through with a farce of a marriage, and that she could not do! Anything, even foisting herself onto Jonathon's mother for protection, was better than being bartered for the estate.

She could rely on the Edelstons. And she would not be alone and penniless on the streets, as her grandfather prophesized, if she disobeyed him. She would have a respectable place to stay, and she had some inheritance from her parents, though she was not sure just how much it amounted to. It would be enough. It had to be.

Even if in the end she had to go as a governess, like Elizabeth, at least she would have retained her self-respect. She was doing the right thing. She repeated this to herself, and knew it was the truth. If she married Lord Ryde—or anyone, for that matter—at her grandfather's bidding, she would only despise her husband, and eventually herself, as well. Such a marriage would be a disaster. Her only chance for happiness lay in thwarting this plan.

"I—I must send for Jonathon immediately," she declared. With quick strides, she crossed to the small tambour writing desk that stood against the wall. From a drawer she pulled a sheet of elegant, pressed writing paper, delicately scented with violets. She selected a pen, then paused, glancing at the small clock that stood on the mantel. She would have to be quick about it. If she took the time to explain her difficulties, the mail coach would have come and gone before she could reach the village.

Hurriedly, she scribbled an urgent plea for help and signed her name. She dusted the sheet with sand, folded it, inscribed the address and sealed it with a wafer. This done, she turned to Miss Westerly.

"Help me change into my habit, please, Elizabeth! I have not a moment to lose. This *must* be on today's mail coach, if Jonathon is to reach me in time."

"What will you tell your grandfather?" her companion demanded, almost wringing her hands in her distress at this turn of events.

"Nothing, at the moment. I shall wait for Jonathon."

"But Lord Ryde is coming, this afternoon!"

Celia laid down the letter and started to unfasten

her gown. “Yes, Lord Ryde.” An imp of mischief suddenly replaced the cold anger she felt for her grandfather’s heartless partner in this detestable scheme for her future. He deserved to be punished for being willing to sell his title to obtain Ranleigh!

“When I have sent this letter,” Celia said softly, “I must prepare to meet him, mustn’t I?”

CHAPTER TWO

"Celia, I beg of you, consider!" Elizabeth pleaded, distraught. "Are you quite sure of what you are doing?"

"Yes, I am. Elizabeth, do you not see? I—I love Jonathon. You cannot expect me to marry someone else, can you? Particularly someone I do not even know?"

Elizabeth gave an audible gasp. "Do—do you love him?" she asked, uncertain.

"Very much." That much was true, at least, she told her guilty conscience by way of a sop—though her feelings were those of a sister for a brother. That part she did not feel it incumbent upon herself to explain. All that was necessary was that Elizabeth should believe her, truly believe that she wished to marry Jonathon, so that her grandfather might be taken in by the plot and not force her to marry Lord Ryde.

"Please help me," she begged. "The mail coach will be coming any time now, and this letter must be on it! I have not a moment to lose if I am to—to secure my happiness!" She was overplaying again. She would have to watch herself; already she was sinking into the depths of melodrama and her little farce was less than an hour old! With hands that shook both from hurry and nerves, Celia dragged off her silken gown.

Elizabeth hesitated, torn between devotion to her charge and duty to her employer. She owed her cousin Roderick loyalty, not a betrayal of his trust. How angry he would be if—when—he learned of her deceitful nature! He would turn her off without a character, and it would be no more than she deserved! But her beloved Celia . . . Refusing to think further, she turned to the ornately carved clothes cupboard and brought out a riding habit of dark green velvet.

Celia pulled this garment over her head, then allowed her chaperone to do up the fastenings. The modish beaver that matched her habit she placed on top of her dusky curls and ruthlessly tucked in strays at random. Elizabeth unearthed her boots from the back of the cupboard and helped her into them. At last, Celia snatched up her gloves and letter and slipped quietly from the room, leaving Elizabeth to seek comfort from the brindle cat.

The hall below was empty as she descended the staircase, but still she moved cautiously so that her booted feet made as little noise as possible. Melodrama again, she told herself in disgust, and forced her steps to continue at a more normal pace. She could not, however, keep from holding her breath as she passed the bookroom door behind which her grandfather worked. She had gone no more than three steps beyond it when that door opened, and she whirled around in dismay.

"Oh, miss." A young maid bobbed a curtsy. "Sir Roderick asked me to tell you that tea will be put off until after his guest has arrived." The girl's bright, eager eyes regarded Celia with avid speculation. Apparently, the whole household knew the reason for the visit. Celia's anger swelled at being the object of servant-hall gossip.

"Thank you," she replied at her most quelling. "If my grandfather wants me, I am going for a ride. You may assure him I shall be back on time."

Turning on her heel, she made her way down the passage toward the kitchens, the shortest route to the stable. Only one scullion was in view, scouring out the massive, scorched kettle that hung near the cavernous hearth.

She wove her way through the large, cluttered room and let herself silently out the far door. Crossing the herb garden that the cook swore had been laid out in Elizabethan times, she entered the cobbled courtyard of the spacious stable. A startled groom, engaged in cleaning a bit, jumped to his feet as she approached.

"I didn't get no message you was wishful to ride, miss," he said, his tone almost defensive.

"I didn't send one, Jem. Saddle Whimsy for me, please."

The groom, a slight, elderly man—long in Sir Roderick's service and by now quite familiar with Celia's lengthy, restless, and occasionally tempestuous rides—regarded her with suspicion. "Yes, miss. Will we be gone long?"

Not just the house servants. Even the grooms seemed to know what was planned for her! She fought down her anger, knowing it was not Jem's fault. "Only to the village," she told him, giving him a coaxing smile. "I want this letter to catch the mail coach, and

I need a good ride."

The man nodded. "Certainly, miss." He set the bit down on the bench and hurried off along the long rows of stalls.

Celia breathed a sigh of relief. She did not particularly wish this expedition to come to her grandfather's ears, as it surely would if Jem suspected there was anything odd or unusual about it. With luck, the need for the groom to mention it would never come up.

Two horses were saddled and bridled in a trice. Jem led forward a tall, restive black gelding and tossed Celia lightly up into the saddle. While she arranged her skirts over the pommel, he swung himself up on his own mount, and they rode out through the arched stone gateway. Just beyond this, Celia turned to enter a field and urged her eager mount into a canter toward the narrow lane which wound along the course of a stream.

Several minutes passed before she slackened her impassioned pace, her temper almost spent. Here, trees lined their route, shading them from the hot sun, and the simple beauty of the lacy patterns of sunlight and darkness that fell across the road worked their magic on her. When she rode she was free, at least for a little while, and she could forget . . . . She slowed her horse to a brisk trot as they passed a lumbering farm cart, and raised a hand in greeting as she recognized one of her grandfather's workers driving the weatherworn vehicle.

The ride to the village was not a long one, but it provided ample time for her to review her impetuous course of action. She was not thinking clearly, she knew. Her grandfather's decree had come as a severe shock to her, and she still suffered from a benumbed reaction to it. One thing stood out in her mind, though, of which she had no doubt. Only misery could result from her obeying him, from her marrying a man who would so meekly do as her grandfather ordered.

They approached the outskirts of the village and, at last, reined in before the tiny inn that served the mail coaches. With one last tug at her conscience for involving Jonathon in her troubles, she released the letter into Jem's waiting hand, then held his horse while he disappeared inside. He returned almost immediately.

"We're in time, miss," he informed her as he received his bridle back from her. "It's not due to arrive for nigh on half an hour yet."

Celia turned her horse toward home, breathing deeply of the clear, flower-scented air. She had taken the first step down what she feared would be a difficult path, but it was a path she must tread if she were ever to find any happiness in her future. She rode on, lost in thought, trying to formulate her next move.

She would have to bring up Jonathon's name today, to begin preparing Sir Roderick for his arrival and subsequent request to marry her. She would figure out how to get out of that later, when the time came. Avoiding one marriage at a time was all she could handle.

And once Jonathon came, she would have his support. Her heart warmed for the first time that day. Dear Jonathon. He would probably enjoy his role of knight errant immensely. She only hoped he would not overplay his part of eager suitor and arouse her grandfather's suspicions.

They continued in silence, Celia's thoughts of Jonathon leading naturally to memories of her brother Charlie. So unlike they had been, yet inseparable to the very end. She swallowed the lump that forced its way into her throat. If only Charlie had not died! Then her grandfather would have the heir he so ardently desired. Lord Ryde could disappear back into the shadowy mystery of his dealings in France, and no one would miss him—least of all her! But Charlie was not alive, and Lord Ryde was no longer engaged in intrigues on the Continent. He was bearing down upon her at this very moment, bent on destroying the secure peace of her world.

When at last they rode into the yard, Celia pulled up abruptly at sight of a sleek racing-curricle standing before the low, stone stables. Two bays, matched to a shade, were just being taken out from between the shafts. Lord Ryde? Somehow this decidedly sporting vehicle did not quite fit in with her image of the unknown man, but she did not have time to worry over it just then. She would have to hurry to get ready, for making her grandfather angry by being late would not help her in the least.

She dismounted quickly and turned her reins over to Jem with a smiling word of thanks. Almost running, she retraced her route through the small herb garden and back into the house. Although she knew she should not, she paused to listen at the bookroom door and was reassured by the muffled sound of deep voices coming through the heavy paneling. That meant the Great Hall would be empty and she could get up to her room without being seen.

She darted up the staircase, then along the lengthy course of hallways that led to her bedchamber. Once safely inside, she started to ring for her maid, then changed her mind. Instead, she threw open the doors of the carved cupboard that contained her dresses. An unfashionable dark gray from her mourning caught her eye. It was the most unbecoming garment she possessed. Pulling it out, she held it up before her and smiled grimly at the high neck and the narrow, tight sleeves. With her curls smoothed back into a semblance of the severe chignon that her companion always wore, she would look positively dowdy. That should put Lord Ryde off!

The door opened, and Elizabeth peeped in. "Oh!" she exclaimed. "Thank heaven you are back!" She regarded her charge critically. *"With sackcloth shirt and iron belt, And eyes with sorrow streaming?"* she demanded with a touch of exasperation, quoting from Sir Walter Scott's *Marmion.*

That drew a reluctant giggle from Celia. "How unkind! Did that not refer to the Scottish king?" She considered a moment. "No, I think the line when Marmion rode to Crichtoun is more appropriate. You remember, *With eyes scarce dried, the sorrowing dame To welcome noble Marmion came."*

"Oh, Celia." Elizabeth sank down onto the bed. "You had best not, you know. Your grandfather wished you to wear the muslin."

"I know. It is the only dress I have that does not bespeak either mourning or the schoolroom. I suppose you are right." She laid aside the dark gray gown. "I do not want to make him angry. Let it be the muslin, then."

She hurried out of her riding habit, tossing the garment casually across the arm of a chair and drawing a disapproving exclamation from Elizabeth. With hands that trembled slightly in her nervousness, she pulled the soft flounces of the new dress over her head and shook out the skirts so that they fell about her ankles. Elizabeth set to work on the fastenings.

It had been a very long time since Celia had donned anything but the blacks and grays of mourning, and in spite of herself, a thrill flickered through her. A narrow ruffle of blond lace lined the rounded neckline that was cut low to reveal the ivory creaminess of her skin. Blue satin ribands adorned the little puffed sleeves and circled the high waist just beneath her bust. This was no simple dress for a schoolroom miss, but her first truly fashionable gown.

"How lovely you are," Elizabeth sighed. A dreamy expression crept into her gray eyes. "It would be terrible to force you to marry a man who only wants the estates!"

"It would indeed!" Celia agreed, though not out of any admiration for her own beauty. "But it will not come to that! Jonathon will save me."

"How fortunate you are to have someone who loves you!" Elizabeth tried to keep the touch of wistfulness out of her voice. "I am so glad you will be happy."

If only that were true, Celia reflected. Although not possessing as romantic a nature as her dear companion, she was not wholly without dreams . . . though at the moment, her future bore more the appearance of a nightmare. If Elizabeth but knew it, Celia's problems would only really begin once she was free from the threat of marriage to Lord Ryde. Firmly, she thrust this thought from her. One hurdle at a time, she reminded herself; take them as they come.

At the moment, she would have to meet Trevor, Lord Ryde, placate her grandfather, and prepare the ground for Jonathon's arrival. A fiery termagant, spitting challenges and refusals, would hardly win sympathy. Instead . . . should she try to teach Lord Ryde a much needed lesson? Try to attract him, make him want her just a little, so that he would regret the cold-blooded nature of his offer when Jonathon whisked her away from his clutches . . . ?

She sank into the chair before her dressing table and allowed Elizabeth to brush out her unruly ringlets. These, the woman arranged with artless abandon about her oval face, then threaded a blue riband through the dusky curls.

"And ne'er did Grecian chisel trace A nymph, a Naiad, or a Grace of finer form, or lovelier face," Elizabeth quoted.

Celia looked at her, startled. "Do you really think so?" She turned to peer into the mirror. "No," she shook her head, having little regard for her own loveliness. "They are the most romantic lines, though, are they not? It would be above anything wonderful if only some gentleman would write such things about one."

"Would not Captain Edelston . . . ?" Elizabeth asked hesitantly.

Celia bit her lip, forcing back a smile at the thought of the cheerful, occasionally vacuous Jonathon ever suffering in the throes of a poetic muse. No, as fond of him as she was, she could not but recognize his shortcomings. He was no Lochinvar, and his was not the hazy, only dreamt-of image for which she yearned.

Her sudden longing must have clouded her expression, for Elizabeth continued more crisply. "Well, it is Lord Ryde we must convince to pity you. *Lovely, and gentle, and distressed—These charms might tame the fiercest breast,*" she quoted.

"Well, I suppose I am a maiden in distress," Celia agreed, rather flattered by the comparison. "Elizabeth, I believe you must have committed the whole of *Marmion* to memory!"

Elizabeth's half-smile was somewhat embarrassed. "I make a game of it. Now, how do those lines go on? Something about *where errant-knights might see Adventures of high chivalry, Might meet some damsel flying fast, With hair unbound and* . . . oh dear, how does it end?"

"And looks aghast," supplied Celia, also quite familiar with Sir Walter Scott's epic poem. "It sounds as if the poor creature must have looked a fright."

"Well, that you do not!" Elizabeth asserted fondly.

Celia glanced again at the mirror before her. Pale from nervousness and with her hair arranged *à la Titan,* she looked more like a schoolroom miss of sixteen than a young lady of fashion long overdue for her first Season—a frightened, hesitant child, in fact.

Her eyes widened slightly. Elizabeth was absolutely right! Lord Ryde must be brought to pity her! That would teach him a lesson! She would do her best to make him feel as cruel and heartless as he was! She would play the martyr, with lips trembling and eyelashes fluttering with unshed tears. And when Jonathon arrived she could throw herself into his arms, weeping, sobbing that he was her true love. She contemplated the scene, ignoring its shocking impropriety, dwelling solely on Lord Ryde's subsequent and inevitable embarrassment.

This role called for simplicity. Simplicity and innocence. She opened the small, inlaid jewelry case that stood on the dressing table and brought out the single strand of pearls that had been her mother's. She clasped them about her neck, then approved the result. If she were careful, she might have a little bit of fun, take a certain measure of revenge, before calling this farce to a close.

A knock sounded at the door and Celia stiffened. The first hurdle. Carefully, she schooled her features into an expression as heart-rendingly pitiful as she could manage.

"Yes?" she called, trying to inject a hint of deep tragedy into her voice.

The door opened to reveal an upper housemaid who bobbed a quick curtsy, her wide eyes regarding her mistress. "If you please, miss, Sir Roderick desires you to go to him in the bookroom."

"We shall be down in a moment, Mary." Celia lowered her eyes in a dejected attitude.

The maid curtsied again, her face alight with excitement. In a moment, she hurried off.

"She can hardly wait to get to the servants' hall, to tell them how you looked and acted!" Elizabeth protested. "Oh, Celia, do—do behave yourself! You are giving them something to gossip about below-stairs."

"Let them." Celia slipped her feet into a pair of delicate white sandals which Elizabeth produced from the bottom of the cupboard. "I want Grandfather to know how unhappy I am with his arrangements. I—I want to make things easier for when Jonathon arrives."

Together, she and Elizabeth hurried along the maze of hallways, down the main stairs and across the Great Hall. At the bookroom door, Celia hesitated, again composing her features to a demure expression, eyes downcast and lips trembling just a little. The last was easier than she expected. She always felt uncomfortable when expected to act out charades, and this was a much more important performance. Gathering her courage, she knocked on the door, then entered without waiting for an answer.

Elizabeth slipped quickly by her to take her usual seat in the farthest corner. The workbag, which she always carried, she set by her feet, then drew from it her customary embroidery. She forced herself to concentrate on this work as befitted her lowly position.

Celia stepped forward. Sir Roderick sat behind the large desk, with the pile of papers pushed to one side to clear the space before him. She glanced up at him through her long, dark lashes as she came to stand demurely before him, and was irritated by the smug satisfaction she read in his face. What did it matter? she reminded herself. He would learn soon enough he could not force her against her will.

Surreptitiously, her gaze shifted to the figure seated in the overstuffed armchair near the desk, and her head came up slowly. Her gaze moved across a surprisingly compelling countenance, noting the firm chin, and encountering dark, luminous pools as she met his eyes. To her shock and dismay, they held hers until she felt herself floundering in their vast depths, and somewhere within her, she became aware of a quivering sensation. He did not rise, but at that moment, Celia was beyond criticizing him for this omission of so fundamental a courtesy.

Lord Ryde's appearance rivaled that of her favorite heroes from the romance novels to which she subscribed. He sat proudly, his head held high, his tall, muscular frame erect, even in the padded softness of the chair. His thick black locks, which were carefully cut and combed into the Brutus, tapered to a widow's peak low on his brow. The compelling eyes were widely spaced above his aristocratic nose, and his mouth was set in grim lines. His coat of blue superfine lay smoothly across his shoulders and the yellow pantaloons displayed an excellent leg to advantage. His cravat was neat, his shirt points moderate, and he favored only a single fob. His top boots gleamed in a way that would be the envy of many a tulip of the *ton*. There was a suppressed tension about him that Celia could feel. He looked, in fact, as annoyed as she felt.

Slowly, he raised the quizzing glass that hung from a black riband about his neck, giving her the briefest of surveillances. A muscle tightened at the corner of his mouth, and he turned back to Sir Roderick.

"Very pretty," he commented, his voice devoid of any emotion or interest. If anything, his tone was one of accusation!

Celia's temper rose. Had he no interest in the girl he had agreed to marry? Even allowing for his not liking the arrangement any more than she, this was beyond anything! She might have been a farm horse offered for his inspection—though she strongly suspected he would show more enthusiasm over the selection of a work animal for his estate.

His attitude was almost contemptuous! Bitterly, she

regretted the wave of attraction that had swept through her on first seeing him. He made it abundantly clear that he was here strictly for business, and she meant next to nothing—a necessary evil to be endured in exchange for considerable gain. She could detect in those disturbing eyes no hint of a desire that the proposed marriage should be anything other than one of simple convenience. If he had set out to alienate his future bride on purpose, she thought savagely, he could hardly have done it more effectively.

Sir Roderick rose, smiling his approval at Celia. He crossed over to her, taking her hand and patting it fondly as he led her up to Lord Ryde. "My little Celia," he said, a note of pride in his voice. "And this, my dear, is my godson, Trevor. I know you two will deal very well together. A chair, my dear?"

He waved her to the straight-backed chair that had been placed beside Lord Ryde's. Silently, she lowered herself into it, copying Elizabeth's prim posture, crossing her ankles and folding her hands in her lap. Feeling Lord Ryde's gaze upon her, she lowered her head demurely, but glanced up at him from the corner of her eye.

Again her anger surged. Lord Ryde regarded her with a long, appraising stare in which she could detect no sign of either pleasure or approval. When he spoke, his remarks were directed to her grandfather.

"She is very young," he said.

"She is nearly nineteen." Sir Roderick shook his head.

"I assume the situation has been explained to her?" Again, Ryde ignored her.

Sir Roderick nodded. "I thought perhaps we would not hold the wedding until two or three months from now. That should give her time enough to adjust to the idea. Do you care when or where it should be?"

Lord Ryde shrugged. "Whatever you wish. It does not matter."

Elizabeth gasped, but bit her lip firmly to prevent herself from breaking into incautious speech.

Celia showed none of her companion's reticence. "And what if it matters to me?" Celia demanded indignantly, her firm resolve to be sweet and demure vanishing rapidly in the face of his lordship's indifference.

He turned to look at her, surprise registering in his raised brow.

"Celia!" her grandfather said sharply.

She rose, taking a couple of quick strides, stopping before his desk. "I won't be quiet. You treat this as if it has nothing to do with me whatsoever! Has it not occurred to you that I might have some feelings about my own wedding?"

Ryde frowned, but his eyes gleamed with a new interest. "I'm sure your grandfather knows what is best," was all he said.

Celia glared at him but lapsed into an angry silence. Those were the first words he had actually addressed to her, and somehow they did not bode well for a happy future together. She was glad she had summoned Jonathon! Nothing on earth could ever make her marry anyone as inconsiderate as Lord Ryde!

Sir Roderick waved her back to her chair, and, clenching her teeth, she went.

"I would like to take Celia to visit her future home," said Sir Roderick. "She might feel more comfortable when she is taken there as a bride, and you will be able to get to know one another a little better."

Celia's eyes flew to her grandfather in surprise. She was rather moved by this show of consideration for her on his part. She studied the tired lines of his face, the erect posture of his wiry body. He had been a strong man, and age was not conquering him easily. He really does believe he is doing the best thing for me, Celia thought. But there was no excuse for Lord Ryde's lack of interest in her. Sir Roderick must be gravely mistaken in his godson's character.

Ryde shrugged a shoulder. "As you wish," he replied. "Why don't you return with me at the end of the week? It will be no trouble to make the arrangements."

Sir Roderick nodded his approval, but Celia's mind was in a whirl. "No trouble" to make arrangements for the reception of his future bride at an estate described as falling apart? He was certainly going to no trouble to hide his indifference to her. Jonathon! she suddenly remembered. Jonathon would be arriving by the end of the week, with luck. She could not possibly go now to Lord Ryde's estate outside of Brighton.

"No!" she blurted out, then blushed as both Sir Roderick and Ryde turned toward her. "I. . . . " she stammered, suddenly embarrassed. "It is not at all convenient for me to leave next week."

"Celia," her grandfather said softly, a note of warning in his voice.

There was a trace of amusement in Ryde's expression as he studied her. "If it is convenient for your grandfather, I am sure you will work it out," he said coolly, but his eyes lingered on her vexed countenance.

"No, Grandfather." She turned to him. "There is someone coming to visit me. I only learned this afternoon, and I have not had a chance to tell you yet."

His stern features relaxed and he glanced at Ryde. "Perhaps her friend could come with us? Celia has been very much alone since she has lived here. A friend would be good for her."

Ryde glanced at Celia, who was frowning. "That does not please you?" he asked.

Sir Roderick also noted her hesitation. "Who is coming? Is it that Miss Carlyle, the one who writes so often?"

Celia shook her head, threw a quick glance at Elizabeth, then braced herself for the trouble she knew would follow. "It is Jonathon Edelston, Grandfather. You have heard me mention him many times. He has been promising to come this age, but this is the first chance he has had to get away."

Lord Ryde raised his eyebrows slightly, glancing from Celia's nervous face to her grandfather's frown.

Sir Roderick picked up a pen, examining it with care. "Captain Edelston," he told Ryde, "has been like a brother to Celia. I am sure he would like to meet her future husband. Perhaps"—he turned his stern gaze on Celia, commanding her silence—"we could arrange to hold the wedding while he is still here. Would you like that, my dear?"

Celia bit her lip, not daring to look at her grandfather. Take this slowly, she warned herself. She had mentioned Jonathon; his visit would be accepted. That was enough for now. Hints at a romance could wait for convenient moments, or even until after his arrival.

Sir Roderick nodded. "We will go to Hastings, as planned, then. When your friend arrives he will be given directions on how to find us, and we will make arrangements for him in Brighton. And now"—he turned to Trevor—"shall we leave the discussion of the business matters until later? Would you care to tour the home farm?"

"Why not discuss your financial arrangements now?" Celia asked sweetly, not in the least bit deceived.

"That is none of your concern, my girl," her grandfather chided her gently.

"None of my concern," she repeated. "And yet these 'business matters' of yours are deciding my life!" Her temper, always volatile, flared again. "I am perfectly capable of discussing arrangements on my own behalf. I am not a child, you know."

"Then stop acting like one," suggested Ryde mildly, before Sir Roderick could speak. Amusement at her anger glinted in his eyes. He turned back to the older man. "I would enjoy seeing the experimental work you have been doing since I was here last."

Celia was on her feet, the last shreds of her control giving way. "Grandfather!" she exclaimed, demanding his attention. "I will not go through with this! I will never marry such a—an impossible, odious man." Words really bad enough to describe him fortunately failed her. "He has absolutely no feelings or consideration whatsoever. You cannot possibly expect me to marry him!"

To her fury, Sir Roderick merely rose, taking her hand and patting it. "You must forgive her, Trevor. She is overwrought, nervous. This first meeting was bound to be a strain."

"As far as I am concerned, this can be the last meeting!" she exclaimed. Pulling away from him, she strode toward the door.

Ryde was behind her, swinging her easily around to face him. His fingers dug into the soft flesh above her wrist, and she cried out involuntarily. Immediately, the intensity of his grip eased. Soft color flooded her cheeks and her breast rose and fell with her suddenly rapid breathing. The traitorous trembling started within her again as she encountered the compelling depths of his eyes.

Tiny lines of humorous appreciation showed at their corners, and his lips twitched with a suppressed smile. His hold shifted on her arm, but allowed no chance of escape.

"Your manners, child," he reproved her. "You should not speak so to your grandfather."

Celia glared up at the figure towering above her, her pulse racing more from his nearness than from her anger. "I have no intention of marrying you," she whispered, so softly that only he could hear. "You might as well get that idea out of your mind, right now."

Ryde's smile won out, and his eyes lit with a spark of enjoyment. "Hurling down the gauntlet, my girl?" His whispered tone matched hers. "I accept your challenge!" He dropped her wrist and turned away. "Her manners will need to be improved, but I am sure she will not give me much trouble," he told Sir Roderick.

Celia glared at his back. Accept her "challenge," would he? This was no game! This was out-and-out war, and she was going to win! At least she had broken through that complete indifference of his. A certain smugness settled over her at this feat. The first skirmish, it would seem, went to her. Perhaps—just perhaps—she might have some fun before Jonathon arrived and the battle ended.

Sir Roderick Marcombe frowned thoughtfully at her. "You are tired, Celia. Why do you not go up to your bedchamber and lie down for a while? We shall see you at dinner." He crossed the room and opened the door for her.

Celia stood, looking irresolutely from him to Lord Ryde. Not much more could be accomplished now, she decided. Turning, she made what she hoped was a majestic exit from the room. Elizabeth rose and hurried out in her wake, clutching the dangling threads of her work.

"You must forgive her, my dear Trevor. She is not usually given to megrims or missishness." Sir Roderick's words came to her as the door swung closed. Celia's fists clenched. Missish, was she? She would show them she was not to be ignored!

She stormed across the Great Hall, but as she started up the staircase she paused, carefully bringing her temper under control. Anger clouded her thinking, and she stood in need of having all of her wits about her. Trevor, Lord Ryde, was not going to be easy to handle, but handle him she must!

His attitude puzzled her. Irritated, grim, then that

sudden amusement, accepting her "challenge" . . . She would have a difficult time trying to understand him, but that was something she would have to do if she ever hoped to gain the upper hand in this situation.

Most frightening of all, however, was the effect his mere presence had upon her. It was a shame he was so infuriating. She blushed at the thought that rose to her mind, of being held in those strong arms. Never! she told herself. Lord Ryde was the enemy in this battle of wills, and she would never give in to him. She was not a commodity, to be traded or bartered, and he would learn it before she was done!

CHAPTER THREE

Trevor, Lord Ryde, watched as the door swung closed behind Miss Marcombe and Miss Westerly. His eyes, half-lidded, retained a hint of lurking enjoyment at his encounter with the raging little spitfire. A determined will and lively spirit were not qualities he had expected to encounter in this young lady. But then, neither was beauty. She was not in the least what he had imagined. His jaw tightened and his amusement faded away. On the whole, he was not at all sure he cared for the way things were turning out.

"I fear she needs a strong hand to her bridle," Sir Roderick Marcombe informed his godson.

"She does, indeed." Trevor turned his now-frowning gaze on Sir Roderick. "You may be sure I shall see to it." Even to himself, his voice sounded cold and forbidding.

He returned to his chair and sank back against its cushions. His dark brow lowered, lending him a saturnine expression. He had given his word, he reminded himself. A man of honor did not go back on that, no matter how many regrets or second thoughts he has had in the interim. He was prepared to face what he must—no matter how little the prospect pleased him.

But for a moment—just for a very brief moment—he had experienced a slight lessening of his intense displeasure. He could never resist an invitation to do battle, especially when it was hurled at him with all the passion and disdain that his opponent possessed. Slowly, he brought his forefingers together and rested his elbows on the arms of his chair. He would go through with this arranged marriage because he must, and for no other reason. But he would make certain it would be on his terms, not hers.

"How did your last journey fare?" Sir Roderick asked, breaking into Ryde's dark reflections.

Trevor took a deep breath and exhaled slowly. "I've done my part," he said shortly. It was not something he cared to talk about, nor had the outcome satisfied him. No more than any other man did he like to leave unfinished business in the hands of someone else, but this time there had been no choice. His role had been strictly that of organizer, and his instructions had been to leave the captured agent's daring rescue from the French gaol in the hands of another. It grated on him not to take a more active role, but his mysterious contact had more experience with this sort of undertaking.

He looked up at his godfather, saw another question forming on the man's lips, and stood abruptly. "Come, let us see this new hunter you say is shaping up so well. And that colt, what do you think of him?" The ploy worked, and they left the room, deep in a discussion of horseflesh.

Lord Ryde's mood was no more grim than was Celia's as she dressed for dinner a short while later.

Now that she had met him, it was time to rethink her strategy before deciding on a viable course of action. Lord Ryde was obviously not pleased about the proposed marriage, either—at least not until she threw such a blatant challenge at him.

Nor was his character in the least bit weak, in spite of her first assessment of the arrangement. Irritatingly, she found herself drawn to a man who would so readily pick up the gauntlet hurled at him. All in all, he was not in the least what she had imagined.

But still, he had agreed to offer for her, solely at her grandfather's bidding. That she could not forget—or forgive. Or was he, in some unfathomable manner, being forced as was she? That idea gave her pause. There was only one way to be sure of the motives that propelled him to accept this alliance. She would have to approach him and ask directly. There might be a chance that she could win him over to her side, that together they could go to her grandfather and see if they could convince him to abandon this ridiculous idea of marriage.

These deliberations resulted in the decision to be at her most pleasant, to enact the role of a cordial and helpful hostess when she went down to dinner. She would even try to look her prettiest. That always put her grandfather in a mellow mood. Perhaps it would have the same effect on Lord Ryde.

The problem of what to wear was settled by the simple expedient of selecting the most becoming of her half-mourning gowns, a lilac crepe trimmed in black ribands. There was little she could do along that line, she reflected regretfully, until she could visit a *modiste* or seamstress. Her hair she allowed her maid to brush into soft ringlets that framed her oval face. When she at last descended the stairs, it was in a mood of hopeful, if somewhat nervous, expectancy.

The others were ahead of her, already gathered in the elegant Green Saloon that stood opposite the informal dining room normally used by the family. As Celia paused on the threshold, Sir Roderick was pouring wine for himself and Lord Ryde.

The latter leaned negligently against the mantel. He looked up at the sound of the door, and Celia found herself staring into the most remarkable eyes she had ever beheld. Had she been too angry to appreciate them earlier? she wondered as she forced herself to resume breathing. They were of a deep, glowing color somewhere between mahogany and ebony, and could be as cold as ice, or sparkling—as they were now—with an unshared amusement. They held her captivated—until he looked away almost at once. Paying Celia no further attention, he agreed politely with whatever remark had been addressed to him by Elizabeth, who sat in one of the Queen Anne chairs near the small fire.

Celia's initial impression of him returned, stronger than ever. He might have stepped out of the pages of any of the novels or romantic poems that she read of late. There were the rugged good looks, the air of command and breeding, the supercilious manner in which he looked down his nose at her—and then ignored her. Enthralled and infuriated, she vowed he would not ignore her for long. She swept regally into the room.

"Ah, Celia." Sir Roderick came toward her, taking her hand. "Have you rested, child?"

"Yes, Grandfather." She lowered her eyes with becoming modesty. "And I am truly sorry. Did—did you have an enjoyable ride about the estate?"

"We did not go out, after all," he told her as he guided her to a chair.

"I am sorry to hear that." She turned so that she faced Lord Ryde and forced herself to smile shyly up at him. "The estate is at its most beautiful at this time of year."

He inclined his head. "So I believe."

"If Grandfather is busy tomorrow, perhaps you will allow me to escort you around? The—the countryside is much admired, I believe."

Ryde's eyebrows raised a fraction, and a muscle at the edge of his mouth twitched. "I shall be honored." He gave her a slight bow.

Out of the corner of her eye, Celia caught her grandfather's frowning gaze resting on her. Well, he could be as suspicious as he liked, She offered this olive branch in all sincerity—though for her own purposes, not his.

"You—you might even enjoy the ride into the village." Elizabeth rushed into speech to prevent her Cousin Roderick from commenting on Celia's unexpected cooperation. All eyes turned on her in surprise at this unprecedented entrance into a conversation, and she flushed a fiery red.

The butler entered at that point to announce dinner, and Elizabeth was granted a respite in which to recover her countenance. Celia rose at once and accepted Ryde's escort, though she carefully avoided meeting his gaze. Elizabeth, to her further discomfiture, followed on Sir Roderick's arm.

Conversation during the meal remained mercifully on neutral grounds, but the chances of this continuing throughout an entire evening did not seem good. Therefore, for the sake of her plan, Celia pleaded a headache and excused herself immediately upon completion of the meal. Her manner was apologetic, preventing even her grandfather from issuing a stern reproof to her for absenting herself from the drawing room. After fobbing off Elizabeth's concerned questions, Celia retired to bed with her copy of *Marmion* and, to prevent herself from indulging in fruitless thought, proceeded to read herself to sleep.

Morning, though, brought her companion tapping at her door at an early hour. Celia called to her to enter, just as Seddons, her maid, started fastening up her riding habit.

Elizabeth, garbed in her usual black and with her pale blond hair pulled back unbecomingly from her angular face, peeped into the room.

"Oh, dear," she exclaimed, vexed. "You are dressed for riding already. Shall I change now, too?"

"That won't be necessary," Celia said quickly. "There can be no need for you to chaperone me while we are on the estate, or indeed even if we go about the surrounding countryside. It will be quite all right."

"But will it not be awkward for you?" Elizabeth's soft gray eyes clouded with worry.

"Indeed not. I—I wish to speak to Lord Ryde, and—and it is rather a delicate situation. It would be far more awkward with another person present."

Elizabeth hesitated, her suspicious gaze resting on her charge. She met the blandest of looks which only succeeded in confirming her uneasiness, but in honesty she had to allow the justice of Celia's desire for privacy. She waited while her charge put the finishing touches on her toilette and picked up her beaver and gloves. Together, they made their way downstairs to the breakfast parlor.

Ryde sat near the sideboard with the remains of a hearty breakfast on a plate before him. He drained a tankard of ale as the two ladies entered, then stood.

"You are ready," he commented. His tone was merely polite. If he were surprised or pleased, it did not show.

"Of course," Celia forced herself to smile at him. "There is nothing more tedious than to be kept waiting."

"Then with your permission, I will bespeak the horses." He bowed to the ladies and left the room, leaving Celia to glare at his retreating back.

"Are you sure you would not like me to accompany you?" Elizabeth murmured, her tone skeptical.

"No, I promise I shall not murder him." Celia crossed to the sideboard and began to fill her plate absently. "At least, not while there is a chance of talking him over to my side."

"Do you think there is any possibility?" Elizabeth looked out the window, watching as Ryde's tall, imposing figure strode across the gravel with restless energy. She was quite glad she was not to accompany them. His air of barely disguised displeasure left her jumpy.

Celia kept her back firmly turned, refusing to indulge herself by watching him. "There is only one way to find out if I can," she replied flippantly, thus betraying her frayed nerves to her understanding companion.

Elizabeth gave her an encouraging smile. "He looks to be a reasonable man," she said generously. "But proud. He will not care to be rejected."

Celia nodded, grateful to have someone's support. She found she had less appetite than usual for her breakfast and picked at the food, contenting herself finally with nibbling on a roll. She sipped her tea slowly, and had not even drained her first cup when the door to the parlor opened and Lord Ryde came back in.

"The horses have been brought around. If you are finished?" He took hold of her chair and drew it back for her without awaiting an answer.

Celia rose. "Please excuse me, dear Elizabeth. We shall not be gone overly long, I am sure."

Her companion caught her hand and gave it a heartening squeeze. Hurriedly, Celia disengaged herself and left the room, followed by Ryde.

Jem stood in the circular drive before the front door, holding the bridles of Whimsy and her grandfather's second hack, a raw-boned chestnut with sloping shoulders and powerful hindquarters. The animal sidled impatiently. Too long in the stall, Celia diagnosed, and, knowing the chestnut's propensity for playing off his tricks, began to look forward to Ryde's attempts to stay in the saddle. She would soon see his abilities—or lack thereof—as a horseman.

If she had hoped he would be thrown, she was to be disappointed. Within a few minutes of his swinging himself onto the animal's back and taking up the reins, Ryde's mastery was established. Celia watched with grudging approval as he brought his dancing mount under control, then maneuvered him into position beside her. He enjoyed the battle, she could tell, and his exertion of command, the sheer power of the man, had a disturbing effect on her that she strove to hide.

"I fear he has not been getting enough exercise of late," she commented, keeping any trace of apology out of her voice.

"Then, that makes two of us," Ryde said briefly. "And now, Miss Marcombe," he added as they left the graveled drive and started sedately across the fields, "to what do I owe the honor of your company this morning?"

"I should have thought that was obvious," she almost snapped, not pleased to discover he had guessed she was up to something.

"Not to me," he replied, his tone one of gentle regret. "Please, do enlighten me."

She rode in silence for a moment, then turned to look squarely at him. "Do you find my company so objectionable, then?"

"As I do not know you, I am in no position to judge."

He apparently also had little desire to rectify that situation. If anything, she decided, he was laughing at her! That did not please her, either. As far as he knew, he was to marry her. She would teach him she was not to be scorned or ignored! Somehow, she determined, she would drive that lurking amusement from his eyes and replace it with interest—or even something more!

"You are having very little trouble with Rufus," she tried, and hoped only admiration sounded in her voice. "He can be very difficult to control when he wishes."

"Oh, we're old friends," Trevor said with a casualness that neatly denied her intended compliment. "There is a ditch just ahead, but I believe there is a safe place for you to cross, just a few hundred yards along here."

Celia threw him a glance filled with scorn, for the moment forgetting her intention of flattering him into a compliant mood. Urging Whimsy into a canter, she cleared the ditch with ease, then pointed her mount toward the hedgerow and jumped this as well. Trevor and Rufus landed beside her a moment later.

"We are approaching the south fields," she said. "But then, I believe you know that, do you not? Perhaps it is you who should be giving me a tour of the estate."

"Perhaps," Ryde said enigmatically. He nudged Rufus forward and took the lead. He did not glance back to see if she followed.

She fought down the urge to ride away from him. She had proposed this outing for a purpose, and at the moment, if he continued in this disagreeable vein, she saw little way of accomplishing it. By some means, she had to establish a friendlier atmosphere.

She pressed her horse forward to join him. "Is Hastings a large estate?" she asked with polite interest.

He looked down at her, his eyes cold. "It does not compare with Ranleigh."

"Little does," she said immediately. "Especially now, when everything is coming into bloom." His expression did not change, and Celia cast her mind about for another topic of conversation with which to penetrate his harsh exterior. "You—you must hunt," she attempted at last. "You ride so very well."

"Because Rufus cannot unseat me?" he asked. "But then, I know his tricks." They lapsed into silence again for several minutes as they rode on. "Yes, I do hunt," he said suddenly, just when she was desperately seeking another question to ask. "Though not recently. Do you?"

"Like you, not recently. Grandfather did not think it proper while I was in mourning."

"How boring for you."

"It has been!" she exclaimed, momentarily diverted. "It is no pleasant thing to suddenly be denied even the most harmless of outlets for one's energy." She looked up at him and bit her lip, for a mocking expression was back in his eyes, clear to be seen.

"If we take the fence just ahead, we can ride down to the stream," she told him through clenched teeth. Without awaiting his answer, she headed her horse into it, taking the five-foot fence from a trot. *That* should show Lord Ryde!

If it did, he did not acknowledge it by a single sign. Rufus took the fence, flying, then pulling up neatly at her side. "Has the bridge been replaced yet?" he asked casually.

"No, but the stream is not deep. If you wish, we can ford it easily."

They continued for some time without speaking, Lord Ryde apparently unwilling to initiate a topic of conversation and Celia unable to think of an approach that would work with him. So involved was she that she rode on for several yards before she realized that Trevor had stopped. She turned, looking inquiringly back at him.

"You must excuse me from going farther," he said. "There is something I promised to go over for your grandfather, and I wish to have it completed before luncheon."

He was going to leave her? How dare he—when she had only endured his intolerable company in order to speak to him! And now, she would not have the opportunity, after all. Her fingers tightened on the reins, causing Whimsy to back up a few steps.

"I wouldn't dream of keeping you from it," she informed him with chilly politeness. "Do go back. I believe you know the way."

"I fear I am your escort. As much as you may dislike it, I must ask you to accompany me."

His expression was taunting as he sat back with that half-smile curving his firm lips. It was as though he waited to see if she would rise to this challenge. She would not give him the satisfaction, she vowed.

"By all means, then, let us return." Bestowing a sweet smile on him, she guided her horse through the trees and headed back toward the estate.

She led the way into the cobbled stableyard. Drawing up before the long rows of stalls, she freed her skirts and knee from the pommel. The brush of nailed boots on the stones warned her, and she looked down as Ryde reached up to help her from the saddle. It was more dignified to submit gracefully, so she suffered his hands to grasp her about her slender waist. He lifted her with no visible sign of effort and set her lightly on her feet.

She took a deep breath, steadying her unaccountably chaotic reaction to him. "Thank you," she managed to say with a semblance of calm.

He bowed deeply, then turned and walked away from her.

Her fingers tightened on her crop, and she experienced a momentary and highly reprehensible urge to slash it across his back. He still laughed at her! He was not even interested enough to try to get to know her! He was so sure of himself, he made absolutely no effort!

Luncheon, as might have been predicted, proved to be a strained affair. Celia sat at the end of the table, once again wearing her new sprigged muslin. Irritation with herself for her morning's failure caused her to glower at both her grandfather and Ryde. She had made a fine mess of her plans. Ryde was as far as ever from being open to any suggestion she might make. Somehow, she still had to establish friendly relations so that she could request his help. But how? He had been singularly unresponsive to her attempts so far.

As the meal drew to a close, Sir Roderick Marcombe stood. "Will you join me in the bookroom, Trevor? There are several things on which I would like your opinion."

Trevor stood at once, and Celia's eyes flew to him in dismay. To her indignation, he smiled slightly to himself as if pleased that she did not want him to go. She looked away. Well, what did it matter if he thought she was succumbing to his spell? She was willing to cater to his vanity if it meant he would listen to her.

Restless, she went outside, walking around to the back of the house where a meticulously cultivated formal garden was situated. Seating herself on one of the long stone benches, she leaned forward with her elbows resting on her knees and her chin in her cupped hands. She let out a deep sigh, then set to work, planning a new strategy.

A slight rustling disturbed her thoughts, and she looked up to see Elizabeth approaching with her inevitable workbag. The woman seated herself at Celia's side and drew out her embroidery hoop from which trailed the long ends of a table shawl.

"Did you make any progress this morning?" Elizabeth asked. She set a stitch carefully. "He—he can be a charming man when he wishes, can he not?"

"Charming?" Celia demanded, surprised. "That is not a word I would use to describe him. 'Impossible' comes closer!"

"Oh, dear. I—I had hoped . . ." Her sentence trailed off. "I thought he smiled at you after luncheon."

Celia spun to face her. "Not you, too, Elizabeth! You cannot want to force me into this hateful marriage! Surely you know how I feel, and can sympathize."

"I do, but . . ." She broke off under her charge's indignant eye. "Would—would it not be best to consider him without prejudice? To try to get to know him? You must not be frightened by his harsh features," Elizabeth went on in reasonable tones. "He—he may look a very satyr, but he is not that at all, I am sure."

"A satyr?" Celia considered Ryde for a moment and a peculiar tingling sensation ran through her. She did not consider his features unpleasant. Dynamic, yes, and strangely appealing. She could be strongly attracted to such a man . . . if the circumstances were different. But they were not, she reminded herself with a certain regret. "He has most unpleasant features!" she declared forcefully and untruthfully. "How could anyone admire a man who looks like that, when they had known my Jonathon?" She sighed with rapture.

"Is Captain Edelston handsome?" Elizabeth asked, taking the bait.

"A Grecian god," Celia rhapsodized. "He is tall, with blond curls and so very good-looking." It was all quite true, but Jonathon's classical perfection had never sent the least shiver through her the way Ryde's imperfect, severe features could.

"My dear Celia!" Elizabeth exclaimed, dismayed. "Oh, when your grandfather sees him beside Lord Ryde, he *must* realize that his godson cannot bring you happiness, not when there is someone like Captain Edelston!"

"He cannot help but be struck by their difference," Celia agreed. She stood, no longer able to sit still for some inscrutable reason. "I—I think I shall return to the house. Do you come, Elizabeth?"

Her companion shook her head. "Do you need me? Then not just yet, I believe. It is so pleasant here in the sun."

Elizabeth raised her soft gray eyes, watching as her charge walked slowly back to the house. The poor child! What chance did the girl really have for happiness? Elizabeth might have known her Cousin Roderick Marcombe for only six short months, but it had not taken her long to realize that he would brook no opposition to his plans.

There was the slightest possibility that the rigid old gentleman might relent in this matter, since the affection between Celia and Captain Edelston was of so long a standing. Somehow, though, she doubted it. Sir Roderick Marcombe was not one to allow his mind to be changed. *Alas, that lawless was their love . . .* she quoted to herself, her gentle heart crying out for the tragic lovers.

Here, in spite of herself, a touch of envy crept in. Celia—beautiful, young and an heiress—with the handsome and romantic Captain Jonathon Edelston very much in love with her and with the masculine, rugged Lord Ryde determined to make her his bride . . .

She sighed. This, to her, was the ultimate of romance. If only something of this order might happen to her! But here, her common sense took over. No, all she wanted, all she had ever longed for, was for just one man to look her way. One gentle, tender man who would overlook her lack of fortune, see through the unbecoming disguise she had been forced to adopt to pass for a governess, who could love someone as insignificant as she.

But she was only a poor relation of the honorable house of Marcombe, taken in out of charity by her distant cousin Roderick. She had never been presented, never been to London, always known that her lot would be one of genteel servitude. She knew herself to have been lucky beyond her hopes to have been rescued from her grim lodgings and brought to be the companion of the lovely Celia. Fortunately, she had been raised from childhood to know her lowly position and accept her drear lot. Her romantic nature she had long ago learned to keep under firm check.

It was just as well, she decided. She did not possess the disposition to be a heroine. She had a strong suspicion that such a role would be extremely uncomfortable and lead one into the most shockingly improper situations. Besides, she doubted she had the ability to swoon gracefully at the first sign of danger, which, according to the novels she devoured, seemed to be prerequisite for the part.

Laugh those that can, weep those that may . . . She recalled Scott's words with a sigh, but a slight smile lingered on her lips from her fanciful thoughts. Now, if only Celia's problems could be dismissed as easily as her daydreams! Here was a young lady eminently suited to the role of heroine—except, perhaps, for the fainting.

Celia should—must!—be happy. For her beloved charge, Elizabeth wanted everything that she herself had been denied. That hers was a vicarious existence, that she was living an exciting, fantasy life through the girl, she tried to ignore. Celia must find true love—but Elizabeth had to admit she did not see how this was to be brought about. She would do all that she could—anything in her power to help Celia and her Jonathon.

Elizabeth remained in the peace of the garden until the westering sun recalled her to a reluctant sense of the time and her duties. It must have been several hours since Celia had left her, and she had no idea what the impulsive girl might have been getting up to. Stowing her work safely away in her basket, she made her way quickly back to the house and up to her room.

Dressing for dinner presented no great problem. To have more than just a very few gowns was an unnecessary extravagance for a female in her position, and one in which it would have been unwise for her to indulge. It was no easy thing when one was only nine-and-twenty to present a respectable picture of a mature and capable chaperone. Of the four gowns she possessed, three were black, unrelieved by so much as a single riband or band of lace. The severe monotony of her raiment, combined with her unbecoming hair style, managed to add at least ten years to her appearance.

She changed into her high-necked dinner gown, smoothed her hair back into its tight chignon, then crossed the hall to Celia's room. There she found the girl, garbed only in a long chemise, pouring over the contents of her clothes cupboards.

She looked up as Elizabeth entered the room. "Oh, dear! I am not late, am I? I have not heard the gong! Seddons," She turned to her somber-faced maid who stood near the bed, holding a gown, "we must hurry!"

"No, I am early," Elizabeth assured her. She moved about the room, looking over the meager selection of dresses that lay across the chairs.

"Unless I wear the gown I wore last night, I fear Grandfather will accuse me of decking myself out like a crow," Celia said ruefully. "I have only my mourning clothing."

There was considerable truth in this statement. While it was proper for Elizabeth to dress in the dark colors, it was not at all the thing for a girl of Celia's age and position. The gentlemen could be pardoned if they suspected that she intentionally dressed in this manner to make herself appear unattractive.

"This is a problem," Elizabeth murmured, fingering a black crepe. "Do you have other dresses, from the schoolroom, that we might unpick and make over for you?"

Celia shook her head. "Grandfather gave them away, saying I should not need them again. And even if there were any left, we could not do anything in the next half hour."

"Oh!" Elizabeth exclaimed, vexed that her charge should not have so basic an item as a suitable gown. "You must have new dresses, and as soon as possible. You ought to look your best for"—she met Celia's eyes in a secret look of understanding—"for your intended husband."

"That still does me no good for tonight." Celia picked up a half-robe in dove-gray crepe, then the accompanying slip of darker gray muslin. "These shall have to do. Support me, dear Elizabeth, when Grandfather rants at me for choosing so drab a costume."

Elizabeth awarded this sally a slight smile, but her mind was preoccupied with the practical aspects of the situation. "He is taking you to visit Lord Ryde's estate at the end of the week, is he not? You really must have something more appropriate to wear." She considered. "Gentlemen so rarely think of such necessities."

Celia, emerging from beneath the folds of the slip that her maid had just tossed over her head, turned her large golden-brown eyes on her companion. A sudden gleam lit their depths. "We might quite easily pass through London on our way to Brighton, might we not?" she asked.

"We might," Elizabeth agreed. "*If* your grandfather agrees."

"Now, how to talk him into it," Celia murmured. "I believe he would more readily listen to you than to me." She donned the half-robe, then allowed her maid to do up the fastenings. The soft material fell about her ankles in long, graceful folds.

"All right," Elizabeth smiled fondly at Celia. "I shall warn him that if he does not desire to have two crows hovering over his dinner table, he must do something about it. That should get results."

With Celia's heartfelt thanks ringing in her ears, Elizabeth left her and proceeded along the numerous corridors and down the stairs. The door to the Green Saloon stood slightly ajar, a sure sign that someone was down before her. She entered, and was relieved to find Sir Roderick the sole occupant of the room.

He rose as she entered. "Ah, good evening, Cousin Elizabeth." He looked beyond her, as if he expected to see Celia as well.

"I—I am glad that I have found you alone, Cousin Roderick. There is a matter of some delicacy I wish to discuss with you." Quelling the nervousness that always overcame her in the presence of her overpowering relative, she came forward into the room.

Sir Roderick looked at her in some surprise. He gestured for her to take a seat on the sofa, then pulled a chair up opposite her. "And what is this momentous topic?"

"New gowns. For Celia." Now that she had begun, it suddenly became much easier. "She is distressed that she has nothing suitable to wear while Lord Ryde is a guest in this house. And the matter will only be worse when she, in turn, is a guest in his home. She has nothing, except the one sprigged muslin."

Sir Roderick frowned, then nodded. "She will need a trousseau for her wedding, of course."

"And a few dresses immediately. She—she only has black and gray, at present."

His eyes narrowed and he regarded Elizabeth closely. "Just what is my granddaughter up to?" he demanded.

Elizabeth blushed furiously. "Nothing! That is—no, nothing! I—I believe it upsets her that Lord Ryde does not admire her. She hopes that if she is becomingly attired he might notice her."

"Could be," Sir Roderick amused himself, though Elizabeth had the distinct impression her clumsy excuse had not fooled the elderly gentleman. "Has she come to her senses about this marriage, then?"

"I—I am not sure." The only thing of which she was sure at the moment was that she regretted approaching her formidable cousin. If she were not careful he would have the truth from her, and that would surely put a period to Celia's hopes! "I—I believe the proposal has rubbed against her independent spirit," she said in all honesty. "She just needs time to adjust to the idea."

She broke off as the door opened and Lord Ryde entered the saloon. Elizabeth stood immediately, flushing once again in embarrassment, and darted to an inconspicuous corner of the room. There, she took her accustomed seat and drew out her embroidery, hiding behind this familiar and soothing occupation.

Celia arrived only a few minutes later. In spite of

the drab color of her gown, the girl looked radiant. Her maid had brushed her dark brown curls until they glistened, framing her face in a glowing, dusky halo. And nothing, Elizabeth thought, could disguise her dainty figure, her graceful carriage, or her springing, almost dancing step. She experienced both a spark of pride and a disturbing pang of jealousy as she looked at the girl. Her own youth slipped farther away every day and never, even by the wildest stretch of the imagination, could she have been considered lovely.

Lord Ryde turned at Celia's entrance, then paused, his eyes resting on her. Slowly, intently, his gaze moved from the top of her burnished curls to the toes of her sandaled feet, not missing any of the highlights in between.

Delicate color suffused Celia's cheeks. She seemed unable to move, as if mesmerized by his lordship's unwavering regard. Her breast rose and fell as her breath came more quickly.

Elizabeth stared from one to the other, startled. There could be no mistaking Celia's reaction to the gentleman, the attraction that held her almost spellbound. And as for Lord Ryde, there was a gleam in his dark eyes that spoke of an awakening interest. Perhaps there was a chance this marriage could work out after all!

Oh, how Elizabeth hoped it would! A troth plighted in the schoolroom might be sweetly touching, the sort of arrangement that made a lonely spinster sigh deeply and shed a misty tear, but it was as nothing compared to the electrical charge that almost shimmered in the air between these two. Now here was romance, indeed!

Without a second thought, she dismissed the prior claims of Captain Edelston. He was personally unknown to her; all that truly mattered was that Celia should be happy, and this seemed most likely if she could accept her grandfather's decrees. Elizabeth glanced back at Celia, saw a trembling smile forming on the girl's lips, and her hopes surged.

In another moment, they were dashed down. Ryde's own lips quivered with an emotion that could only be amusement. Celia stiffened and sparks flashed from her large, furious eyes. She gave him a scathing head-to-toe look of her own, then pointedly turned her back on him. Elizabeth sighed, seeing her half-formed dreams crumbling about her.

CHAPTER FOUR

Celia stretched in her bed, coming slowly awake out of an uneasy sleep. Something was wrong, terribly wrong, but for the moment memory evaded her. She rolled over, encountered an unmoving lump on top of her coverlet, and absently reached over to stroke the brindle fur of the cat Jasper, who should not have been in her chamber at all. Loud purrs rewarded her effort. She tried to focus on the source of her disturbed feelings, and unwelcome images of the night before flooded back to her.

The second skirmish undoubtedly went to Lord Ryde, with all honors. She had behaved badly, allowed her anger to get the better of her and spoken heated words without thinking. Her temper and unruly tongue were her greatest faults, she knew, but just admitting that fact did her little good, and certainly did not mend the damage she might have done.

But he had mocked her! And what was worse, she feared he guessed the overwhelming power that his sheer masculine attraction could so easily have over her. What had set her off last night was the realization that this was a matter of the most complete indifference to him. So, she had been cold and almost rude to him, trying to repay the hurt and salvage her pride.

All it had amounted to, she realized in the more rational light of morning, was that she had once again allowed herself to be diverted from her purpose. She had not been able to penetrate the hard shell that seemed to make him impervious to her jibes. She had made no progress whatsoever—and perhaps had even lost ground.

She must do better, and soon. Only a few days remained before their impending departure to visit his estates, and that was a journey she would rather not make. It would be best to settle the matter with him here, before either of them were forced any deeper into this marriage sham.

She drew back the heavy silk curtains from her massive four-poster bed and looked out into the room. Only a very pale sunlight filtered through a crack in the drawn drapcs, casting a shimmering streak across the carpet. It must still be very early.

A ride was what she needed to clear the cobwebs from her mind, to rid herself of her frustration, ease her distress, and put her in a better mood. An early morning gallop, to allow Whimsy to stretch his legs. She rose and rang for Seddons, her maid.

Less than half an hour later, Celia almost ran down the steps, out the front door, and around to the stable. There she drew up short, her enthusiasm suddenly dampened.

Ryde was there before her. As she watched, he swung himself up easily into Rufus's saddle. He collected his reins from the groom, then saw Celia for the first time. His eyebrows rose in surprise, and he guided the sidling, skittish horse up to her.

"Good morning," he called as he approached. "I felt in need of a good, long gallop."

"So did I." She had not expected him to share this passion of hers. They waited in silence while Jem saddled Whimsy and threw Celia up into the saddle. As soon as her skirts were arranged to her satisfaction, she turned her horse out of the cobbled yard. Trevor and Rufus followed.

She veered to the left, breaking into a trot as they headed across the field that led to the lane. She was forced to restrain her mount to give him time for a brief warm-up, then at last allowed him his head. He immediately broke into a canter, crow-hopped twice, then lengthened his stride into a gallop.

Thundering hoofbeats behind told her that Ryde had given Rufus his rein as well. In moments, the larger horse moved up beside her, then inched into the lead, challenging. Whether the answering spirit came from herself or Whimsy, Celia had no idea, but in a moment they were racing, neck and neck, an all-out run for a nonexistent finish line.

They took the first fence they reached without so much as a check. Rufus, with his longer stride, landed ahead, where he remained until they scrambled up a short bank. Here, Whimsy had the advantage and they pulled even again. The next fence seemed to dash toward them, then was left behind as they raced on. A crop grew in this field, and, as one, they turned to follow the rails, leaving the maturing plants unscathed.

A stone wall lay ahead of them. Celia checked Whimsy, gauged his stride, and they cleared the wall, flying. Rufus again landed ahead and Celia, laughing in exhilaration, urged her tiring mount in pursuit. A few hundred yards ahead a wild tangle of underbrush closed about them and the ground sloped downward.

"There—there's a gully up there!" Celia managed to shout.

"To the line of trees, then!" Trevor called back.

So came the dash to the finish line. Celia leaned low, urging Whimsy on, and they closed the gap that Rufus had created. Trevor threw them a glance, his eyes dancing as unleashed energy radiated from him. He returned his concentration forward, watching the treacherous ground beneath his horse's flying hooves, and pulled into the lead again.

Trevor passed the first line of trees with Celia barely inches behind him. He reined in and his deep laugh of exultation boomed forth, sending a responsive shiver through her. She brought Whimsy to a halt beside Rufus, both horses blowing.

Trevor reached across, grasping her hand. "Well done!" he exclaimed. His power and vibrancy were a tangible force, washing over her, leaving her as breathless as had their mad ride.

"It was a wonderful race!" she exclaimed, returning the pressure of his fingers. Her eyes met his, and she began to sink into their mysterious darkness. She looked away, nervous, suddenly afraid of she knew not what.

"We—we shall have to cool them, the poor dears." She patted Whimsy's neck affectionately. "What a workout we have given them this morning!"

"And us," Trevor agreed. He looked about. "I don't remember this area well. Is there a gate heading in the right direction, or do we go back over the fences?"

"There is a gate, just beyond that slope, that will take us onto the lane. That will give them a quiet walk back."

"I have not had such a run in an age," Trevor declared. He sat at his ease, swaying comfortably with the horse's stride, his reins held loosely in one hand.

"I doubt if Rufus has, either," she laughed. "It was good for all of us."

"Do you do this often?"

"Occasionally," she admitted. "Once in a while I need an outlet. But it is so much more fun when you are not alone!" She broke off, but the look he directed at her was far from sneering or mocking; it held a world of understanding.

"Does your companion ride?" he asked.

"Indifferently, I fear. She has never had much opportunity, in the past. Jem—our head groom—and I have given her lessons, but she does not yet care for hunting or—or careering over the countryside."

A soft, rumbling chuckle shook his large frame. "She is to be honored for attempting at all, learning so late. And pitied, if she tries to keep up with you."

Warm color rose to Celia's cheeks, for there was no mistaking the hint of honest admiration contained in his voice. For the first time in their short, two-day acquaintance, Celia experienced a sensation of camaraderie, of being drawn to this strange, difficult man.

"I feel all tingling and alive!" she declared. "There is

nothing on earth as wonderful as riding like that!"

"Do you really think so?"

She turned to look up at him and found him watching her with an odd, enigmatic smile.

"Do not you?" she asked. Puzzled, she tried to fathom his meaning.

Tiny lines of amusement crinkled at the corners of his eyes, and a deep chuckle of genuine amusement escaped him. "Yes, child, it's an experience like very few others. But you are young yet; there is still much for you to discover."

It was on the tip of her tongue to ask him what he meant, but he seemed to withdraw somewhat from her, closing off this avenue of discussion. They rode on for a few minutes in a silence that was not quite companionable, yet not quite strained. They started down the slope, then followed the flat verge until they reached the gate. Trevor moved Rufus forward and leaned down to unlatch it. Carefully, he backed his horse, then held the gate wide for Celia to precede him into the lane.

A lumbering wagon approached, driven by one of the tenant farmers. The man reined in his draught horse, waving as he recognized the pair on horseback. Trevor locked the gate, then urged Rufus forward to exchange greetings with the farmer.

Celia brought Whimsy up to join them as the man drove on. "Do you know him?" she asked, surprised.

"I know most of the people here," he answered. "I spent most of my school holidays at Ranleigh after my father was sent to India."

"Military?" she asked, surprised.

"Worse. Diplomat. I think he must have been posted all over the world. I knew Uncle Roderick better than I knew my own father."

"Uncle?" she asked, trying to place a possible connection.

"By courtesy only." There was a note of amusement in his voice. "We are not related."

"He said you had helped him before, when he had been ill."

At that, Trevor laughed outright. "That is his polite way of saying he issued a royal decree commanding my presence, then dictated his orders through me while he lay abed."

"And you put up with it, calmly doing as you were bid?" she demanded.

He looked down at her, frowning thoughtfully. "You are so ready to see weakness," he said gently. "Say rather that I was quite willing to humor an elderly man who has shown me nothing but kindness. If loving that exasperating old dictator is a fault, then I am guilty. I respect him," he added. "And he has had the goodness to respect me. He asks my opinion and has the courtesy to listen to my replies. He is a good man, strong-willed and proud."

The last could be said about Ryde, she reflected ruefully. By no means could he be considered weak. Her grandfather must have detected in his godson characteristics that they shared, respecting a pride and a will equal to his own. And being so similar, they would either hate or love each other, depending on their basic natures. It gave her momentary pause to realize that it was the warmer emotion that ruled them.

Yet, Ryde was also a man capable of who knew what daring. She glanced at him, wondering. "My grandfather said you had been in France recently," she said before she could stop herself.

Lord Ryde stiffened, then seemed to force himself to relax. "Oh, I get around a bit," he replied in a tone that did not encourage her to pursue the subject. Her curiosity naturally stirred, but she stifled it, respecting his reticence. Sir Roderick had spoken of danger. . . . Instead, she cast about in her mind for another topic.

"Did my grandfather ever speak of my father?" she tried instead.

"Often. I gathered that they were not much alike, that they preferred to live quite differently. The only things they shared were their pride and stubbornness."

"Those—those are family failings. I fear I have them as well."

"Your grandfather respected your father for the stand he took, you know. I think he was sorry for the estrangement between them, though it was inevitable."

Celia remained silent, her brain whirling. If that were true, then there was a chance—a very good chance—that she could defy him, too. It was possible her grandfather had learned a bitter lesson with his son. If she could convince Ryde to help her, so that the marriage idea might be abandoned without the old man having to give in or lose face, there was every hope she would not have to do anything drastic at all! She could continue to live here at Ranleigh, be presented to London society, and allow her life to take its proper course.

Ryde took a deep breath, exhaling heavily in contentment. Celia glanced over at him, surprised to see his relaxed, easy expression. His gaze rested beyond her, on the crops growing in the fields, or perhaps beyond them to the thicket where the deer grazed.

He belonged in the country, she realized suddenly! She had expected, from those references to his secret work, that he would prefer a life of danger, of excitement. True, he was completely at home on a horse as difficult as Rufus, but somehow she guessed he would be one to tramp happily for hours through damp underbrush in a freezing wind, carrying a gun and a brace of partridges. He would be present for the lambings, and work long and hard beside his laborers to accomplish his goals. He had boundless energy that she could feel, and he would devote it all to an estate that he loved.

This was what her grandfather would have wanted for a son, not her own father who loathed the fresh, clean air and who only felt at home behind a green baize cloth with a pack of cards or ivory dice in his hands. It was no wonder that the old man wanted to see his estate safe with Lord Ryde. And she, it dawned on her with a blinding flash, was the means of reconciliation between the two. Through her, her grandfather sought to recapture the son he had lost.

If Charlie had lived . . . Everything might be so different! But his grandson had not survived, and now the old man sought to bring his godson into the family to become his heir.

She could understand it now—but she would not submit to it. She was not a pawn to cooperate meekly just so that her grandfather would be satisfied. She wanted more out of life than to be a business transaction. Her pride could never tolerate it.

They turned in at last at the open gate and proceeded up the graveled drive. Jem and Coxly, Ryde's groom, came hurrying forward as they drew up in the stableyard, and Trevor jumped lightly to the cobbled stones. He handed his reins to the waiting groom, then turned to hold out his hands to Celia. She hesitated a moment, then again allowed him to clasp her slender waist and lift her to the ground. A slight smile played about his lips but he released her almost as soon as she found her footing. Offering his arm, he escorted her back to the house.

They parted company at the foot of the stairs. Celia ran quickly up, her heart light for the first time since her grandfather broke his fateful news. There was hope, real hope, that Ryde would understand when she appealed to him for his support, that he would withdraw his suit. And after that . . . well, she would not be adverse to getting to know him a bit better.

She descended to the breakfast parlor a short half hour later, once again dressed in the sprigged muslin. The others were already gathered there, just finishing their meal. Ryde glanced up and smiled as she entered.

"Good morning," she said to all in general. She walked around the table to the sideboard, pausing by her grandfather's chair to drop a kiss on his cheek, a sign of affection she had neglected for the previous two mornings. Ravenous after her exercise, she filled her plate with an array of eggs, sausages, and rolls, then took her place at the table.

Sir Roderick watched her for a moment, his eyes thoughtful. At last, he stood. "Trevor, would you join me in the bookroom when you are done?" he asked. Ryde's eyes rested momentarily on Celia, then he nodded and stood also. The two men left the parlor.

It was not until luncheon that Celia saw either of them again. They came in together, apparently deep in a discussion of the fate of the west fields. This they continued throughout the cold meal. Twice, Trevor's eyes strayed to Celia, and it was not purely coincidental when they met her gaze. She encountered a warm smile lurking in their dark depths, a smile of friendship, not of amusement. A pleasant glow seeped through her, for she was sure at last that she was well on her way to accomplishing her purpose.

For the afternoon, Sir Roderick again claimed his godson's company, this time to ride out to inspect the fields for themselves. Celia watched them depart with something disturbingly akin to disappointment.

"Celia," Elizabeth called to her softly.

Celia turned away from the window where she could see the two men disappearing toward the stable. "Yes?"

"I spoke to your grandfather again this morning, before you came down. He has agreed to allow us to stay in London for a week on our way to Lord Ryde's estate."

"A week?" Celia brightened, forgetting for a moment that she hoped not to be making that trip at all. "A whole week? How ever did you manage it?"

Elizabeth smiled proudly. "I pointed out that it

would be impossible for you to have dresses made up any faster than that. He could not, after all, wish you to appear in ready-made clothing! And he saw the wisdom of not presenting you to your future servants unsuitably clad."

"I—" Celia hesitated, then went on. "I don't intend to go through with this marriage. You know that, Elizabeth."

"Yes, I know it. But until your wardrobe has been replenished, I see no need for your grandfather to be informed. Do you?" Her lips twitched slightly, but she managed to maintain an expression of bland innocence.

"That—that is deceitful!" Celia exclaimed, but could not suppress a giggle of delight at her companion's tactics. Elizabeth, mousy little creature that she appeared, had hidden depths.

"Let us make a list of the things you will need," Elizabeth urged, succumbing to the feminine pleasure for clothing in which she could not indulge herself.

Celia agreed. There was always a chance that she would have to make this journey before she and Ryde could convince her grandfather that they were in earnest. And a week in London! That was bait difficult to resist. She could visit the shops, spend hours with a *modiste*, buy new stockings and chemises and gowns for walking and dining and dancing. Perhaps she could go anyway, even if they were not traveling on to Hastings.

The next two hours were beguiled in the most pleasant manner. Celia and Elizabeth, assisted by Seddons and the playful cat Jasper, threw open her wardrobes and went to work. It took only a few minutes to determine that all her current dresses were wholly unsuitable, and these were laid aside, much to the cat's delight. He pounced onto the pile of clothes that lay on the bed, his tail twitching, and began to attack each billowing fold.

"Jasper!" Elizabeth exclaimed and swooped down on the indignant animal. "Miss Celia still needs those yet a while," she informed the furry armful she now held tightly. Jasper's only response was to purr and rub his head against her arm. Elizabeth laughed, but put him out of the room. He sat down, gave her a baleful glare, then proceeded to take a thorough bath to smooth down the hairs she had ruffled.

The work went more easily after that. Seddons returned the gowns to the cupboards for safety, then left Celia and Elizabeth to make lists of everything necessary for a young lady of quality to present a creditable appearance to the world. Their sole guide in this endeavor was the most recent issue of *La Belle Assemble*, obtained by Celia, as her mourning drew to a close, in the hopes of this very occupation.

By late afternoon, Celia tired of remaining indoors. The spring sunshine beckoned her outside, and armed with her much-read copy of *Marmion*, she headed for the rose garden. She was nearing one of her favorite sections, the song of Lochinvar, and she settled down on the long stone bench prepared to enjoy herself. Barely moments later, Jasper insinuated himself into her lap. Resting the book on his back, she found her place.

Lochinvar. Now here was a figure of romance, sure

to inspire the heart of any young lady. *So faithful in love, and so dauntless in war. There was never knight like the young Lochinvar.* She closed her finger in the book, holding her place as she laid it in her lap. For true romance there had to be difficulties to overcome, but that was what made it so exciting, so thrilling—as long as there was always a happy conclusion. And there had to be a dashing hero who would risk all for love and win out because of his daring deeds.

Every woman, in her heart, must want such a man, one who would not only try, but actually succeed, in rescuing her from her sea of troubles, preferably from the very jaws of disaster. She wanted a knight errant to fight a battle for her, then sweep her up onto his charger and race off with her. That such a ride would undoubtedly be most uncomfortable she did not allow to weigh with her.

Jonathon, a dear though he was, did not fit this mold. And in reality, she strongly suspected, few men did. Lord Ryde . . . She paused, considering. Now there was a gentleman with distinct promise in the romantic line. Somehow, she could see him doing something so outrageous as stealing his love away from her wedding. He would go at it wholeheartedly, reckless, heedless of danger, and, all the time, his deep laugh would vibrate through her as he fought for her with boundless energy and joy.

There was only one thing wrong with this picture she conjured up. It was Lord Ryde from whom she had to escape.

This presented a rather disturbing situation. In all honesty, she had to admit that Lord Ryde was a devastatingly attractive man. The more she saw of him, the more sure she was that his thick, curling black hair, his harsh features, and those dark, luminous eyes were exactly to her taste. And in the brief time they had spent riding together that morning, she had sensed a kindred spirit hidden within him.

Thoughtfully, she rubbed the cat's head. Ryde had agreed to marry her solely at her grandfather's bidding, before ever setting eyes on her! She could never let herself forget that fact. And she could never accept a proposal that was made at the instigation of a third party.

If only he would withdraw his offer now, and then seek to know her better. If he would pay court to her of his own accord instead of on her grandfather's instructions, she could not deny that she might be willing to listen to him. But not under the present circumstances!

A scuffling in the gravel caused her to look up. There, less than twenty feet away, came the object of her thoughts. His tall, rugged figure moved with surprising grace, as of power strictly held in leash. Yes, if he would only approach her on his own, she would be very willing to listen.

"Do I disturb you?" he asked.

"Not in the least." She slid over on the bench, making room for him to join her. "Did you have a pleasant ride?"

"And an instructive one. There is much I still need to learn about the management of an estate." He must have come straight from the stables, for he was still dressed in buckskins and an olive-green riding coat.

Chestnut hairs clung to both, and an unmistakable aroma of horse reached her, pleasantly pungent.

Jasper stood and stretched, then headed for Ryde with the unerring instinct of a feline who senses clothing not yet honored with stray cat hairs. Horses provided a poor substitute in his prejudiced eyes.

"Did you solve Grandfather's problem?" Celia asked, watching with interest as Trevor settled the cat on his lap.

"You mean, did he solve mine. I hope so. I won't be able to tell, though, until I return to Hastings and put his ideas into effect." He glanced down, saw the book, and idly picked it up and began to leaf through the pages. *"Forward and frolic glee was there, The will to do, the soul to dare.* That sounds like our ride this morning, does it not?"

"It certainly does. *And the stern joy which warriors feel In foemen worthy of their steel,"* she quoted. "Or was poor Rufus tired from his morning run?"

Ryde laughed, softly this time, but the deep undertones of the sound wreaked their damage on Celia. "Poor Rufus," he declared. "He was quite a gentleman. Most unlike himself, I fear. *Of manners gentle, of affections mild."*

Celia's brow furrowed as she tried to place the quote. "That is not Scott," she finally said.

"No, Pope. One of his lesser known works."

She looked up at him, surprised. "You read poetry, then? I did not think gentlemen usually did."

"Well, I am afraid I do," he told her apologetically. "Occasionally, at least. On the whole, I much prefer to be doing rather than just sitting and reading."

She sighed. "I know. Oh, there are so many things I would much rather do than just read about them! You can have no idea how frustrating it can be to long for activity."

"Then why do you not do something about it?" he asked, smiling.

"That is easy for you to say. You are a man. It is not proper for ladies to have grand adventures."

His lips twitched and it took an obvious effort for him to control his amusement. "Is that what you want? Adventures?" A curious note lurked in his voice and she detected no offense.

"Well," she considered. "It surely must be more interesting than just sitting about doing needlework!"

"Now, that is something I have not seen you do!"

"You are laughing at me," she pointed out, though she knew there was no unkindness intended. "And you are quite right. I do not do needlework. Or rather I do, but it is quite shockingly bad. I leave that to my dear Elizabeth."

"What do you do, then?"

"At the moment, very little. I ride, I play the pianoforte, and I dream of being free. All forms of escape, I fear."

"Is that what you wish? To escape?" He watched her, curious.

She bit her lip. Now, if ever, seemed to be the time to broach the subject. His mood was sympathetic and understanding. Surely she could talk him around, now!

"Not escape, exactly. But I long for a purpose, something to accomplish. And I—I don't want to be anyone's pawn!"

"Now we come to it," he murmured, the lurking smile back in his eyes. He removed Jasper's claws from his leg and held his front paws in one hand where they could wreak no further damage on his buckskins.

She took a deep breath. "My lord, does it not irritate you when someone tries to order your life?"

"No one would dare," he said simply.

"But—" She broke off and stood, too nervous to remain still. "Would you not wish to choose your own wife?" she demanded.

"I thought I had," came the calm reply.

"But you had not even met me! Grandfather ordered you to marry me!"

"No, no one orders me to do anything."

She blinked at him, momentarily nonplussed. "Do you deny that my grandfather has asked that you marry me?"

"I do not deny it." His smile was tighter, almost forced. He shifted Jasper unnecessarily in his lap, but the cat did not object. He merely stretched and yawned, displaying an impressive set of teeth.

"But you yourself could not have wished it when he first suggested it!" Celia exclaimed, paying the cat no heed. "When you arrived here, I would swear that you were not pleased!'

Ryde stiffened slightly, but the smile remained firmly in place. "I admit I have felt certain regrets, but at the time I gave my word, I was quite willing."

"Why?" She could not prevent herself from asking the question that haunted her.

"I had my reasons," he said evenly.

"What are they? I—I think I have the right to know."

He ran one finger slowly down the cat's back. "All right, if you want plain speaking you shall have it. I have just inherited an estate and a barony. I am the last of my name." He paused, letting this sink in.

She felt the blood rush to her cheeks. His implication was obvious. He needed a son and heir, and for that he needed a wife.

He nodded and she tried to erase some of the shock from her face. "There was no lady of my acquaintance with whom I felt I could live for any length of time," he went on. "There seemed no reason why I should not oblige my godfather in this manner when he requested this favor of me."

Her legs no longer seemed capable of supporting her, so she sank back down on the bench. Jasper, apparently feeling that his obligations as far as Ryde's breeches were concerned had been fulfilled, returned to the cool crispness of Celia's muslin skirts.

"You wanted the truth," he pointed out.

"Yes, I—I did. And I am glad you told me. There should be no pretense when one is arranging business matters, should there?"

His smile was back. "Most assuredly not," he agreed.

"And since you have spoken plainly, you will not object if I do the same?" She gathered the cat against her as if for courage.

"By all means, please do."

"Then—my grandfather will not hear of my oversetting his plans and refusing to marry you. I ask you, my lord, not to offer for me at his instigation. I cannot and will not marry you—or anyone!—when he has ordered the whole thing."

She bit her lip, watching him through wide, worried eyes. Would he catch the inflection in her voice, the meaning that underlay her words? If he told her that he had changed his mind, that it was on his own initiative that he stayed now, it would make all the difference in the world to her.

"My dear Miss Marcombe." Dancing sparks of laughter lit his dark eyes as he shook his head in apology. "It pains me to be so disobliging."

"But . . ." She broke off, staring at him in growing horror.

"I never go back on my given word. And I have given my word to your grandfather that I will marry you."

CHAPTER FIVE

Celia sat hunched in a corner of the traveling chaise, frowning out the window upon the green fields that slipped slowly by. Three days had passed since her interview in the rose garden with Lord Ryde, and she still seethed and fumed at his treachery. The nerve of that infuriating, odious, calculating man! Obtaining Ranleigh was his only concern. He had shown her of what little matter she was.

His sole purpose in talking with her that day must have been to assure her compliance in marrying him. He must have realized how bitterly she objected to the idea and seen the need for a little persuasion. He could hardly drag a kicking and screaming bride to the altar!

And where was Jonathon? Her letter must have reached him by now! Would he arrive at Ranleigh that morning, or perhaps the next, and discover her gone? More than ever was she glad she had written that impetuous note to him. She could hardly count on Elizabeth remaining strong in the face of Sir Roderick's rage, so without Jonathon she was virtually on her own. And her grandfather and Lord Ryde, united, posed rather a daunting front for a young lady alone.

At any other time, Celia would have thought poorly of Sir Roderick's decision to take as much as two days to accomplish the forty-five mile journey to London. Now, she welcomed any delay, anything that might allow Jonathon to catch them up and prevent her eventual arrival at Ryde's Hastings.

She peered ahead as another village came into view. She might not want to reach her destination, but she was heartily bored with traveling. London could be only an hour or less away.

"That must be Whetstone." Elizabeth, who sat opposite her on the forward seat, consulted a guidebook. "We must be almost there!"

She proved to be correct. Next came the turnpike, followed by the infamous Finchley Common, and they drew closer and closer to London. Beyond the Common lay East End, and then it was only a short distance on to Highgate and their first glimpse of the sprawling tangle of buildings that was the great city itself.

From here, their way led down a long descent until they reached Islington Spa and then, the last toll booth. This passed, it seemed a surprisingly short time before the carriage wheels struck cobbled stones, and buildings lined their way.

Celia took a deep breath of the familiar London smells with which she had grown up, and she drew back, repelled by the acrid unpleasantness that met her nostrils. Had it always been this way, and she had not known it until she breathed the clean air of the country?

"It is so very large," Elizabeth murmured in awe. She peered about as the traveling chaise made its way through a maze of streets. There seemed to be an inordinate amount of filth. Street sweepers waged a constant war, but were up against horse-drawn wagons bearing produce, vendors hawking their wares and a myriad of people going about their business. Mostly, though, there were beggars and ragged urchins, huddling in decaying doorways, darting between the traffic, importuning anyone who seemed to be better off.

Celia sank back against the squabs. These streets, outside the fashionable quarters where she had lived, presented a very different picture of the city she had always loved. It was a disturbing sight, one she had almost forgotten in her nineteen-month absence.

The carriage slowed, made another turning, and the scenery was transformed as if by magic. Large, stately mansions now lined one side of the wider street, and a garden, surrounded by an iron fence, lay on the other. They entered another block and the houses diminished in size but were no less respectable.

At last, when Celia was finally getting her bearings and recognizing familiar streets and landmarks, the carriage made one last turn and pulled up before Grillon's Hotel. A footman hurried forward, opening their door and letting down the step. He offered his hand and helped first Celia and then Elizabeth to alight.

In a very short time, Celia found herself in a large, pleasant apartment with a window that looked out over the street. Beyond her door lay an elegant little drawing room, which also led to the rooms allotted to

Elizabeth and Sir Roderick. Celia turned away from the window and watched while Seddons, her maid, unpacked the last of her few belongings. Tomorrow she would begin the enjoyable task of filling the many gaps in her wardrobe.

For the moment, she was content. Grillon's Hotel had one advantage that would never appear on any advertisement. Lord Ryde did not stay there.

This fact, more than any other, contributed to Celia's present rise in spirits. She was free of him, free of his hateful, deceitful presence, for as long as they remained in London. They had parted company with him at the gates of Ranleigh, they to proceed at a slow and stately rate, he to dash off at a spanking pace in his gleaming curricle with the intention of making London that night and Hastings the next, with many changes of horses along the way. That she envied him his speed and sporting mode of travel, Celia would never admit.

They dined early in the hotel's luxurious restaurant. As the meal ended, Sir Roderick suggested that the ladies might like to retire to their suite and rest after the fatigue of their journey. He, on the other hand, had formed the intention of going to White's, where he was a member, to spend the evening playing cards. Celia thought poorly of this plan, for during her absence from the city she had sorely missed the many plays and other entertainments to be found at the height of a Season. Elizabeth, though, an indifferent traveler, seconded Sir Roderick's scheme, and she was forced to give in with a good grace.

The evening did not prove as grim as she had feared. Upon inquiry, she discovered that the hotel possessed any number of fashion magazines. These she requested to be brought to her room upon the instant, and she sat up late, pouring over each one, scribbling numerous notes on the list that she and Elizabeth had made at Ranleigh.

As soon as they had breakfasted the following morning, Celia and Elizabeth set forth on their first shopping expedition. No limit had been set on her spending. In fact, Sir Roderick's sole comment concerning the matter was that he wished his granddaughter to obtain an appropriately elegant trousseau. It was therefore with thrilled anticipation that Celia, upon stepping into the hackney cab, gave the driver the name of one of the most fashionable *modistes* in town.

Elizabeth appeared to suffer certain qualms upon entering the elaborate show rooms, but these soon dissipated in the unparalleled experience that followed. Celia might not be known to Madame Yvette, but any young lady who swept in with so regal a manner and demanded to be shown so wide a selection of gowns for every occasion was deserving of Madame's personal attention. This Celia received, and in a short time endless arrays of gowns were being displayed before her.

The first to take Celia's fancy was a walking dress of rose Circassian cloth, ornamented with bands of white lutestring and edged with corded lozenges. It was cut *à la blouse*, and confined into shape with Athenian braces of the lutestring. This confection was carefully set aside to be fitted.

Next, she turned her attention to a carriage dress of Parisian green grenadine, but she set this aside upon sight of the loveliest morning dress, a simple round gown of pale yellow jaconet muslin. Several rows of easings, pulled with white riband and narrow lace, trimmed the bottom of the full skirt, the high waistline, and the cuffs of the long, loose sleeves which, she was assured, were just coming into fashion. Celia, slipping into this enchanting creation, felt herself a fairy princess and knew, whatever the cost or sacrifices she would have to make in her remaining purchases, she must have this one dress.

At the end of two and a half hours, Celia had added an evening gown of white crepe to the two dresses already selected, and had undergone a lengthy fitting for the alterations to all three. These, the beaming proprietress promised, would be delivered within two days' time. Celia left the shop, in alt over her morning's work.

She came back to earth with a crash. She had no idea what the bill would come to but she had a sneaking suspicion it would be substantial. Guilt afflicted her vulnerable conscience. She was accustomed to managing on a meager allowance when it came to her clothing. Her grandfather's generosity sprang from his belief that he was purchasing her trousseau. She knew he was not. She made a vow, then and there, to practice the strictest economy in the remainder of her acquisitions.

And she needed to make many more. While three gowns might have sufficed during her mourning, they would hardly be sufficient to see her through more than the immediate future. Sir Roderick, a stickler on matters of dress, would be most sincerely displeased if she came down to dinner every night in the same gown.

"Where should we go next?" asked Elizabeth, looking somewhat dazed from the morning's visit.

Celia stood on the street, looking about her uncertainly while one of the shop assistants flagged down a hackney cab. "I do not know," Celia finally said. "A seamstress, I suppose. My mother always had her dresses made up, and quite inexpensively, I believe. We must go to a linen draper, of course. And you, my dear Elizabeth, shall have a new dress or two, as well. No, do not protest. And no, I shall not allow you to make over my mourning dresses. You are quite four inches taller than I am. What a figure you should look, with skirts much too short!"

The hackney pulled up and the two ladies climbed in. Celia directed the driver to Bond Street, where they presently alighted. She and Elizabeth started strolling slowly, gazing into the shop windows.

"There are so many things we must get. We need a haberdasher, I suppose, and . . ." She broke off, staring into a milliner's shop. In prominent display stood a white crepe toque, ornamented about the front with chenille and topped by a diadem of white crepe roses. She shook her head and moved on. "I shall need hats, of course, though I think I can retrim my old straw bonnets so that they will look quite the thing. I—I do not think I care for the more fashionable new hats."

"We shall find ribands and satins, and set to work on your bonnets in the evening," Elizabeth assured her. "I am quite accustomed to making things over. You shall see how beautifully they will come out."

They continued walking, peering into the windows

and discussing the items that met their fascinated gaze. London was quite familiar to Celia, who had known no other home until nineteen months ago. But the interests of a young lady were quite different from those of a young girl, and the shops held new and exciting discoveries for her.

"Grafton House!" she suddenly exclaimed. "Mamma always used to shop there, and could find the most amazing things! You will adore it, Elizabeth. I am sure we may find all that we need there, and for the merest song!"

"Is it far? Can we walk from here?"

Celia laughed. "Not now. In the morning. Before breakfast. It is always shockingly crowded, but we shall get there at the most indecently early hour. Now, are you tired, or shall we visit a linen draper? If we are to leave London in only six more days, we must waste no time in contacting my mamma's old seamstress."

Although Elizabeth denied it, she did look somewhat tired. It must be the unaccustomed noise and bustle of London, Celia decided, and vowed to herself to make this next stop a short one. They would return to the hotel early, consult with the seamstress, then spend a quiet evening in their rooms.

They located another hackney with ease, gave the direction of Layton and Shear's, Bedford House, and were soon trotting briskly down the street. Elizabeth sank back against the seat, her eyes closed. Celia watched her carefully, then decided it was no more than weariness.

The signs of fatigue dropped away from her quickly enough, though, upon entering the magical emporium. In a surprisingly short time, Celia found herself in possession of dress lengths in celestial-blue mull muslin, amber crepe lisse, sea-green gauze, and peach cambric. Only their surprisingly inexpensive prices prevented her from succumbing to guilt at being so extravagant. So reasonable were they, in fact, that she was easily able to add a length of olive green kerseymere, that would make up beautifully into a pelisse. A rather stunning brown *Gros de Berlin* followed, intended for a spencer.

Elizabeth, over her repeated protests, was persuaded to allow her charge to purchase for her a lavender grenadine and a quite affordable levantine silk in a soft, warm brown. Also added to their purchases were a selection of necessary trimmings, such as blond lace, Brussels sprigs, letting-in lace, and a selection of ribands and scraps of satin for lining the bonnets.

They returned to Grillon's, tired but pleased. Recalling the address of the seamstress most recently employed by her mother, Celia sent a message to this woman. They barely had time to refresh themselves with tea and cakes, not having had anything since breakfast, when the seamstress arrived, armed with fashion plates and a zeal that bordered on the fanatical. Celia's head whirled by the time the woman finally departed, armed with several packages of their newly acquired cloth.

The following morning saw Celia and Elizabeth at Grafton House at an hour when the majority of fashionable London was not yet astir. Even then, this bargain establishment was busy. Elizabeth, keeping quite close to her charge, expressed in hushed accents her shocked disapproval of the vulgarity of many of the patrons. They did not allow this to disturb them, however, and soon were lost in the delight of hunting out bargains. Here, they found everything from silk stockings, at only twelve shillings the pair, to an array of untrimmed bonnets, handkerchiefs, slippers, and shawls, all quite ridiculously inexpensive. A particularly lovely blue paisley shawl, so soft Celia could not detect its difference from cashmere, caught her eye. Nothing would do but that she should purchase this, and bestow it on her protesting chaperone.

By the time they returned to the hotel, both ladies were exhausted. They ordered a light nuncheon, then sank back into their chairs to consider the remainder of the day.

"I cannot face another shop at the moment," Celia sighed. "My head aches dreadfully."

"It is all so very noisy, is it not?" Elizabeth agreed. "How I do miss the quiet of the country! Thank heaven we shall only be here a few more days."

Celia could not agree with that last thought. She had no desire to continue their journey—for their next destination was the estate of Lord Ryde. Had they been returning home, to Ranleigh, she would have had no objections to leaving the city. Purchasing new gowns must always be exciting, and London during the Season thrilled her with its throngs of fashionables and numerous entertainments, but to her surprise, the peace of the country beckoned.

"I do long for a breath of fresh air," Elizabeth continued.

"Then let us go to the Park!" Celia exclaimed on inspiration. "This afternoon, at the hour of the Promenade! You will like it of all things! And we may inspect all the latest fashions, for that is where the *ton* goes to be seen!"

After they finished eating, both ladies retired to their chambers to lie down upon their beds and recuperate their strength. Celia drifted off into a sleep that lasted for more than two hours. When she finally rose, she felt quite refreshed and much more the thing. She rang for her maid, then began to prepare for her outing in Hyde Park.

When Elizabeth finally tapped on her door, Celia had on the new walking dress of rose Circassian cloth. An old bonnet with a high poke, now adorned with clusters of matching rose ribands, rested on the table beside her. Celia pulled this on over her dusky curls and tied its strings beneath one ear.

"Quite dashing," Elizabeth told her, smiling.

Celia regarded herself in the mirror, turning slightly to admire the reflection. "I have never had a dress so lovely before. It will be such fun, walking in the Park, looking as though I belong there with the Polite World."

"If Lord Ryde saw you now, he would not be so indifferent!" Elizabeth avowed, most unwisely.

Celia bristled. "I am sure I do not care what he thinks! Grandfather may believe I am buying this finery for him, but I assure you I am not! It—it is for Jonathon! He has only seen me as a schoolroom miss before, and yet he loved me. Do you not think he will be pleased with my transformation?"

That mention of Ryde continued to irritate Celia. Throughout her shopping, as she stood for hours having the new gowns pinned to fit her slender frame, his image had been at the back of her mind. Always, the question of what he would think when he was privileged to see her in these beautiful creations haunted her. Would he maintain his amused disinterest? Or would she see the laughter fade from his mysterious, compelling eyes to be replaced by a smoldering glow of desire? Oh, if only she could make him regret that he ever thought of her as a piece of "property"! He must be made to appreciate all that he lost when Jonathon rescued her from his calculating clutches!

With these ignoble thoughts still in her mind, they set off for the Park. They were put down at the Stanhope Gate, and eagerly they headed for the path that took them along Rotten Row where the *ton* either drove or rode to be seen by the rest of the *beau monde*. Nor did they find themselves the only ones on foot. The Season was in full swing, almost everybody who was Anybody was in London, and the majority of them flocked to the popular Promenade.

"*And in its park, in jovial June, How sweet the merry linnet's tune*," Elizabeth murmured in contentment, drawing, as was her wont of late, upon *Marmion* for inspiration.

"It is but barely turned May," Celia pointed out. "If it were June, the Season would be almost over. Do you know," she went on musingly as she eyed a small group of young ladies who were all garbed in the latest fashions, "I really looked forward to being presented. I should have been, last year. And now," she continued, warming to her theme, "I cannot be, because of Grandfather and his odious godson."

"Once you are married, you may spend every

Season in town," Elizabeth pointed out.

"I am not marrying Ryde!" Celia exclaimed, "I—I shall marry Jonathon, but, oh, how I should have liked a real Season, with the round of parties, and to have gentlemen pay me court! This just seems so—so abrupt!"

"I am sure Captain Edelston will make it up to you," Elizabeth said soothingly.

Celia lapsed into silence, for she could not confess the truth to her companion. What would become of her? Had things only been different, had her parents not died, she would right now be one of the fashionable throng being paraded on the Marriage Mart, having wonderful fun—and being able to select a dashing husband who would love her for herself, no matter what her grandfather predicted about fortune hunters. She added this to the growing number of grudges that she held against Ryde. It was all his fault that she could only enjoy the Season vicariously, and for only a precious few days.

These thoughts continued to dominate her mind as they strolled along the path beside the tanbark. Notables passed her on either side, but so involved was she in heaping more and more blame onto Ryde's absent head that she failed to notice who they were or what they wore.

A startled cry recalled her from her abstraction, and she looked about vaguely to see the source of it. A gentleman reined in beside her, staring down with a humorous, incredulous expression.

"Cilly!" he exclaimed. "By all that's holy! Cilly, my little love!"

She looked up into the classically handsome face of

a tall, blond man astride a large, quiet black gelding. He gazed down, a warm smile lighting his bright blue eyes.

"Jonny!" she almost screamed. "Oh, Jonny!" Her delight in seeing her old friend again crumbled as she remembered the part she had to play. "Thank heaven you have found me!" she exclaimed dramatically. She rushed up to him as he swung easily down from the saddle.

He caught her arms, holding her off. "Really, Cill. Not in the middle of the Park! Remember where you are."

"Safe, with you!" she declared, accompanying her words with an intent stare and a meaningful squeeze of the hands she now held.

"Well, of course you're safe," he declared, surprised. He pushed her slightly away so that he could get a better look at her. "What a little beauty you've turned into! Have you come to town to snare a beau at last?"

"You haven't received my letter?" she demanded. "Oh, Jonny! How just like you! But at least you are here, so there has been no harm done."

"No!" he assured her, shocked at such an idea. "Never did anyone any harm in my life, except a few of Boney's troops," he added conscientiously. "How can you say such a thing, love?"

Although he used the term of endearment for her, his attitude was conspicuously unlike that of a lover. She threw him a speaking glance, which appeared to have no effect on him whatsoever. This called for resourcefulness.

She gripped his arm, giving it a hard pinch. "Oh, Jonny, I am so glad to see you again," she sighed, moving closer and pulling on him so that he bent closer and her lips came nearer his ear. "Play along," she hissed softly.

He looked down at her, perplexed. "I say, Cill, is something the matter?" he asked as the odd nature of her manner finally dawned on him.

"I'm in the most dreadful trouble," she whispered. "You must help me!" In a normal speaking voice, she said: "Dearest Jonathon, allow me to introduce you to my companion." She turned, and found that Elizabeth, sweet, discreet creature that she was, had stepped back several paces to allow the reunion to take place undisturbed.

"Jonny, I want you to meet my chaperon, companion, and dear friend, Miss Westerly." Carefully, she schooled her features into a totally besotted expression and gazed up at the gentleman she held firmly in tow. "Now that you have seen him, Elizabeth, you can understand how I could never love another!"

Jonathon blinked at her tragic accents, aware that something was obviously expected of him. "Of course not," he declared in heartening tones as he patted the hand that gripped his arm firmly. "How could you?"

Elizabeth, gazing up into that tanned face with its classical features and deep blue eyes, topped by the dark blond curls, could only agree. Never had she thought to behold the embodiment of her own private romantic fantasies. But here stood her secret hero, the reality more perfect than even her hazy imaginings could make him. It was no wonder Celia loved him. Anyone would!

She held out a hesitant hand and he took a stiff step toward her, then bowed low over her fingers. She kept her eyes lowered, hoping frantically that no one would notice her heightened color.

"May I escort you a ways?" he asked. They stood at a stretch of the path that bordered the tanbark, and he could easily lead his horse for a distance. He fell into step beside them, limping slightly.

"Does it bother you much?" Celia asked solicitously.

"What? Oh, the knee. No, not much. I never cared for dancing, you know, and this way no one expects it of me. I can make my excuses early and escape the dullest parties!"

"If you didn't come in answer to my letter, what brings you here?" Celia asked, curious. "I did not think you liked London."

"Don't. But my mother took a fancy to come up for a few weeks, and I couldn't let her stay alone at an hotel."

Elizabeth gazed admiringly up at his amiable and undeniably handsome countenance. She could only approve wholeheartedly of a gentleman who would put the needs of another before his own preferences. Captain Jonathon Edelston would make any woman a wonderful husband. How glad she was that it was her darling Celia who should have won his love! She repeated this thought, fighting down the unworthy pangs of jealousy and yearning that tugged at her.

"You—you received your injury at Trafalgar, did you not?" Elizabeth rushed into speech, trying to divert her thoughts from their dangerous and unhappy direction.

Jonathon nodded. "Just a ball lodged near my knee. Came off pretty light, really. Not like a lot of them."

"Alas! to whom the Almighty gave, For Britain's sins an

early grave!" Elizabeth quoted. Such bravery set the final seal of perfection on the inestimable Captain Edelston.

Jonathon blinked, totally unaware of his rise to near hero status in Miss Westerly's eyes. "Uh . . . quite," he managed. Poetry was not one of his passions. If asked the identity of Scott's noble Marmion, he would have answered, after subjecting the matter to earnest consideration, that he rather fancied the fellow must be that new boxing cove everyone was making such a fuss over.

"You may be proud," Elizabeth asserted. "Your limp is a—a badge of honor."

Jonathon turned to really look at her, approving of such proper sentiments. "Are you enjoying London?" he asked.

"Oh, yes, but it is all so—so busy and noisy!" She blushed, unused to encountering such deference in a gentleman. Companions, in her experience, were ignored, especially when there was a young lady of Celia's beauty and liveliness in the vicinity. Her treacherous heart warmed even more to him.

Jonathon nodded. "Prefer the country myself." He considered for a minute. "Don't mind Bath, though. No one expects a fellow to dance all the time, there. Ever been to Bath?"

Elizabeth reluctantly had to admit that she had not. He assured her she would like it of all things, for one could attend plays and concerts, just like in London, but without the crowds. She agreed, then lowered her eyes. It seemed odd to her that in all the years of her genteel servitude she had accepted the snubs and insults she had received without a blink. But the moment a gentleman spoke kindly to her, treated her as her charge's equal, the inferior nature of her status pained her.

Celia, who had been unaccountably silent, suddenly spun about to face her. "Elizabeth, could I—we—have a moment, just a little moment, alone? It has been almost nineteen months since I have seen my Jonathon, and I must tell him what Grandfather is planning. Please, dear Elizabeth?"

"I—of course," she stammered, guiltily aware that she had been monopolizing the gentleman in conversation in the most improper fashion.

Celia looked about. "There! Jonathon, there is a bench, down that path!"

"Cill, really! My horse!"

"Let Elizabeth hold him! He looks quiet enough. Will you, dear Elizabeth? Just for a few moments?"

Elizabeth took the reins, looking up at the massive gelding somewhat uneasily. His large head turned toward her, and she looked up into an eye that reflected nothing but docile patience. Reassured, she watched Celia lead Jonathon the short distance to the bench.

So, this was why Celia had cried out so fervently against marriage with Lord Ryde. Seeing Jonathon, Elizabeth could understand. In her mind, bright blue eyes were infinitely preferable to dark, brooding ones. She let out a wistful sigh. He seemed the embodiment of every amiable quality. Her last thoughts of encouraging Celia to consider Ryde as a husband vanished. No man could compare to Captain Edelston!

Celia, meanwhile, sat down on the stone bench and patted the place beside her. Jonathon seated himself.

"What are you up to, Cill?" he demanded. "You're in some scrape, aren't you?"

"Oh, Jonny, do be quiet!" she hushed him. "I am in trouble, but it is not of my making. Grandfather is forcing me into a marriage, and I want no part of it!"

"Forcing you!" Jonathon exclaimed. "Doesn't seem possible! You sure that's what he means?"

"Very sure!" In as few words as possible, she explained the situation to him.

"Trevor Ryde," Jonathon mused. "Noted Corinthian, you know, Cill. Quite popular, by report. And inherited the barony just recently. Don't know him personally, of course, but I've heard nothing but good about him. Any female would be glad to take him!"

"Well, not this female!" Celia declared, forgetting to keep her voice low.

"Oh, you're thinking of that pile of debt he inherited. Shouldn't trouble you. Sir Roderick's got the blunt to stand the nonsense."

"If you mean my grandfather is wealthy, I believe he is. But the money is all tied up in Ranleigh. Were you not listening to me, Jonny? Grandfather wishes to give Ranleigh to Lord Ryde, and I am merely part of the deal! I am being forced into this arrangement as part of a business proposition to salvage Ryde's estates!"

"What?" Jonathon exclaimed, shocked as the true situation dawned on him. "Never heard anything so shabby! I'll tell you what, Cill, I'll not hear of it! Won't have you treated like that! Promised Charlie I'd take care of you, and a fine thing it would be if I let you be married off in such a ramshackle fashion! What do you want me to do?"

Celia closed her eyes for a moment. It had been Charlie, she remembered, who had instigated all of their more outrageous boyhood exploits. And Charlie, not Jonathon, had been the one to suggest their enlistment in the Royal Navy. She loved Jonathon dearly, but was not blind to his faults. Whatever planning had to be done would be up to her. Jonathon might be a kindhearted soul, loyal as they came, but his intellect was not staggering and his leadership abilities apparently had begun and ended with his naval command.

"Jonny," she said carefully, "I want you to pretend to be betrothed to me."

"What? No, really, Cill! Marry you? I'll do anything in my power to help, but really, is that necessary?"

If the situation had been less serious, she would have laughed at his distraught expression. Not being vain, it did not bother her that the idea of marriage to her should horrify him. Being tied to him did not exactly appeal to her, either. She had by far the stronger will, and would run roughshod over him. He was definitely not the husband for her.

"Absolutely not!" she assured him. "I just want you to *pretend* to be betrothed to me. Tell my grandfather you want to marry me. Once he knows I will be taken care of, he won't have to include me in his arrangements with his godson."

"We won't have to announce the engagement or anything, will we?" he asked, worried.

"No! It will be private," she promised him, exasperated. "And it will just be for long enough to extricate me from this situation."

"What happens then?" he asked vaguely, voicing the one question that she had tried to ignore.

"I don't care! Just as long as I do not have to marry Lord Ryde. I—I have some money, from my parents. And your mother will take me in for a short time, will she not? I shall manage, if you will only help me! All you have to do is convince Elizabeth and my grandfather that you are in love with me."

Jonathon nodded, his expression abstracted as he tried to assimilate all the details of this plot. "Uh, Cill," he finally said. "This business about giving Ranleigh to Lord Ryde. Must be all a hum. What I mean is, can't do it, can he? Thought the estates were entailed."

"They are. Or at least they were. Charlie and my father were the last of the line. Now that they are both dead, Grandfather can break the entail and leave the property as he wishes."

Jonathon looked acutely uncomfortable. "Are you sure? I mean, aren't there any cousins or anything who can inherit?"

She shook her head. "Grandfather has had his solicitor checking ever since Papa died. There is no one. He can do as he wishes with Ranleigh now." She suddenly frowned at Jonathon's uneasy expression. "What is the matter?" she demanded. "Oh, Johnny, surely you will not desert me!"

"No!" he exclaimed, obviously shocked at such a suggestion. "That is. . . ." He broke off, his expression vexed. Then he appeared to come to a decision and reached over and took a firm hold of both her hands. "Look, Cill, I'm going to tell you something in the strictest secrecy. Understand? Don't go setting up a screech or anything."

He waited as if for her to acknowledge what he had said, so she nodded. "You know you can trust me, Jonny."

His lips twisted into a slight grimace. "Actually, Cill, it's the other way around. I wanted to tell you long ago, but Charlie wouldn't hear of it. Insisted no one was to know. But this . . . Your grandfather has to be stopped!"

"What are you talking about, Jonny?" Celia demanded. "What does this have to do with Charlie?"

His grip tightened on her hands. "That entail can't be broken. Charlie's alive, Cill."

CHAPTER SIX

The blood drained from Celia's cheeks, leaving her chilled and trembling. Jonathon's hands tightened on hers for support and she clutched at them as if they were her only tie to reality.

"But . . ." she whispered, shaking her head slowly.

"Steady, Cill. Charlie's alive."

"You—you were at his side when he died! You told me!"

Jonathon shook his head. "I told you what Charlie asked me to say. He didn't want you to know the truth. Didn't like it much myself, but he's my friend. He wanted to spare you."

"Where is he? And—and *why?* What happened?"

Jonathon turned away from her, looking acutely uncomfortable. "It was just after the battle ended. A lot of men were dead, friends of ours." He shook his head, remembering. "I was in a sort of makeshift hospital with the wound in my knee. Charlie slipped in one night after everyone was asleep. Woke me up, told me he was leaving, wanted it spread about he was dead. Tried to argue with him, but you know what he's like. Just laughed, real soft so he didn't disturb anyone. Made me vow I'd never tell a soul. Then told me to look after you and slipped off."

"He—he deserted," Celia whispered. "I just can't believe it of Charlie! There must be some other explanation!"

"You weren't there, Cill. You didn't see your friends or the men under your command dying. Don't judge him."

"No. But—I always thought he was so dashing and brave!" Her voice broke on a laugh that turned into a sob. "Oh, Jonny, he was such a hero to me! And all this time he has been hiding, ashamed to come home!" She sat up slightly. "Where is he?" she demanded.

Jonathon shook his head again. "No idea. Got a letter from him about a year back, saying he was in Italy. He knew your parents were dead, wanted to make sure you were all right. Didn't give any address where I could reach him, though."

"Oh, Jonny! What a mess we are in! What can I tell Grandfather?" Her eyes gleamed suddenly and a slight smile twitched the corners of her mouth upward. "Well, this certainly puts a period to Grandfather's plans for my marriage! Lord Ryde won't want any part of me without Ranleigh!"

"I—I don't think we'd better tell your grandfather," Jonathon said slowly. "Not unless we have to, that is. Promised Charlie," he added conscientiously.

Celia considered, then nodded. "It would destroy him. He is so proud, Jonny. To find out his only grandson is a deserter . . . I would hate to think what it would do to him." She fell silent for a moment, thinking. At last she said: "We shall have to find him, Jonny."

"Your grandfather?" he asked blankly.

"No, Charlie. Surely we can concoct some story about his being injured, maybe losing his memory. But we must bring him home!"

"How are we going to find him?" Jonathon asked, apparently accepting his role in the search.

"I don't know," she admitted. "You must tell me everything he said, everything you can remember. Has he written any other letters? Anything that might give us a clue as to his next move?"

Jonathon turned his mind to it, but came up with nothing. "It'll take time," he said sadly. "Didn't bring his letters to town with me."

"Has he written many?" she asked, eager.

"Only four. About one a year."

"But the last was after my parents died?" she pursued.

He nodded. "About six months after. Took him a while to get the news, he said."

"Then he should be due to write another letter soon!" she exclaimed.

"Maybe. He's never been very regular."

"Well, we can hope!" She chewed on her lower lip, searching for an idea. "Jonny!" she cried suddenly. "I have it! You could approach someone in the Navy and say that someone you know thought they saw Charlie! If you say he might have had a head injury during the battle they might believe he lost his memory and just wandered off! His body was never found, so they will have to admit there is a chance of his being alive. And he was an officer, of good family. Surely they would help us look!"

Jonathon agreed to this, but somewhat reluctantly. "There is a war on, Cill. Makes searching the Continent a tricky matter. Charlie would hardly answer an advertisement placed in a paper! And how are we to let him know he's not supposed to know who he is?"

"Jonny, we've got to find him, and that's the only thing I can think of! Now, please! Promise me you will start inquiries!"

"I don't know if Charlie would like this, Cill," Jonathon caviled.

"Do you not think he would like to come home if he could? What about Ranleigh? It is not as if there is nothing in England for him, you know. He has a sizable inheritance. If we can clear his name, he will be quite grateful, I assure you!"

"All right, Cill," Jonathon agreed reluctantly. "I'll stop by headquarters and ask questions."

"You will be careful, won't you? Not give the truth away?"

He regarded her scornfully. "I've kept his secret for almost five years, Cill. I'm not likely to cause him trouble now!"

She grasped his hands. "Thank you, Jonny! I knew I could count on you." She sighed. "I suppose it will all take a dreadfully long time, though. In the meantime, we will have to stall my grandfather, keep him from breaking the entail until we have found Charlie!"

"What are you going to do?" Jonathon asked.

"Not marry Lord Ryde, for one! I think we had best fall back on my original plan, Jonny. You must pretend to be my suitor. That should upset things for a while. If we can get Ryde to withdraw his suit, that will solve the immediate problem. Then we can concentrate on Charlie."

"What if your grandfather insists that you marry me?" Jonathon demanded, worried.

Celia controlled her exasperation. "We will stall him. I don't want him to know the truth about Charlie until we can cover up the reason for his disappearance. Oh, Jonny, you must help me fool Grandfather! It is for his own good!"

This, Jonathon seemed to accept. After giving him repeated instructions on how to behave as a long-time suitor, Celia felt prepared to face Elizabeth, who still stood holding the horse, peering anxiously over at them.

To Celia's relief, Jonathon's manner was far more attentive as he returned her to her chaperone's side. He even remembered to kiss her hand, though the eyes he raised to her sparkled with little-boy mischief at their conspiracy. Celia gave him a reproving frown, and immediately his expression became more serious, as befitted an ardent suitor.

"You will take me driving tomorrow afternoon, will you not?" she prompted him.

"Of course!" he responded nobly. "Drove to town in my curricle. Could leave my groom behind, and take Miss Westerly, too." He looked questioningly at this lady, who blushed and stammered a disclaimer that she desired to join them.

"At four o'clock tomorrow, then? We are staying at Grillon's."

On this, they parted. Celia guided Elizabeth back toward the Stanhope Gate where they could be assured of locating a hackney. Her mind was in a whirl, but she firmly tried to put thoughts of her brother aside until she could be alone. She still had a marriage to avoid, now more than ever, and that meant convincing Elizabeth that her heart was already engaged.

Her companion gazed back over her shoulder to where Jonathon, once more astride his black gelding, rode off. "Oh, Celia," Elizabeth sighed. "He—he is everything that I—that a woman could desire in a man! You are so fortunate!" In spite of herself, a touch of envy crept into her voice.

"He is wonderful!" Celia agreed, bemused. It seemed this was one problem that was taking care of itself. Elizabeth was already predisposed toward Jonathon's handsome countenance and gentle air. She would believe in the long-standing engagement because she wanted to—and because she would never suspect that he might be capable of telling untruths or of being party to a deceit!

As they crossed the Park toward the gate, Celia managed to babble happily on about Jonathon's charms, his elegance, and his dashing naval career. This last caused her an uncomfortable ache, reminding her of Charlie's less than honorable method of leaving the service, but she kept stoically at her plan. She also kept a surreptitious eye on her companion, trying to fathom her thoughts.

Elizabeth seemed strangely quiet, even for her. Did she sense anything odd in Celia's manner? Or was her current worried attitude just due to the confirmation that Celia would never bow to her grandfather's will? Now that she had actually met Jonathon, she would no longer doubt the existence of a legitimate and prior suitor to whose claims Sir Roderick must listen.

When they returned to the hotel it was to discover that her evening gown had arrived from Madame Yvette. This instantly had to be tried on, and for a few minutes Celia was able to banish her worries from her mind. The gown was of white crepe over a sky blue sarsenet slip, decorated about the hem and rounded neckline with deep pointed Vandykes of blue velvet. The short, full puffed sleeves, of mixed blue and white crepe, were confined in three separate folds by more of the velvet Vandykes. Celia found the white shawl of Norwich silk purchased that morning at Grafton House and draped it over her arms. With the pearls clasped at her throat, the effect was delightful, exactly appropriate for a young lady of Celia's tender years.

Just seeing herself in this beautiful creation sent her confidence soaring. She felt a lady for a change, no longer a child. Somehow, she would find Charlie and together they would think of a way to bring him safely home! And until then, surely her grandfather would be moved by her story of Jonathon's love and postpone any legal action concerning the entailed estate.

Picking up her gloves, Celia went out into the sitting room to await Elizabeth and her grandfather. He would dine with them, she knew, before making his way to his club for a quiet evening of cards.

She did not have long to wait. Both joined her in a

very short time, and, as she had hoped, her gown met with her grandfather's beaming approval. He offered her his arm, and the three made their way down the stairs to the small dining parlor he had reserved.

Sir Roderick appeared to be in an affable mood that evening, ready to be pleased by the selection of dishes that the hotel offered. Celia waited to spring her news until a delectable platter of fish in cream sauce was set before the elderly gentleman.

"Grandfather," she began as soon as the waiter left the room, "Jonathon has arrived. We met him in the Park this afternoon."

Sir Roderick's fork hesitated for a moment as a somewhat fixed smile settled over his face. "I am glad he was able to find you. Does he go on well?"

"Quite well," Celia assured him, trying to gauge his reaction. She had to convince him, stop his plans for the marriage! "He wishes to take me driving on the morrow."

"Of course, it will be pleasant for you to talk over old times and catch up on all you have been doing."

"You do not mind, then?" Celia asked, hoping he would realize from her tone that there would be more involved than he mentioned.

"I have no wish to deprive you of your old friends, my dear," Sir Roderick declared. He looked up, meeting her gaze squarely. "And I am sure Trevor will feel the same."

A silence that vibrated with unspoken words engulfed them.

"When, musing on companions gone, We doubly feel ourselves alone," Elizabeth injected in an attempt to ease

the suddenly strained atmosphere. For her, it was a feeble offering, for her knowledge of *Marmion* must have provided a more appropriate quote. Its sheer inadequacy merely emphasized the fact that her wits had been woolgathering throughout the meal and her attention far from the conversation.

Celia bit her lip, looking from Elizabeth to her grandfather. If her chaperone, in her uncharacteristic abstraction, said too much . . . It would be best, if possible, to let the subject drop. She did not want to antagonize Sir Roderick at this point. There should be time enough to suggest that Jonathon was a great deal more than a friend, time enough for him to accept this as an inevitability and abandon his own plans.

It was Ryde, after all, who most needed to be convinced. He would hardly expect her to marry him if she loved another. His self-esteem would not accept her turning him down for his own sake, but a previous long-standing affection might alter the matter. There was a chance, if he believed her heart to be already engaged, that he could back out gracefully with his masculine pride intact.

Just meeting Jonathon, then having her explain the situation, might very well do the trick. He would withdraw his suit, and then she would be free to search for Charlie.

For the briefest moment, she experienced a touch of pity for Lord Ryde for losing the money he counted on to repair his own estate. But she was not the only heiress in the world. He could find another, quite easily, one who would be only too glad to buy his title.

And it was not as if that were the only thing he had to offer. His masculine charm was overpowering. No, he would have no trouble replacing her as his bride. Somehow, that knowledge did not please her as much as it should.

CHAPTER SEVEN

A late afternoon haze dulled the brilliant blue of the sky as Lord Ryde turned off the Brighton Road and directed his horses up the long, winding, unweeded drive. His brow lowered in displeasure. He had left strict instructions that the undergroom was to look after the drive during his absence.

Nor had the hawthorns been trimmed. Overgrown and straggling, their trailing tips reached out toward him, brushing the wheels of his curricle. Unsightly weeds poked through yawning gaps in their unkempt branches. Only the scattering of tiny pink flowers that covered the shrubs eased the feeling of neglect that met his irritated eyes.

The unraked gravel crunched beneath the horses' hooves, and his near wheel slid and bounced as it pulled through a deep rut. He steadied his pair, then urged them on. They passed the broken gate that lay to one side, then continued along through the sorry remains of what had once been an elaborate formal garden, laid out in a mirrored pattern on either side of the drive.

Directly ahead of him lay the house, and the sight of it afforded him no pleasure. A medium-sized but stately home, Hastings Manor should have been a delight to any eye with its worn, gray stone front, arched entry, bay windows, and reaching tower. Built in the late fifteenth century by a more affluent Ryde, the structure had been weathered by time, which gave it a grace and majesty that only the neglect of the last few decades had managed to mar. Trevor never saw the decayed beauty without experiencing a surge of anger that anyone could have allowed the place to fall into such a state of disrepair. And it galled him that he had not the means to set it to rights.

He drew the horses up before the entryway and swung down from the curricle. Coxly, his groom, sprang lightly to the ground and ran around to take the pair's heads. Lord Ryde stripped off his driving gloves and started up the uneven flagged walk to the door.

It opened as he approached. Gosson, the elderly butler who had served his father for more than thirty years and now presided over Hastings, bowed deeply to him.

"Welcome home, sir." Gosson took his gloves and hat, laid these aside on a small table that stood against the wall, then set about helping him out of his driving coat.

"Thank you, Gosson. Though I doubt you thank me for bringing you here. It is not much of a home."

"Not yet, perhaps, sir, but you will make it one in time." He hesitated, then coughed in an apologetic manner. "The undergroom was not able to attend to the drive, I fear, sir. Part of the stable roof collapsed, and he has been somewhat occupied."

A muttered exclamation escaped Trevor's lips. The house was literally falling down about their heads, and his predecessor's creditors dunned him constantly, demanding what little remained of his own competence, the money he needed to prevent the rest of the place from crumbling into ruin.

"If you will excuse me now, my lord, I will see to your luggage."

"Where is Wrenn?" Trevor asked, looking about for his valet.

"I believe he is in the stables at the moment, my lord. He said something about repairing the legs on the chairs from your dressing room."

Trevor nodded, grateful not only for the many hidden talents possessed by his gentleman's gentleman but by that man's willingness to utilize them. Being valet to the master of the house gave him an exalted position in the servants' hierarchy, and such menial tasks as carpentry were far beneath him. In a more orderly household, Trevor reflected, Wrenn would be wasted.

"Excuse me, my lord," Gosson repeated.

"Let Coxly bring it in. Hold the horses for him, but do not lift anything heavy."

The butler went out front, and Trevor glanced about the hall as he started toward the stairs. He paused in surprise. The exterior of Hastings might be as disreputable as ever, but the inside showed distinct improvement. Mrs. Gosson, his inestimable housekeeper, had been busy to a purpose.

The clutter that had lain about in piles had been

cleared away and the wooden furniture dusted and polished. The floor of marble tiles beneath his booted feet had been scrubbed until it shone, silent testimony to the industry of the village girl hired by the zealous housekeeper. Everywhere was the odor of lemon and beeswax, a refreshing change from the mildew he had encountered upon his first visit to this ramshackle ruin less than two months ago.

He opened a door at random and found himself standing in a long saloon. Here, also, the village girl had been at work. The carpets had been beaten until their original patterns could be detected, though nothing would restore the faded colors to their one-time brilliance. The furniture was hopelessly out of style but comfortable nevertheless, and now presented an inviting aspect. The layer of soot had been removed from the paintings nearest the inglenook hearth, and that, he found, gave the room a lighter and more cheering air. Even the drapes at the window did not appear quite as hopelessly threadbare.

He returned to the hall, thoughtful. They had a week, at best, to ready the house for the reception of visitors. Under the circumstances, they had best close off most of the rooms, stripping them of anything usable to fix up the few that would remain open. He could leave most of the task to the Gossons. With their help, the house could be made to look more habitable—but he still did not relish the idea of welcoming his godfather to such squalor.

And as for his intended bride . . . He crossed the hall and entered the bookroom, almost slamming the door behind him. Here, at least, the general air of shabbiness was less noticeable. The layer of dust and dirt had been removed, the furniture polished, but little else needed changing. The aroma of beeswax and old leather met his nostrils, a mellow fragrance that he found rather pleasant. This was a quiet, restful room, lined with shelves filled with numerous volumes. A large cherrywood desk stood to one side. On the other, a sofa and two wing back chairs were arranged about a low table. A fire crackled merrily in the hearth just behind this grouping.

A decanter of Madeira rested on the low table, along with a glass of delicate cut-crystal. Trevor filled the glass, then sank down into one of the chairs. In a week, he must be prepared to receive the future mistress of this rotted pile. If she had objected to the marriage before, he could imagine her response upon being privileged to view her future home. Well, he had a week, and would make the most of it.

He stood, refilled the glass, then went in search of his account books. An hour of pouring over these was enough to send him into a deeper dudgeon. How anyone could have mismanaged the place so badly and for so long was a mystery to him! The estate could not be made productive again without a considerable outlay of money, but the only source of money lay in the dilapidated tenant farms and the unplanted fields. Frustrated, he sank his head into his hands.

There was a source of money, of course. Sir Roderick had offered him a substantial amount, masked as a wedding present. It was his granddaughter's dowry, too, however. As such, Trevor did not feel justified in touching these funds. He was not a man to marry for gain. They would be left intact as a safeguard for the girl's future.

And why had he ever agreed to this marriage? The reasons he had given Celia were quite true, though he had omitted the major one: a bout of determination, a spirit soaring to meet an insurmountable challenge. At the moment Sir Roderick's letter had reached him, proposing the scheme, he had just recovered from the initial shock of seeing his crumbling inheritance and was preparing to set out and conquer the world—or at least his corner of it. From the wording of the message, he believed his godfather to be at his wit's end in trying to establish the girl creditably. In that fit of crusading zeal, he had recklessly agreed to take on his mentor's problems as well as his own. He did need a wife, and since he doubted he would ever meet a woman he could love, why not offer this one the protection of his name and newly acquired title? There had been ample time since to regret his impulsive decision.

He leaned back in his desk chair, one finger tapping lightly against his strong chin, considering the girl he had promised to take to wife. He had expected a dowdy little mouse of a creature with a poor complexion and a squint, one whose fortune would be her only attraction on the Marriage Mart. He had never expected a veritable beauty, and certainly not a little minx with a fiery, independent spirit. It had not pleased him. He had intended to play Prince Charming to a grateful Cinders. The potential reversal of these roles galled him.

A muscle twitched at the corner of his mouth. He had suspected her of wanting to marry him for the title. Instead, she believed him to be selling his title for her money! Life with this lively little vixen would never be dull. To his surprise, he found he rather liked a girl unbroken to bridle.

All traces of amusement faded from his face, leaving it grim. It was not a characteristic that he could admire in a wife. He wanted a woman he could rely on, who would help him in his work—not a flighty chit straight from the schoolroom who would challenge his every utterance, set up her will against his, do outrageous things just to shock him. And Miss Celia Marcombe appeared more than capable of doing just that.

If he were honest, though, he had to admire her courage and fighting spirit. These very same characteristics in himself had gotten him into this mess. If she were less antagonistic, less ready to rip out at him for the mildest provocation, she might be an entertaining companion. And he admitted to enough interest in her to want to tame her. He could only hope that she cherished no silly romantic fancies of entrapping him into developing a *tendre* for her. He was a proud man, not to be ensnared by a green girl. His heart was not so easily touched.

He set down his glass and rose. He had only a few more days to make the place look less like a run-down charity house, and not a spare groat remained for hiring any additional help. Well, he would not allow Celia Marcombe to view his dilapidated inheritance in its present condition. It would look more like a gentleman's estate by the time she arrived if he had to pull every weed with ihs own hands. He left the bookroom and headed for his chamber to change into clothing more appropriate for the tasks he had in mind.

He had stripped off his coat and begun to search in his wardrobe for his oldest attire when a gentle tap sounded on his door. It opened immediately to admit a medium-sized King Charles spaniel. The dog's whole body appeared to wag in ecstatic delight upon seeing his master, and nothing would do but that Trevor must sit in a chair upon the instant and receive the besotted animal's head into his lap.

"Really, Adolphus," he told the liver and white spaniel with feigned reproof. "You must strive for a little dignity." He caressed the dog's ears, and its tongue lolled out the side of its mouth.

A discreet cough sounded from the threshold. A small, lightly built man of indeterminate years stood there, a warm smile on his sharp-featured face. He came into the room and collected the coat from where Trevor had allowed it to drop. With a few deft strokes of his expert hands, he brushed it off. "Did your lordship have a pleasant journey?"

"Tolerable. But you have spoiled me. I missed your constant attentions." Trevor stood and Adolphus withdrew to the fireplace, circled twice and collapsed. The spaniel dropped his head onto his paws, but kept an intelligent eye cocked on his master.

Wrenn permitted himself a prim smile. "It was your suggestion that I remain here."

"True, and if you have managed to do anything with those chairs, it was a sacrifice worth making."

"I went through the attics, my lord." Wrenn broke off while he assisted his master into stained buckskins and a frayed riding jacket. Adolphus perked up his ears, watching this change of wardrobe with interest. There might be a walk in the offing, with a chance for a good run after a squirrel.

Wrenn smoothed the jacket carefully over Ryde's broad shoulders, but the result could not please him. His expression was pained as he stepped back at last. "I found two small tables and a dresser that appear to have been stored for a great many years. They were in considerably better condition than what I have seen in the rooms, so I have brought them down and fixed them."

"Inestimable man," Trevor murmured, smiling. He regarded his reflection in the long cheval glass. "I can only be glad no one will see me, I suppose. Now, shall I begin on the weeds or painting the rooms? We are to have guests in a week's time."

Over the course of the next three days, Trevor discovered himself capable of performing a wide range of chores that had never before come in his way. He strongly suspected that his servants had never set their hands at some of the tasks that now befell them, but not one word of complaint or disgust crossed their lips.

By the afternoon of the fourth day, the approach to the house looked much more presentable. Trevor, accompanied by his undergroom Ketter and the ever-hopeful Adolphus, walked slowly up the drive, inspecting for lurking weeds or branches that had been missed by the pruning shears. On the whole, he decided, this section of the yard was as ready as it could be for the critical eyes of visitors.

These were to arrive sooner than he expected. As he paused to inspect the gate that now hung on new hinges, the sound of a heavy carriage drawn by four horses reached him. It pulled into sight, checked its progress, then turned onto the newly raked drive.

Adolphus set up a low growl and advanced several slow steps. Trevor straightened from where he had knelt by the broken post. The coach was a large traveling chaise, its panels smooth and unmarked, and it had curtains drawn tightly at the windows. He could detect no clue to the identity of the passengers. The coachman drew up his team so that they came to a halt abreast of Trevor, and the dog sprang toward it, barking vociferously.

"Dolph!" Trevor silenced the dog, then called him to heel with a snap of his fingers. The spaniel went to his side but kept a suspicious eye turned on the intruders.

The coachman looked Trevor over, then jerked his head in a manner that indicated that he desired speech with him.

Ryde stepped forward, somewhat irritated but mostly amused by the driver's supercilious manner. "Can I help you?" he asked.

The coachman seemed somewhat taken aback by the gentlemanly accents of Trevor's voice, but a closer examination of his dress seemed to reassure him. "This the home of Lord Ryde?" he asked.

"It is," Trevor admitted.

With only a nod to indicate thanks for the information, the man gave his horses the office, and the large carriage moved forward at a brisk trot. Trevor, with Dolph just ahead of him, followed more slowly on foot.

By the time he reached the house, two men had climbed down from the chaise. One, a short gentleman of stocky build and slow, deliberate movements, turned back to the door and extended his hand into the vehicle. A moment later, a lady—heavily cloaked and with a hood pulled low to hide her face—stepped down to stand beside her companions. Her head turned quickly from side to side as she inspected her surroundings. Dolph growled with low, menacing intent.

The door to the house swung open and Gosson emerged. He regarded the new arrivals calmly, waiting for them to state their requirements.

The lady went up to him. "Milord Ryde, is he in residence, *s'il vous plaït?*"

Her voice was soft, but the heavy French accents carried clearly. Trevor frowned, then stepped forward quickly with Dolph bounding at his heels. All three of his visitors spun about to face him as the dog let forth with a savage challenge, which Trevor stopped with a sharp command.

There was complete silence for a moment, then the lady exclaimed in delight.

"Ah, *mon cher* Trevor! But almost I did not recognize you!" She ran lightly toward him, her hands outstretched to throw herself into his arms. As she raised her face to kiss him, her hood fell back to reveal masses of fluffy guinea-gold curls. Dolph growled again, his hackles raised.

Trevor gently disentangled himself, then held the lady slightly away so that he could look at her. "Thérèse! What the devil is going on?" He looked over at her companions who now stood somewhat more at ease, though keeping a wary watch on the spaniel. "Harding, is that you? What's happened? I did not expect her to come here!"

The short man moved forward, encountered

Dolph's threateningly curled lip, and returned hastily to his place. "We had some trouble, m'lord. Her courier was shot and may have been captured. We barely got her away. Me and Wiggins here thought it best to bring her straight to you for hiding."

"When did this happen?" Trevor demanded, frowning. With a snap of his fingers, he recalled the dog who had begun to creep slowly toward the men with lowered head and menacing posture.

"Three days ago." Harding's gaze never left the spaniel. "We crossed to England night before last, m'lord, on a smuggler's craft. We've been traveling ever since."

Trevor looked down at the petite armful who now curled herself snugly against him. "You must be exhausted. Harding, send your coach around to the stables. Ketter?" He turned and found his under-groom standing several paces off, watching them with wide, fascinated eyes. "Show the driver the way, then bring him to the kitchens. And take Adolphus with you." The spaniel showed some reluctance at being led away from his master, particularly with so many strangers about, but he was at last induced to follow Ketter.

Ryde turned back to his guests. "We'd best get inside."

Gosson had disappeared. Trevor led his unexpected guests into the house, then opened the door into the Gold Saloon, the one room that was fit to sit in. He gestured for them to take chairs, then rang for the butler. He had barely released the bell pull when Gosson entered the room bearing a tray laden with decanters and wineglasses. This he set on a table near the wall, then withdrew to forage in the kitchen for anything else that might be suitable for refreshments.

The lady took off her traveling cloak and dropped it casually on a chair. Her curvaceous figure was draped in a high-necked carriage dress of black bombazine which managed to be alluring in spite of its stark simplicity. She eyed the room critically, then turned her brilliant smile on Trevor.

"So, *mon cher,* you have become Lord Ryde since last I saw you."

"You see for yourself the grandeur of my inheritance," he responded with a sweeping gesture that indicated their surroundings.

She laughed, a lovely, musical sound. "But it is *merveilleuse!* It shall give you something to do for so very long. You will have not the time to suffer from *ennui!*"

His smile was a bit grim. "That, I assuredly shall not. But I think you had best tell me your story. Are you being followed? Does anyone know you were coming here?"

It was Harding who answered. "No one knew our plans, m'lord, but I'll not swear to it we weren't followed. We were as careful as could be, but I've had a sort of uneasy feeling. Best not to take chances."

"No." Trevor considered for a minute. "You and Wiggins had best leave here very soon." He regarded Thérèse's delightful figure for a moment. "You will take Ketter, my undergroom, with you, wrapped in Mlle. de Bourgerre's cloak. They are about the same height. I would suggest you head for London."

"And Ma'mselle?" Harding asked quickly.

"She will stay here, until other arrangements can be

made. Have you contacted Headquarters yet?" Harding shook his head, saying there had been no time. "Then we must arrange a meeting as soon as possible. Once she has given them all the information they desire, there should be no more reason to try and assassinate her."

"Do you want the meeting to take place here?" It was Wiggins who spoke, and he sounded skeptical.

"Certainly not! Nor in Brighton. It must be nearby, though. We will think of something."

Gosson returned and the conversation was broken off while he placed a tray of biscuits and pastry on a small table beside Mlle. de Bourgerre. As he started to leave, Trevor stopped him.

"Will you have Mrs. Gosson come to me, please?"

"Very good, my lord." Gosson left the room, and Trevor turned back to his guests.

"We must trust my servants, of course, but you will be quite safe with them. But we need to make other arrangements soon. I will be having some guests coming to stay with me for some time, and I cannot put them off. Nor do I wish them to know of you, my dear Thérèse."

"Mais, quelle intrigue!" the lady murmured, fluttering provocative lashes at Trevor. "Would they be a danger to me, then?"

"The fewer people to know you are here, the better," Trevor told her repressively. He turned to Harding and Wiggins. "It will be best if you leave quickly, and get as far away from here as you can tonight. And keep up the pretense of having Mademoiselle with you as long as possible."

The door opened and the plump, motherly figure

of Mrs. Gosson bustled in. She threw a quick, speculative glance at the occupants of the room, then turned to Trevor to await his orders.

"I wish Mademoiselle to have a room where she will be well-hidden," Trevor said slowly, choosing his words with care. "No one is to know that she is here. Can that be arranged?"

"But of course, my lord. Does Mademoiselle have any luggage?"

Trevor looked questioningly at the lady.

"Only a small valise, provided by M. Harding. My luggage was lost with my courier."

Trevor nodded. "Do you have anything Mademoiselle can use for the night? Tomorrow I will need you to go into Brighton and purchase additional items for her—discreetly, of course."

"As you wish, my lord. If you will excuse me, I will see to a room at once."

"Please send Ketter to me, Mrs. Gosson." He turned back to Mlle. de Bourgerre. "If you do not mind, Thérèse, I fear I must ask your cloak of you."

She picked it up from the chair where she had dropped it, then carried it over to him. "As you wish, *mon cher* Trevor. Would you like my dress as well?"

He glanced at the two men who would have to assist with the impersonation. "Do you think it would help?"

Wiggins appeared extremely interested, but Harding's sandy complexion had taken on a distinctly reddish hue. "Won't be necessary," he said hurriedly. "The cloak should do the trick. But if your man could perhaps wear a pair of slippers rather than boots . . . ?"

It took half an hour, but at last Trevor had the satisfaction of seeing the two men back into their coach, accompanied by Ketter wrapped securely in the thick black cloak. He stood in the drive until the vehicle passed beyond his sight, then returned slowly to the curtained room in which his unexpected guest sat.

She looked up as he came in. "They are gone, then? That is good. Trevor, *mon cher,* there is something for which I need your help."

Ryde crossed to the table and poured himself a glass of brandy from the decanter. "Well, my Thérèse?"

"They would not assist me. They are good men, in their way, but imagination—they have none! They did not think this could be achieved."

Trevor took a sip from his glass and waited. Mlle. de Bourgerre watched him through half-lidded eyes.

"I wish you to find my courier," she said softly.

"The man who was shot?"

She nodded. "He was not killed, of this I am sure. And he is very clever; he will not have been caught. Find him for me, Trevor."

"Who was he?"

She shook her head. "I knew him only as *Le Maniganceur.*"

"The Intriguer? How theatrical. But it is not much to go on, you know."

Mlle. de Bourgerre did not appear pleased. "But it was not his choice of names. It is his *nom de guerre,* his code name. Surely his people will send him aid if they know he is in need?"

Ryde nodded. "Wiggins and Harding, could they

not do this?"

"Bah! Not without orders, it seems. All they would say is that they must see me safely in hiding, and then they would consider what to do next. But you, *mon cher* Trevor, they say it was you who planned my rescue from the Paris gaol. Surely you can help *mon Maniganceur?*"

CHAPTER EIGHT

Celia's precious week in London slipped rapidly away. There was too much that had to be accomplished, too many plans to be made, and nothing seemed to be working aright for her. In accordance with her plot to have Sir Roderick abandon the proposed marriage to Lord Ryde, Celia commanded Jonathon's almost constant attendance. And when he was not at her side, she directed him to pursue his inquiries on the possible whereabouts of her brother Charlie.

So far, neither course of action had borne any fruit. Sir Roderick, she had to admit reluctantly, proved a masterful general, and all honors in their battle went to him. She had driven or walked with Jonathon daily, visited the theater in his company and even, on several occasions, steeled Jonathon's nerves to a confrontation with her grandfather. But through all of this, Sir Roderick maintained an impassive front. Nothing could exceed his pleasure in meeting his granddaughter's oldest friend—and not a single opening could she find to tell him of her supposed marriage plans. He remained pleased at Jonathon's presence and accepted his constant squiring of Celia and Elizabeth with a complaisance that worried the girl more than she cared to admit. Her grandfather lost no opportunity to make it clear that he did not consider Jonathon as a rival to Lord Ryde.

Nor could Jonathon's foray into government circles be considered a success, for it produced disturbing results at best. His first step had been to look up an old friend who now occupied a position of some importance in the Naval Office. His casual question of how one would set about finding a missing person at first produced only mild interest. His friend, quite naturally, requested more details, so Jonathon mentioned the chance that Captain Charles Marcombe might be alive but possibly suffering a loss of memory.

At that point, things began happening with surprising rapidity. In a very short time, Jonathon found himself seated in a discreet office up a back stair, facing two men previously unknown to him but bearing a disturbing air of authority. What had put that idea into his head? they wanted to know. Who was it who thought they had seen Captain Marcombe? And where had that been, and when?

Jonathon became acutely uncomfortable. He hedged a bit and fumbled for details he had not prepared. He had assumed it had been officially accepted that Charlie had died and his body been claimed by the sea. But the inordinate amount of interest created by his question alerted even his tentative intellect that something was amiss. The Naval Office must have suspected that Charlie was a deserter, and he cursed himself for giving any credence to their suspicions.

The report he gave to Celia could not please her. Like Jonathon, she feared that she may have done her brother more harm than good, and that an official and serious investigation on him might soon be underway. But the problem of the entailed estates still remained, and she could think of no other way to locate him. Charlie must be found. Celia could only trust in the quick wits of her brother which had kept him alive and hidden. He must, surely, have prepared a story to protect himself in the event he was seen and recognized.

There was little more she could do, she realized, and that fact depressed her. To counter this, she threw herself into a frenzied round of fittings, shopping, and outings in the Park. Anything was better than sitting around and thinking, or dreading the approaching visit to Lord Ryde's home and having to see that detestable man again.

Her fear of this event increased as it grew nearer. Toward the end of the week, Sir Roderick ordered their horses sent ahead to the last change along the New Road. All too soon their bandboxes and portmanteaus were packed and loaded into the fourgon, and their servants departed with this vehicle to begin the journey. Then came their own turn to leave the temporary sanctuary of Grillon's, and Celia reluctantly allowed herself to be handed up into the post chaise. The coachman climbed onto the box, the ostlers stepped away, and they set forth on the six-hour journey toward Brighton.

The miles passed slowly, leaving Celia ample time to indulge in the reflections she had tried to avoid. Thoughts of Charlie haunted her—and worse, fear of his exposure. Until he could come safely home, she had to prevent her grandfather from entering into any legal agreements—and without telling him the truth. That posed a problem. If she defied him, he was more than capable of forcing her into the marriage. Her only recourse would be to reveal Charlie's shameful secret, which she wanted to avoid at all costs.

She stole a glance across at the rigid lines of the elderly man's face. If he only knew what was at stake . . . but that was what she wanted to prevent. And she definitely did not want Ryde to know of her brother's cowardice, either. The whole situation was so unnecessary! She fumed. He was a hateful man to press a suit that was obviously distasteful to her.

At least Jonathon would be following along behind them. Much to Celia's surprise, he had, on his own initiative, arranged for his mother to become the house guest of old friends, then procured lodgings for himself in Brighton. He would be near enough to play the suitor, to come to her aid, to take her away if the situation became intolerable.

The moment she dreaded came at last. The traveling chaise slowed, then made the turning between the high hedges onto the drive at Hastings. By this time, Celia's nerves neared the breaking point, and she was not in a mood to be pleased by anything. In fact, she actually wanted to dislike everything that was remotely connected with Ryde, and the decayed neglect that met her eyes made it surprisingly easy.

The hedges had been trimmed, but as this had also removed the majority of the pale pink blossoms that had relieved their dreariness, it could not be considered much of an improvement. The drive was smoothly raked and no weeds marred its neat surface, but the grass verge that rimmed it showed brown bald spots where gophers, weeds and neglect had taken their toll.

They approached the gate which stood wide for them, hanging securely from its new hinges. The stone columns that supported it, though, were somewhat crumbled, having defied the grooms' attempts to rebuild them. This passed, Celia received her first sight of the gardens and the house beyond.

She wrinkled her nose in distaste. Little remained of what must have once been impressive formal shrubbery. She glimpsed benches and dry fountains. Once, it must have been beautiful. Now . . . She shivered slightly. She could easily imagine headless specters flitting among the dead bushes in the pale moonlight. The grounds were as sinister as anything she had encountered in a lurid romance novel.

She turned her attention to the manor house itself, and was somewhat mollified by its pleasant aspect. This state lasted less than one minute, though, for as they drew nearer she was able to see the signs of disrepair more clearly. The ivy that had clung thickly to the gray stone walls had been cut back in places, leaving a tracery of dark lines everywhere that it had been. Near the top, long tendrils that had been left reached out across the paned windows, covering them with a tangle of green leaves that effectively blocked the sunlight. Shutters, hanging at drunken angles, did little to improve either her impression or her mood.

"*Remains of rude magnificence,*" Celia quoted softly from *Marmion.*

Elizabeth gave her a quelling glance. "You forget.

It goes on to say something about *Still rises unimpaired below The courtyard's graceful portico.* We were warned the estate had been allowed to fall into ruin, you know. We may find it is better inside."

Celia merely sniffed to indicate her disbelief, and the carriage rolled to a halt, effectively stopping any further discussion. If she were to admit the truth, Celia's only true objection to Hastings, even with all of its dilapidation, was that it belonged to Ryde. She sat back in her seat and waited. In another moment, the massive front door swung wide within its recessed arch and the elderly butler sailed forth. He approached the chaise and opened the door for them.

"No footman?" Celia murmured under her breath to her grandfather as he joined her on the graveled drive.

"Trevor is practicing certain economies here until he can bring the place about," came Sir Roderick's whispered answer. "You will find him sadly understaffed, I fear."

"Why? Do I not bring him enough money?" she asked sweetly, hoping it would give the elderly man pause.

She turned her back on her grandfather before he could reply and looked about as Elizabeth joined her. Certain economies indeed! The state of affairs at this dreadful house were not to be tolerated. Her scathing glance swept across a flower bed that showed recent weeding, then passed on to a small stretch of lawn to which someone had taken scythe and shears. Pretty meager attempts to render the place less hideous, she thought, her anger rekindling at these obvious signs of Ryde's reasons for offering for her.

"Uncle Roderick! Allow me to welcome you to Hastings."

Celia spun about, startled. She had not heard his approach. Lord Ryde, followed by his spaniel, stepped out of the dark reaches of the stone arched entry into the late afternoon sunshine. The warm light glinted off Ryde's thick, dark curling hair, and Celia found it strangely hard to breathe. He was so very tall, so very broad-shouldered, so very irritatingly masculine in every line of his muscled build.

"I hope you have had a pleasant journey." He took his godfather's hand in greeting. His voice was as cold and as forbidding as his frozen expression. The dog came forward with a low growl and sniffed the hand Sir Roderick extended to him. Apparently satisfied, the spaniel turned his attention to the ladies.

Celia sank down as gracefully as could be managed in her narrow skirts and held out her own hand. The dog growled and advanced on her.

"Dolph!" The tone of Ryde's voice brought the animal to a halt, cowering.

"He is quite all right," Celia told him. "Dolph? Is that your name? Come here, boy."

The dog, fearful of incurring his master's further displeasure, slunk forward. Emboldened by Celia's gentle words, Dolph inspected her thoroughly. When she ventured to stroke his head and caress the floppy ears, he submitted with the fatuous expression of a dog who experienced sheer bliss.

"He does not usually make friends so easily," Ryde said, addressing Sir Roderick.

So much for his greeting her, Celia reflected. He was as stiff and formal as the first afternoon they met!

Perhaps he was embarrassed at bringing his supposed future bride to such a dilapidated property. She permitted herself the savage hope that the situation mortified him, never suspecting that this was, in fact, the truth.

Ryde nodded briefly to Celia, then turned to escort Sir Roderick into the house. The two ladies were left to follow, with Adolphus keeping an eye on them. Furious, but determined not to let him see that his slight offended her, Celia strode after the two men, with her companion in her wake. Could that odious, insufferable man not even speak to her? Could he not at least apologize for the wretched state of disrepair? This was supposedly her future home, and he had made no attempt to welcome her to it. His words of greeting had been carefully directed to her grandfather, and to her grandfather alone.

She stopped in the wide hall, looking about with curiosity in spite of wanting to dislike all she saw. The floor, tiled in a pleasing geometric pattern of green and white marble, shone with the loving attention that had been expended on it. A large Chinese vase, holding several long-stemmed roses, stood on a polished table. Sunshine flooded in through the open door, bathing the room in a warm glow.

"*Nor wholly yet hath time defaced Thy lordly gallery fair.* It is really quite pretty!" Elizabeth whispered, but not softly enough. Ryde turned to look at her, a sudden smile touching his dark eyes. Elizabeth blushed furiously.

"I suppose it is," Celia said with an attempt at indifference, though she feared her own approval sounded in her voice. Lord Ryde turned his gaze fully on her for the first time since they arrived, and she stiffened against the wave of attraction that washed through her. The smile in his eyes spread to his harsh mouth, almost as if he guessed the effect he had on her.

"You must be tired after such a long journey." His eyes held Celia's for a moment, then returned to Sir Roderick. "Come into the front saloon and have some refreshments. Your baggage arrived a short while ago, and your things are still being taken up to your rooms."

He opened a door to their left and escorted them into the Gold Saloon. Here, every attempt had been made to make the room pleasant and welcoming, with quite satisfactory results. If several pieces of furniture had been borrowed from other, unused rooms, and the drapes at the bay window actually belonged in an upper bedchamber, these discrepancies were not immediately discernible. Ryde gave a gentle tug on the bell pull that hung near the doorway, summoning the housekeeper.

Celia, at the moment, looked no farther than the long, comfortable proportions of this apartment and found herself impressed against her will. She sank into a Queen Anne chair that until recently had stood in the bedchamber allotted to the mistress of the house.

"You have made some progress," remarked Sir Roderick. He seated himself on the long sofa, one of the few pieces of furniture originally intended for this room. Elizabeth retired into a far corner and sat primly on the edge of a wing back chair that had come from the Red Saloon, which was now closed off.

Ryde, with Adolphus at his heels, crossed to a small writing desk that stood against a wall. On its top stood a chased silver tray that held two cut-crystal decanters and several glasses. He poured ratafia into two of the glasses, then carried one to Elizabeth and the other to Celia. Apparently without hearing Celia's surprised "thank you," he returned to the table and poured out glasses of Madeira for his godfather and himself. The spaniel retired to lie on the carpet before the fireplace, nose on his paws.

The door opened to admit Mrs. Gosson, who carried a tray laden with tiny sandwiches and cakes. Dolph raised an interested head, watching as the housekeeper placed her burden on the table before Celia, curtsying slightly as she did so. Her wide eyes took in every detail of the girl's appearance, and she smiled broadly at her.

"Well, how pleased I am to welcome you to Hastings, miss—so looking forward to your visit as we have been," she declared, positively beaming. "Now, your trunks have been carried up to your room and your woman is seeing to your things. Don't let Master Trevor keep you talking down here when you must be longing for a nice lie down after such a tedious drive." She curtsied again to the other occupants of the room and hurried out.

"You must forgive my housekeeper if she seems a trifle forward," Ryde said evenly.

"I could hardly consider such kind words as unwelcome," Celia told him with careful innocence. "It is quite a relief to know that someone is pleased that I have come."

Lord Ryde's eyes flashed for a moment at this

rebuke before a grudging twinkle acknowledged its justice. "As you say," he murmured provocatively. "I do most sincerely hope that we may make you feel—at home, here."

Celia sat up, pressing her lips firmly together to prevent her speaking hasty, unwise words. This would never be her home, be it ten times as lovely! The man was impossible, marriage to him unthinkable—even if there were not this business of Charlie to be considered! Ryde's shoulders shook slightly with repressed amusement, and Celia turned her back on him with pointed nonchalance.

She maintained what she hoped was a dignified silence while Lord Ryde and her grandfather discussed such harmless topics as the superb weather and the surprisingly easy drive. Her eyes fell on the plate of delectable pastries, and she selected a ratafia biscuit. She took a delicate bite, discovered she was hungry, finished it off and selected another.

Adolphus stood, stretched and padded over to her chair where he sat down before her. He raised large eyes of a beguiling pansy brown and assumed the mien of a neglected dog who has not eaten in a week but who would never presume to beg. The next biscuit found its way into his mouth.

Celia cast a guilty glance about but decided she had been unobserved. Elizabeth, she noted, remained in her corner. Smiling at her companion's rigid adherence to what the young woman persisted in believing to be her lowly position, Celia picked up a napkin and filled it with an array of easily carried pastries, macaroons and biscuits. She then changed her seat to one beside Elizabeth and opened up the linen that covered her hoard. Adolphus joined them, and in an indecently short period of time, the napkin lay empty between the two ladies.

Celia got up to make a second raid on the tray, but the door opened and forestalled her. Mrs. Gosson again bustled into the room. Her worried gaze fell on the tray, and she beamed to see so many of her treats gone.

"Now, miss, your room is waiting for you. If you will come this way, please? And you, sir? Miss?" She looked expectantly at Elizabeth, then stood back to allow the guests to precede her from the room.

"You must excuse the state things are in, miss," Mrs. Gosson continued as she led them up the polished oak stairway that curved gracefully toward the next floor. "Such a fuss as we've been in, yet it still looks like gypsies have been living here! And Master Trevor so distressed for you to see it like this!" She clucked like the mother hen she resembled.

She traversed a long, dark hallway, then opened a door at the far end. "We've put you in here, sir, in the Red Room. If you're needing anything, you just ring for the maid. She's a new girl, but hard working. And now, miss." She turned a corner and entered a short passage. "You will be in the Blue Room, here," she told Elizabeth, opening a door. A startled, youthful maid looked up from where she unpacked Elizabeth's meager trunk. Miss Westerly threw a bemused look at Celia, murmured a choked "thank you," and entered the chamber.

Disliking this house and the people in it was becoming harder and harder, Celia reflected ruefully. Such thoughtfulness to a mere companion was a very rare thing. But whether the idea had been Ryde's or his motherly housekeeper's, Celia could not be certain. Uncharitably, she suspected the latter.

Mrs. Gosson turned to the door across the hall. "And now, miss, you are in the Green Room." She opened the door and stood back to allow Celia to step in before her.

The apartment was not large, but would have been roomy and comfortable had it not been overpowered by massive furniture. An ancient hearth was cut into one wall, opposite a large canopied bed. The hangings around this were of a heavy brocade in an ugly dull green. A diamond-paned bay window arched outwards, beckoning Celia away from all the oppressive darkness to what she guessed would be a view over the back of the house.

She closed her eyes for a moment. Her taste ran to light, bright colors, and she could not help but wrinkle her nose in distaste. This one room went a great way toward reversing the favorable opinion she had started to form. If they thought they could force her to remain in this house, they were quite wrong. She now decided that she disliked it intensely.

A movement at the window caused her to look more closely. Behind a lace curtain, a huge black and white cat lay in the sun on the sill, sleeping peacefully. Celia pushed the flimsy drape aside and stroked the glossy, mottled fur. The cat blinked, then opened eyes of different colors, one blue, the other green, set in a patchwork face.

"Well, what a love you are," Celia informed him as he arched his generous back into her smoothing hand.

"Is he here?" Mrs. Gosson exclaimed. "I am so

sorry, miss, he must have slipped in with me earlier. We have been letting him have the run of the house, you see, because Jane—the maid—swore she heard mice."

"It is quite all right," Celia assured the anxious woman. "I would rather have a cat than a mouse in my room any day!" She picked the animal up, surprised by his weight and bulk. "He must be a very good mouser."

Mrs. Gosson snorted. "Table scraps, that's what he likes. I doubt he could run fast enough to catch a mouse, these days. He just scares them a little, sitting there like a great statue." She shook her head. "A right merry-andrew, this one is, with his blotchy jester's face."

"Is that what you call him?" Celia almost smiled as the hefty cat arranged himself in her arms so that his head rested on her shoulder.

"Aye, Andrew he is, unless Cook catches him in the cream. Then it is just as well you don't hear the names she gives him, miss!"

The housekeeper excused herself, leaving Celia to wander about the chamber, touching the antiquated furnishings. Everywhere, almost overpowering, was the smell of beeswax and lemon oil. A few straggling roses had been arranged forlornly in a vase on a dresser—probably Mrs. Gosson's attempt to make the room appear less forbidding. She had no doubt that the bed linen would be found to have been mended and darned.

She sank down on the edge of the lumpy bed and lowered the unprotesting Andrew to her lap. Her surroundings were overpowering, making her feel oppressed and miserable. This would never do! She gave herself a mental shake, but it did no good; her spirits remained low. She hugged the cat closer to her. If her grandfather's purpose in forcing her to come here was to let her see what was in store for her, it was a ridiculously bad tactic. She hated this house! At least, she hated the decay and the darkness and the heavy, depressing atmosphere that hung about her.

And the worst was that she couldn't escape—not yet, at least. She had to stay here, no matter what her feelings were. She dared not force her grandfather's hand.

If only she could improve this chamber, do something to make it less somber . . . She looked about once again, this time seeing the room itself instead of reacting to its furnishings. There was nothing wrong with this apartment, basically. The bay window and the hearth were actually quite beautiful. With light paint and bright hangings it would be almost unrecognizable. And the cabinets would have to go, of course. Perhaps delicate Queen Anne chairs and plain, uncarved wardrobes . . . She lost herself in the delightful—and potentially expensive—pastime of fixing up this chamber in her mind.

A soft tap sounded on the door, and Elizabeth entered almost immediately.

"What a—what a magnificent room!" she exclaimed, obviously searching for something good to say about it.

"It could be," Celia agreed. She told her companion of the changes she felt ought to be made.

"It would improve it beyond anything!" Elizabeth nodded. She seated herself on the bed beside Celia, who promptly introduced her to Andrew. "What a pity the last occupants did nothing about the upkeep!" Eizabeth went on as she pulled gently at the cat's twitching tail. Playful paws batted at her hands. "Such a disagreeable situation for Lord Ryde to have to live here, but not to be able to fix it up and make it more pleasant."

"It could be a lovely old house," Celia agreed. "It has been allowed to fall into a shocking state!"

"Just think how much fun you could have, ordering the redecoration," Elizabeth sighed. "It is almost a pity you will not be able to do it."

"Not if it means marrying that man!" Celia assured her, but felt a flickering moment of regret. Elizabeth was right! What a challenge this place would be, seeing it all set to rights, picking color schemes and hangings and furnishings. And she suspected it might all be worthwhile. The house itself was quite small when compared to Ranleigh, but she had detected a noble beauty in the facade, an impression that was carried out in the few rooms she had so far seen.

But then, that was the whole reason for her being there. She stood abruptly, pushing Andrew into Elizabeth's lap as she did so. Suddenly restless, she strode to the window and looked down on a rose garden in which only a scattering of blooms managed to raise their heads. This entire house was nothing but one gigantic graphic demonstration of just how much Lord Ryde needed the income from Ranleigh. Her anger surged, leaving her frustrated at the hatefulness of her position. Before it might have been merely supposition, but here, in this house, it became blatantly obvious to her that on his side she was nothing more than an evil necessity in a business arrangement. How glad she was he could never profit from his schemes!

A distant gong sounded somewhere in the reaches below, startling Celia out of her brooding abstraction.

"What was that?" she asked.

"The signal to dress for dinner, I believe," Elizabeth suggested. A knock sounded on the door, which opened to admit Celia's maid. "Yes, here is Seddons. If you will excuse me, my dear, I shall change." Elizabeth set down the cat, who jumped back onto the windowsill to catch the last failing rays of the sinking sun.

A half hour later, Celia emerged from her room dressed in the amber crepe lisse, which had been made up to perfection into a round dress worn over a white sarsenet slip. Full puffed sleeves set off the low neckline, and a three-quarter length apron, bordered with embroidery, hung from the high waist. She could find little satisfaction in this lovely gown, though, for it would be wasted on Ryde, who she was sure would barely spare a glance for her.

She navigated two short passageways, then hesitated at a crossing, unsure which one to take. She could hear the sound of movement coming from her right, so she went that way. It was possible she was heading toward the servants' hall, but at least there she could ask directions.

She had gone quite a ways when she heard a door open behind her. She turned in surprise and caught just a glimpse of a female figure garbed in a dark gown disappearing around a corner. A maid, Celia decided, but with such profuse golden ringlets. If the girl had a face and figure to match that hair . . . Celia fought down a pang of jealousy. Not all gentlemen found beauty only in flamboyant blondes. Some admired dusky ringlets like her own. She caught herself wondering where Ryde's preference lay, and firmly banished the thought.

The hall, she discovered, led to the back stairs. She hesitated, wondering where these would take her, then retraced her steps. At the crossing of the halls she tried a different passage and this time she was in luck. Within a few minutes she found the sweeping oak staircase and descended to the main hall below.

She looked about, unsure where to go next, and noticed that the door to the Gold Saloon stood slightly ajar. This would not be a normal place to gather before dinner, but in this house it seemed worth a try. She approached it and was reassured by the sound of the deep voices of the men within.

Sir Roderick and Lord Ryde stood on either side of the hearth, holding glasses of the rich, dark Madeira. Elizabeth, as was her custom, sat discreetly withdrawn. A glass of ratafia stood on a table beside her, but she had not touched it. Adolphus rose from his place by the fire and came to greet Celia, recognizing the source of his earlier largesse.

"How quaint," Celia declared with feigned sweetness. She stooped to rub the dog's head. "You use this room for so many things. Is there not another?"

Ryde stiffened. "Not one fit to sit in," he replied, his voice harsh. "I will have Mrs. Gosson escort you over the house on the morrow, if you wish. I am sure you will want to see for yourself the delightful home which will soon be yours."

The bitterness in his voice surprised her, and she unconsciously moved a step closer, really looking at him. There were deep lines about his face, which at first glance she had unkindly labeled as dissipation. She now saw these to be caused by worry, and her satisfaction at getting a rise out of him vanished. She had touched a raw nerve. He was a proud man, which was something she could understand.

This was his inheritance, his birthright, the home of his ancestors. Had it been hers, she, too, would have done anything to see it set to rights. But why did *she* have to be the one he chose to provide the necessary funds? That would always stand between them. Her pride, she feared, was as great as his. Would he insist on standing by the agreement after learning there would in fact be no money? Neither of them could ever find happiness in a marriage that had been initially based on such an arrangement. For the first time, she experienced an honest pang of regret.

CHAPTER NINE

Dinner was served in a small, cozy apartment that Celia guessed was probably the breakfast parlor. Here, again, there was the impression of the furniture being mismatched, but this time it produced a charming result. She did not feel even the slightest desire to direct a barbed comment about it to Lord Ryde.

As if he felt her self-restraint in this regard, he bowed low to her as he drew out her chair at the table. "At least we do not also dine in the Gold Saloon," he said, his voice cool. "But we must make do in here, since the dining room has suffered considerable fire damage and is unfit to use."

"Forgive me for casting aspersions upon your relatives, my lord, but your predecessor has been criminally at fault!" She could not prevent the words from springing to her lips, then was glad the next moment that she had spoken them.

Ryde's features stiffened, then relaxed into a smile

that was almost warm. "You may be sure I shall rectify his mistakes, in time," he told her. "The situation will be quite different for my heir."

It was Celia's turn to stiffen. Always that business arrangement hung between them, being raised by one or the other, sometimes on purpose, sometimes inadvertently as it was now. That was the sole reason for the marriage, as far as he was concerned, to enable him to set his inheritance to rights. And in repayment, he intended that it would be her son who would be his heir.

As Ryde had no hostess, it was up to Celia to reluctantly assume this role. She stood as the last course was removed from the table, and Elizabeth followed her example.

Ryde looked up at the ladies as they rose. "The Gold Saloon is the only room fit to sit in, I fear," he informed them, a trace of challenge in his tone.

"We shall await you there, then," Celia answered calmly. She led the way from the dining parlor, leaving the two gentlemen to their port.

The Gold Saloon was only a short distance down the hall, but several doors stood between. All were firmly closed, and it was with difficulty that Celia overcame the urge to peek in. That could come on the morrow, when she received the formal tour.

Instead, the ladies entered the door that stood slightly ajar. The long saloon was comfortably warm, heated and cheered by a fire that crackled lazily in the inglenook hearth. Adolphus was no longer there, and must have retired to the kitchens for his own dinner. Elizabeth drew her workbag from beneath the chair in which she had sat earlier in the evening, then settled herself to one side of the fireplace. Carefully, she extracted her nearly completed table shawl and began to set more of her neat stitches.

Celia sank down upon the sofa, then turned to regard her companion. "I suppose I should try needlework," she said doubtfully. Her childhood attempts had produced a sampler of such unrelieved awfulness that she had rarely felt tempted to try again.

Elizabeth smiled. "It passes the time."

That was something with which Celia could have used some help that evening. A magazine lay on the table at her elbow, but as this proved to be devoted to the sporting interests of fishing and shooting, it did not long hold her attention. Placing the magazine back where she had found it, she fell to gazing about the room in moody silence. A new challenge presented itself to her, and she began to guess from how many different rooms the furniture must have been gathered.

Almost two hours passed, but the gentlemen showed no sign of joining them. In growing irritation at being left alone in a strange house, Celia rang the bell. Gosson appeared almost on the instant, rolling in a cart laden with a plate of biscuits and a delicate china tea set with only two cups and saucers.

"Will Lord Ryde and my grandfather not be joining us, Gosson?" Celia demanded, eyeing the number of cups.

"I believe not, miss. They have retired to the bookroom."

"Thank you." Celia forced a pleasant smile to her lips, though inwardly she wondered if this could be a calculated snub on Ryde's part. It certainly stung to be treated of so little account. Her first evening as a guest in his house, and he did not trouble to join her! She poured out tea for Elizabeth and herself, which they drank in silence. When they had finished, they went out to find their candles and go up to bed.

Celia passed a surprisingly comfortable night in the strange surroundings, but came down quite early in the morning, anxious to speak to her grandfather. At the foot of the staircase she hesitated, uncertain where to go. On impulse, she decided to try the room in which they had dined the night before, and made her way there.

She was right. The sideboard in the sunny parlor now held an array of covered dishes from which an inviting aroma wafted out to greet her. The table was set for two.

Gosson entered behind her, carrying a fresh pot of steaming coffee. He poured a cup for Celia, who was taking a tiny sample from several of the selections offered.

"Has my grandfather already come down?" she asked as the butler turned to leave the room.

"Yes, miss. The gentlemen rode out over an hour ago."

Celia sighed, then added a roll to her plate and sat down at the table.

Gosson gave a slight cough. "If you are wishful, miss, Mrs. Gosson will be waiting to escort you about the house as soon as you are ready this morning."

"All right, thank you, Gosson." She knew she should not avail herself of this offer, for she was here under false pretenses. But she was curious to see the full extent of the damage inflicted upon the house—to see how much work would be in store for whatever lady Lord Ryde finally married.

In this desire she was seconded by Elizabeth, who joined her a few minutes later. Like Celia, Elizabeth ate the lightest of meals in the morning, and selected only a single roll and a cup of chocolate. They were just finishing their respective repasts when Mrs. Gosson entered the room. The woman beamed warmly upon Celia as she bobbed a quick curtsy.

"Good morning, miss. And Miss Westerly." She smiled at Eizabeth in a friendly manner. "Is everything to your liking?"

"It was an excellent breakfast," Celia told her. "And my room is most comfortable."

Elizabeth added her assurances, thanking the good woman for her kindnesses.

"Well, I'm pleased to hear you say it, and that's no mistake! The trouble we had, finding things that would be suitable. But there, you will see for yourselves shortly. It's a disgrace, as I told Master Trevor, but he did insist you should see it as it is, so as you wouldn't be suffering under any misapprehensions."

Celia hid her confusion by standing and shaking out the narrow skirt of her sprigged muslin. Was this a mark of consideration on Ryde's part? No, it was more likely that he wanted her to see for herself why it was necessary for him to marry her. He probably hoped to firmly establish their purely business relationship in this manner.

By the time they had toured the bottom floor, Celia had spotted the rooms from which many of the furnishings in the Gold Saloon had been pulled. Those items that had been left were a sorry lot, from frayed drapes to torn upholstery, even to tables with broken legs. Celia had a strong suspicion the damage had been intentional, an idea that was confirmed by Mrs. Gosson's oblique reference to the heavy drinking bouts of Lord Ryde's predecessor. It also, apparently, explained the fire in the formal dining room in which that gentleman had met his end, too foxed to raise an alarm until it was too late.

"And his two sons, both taken off with fever, such a short time before," Mrs. Gosson concluded, shaking her head. "A judgment from Heaven, I say. But in this case it is the sins of the cousin being visited upon Master Trevor."

"Have you been in his service long?" Celia asked.

"Aye, that I have. I came to his father's service when he was just a young man, just after Master Trevor was born. Before Mr. Ryde ever joined up in the diplomatic service, it was. Had the tending of his house while he was away in those nasty foreign places. I married Mr. Gosson when he was but a footman and I a parlor maid, I dare not say how many years ago."

"When did his parents die?" Celia asked, guiltily aware that she could be accused, and quite rightly, of gossiping with the servants. No reproving nudge came from Elizabeth, though, who was apparently as curious as was she.

"Nigh on fifteen years ago, when Master Trevor was naught but a youth. That's when your Sir Roderick really stepped in, guiding him and teaching him the ways of London and the running of an estate."

So there it was again, the long-standing affection between the two men. And Mrs. Gosson, Celia had no doubt, would love unquestioningly where her master did. It disturbed her that the housekeeper had already admitted her into the ranks of Family, regarding her with a motherly eye and a certain speculative interest. Only the best would do for her master, Celia guessed, and wondered suddenly if she were measuring up to this woman's standards for him. She found the idea disturbing, and felt herself a cheat for accepting the kindness of the Gossons when she had no intention of becoming their mistress.

The tour of the upper floors revealed much the same general damage as did the lower. The servants' quarters alone appeared to be in decent repair, which was probably due to the fact that the late master did not venture into that area.

"Thy turrets rude and tottered keep Have been the minstrel's loved resort," Elizabeth quoted from her favorite reading as they descended from the attics.

"Do you think so?" Celia asked, considering. "He has only been here for a couple of months, you know, and I would hardly call Lord Ryde a minstrel."

Elizabeth turned gently reproving eyes on her charge. "It is the sentiment that matters," she explained. "At one time, someone cared for this beautiful old home."

"That they did, miss." Mrs. Gosson nodded emphatically. "And we—Master Tevor, I mean—intends to see it fixed up again as it should be. Now, if you'll come this way?" She led them along a narrow passage that brought them to the service stairs.

"Do you have much of a staff?" Celia asked as they navigated the stairs.

"Not what we need, miss. There is only Cook and

the girl Jane besides Gosson and myself. And Wrenn, of course, who is Master Trevor's man. Then there are the two grooms, but the young one is a good lad, and helps out in the kitchens when there's a need.

Celia's brow wrinkled. Jane was the dark little creature with the big eyes who had unpacked for Elizabeth when they arrived. She had seen her frequently since, performing every sort of duty imaginable. "Is your cook a young woman?" Celia asked suddenly.

"No! Why, Master Trevor would never hear of anyone but his own Mrs. Sandies. But you shall meet her yourself." Mrs. Gosson opened the door that led into the kitchen, and Celia was left perplexed. By no stretch of the imagination could the large female with the grizzled locks stuffed under a mob cap who curtsied before her ever appear as a dainty woman with blond ringlets. So who could it have been that she saw in the passage?

As soon as they had toured the back premises, they returned to the main hall. As they reached it, Celia could no longer contain her curiosity.

"Is there another servant? A blond woman?" she asked.

An odd spasm flickered across Mrs. Gosson's lined face, but it was gone in a moment. "Why no, miss. What made you think that?"

"When I came down to dinner last night, I thought I saw a woman in the upper halls."

Mrs. Gosson shook her head firmly. "You must have been mistaken, miss. And now if you will excuse me, I wish to oversee the laying of the table for luncheon." With a polite curtsy, she hurried away.

"What was that about?" Elizabeth asked.

"I did not mistake it," Celia declared, frowning. "I saw a blond woman last night. It was only a glimpse, but I could not have been wrong. And Mrs. Gosson was lying, I am sure." The two ladies stared at each other for a moment. "I think I shall ask Lord Ryde about her," Celia finally said.

The gentlemen did not return to the house for the light nuncheon set out by Mrs. Gosson, and Celia did not see either her grandfather or Ryde until she came down for dinner that evening. By then, just being in the house upset her. Everything about the place served as an ever-present reminder of Ryde's desperate need for money, and every hour he spent alone with Sir Roderick drove home the fact that this need was his sole purpose in marrying her.

She had selected her most becoming gown that evening, the celestial-blue crepe. She was in rare beauty, as Elizabeth assured her, with her glossy curls brushed until they shone and her color high from her disturbed, turbulent emotions. Not that anyone was likely to notice, Celia thought as she swept into the Gold Saloon with her companion in her wake.

Lord Ryde, leaning negligently against the mantel, glanced towards the door as she entered. Slowly, he lowered the glass he held. His eyes narrowed as they studied every detail of her appearance, moving slowly over her, finally coming to rest in the vicinity of the long strand of pearls that lay against the ivory skin exposed by her low-cut bodice.

Calculating their worth, Celia told herself, but a soft flush rushed to warm her cheeks under his intent regard. She sat down on the sofa and faced pointedly away from him.

In another moment he stood before her, holding out a small glass of negus that smelled deliciously of nutmeg and lemon. He made it impossible to ignore him at times, and the irritating truth was that at some of these times she did not want to. His presence could be rather disturbing. . . . She allowed her gaze to sweep over him, trying to keep her thoughts cool and analytical.

As always, his appearance was impeccable, the neatness and propriety of his dress standing out in sharp contrast to his surroundings. His coat of dark blue velvet fitted smoothly over his broad shoulders, his waistcoat was an unobtrusive flowered brocade, and his black knee breeches set just the right tone. He had arranged his neckcloth with the elegant twist of the Orientale mode, neither flashy nor plain.

"Thank you," she murmured, accepting her drink and tearing her eyes from him with difficulty. Why did he have to be so—so *damnably* attractive? she fumed, borrowing the word from her grandfather's extensive vocabulary. He exercised the most upsetting effect on her, and under the circumstances, she could not let it gain hold.

He bowed to her, then went to pour Elizabeth a glass of the mild beverage. Celia's eyes followed him, watching the easy grace of his movements, his gentle mark of respect to her companion and that lady's blushing acknowledgment of his attentions. It seemed that he could be quite charming when he wished. Why did he not make just that little effort with her?

"Lord Ryde!" She might as well ask about the mysterious woman now. When he came back over to her, she described the encounter in the hall. "Mrs. Gosson had no idea who she might be. That seemed somewhat strange."

"We have had a woman in from the village, doing some sewing to repair the drapes," Ryde responded promptly. "I believe she is blond, but I have not paid much attention to her, I fear." He bowed again and returned to her grandfather's side.

There was something too smooth about his response, and it bothered her. A troublesome doubt occupied her mind throughout dinner, and she still brooded over it when the gentlemen joined them shortly after taking their port. She looked up as they entered, and found to her surprise that Trevor's gaze sought her out, frowning.

"Your grandfather tells me you play the pianoforte," he remarked.

"Yes," Celia acknowledged, cautiously, unsure what he might be leading up to.

"If you will come with me, then? And Miss Westerly? I believe we now have another room that you will not find too uncomfortable."

He led them across the hall to a drawing room at the front of the house. This must be the southeast corner, Celia realized, looking about the long apartment. Closed drapes of faded green velvet now covered windows on two sides. Probably bays, she decided, remembering the charmingly irregular aspect of the facade.

The few pieces of furniture the room boasted were arranged in a comfortable circle about the hearth at the far end. And there, close enough to the fire for warmth but far enough away to prevent damage to the tuning, stood an inlaid pianoforte. Celia moved toward it, drawn by its beauty.

"We discovered it in the barn yesterday." Trevor's deep voice, holding a suppressed note of anger, sounded at her side.

"That's disgraceful!" Celia exclaimed. She sat down on the bench and ran gentle, loving fingers over the fine wood. "But it looks to be unharmed."

" Gosson spent all afternoon cleaning it. He hoped you would enjoy it."

Her eyes flew to Trevor's face. "He—I hope he did not go to too much trouble," she stammered.

"A labor of love, I believe. As far as the Gossons are concerned, nothing is too good for you."

An uncomfortable warmth again flooded her cheeks. "It—it is very kind of them." If only he might feel the same! She ran her fingers lightly over the keys, and her distress faded at the sound of the soft, mellow tones. Next, she tried a chord and found it almost pure. "It is in excellent condition!" she exclaimed.

"It is not quite perfect." He leaned over to listen closely as she tried an A minor. "But piano tuning is not a butler's task. I shall have a man out from Brighton tomorrow."

"That is very obliging of you."

"Not in the least. I enjoy music. I hope you will honor us by playing a great deal."

"Us," not "me." He was not one to give in to her an inch. It irritated her, yet she rose to the challenge. She knew herself to be an accomplished player, though at the moment sadly out of practice. Sir Roderick had not felt music to be an appropriate occupation for one in mourning.

She ran her fingers lightly over the keys once more, striking several chords, trying to find something familiar. In a moment she had it, and began one of her favorite pieces by Bach. To her relief, she moved flawlessly, the many hours of practice over the years coming to her aid.

It had been long, so very long, since she had been able to lose herself in the glorious, soaring notes of her favorite composer. She barely glanced at the keyboard. Frustrations, anger, everything seemed to seep away into the keys, vanishing as each pure note faded away. She paused, allowing the last chord to linger, then surged onward with one of Bach's tributes to joy.

At last she sank back, trembling with the emotion these works created in her. Something warm and moist slid down her cheek, and she was forced to search for her reticule, to find a handkerchief to wipe away the tears that trembled on her lashes.

A handkerchief of fine lawn was pressed into her hand. Startled, she glanced up to see Trevor's face just above her own, his dark eyes shining, his face a mirror of her own wonder at the splendor of Bach's genius.

"It—it has been too long since last I played," she almost whispered. She averted her head, dabbing at her eyes.

"Do you know all your music so well?" he asked, his voice soft, matching hers.

"No. I—some would come back to me, but I wish I had my music."

"Allow me." He moved away to a glass-fronted

cabinet, which he opened. From this, he drew forth a stack of papers which he brought back to the pianoforte and handed to Celia.

"Oh!" The exclamation escaped her in a gasp. Here she held Bach, Mozart, Vivaldi, Telemann, all of her favorites. She selected a minuet by Mozart, placed it on the music stand, and began to play the familiar piece. As she neared the bottom of the sheet, Trevor's hand reached over her shoulder to turn the page.

"Another," he said softly as she finished. This time she selected another piece by Bach, and Ryde, his expression rapt, drew up a chair and sat down at her elbow, gazing off into space as she played.

At last she sat back, exhausted from her involvement in the music. She turned to look up at Ryde, and her hesitant smile faded from her lips. His eyes, which rested on her, were devoid of emotion, containing only an unreadable, impenetrable look. It was as if he calculated his success with her!

Anger welled within her, the more powerful for following hard on the heels of such a spiritually moving experience. It had been a trick! A hateful, hurtful manipulation to bring her under his control!

"You cannot get around me by pretending to be interested in music!" she hissed at him in an undervoice.

"Was that what I was doing?" he asked, his expression suddenly piercing.

"It is wasted effort, I assure you! You will never get so much as a single penny of that money you so ardently desire! You may insult me all you wish, but it will do you no good!" She stood, directed a scathing look at him, and walked over to where Sir Roderick sat in quiet conversation with Elizabeth. "I must wish you good night, Grandfather. I fear I have developed the headache." She stooped to kiss his cheek, then left the room with only a cold, sideways glance at Lord Ryde's frowning countenance.

She went out into the hall, slamming the door behind her. Somewhere above her an echo sounded—or was it another door, closing more softly? *Was* there someone else in this house, someone about whom Ryde wanted her to know nothing? The idea did little to soothe her seething temper.

Nor did the sight of her depressing bedchamber. Why did that insufferable man have to mock her by toying with something that meant so much to her? Was it an attempt at coercion? Did he fear to lose the money?

She sank down onto the bed. In honesty, she realized the matter went deeper than purely monetary considerations. The great Trevor Ryde, noted Corinthian and now a baron, had deigned to sell his name at last. But the lady refused. She must have dealt an intolerable blow to his pride. The smile she allowed herself was tight, for she recognized what this meant. He would use any means, fair or foul, to conquer her, to see her helpless beneath his domination. But her own pride equaled his, and she would never submit—even if she could. Charlie was not the only factor that made the marriage impossible. A battle royal loomed ahead of her, and she doubted even Jonathon would be of much assistance now.

She retired to bed but could not sleep. The night was warm, and restless, she threw off her light comforter. Where did the cat Andrew spend his evenings?

she wondered. She could have used his company. After a half hour of uneasy tossing, she finally rose and relit her candle by the pale light of the moon. What she needed was a book. She slipped on a wrap over her nightdress, picked up the candle and left her room.

A soft glow coming through the long windows lit the gallery as she walked along it toward the main stair. On impulse, she knelt on one of the chairs and leaned on the sill. The straggling garden provided a ghostly setting that only lacked a few flitting figures to make it complete.

At first she thought it was her active imagination. A large dark shape seemed to move by the gate, then disappeared again into the shadows. Celia let out a deep breath that she had not realized she held. Her eyes were playing tricks on her! Then a smaller shape—a person, she would swear—seemed to float through the twiggy shrubs toward the drive. In a moment, it blended into the shadows along with the first shape.

She stared fixedly for some time. Once, she thought she saw movement again but it seemed to be going away from her and not toward the house. She shivered. The oppressive atmosphere of the house was getting to her, she told herself. Her worries over Charlie . . . her anger with Ryde . . . she must be partially asleep.

Nevertheless, she abandoned her mission to the bookroom and returned to her chamber, closing the door firmly behind her. With heroic effort she restrained herself from placing a heavy chair before the door to block anyone's entrance. She was being absurd! There must have been a wind, blowing those ghastly overgrown trees. That was all she saw! It was her own silly fancies that created ghostly coaches and haunting specters. That ridiculous idea must have remained hidden in the recesses of her mind from her thoughts on arrival. And her sleepy eyes supplied the rest of the illusion.

By morning, Celia had developed a headache in truth. She felt depressed, dispirited, and blamed it firmly and solely on her disturbed night. Ryde, and his determination to bring her under his all too powerful spell, she chose to ignore.

Her feeling of oppression increased as she dressed, and her one desire as she descended the stairs was to escape from this house for a while. Perhaps she could borrow a horse and ride. She felt her color rise at the memory of her last ride, with Trevor. She had thought she sensed a kindred spirit in him that morning. Perhaps she had—perhaps they were too much alike to ever get along.

Sir Roderick was the sole occupant of the breakfast parlor. He sat at the table with a plate of red beefsteak and a tankard of ale before him. He took a long draught from the latter and set it down.

"Are you better this morning, my dear?" he asked.

She crossed to the sideboard and stood staring moodily at the selection of dishes before her. "Somewhat. Why have you not ridden out?" She served herself, then sat down across from him.

" Trevor had business in Brighton, and left before I came down."

"In Brighton." She took a sharp bite of her roll. If that wasn't just like him, to so neglect his duties as a host! A sudden thought occurred to her, and she turned to stare at her grandfather. "It is not far, is it?"

"No, not much above five miles, I believe. But he had a number of things to do, and did not expect to be back until the afternoon, Gosson said."

"Could we go, Grandfather? I have never been to Brighton, and I—I would like to get out for a little while." She held her breath. If Lord Ryde did not invite her on an outing, she would arrange her own! She would not be subject to his whims!

Sir Roderick considered. "I do not see why not. Now, really, my dear!" He caught Celia as she threw her arms about him. She settled meekly down again, but her eyes sparkled. "Do you think you can be ready within the hour?"

She nodded. "Sooner, if you wish."

They departed in record time, and after a journey of less than thirty minutes, the team harnessed to the traveling chaise trotted past the first buildings of the seaside resort. Elizabeth peered out the window, as eager to see the sights as was Celia.

Directly before them, situated so that it greeted every visitor to Brighton, stood the Royal Pavilion. Even in its current state of expansion and renovation, this was an imposing edifice—in every way a suitable retreat for the flamboyant Prince of Wales. The remodeling undertaken by Henry Holland, over twenty years before, had produced a pleasing, symmetrical composition, with a circular saloon behind a row of carved columns at its center. Behind it, rising out of the Pleasure Gardens, could be glimpsed the peaked dome of the newly erected stables designed by Porden.

Their carriage continued along the glazed red-brick paving of the Steine until it pulled up before the

Castle Inn. Here, Sir Roderick made arrangements to leave his equipage and prepared to escort the ladies about the town.

Having already glimpsed the Pavilion, the next attraction must of course be the sea. They strolled along the Steine toward the Marine Parade, where they might walk in comfort and observe the ocean at their leisure. They passed only a few fashionable people, mostly those who resided in Brighton for the better part of the year. Almost a full month of the London Season still remained, and only a very few of the *beau monde* had as yet departed its pleasures for the coming summer season here.

Celia walked idly, trailing her grandfather, with Elizabeth at her side. Quite a number of new houses lined the street, she noted, built in response to the increased popularity of the resort since Prinny's patronage had made it fashionable. In a few short weeks, each of these buildings would be rented by members of the *ton* who would flock here to escape the heat of London and find further entertainment. But she would no longer be here.

A barouche drew abreast of them, then stopped. A matronly woman of comfortable proportions leaned across a gaunt lady who sat at her side, and peered intently at them.

"Miss Marcombe? Celia?" the woman called. "Is that you, my dear?"

Celia turned. "Mrs. Andover! And Miss Draycott. How delightful to see you again. I had no idea you were in Brighton." She ran forward to take the hands of her mother's dearest friends.

"We have moved here, dear child," Miss Draycott

told her. "So pleasant as it is, and much nearer to London than is Bath. How do you go on, child? We have not set eyes on you this age!"

Sir Roderick approached the barouche, bowing to the ladies. Celia performed the introductions.

"Are you staying here long?" Miss Draycott asked. "You must come to call and tell us how you have been going on since—since your mamma's sad death."

"My grandfather is visiting his godson, Lord Ryde, at Hastings, which is just outside of town," Celia explained, carefully omitting any hint that she was involved. "Miss Westerly and I shall be delighted to pay you a morning visit."

"We shall look forward to it." Mrs. Andover glanced across at Miss Draycott. "You are looking tired, dear sister. We must hurry along." With renewed declarations of their delight at this unexpected meeting, the two ladies signaled their coachman and drove on.

Celia and Elizabeth turned to follow Sir Roderick, who had already started off. How lovely to see those two old dears again, after so long! It quite took her back to happier times, her mother's card parties, the musical evenings. . . . It was good to know she had friends so close by. A new thought struck her. Their presence might even be useful in her battle with Lord Ryde! She would have to see. . . .

Celia remained lost in thought as they strolled to the end of the Steine and turned onto the Marine Parade. Here, houses lined only one side of the street. The other gave way to the beach, along which a number of bathing machines were lined up.

Ahead of them, Sir Roderick came to an abrupt halt, then stepped up to a bench upon which an elderly gentleman sat. The man looked up, exclaimed in pleasure, and gestured for Sir Roderick to join him. Brighton, Celia mused, appeared to be filled with their acquaintances. It only needed one more, as far as she was concerned, and Jonathon was due to arrive that afternoon.

She and Elizabeth continued their ambling walk, gazing out across the foaming blue-green waves. It felt good to get away from that rambling old ruin of a house for a while. The sea air was delightfully crisp and refreshing, with a tang of salt that Celia found exhilarating. It seemed to blow away the cobwebs that cluttered her brain, enabling her to think more clearly. At least she no longer felt so pitifully depressed! New energy suffused her, leaving her ready to face—and vanquish!— Ryde's next tactic.

She glanced back, found that her grandfather had not yet deserted his crony, and decided to wait. No restless energy drove her on now. She was content to admire the view.

"Would it not be enjoyable to live in a house that faced the ocean?" Elizabeth sighed. "Can you not imagine hearing the lulling lap of the waves as you fall asleep each night, and waking to the cries of the gulls?"

"It would be lovely," Celia agreed. She turned to study the houses. "But not very private. Only look! You can see right into the front rooms of every one of these! Why, you could even see who was visiting whom."

She broke off. There, in the next house down, she could indeed see who was visiting. The tall, broad-shouldered gentleman who stood in profile against the window could be none other than Lord Ryde! Celia moved closer, not quite able to believe her eyes. What was he doing here? This was a home, not a business establishment.

The door into the drawing room where Ryde stood opened, and Celia stared at a petite female, all golden and pink in a diaphanous, flowing robe, who floated into the room. In a moment, the lady threw herself into Ryde's unprotesting arms, locking her own about his neck. She disengaged herself almost at once, apparently laughing. She grasped his hands, led him to a sofa, and pulled him down beside her.

Elizabeth, caught by Celia's intent stance, followed her gaze and gasped audibly.

Celia ignored her. The tiny woman with a halo of golden ringlets seemed more than a little familiar. . . . "Business meetings indeed!" she exclaimed through clenched teeth. "How—how *dare* he!"

Sir Roderick moved up beside them. "I am sorry to keep you waiting. Shall we continue?" He became aware of Celia's seething countenance and the direction of her gaze. He looked over, then frowned in vexation as he, too, recognized Trevor.

"Come along, my girl. This is no place for you."

"Grandfather! Did—did you *see?*" she demanded.

"Well, what of it? Come along, let us not be standing about here all day," he added testily.

"I—I won't! Grandfather, how—how can you condone his behavior?"

Sir Roderick took her firmly by the elbow, motioned for Elizabeth to do the same, and the two of them managed to lead Celia on.

"What you have jut seen is no concern of yours, my

girl," he said firmly. "Remember that. A gentleman has his little adventures; they mean nothing. They certainly do not concern his affianced wife."

CHAPTER TEN

Celia turned and craned her neck to take one last, furious glance at the window. She could not believe such duplicity possible! Business meeting indeed! Or were his arrangements with that barque of frailty—to use a term she should not have known—as straightforward and monetarily-based as were his dealings with her?

Was his lack of money the reason he had housed the high flyer in his own home until Celia's arrival? Memory of the half-glimpsed shadows of the night before returned to plague her. He must have removed her in the middle of the night so that they would not know! How long would he have had the nerve to keep his mistress under the same roof with his affianced bride if Celia had not seen her and asked questions?

And now, he was forced to waste what little money he had on that grasping harpy instead of spending it on the estate where it was so badly needed! But that was where *she* came in, after all! She must never let herself forget that for an instant. It was her role to replenish his coffers. She fumed with impotent indignation. How she looked forward to seeing his chagrin when he learned that Charlie was alive, and he could never touch Ranleigh!

A new thought struck her. He was probably planning on spending *her* money as well as his own on his lightskirt! She dug in her heels, refusing to take another step, forcing her grandfather to look at her.

"Behave yourself, miss!" the elderly man ordered with soft but firm voice. His fingers dug into her arm warningly. "You will not make a scene in public!"

She bit her lip, then walked on again. Perhaps she could use this to further her cause, to put an end to that despicable marriage plan—or at the very least delay it until Charlie could be brought safely home. Ryde would have no further interest in her once he knew Ranleigh to be beyond his grasp.

"Grandfather," she began, but he cut her off.

"Not another word!" he ordered. "I repeat, this has nothing to do with you. I thought every young lady of quality was brought up to understand such arrangements."

"I do understand, all too well!" She took a deep breath. "I thought you said Lord Ryde was a capable estate manager! Yet here he is, keeping that—that . . ." She encountered her grandfather's awful gaze and broke off. "Do you not mind that as soon as he gets control of your fortune and Ranleigh, they will be squandered to support that sort of female?"

"That is quite enough, miss!" Sir Roderick snapped.

Celia forced back her fury, hoping savagely she had given him something to think about. Why was she so angry, anyway? What Ryde chose to do was no concern of hers! And it certainly should not leave her feeling so desolated! She steadied herself, forcing her voice to be calm. "If you do not mind, Grandfather, I wish to go home. I have the headache."

Sir Roderick appeared to feel this was for the best, for he turned on the instant, guiding them back the way they had come. Celia kept her face resolutely turned from That Window.

The journey back to Hastings was accomplished in an uncomfortable silence. Celia stared blindly out the window, trying to sort out her chaotic emotions. How dare Ryde behave in such a manner! For a while she passed the time in heaping unspoken insult and abuse upon his absent head. Never in her young life had she encountered such dastardly behavior! She had been dragged to his estate so that he could fix his interest with her, yet here he was, neglecting even the most common courtesy toward her and instead dancing attendance on one who was undoubtedly his mistress! If he thought he could get away with this, he was very much mistaken, as he would shortly discover!

And why—*why*—did it have to upset her so? She knew Ryde's only interest in her was the income from Ranleigh. There had been no sham of lovemaking between them, so she should not—could not—feel that he betrayed her! Yet, something within her cried out in pain at seeing him in the arms of another woman. Her pride must have been wounded; that could be the only explanation. In his eyes, her dark curls and youthful charms did not compare with that blond flamboyance she had glimpsed.

As the carriage turned onto the graveled drive, her

dejection faded before a resurgence of anger. A single month's rent on that house on the Marine Parade, she was sure, could easily restore the garden that lay in ruins at Hastings. Odious, hateful man, to behave as he did. It was just one more proof that he looked upon marriage with her as nothing more than a necessity—and a not very pleasant one, at that.

To her utter disgust, this last thought brought her close to tears. She stepped down from the chaise and hurried ahead of the others toward the house. Gosson opened the door as she neared, and bowed low to her.

"A gentleman has just arrived, miss. I have taken the liberty of showing him into the Gold Saloon, as I was assured you would return shortly."

She forced her chin to stop trembling. "A—a gentleman?"

"A Captain Edelston, miss."

"Jonny! Th—thank you, Gosson. That was quite right! He is a very old friend." Footsteps sounded behind her, and she turned with her sweetest smile forced to her lips. "What a delightful surprise, Grandfather. Jonathon has come to call!"

Sir Roderick did not even hesitate. "You may tell him I will be down shortly, Gosson. Will you send my man up to me? And a cordial, I believe. It has been a most fatiguing morning."

Celia ran lightly across the hall and threw the door open. Jonathon stood, dislodging the recumbent form of the cat Andrew as he did so, and she hurled herself heedlessly into his reluctant arms.

"I must speak to you!" she hissed into his ear.

He put her gently aside, but patted her shoulder as a sign that he had heard her. He then stepped forward to greet Elizabeth, who followed her impetuous charge more sedately into the room.

"Elizabeth, I—I must talk to Jonathon. Alone, please!" she begged. "If you could sit a little way apart, just for the veriest few minutes . . . ?"

Elizabeth hesitated, knowing she really should not comply with this request. But it was too tempting to remain, to sit and gaze at Captain Edelston's handsome face, to listen to the gentle tones of his voice. Turning away abruptly to hide her softly flushed cheeks, she sought the shelter of the far corner of the room.

Celia waited until Elizabeth took a seat out of hearing, then sank down onto the sofa and gestured for Jonathon to join her. Andrew did as well, and settled himself comfortably on her lap.

"Please, we must speak to Grandfather immediately!" Her hands stroked the cat's black and white fur in agitation. "I—I cannot go on with this for so much as another day!"

"Easy, now, Cill," he urged. "Mustn't do anything rash, you know. What's happened to distress you so? Thought you were being quite calm about the whole business."

"The most dreadful thing has happened. Ryde is keeping a mistress! I actually saw them together!"

Jonathon coughed. "Really, Cill. Hadn't expected you to be so missish. Not with Charlie for a brother!" He leaned over and gently removed the cat from her distraught hold. "You must have known about such things before you were out of leading strings! Happens all the time."

"Jonny," she declared, indignant. "Do you mean to tell me that you actually expect me to put up with the attentions of a man who is keeping another woman? I—I can understand it from my grandfather, but not from you!"

"What does it matter, Cill? You're not getting leg-shackled to him, you know."

She looked down at her hands, which she now clasped tightly in her lap. "I—I know, Jonny. But I cannot like it! *He* does not know that I shall not marry him."

"What exactly did you see, Cill?" he asked, resignedly. He stroked the agreeable Andrew as he watched her, and the cat thrust his head into Jonathon's hand for a thorough rubbing.

Jonathon had no real desire to enter into even a sham engagement with her unless it became vitally necessary, Celia guessed. She described the scene, and his brow furrowed.

"Well, what I mean, m'dear, you sure she was his bit of muslin?"

She blinked at this unfamiliar expression, but had no trouble interpreting it. "What else could she be? No—no decent lady would receive a gentleman in a gown like that, or—or throw herself into his arms!"

"Well, you greeted me in much the same way, just now," he pointed out.

"That has nothing to say to anything!" she informed him crossly. "He—he kissed her!" She was not quite positive on that point, but it seemed a likely thing to have happened.

Jonathon's jaw tightened and Andrew pushed at his hand to remind him of the obligations that attended cat-holding. "Kissed her, did he? I suppose she must be his light o'love, then. Don't worry, Cilly. I won't let him force his attentions on you. You just leave it all to me."

"What do you plan to do?" she demanded.

He hesitated, but was spared the necessity of coming up with an answer by Elizabeth, who came forward at that point, looking acutely uncomfortable.

"Should—should we not send for some refreshment?" she suggested. Her soft gray eyes gave the impression of a timid mouse.

"Yes, of course. Jonathon, I am so sorry."

"No need," he assured her. "That butler fellow brought me a very tolerable Madeira. But get something for yourselves, by all means. Must have been a hot drive from Brighton."

Celia, feeling ill at ease when giving orders in someone else's household—especially Ryde's—rang for Gosson, then sent him for more wine for Jonathon and lemonade for herself and Elizabeth. Andrew stretched, jumped to the floor and followed the butler out. Celia returned to sit quietly beside her companion, who was inquiring after Jonathon's lodgings in Brighton. He had taken a room at the Old Ship, he told them, and found it quite comfortable. He believed Brighton to be pleasant enough on the whole, though rather dull at the moment. Celia listened for a little while, but found no comfort in such inconsequential chatter.

"Jonny," she exclaimed when a momentary lull in the conversation allowed her to return to more important matters. "We must convince Grandfather to listen to us. But how? I cannot be forced into this distasteful marriage."

"Of course not," Jonathan said quickly, though the blankness of his countenance indicated that he had little idea of how to proceed.

"You must speak to him, Celia, and soon," Elizabeth agreed. "The longer you wait, the harder it will be and the more adamant your grandfather will become!" Against her will, her eyes strayed to Jonathon's classically perfect features.

"I will tell him today," Celia decided. Actually, she knew it should be Jonathon who should approach the elderly man to ask his permission to pay his addresses, but she had little faith in her old friend's ability to convince anyone that his suit was sincere and of long standing. She had better handle it herself. If she did this wrong, she would not put it beyond her grandfather to demand that she marry one or the other of the two men on the spot. And then she would really be in a bind, for it was unthinkable for her to marry either, and equally unthinkable to tell her grandfather the truth about Charlie!

"Jonny, do you think . . ." she began, then broke off as the door opened. Gosson entered, bearing a tray with glasses and a plate of cakes and macaroons.

"Do—do you enjoy riding, Miss Westerly?" Jonathon asked at random in an attempt to cover up the sudden silence.

"I am learning to enjoy it, very much," Elizabeth

responded shyly. "It had not come very much in my way, before. But dear Celia is the kindest teacher and is never cross with me when I do foolish things."

"Perhaps we can all ride out together one morning soon," Jonathon suggested. "As I came out from Brighton, I saw several excellent vistas for sketching, if you enjoy that occupation."

"What an excellent idea!" Celia exclaimed. She glanced at Gosson, who appeared absorbed in the straightening of a long runner. Would he never leave? "Elizabeth does the loveliest sketches, Jonathon. Quite beyond anything! I tell her she could have obtained a position at a select academy as an art mistress." They were babbling, all three of them, trying to appear natural before the butler. Celia's sense of the ridiculous threatened to get the better of her, and she fought down an urge to giggle. How absurd this conversation was, when such dramatic matters loomed over them!

"Do you also sketch, Captain Edelston?" Elizabeth asked.

"Avidly," he admitted with a shy, boyish smile that could have melted a hardened heart, let alone Elizabeth's tender one. "And I have had some excellent opportunities. The French and Spanish coastlines, you must know, are a delight to the eye. Serving in the Navy had some compensations."

"How I should love to see your drawings, some day," Elizabeth sighed. "I am sure it would be almost as good as actually going there! I have been so very few places, you see."

Celia stared from one to the other. They were quite serious! Perhaps it was because her own passions lay in music and not drawing that she had little interest in this talk, but she felt there were more important things that desperately needed to be discussed.

"Delighted to show you, any time," Jonathon assured Elizabeth, positively beaming at her. "Only I left them at home."

This was getting them nowhere, and time was precious. Celia turned to the butler. "Gosson," she called.

He straightened. "Yes, miss?"

"I believe my grandfather wished to join us. Do you know if he has come down yet?"

"Yes, miss. He went out, saying he was not sure when he would return." He had apparently either completed his task or decided there was nothing to be overheard, for he bowed to her and left the room.

Celia let out a deep sigh. "How vexing of him! Now, Jonny, you may tell Elizabeth about Trafalgar later, for I can see she is all agog to hear of it firsthand. Grandfather's going out was a calculated tactic on his part. I shall have to consider it!"

"Then I shall take my leave of you. Trespassed on your host's hospitality long enough." He bowed over Elizabeth's hand, turned to Celia and encountered such a look that he was reminded of his role. He raised her fingers to his lips, gave her a wink, and departed.

"Is he not the most handsome creature?" Celia asked for Elizabeth's benefit. "And such a gentleman, so kind and considerate! How could anyone not love him?"

"Very true," Elizabeth agreed in a strangely hollow

voice. "It—it is not every young man who takes the trouble to be kind to a mere companion."

Celia slipped her arm about her, giving her a quick hug. "I would never call you a *mere* anything, Elizabeth, dear. Come, let us escape this house and go for a stroll."

Thus it was that Ryde, returning to the house nearly an hour later, was greeted by the intelligence that the ladies were out but that Sir Roderick desired instant conversation with him. The latter, Gosson informed him, awaited his return in the bookroom in some agitation of spirits.

Trevor doffed his greatcoat and beaver and entered this room at once. Adolphus, who had been dozing by the hearth, rose to welcome him. Trevor greeted the animal, but looked beyond him to where his godfather paced about the long room. The elderly man looked up as Trevor approached, and he directed the full force of his scowl at him.

"Hah! There you are. Want to have a word with you."

"Certainly, sir." Trevor gestured to a chair, but the old man ignored him.

"Difficult situation," Sir Roderick told him. "Not sure it's wise of you, under the circumstances."

"What isn't?" Trevor asked, rather amused by his godfather's habit of never explaining anything fully.

"That damned mistress of yours, my boy. Can't say I blame you, of course. She is a lovely little thing, but Celia don't like it."

Trevor's brow snapped down. "What are you talking about?" he demanded.

"Don't pretend you don't know. I took Celia into Brighton this morning, and we went walking along the Marine Parade."

"Ah!" The word was stretched out, indicating his sudden comprehension. A muscle twitched at the corner of his mouth, and he was forced to repress a sudden smile. "I take it Celia saw this—this lady? And that she was not pleased?"

"Damn it, can you expect her to be?" Sir Roderick snapped. "The silly chit is none too keen on this marriage in the first place! Only looking for an excuse to do something outrageous to call it all off!"

"Is she, now?" Trevor's voice quavered with suppressed laughter.

"This is no joking matter!" Sir Roderick exploded.

"But it is! I am quite delighted she was angry." He half-sat on the corner of his desk, drew his snuff box from his coat pocket, and helped himself to a pinch. Dolph settled himself at his master's feet and let out a deep sigh.

"Have you ever heard of one Thérèse de Bourgerre?" Trevor asked idly.

"Thérèse de . . ." Sir Roderick broke off. "Singer, isn't she? What the devil has she to say to anything?"

"A great deal, under the circumstances. I believe you saw her this morning."

"So you've taken a French singer as mistress," Sir Roderick said slowly. "Don't see why who she is should matter. And if you think because Celia loves music, *that* will make any difference to her, you are much mistaken!"

Trevor laughed outright. "Oh, do sit down. I've

done no such thing. Do you know much about the lady?"

"Only that she's supposed to be quite good."

"She is. I met her for the first time about five years ago, while she was still living in Italy where her family had been forced to flee the revolution. I arranged for her to come and sing in London. But while she was here, she also met with a few members of the Government." He offered his enameled box to his godfather, who waved it aside.

"Go on," the old man said testily.

"The result of those meetings was that she returned not to Italy but to France, where she was an instant success. Her being a member of one of the fallen noble families was excellent propaganda for them, I believe. She performed for the elite of Napoleon's troops—and apparently not only on the stage. I heard she became the mistress of one of his top aides."

Here, he fixed Sir Roderick with a steady gaze. "Thérèse de Bourgerre is a very brave young woman. For the past three years, she has been sending us information on Napoleon's plans."

Sir Roderick straightened up, his eyes widening. "What happened?"

"She was caught. Fortunately, they wished to question her extensively, which gave our people time to rescue her. Unfortunately, her courier was shot before he could get her safely out of the country. The men who took over knew of my connection with the affair and brought her here, to this house, for safety. Celia spotted her the other day, so last night I took her to a suitable house a friend of mine was willing to rent.

There is a certain risk of danger from the French agents who are pursuing her, and I do not want you or Celia involved in that."

The look Sir Roderick directed at his godson held a new measure of respect. "Mlle. de Bourgerre is fortunate to have such friends."

Trevor dismissed this. "We were fortunate that she wished to help. It is now our duty—and privilege—to keep her safe until she has spoken to the people in our Government and her danger has passed."

Sir Roderick stood, then clapped Trevor's shoulder. "Celia will be delighted!" he assured him. "Bound to present you in a new light to her."

Trevor took another pinch of snuff. "I do not believe there is any need to tell her quite yet, is there?" he asked.

"Why not? No point in setting up her back if it can be helped." He shook his head. "Headstrong girl; no telling what she will get up to when she takes the bit between her teeth. Proud, just like her father."

"And her grandfather, sir." Trevor smiled. "And like me."

Sir Roderick directed a piercing gaze up at him. "What are you up to, m'boy? Playing a deep game?"

Trevor smiled slowly. "Devilish deep," he agreed.

After his godfather left him, Trevor crossed to the table where a decanter of Madeira stood and poured himself a glass. He carried the wine to the comfortable wing chair that commanded a view of what should have been a small garden. He would have to put the undergroom onto that when the other, more visible signs of damage had been repaired.

He leaned back, swirling the dark liquid in his glass, watching it with a contemplative smile. So the chit was furious, was she? He considered the possibilities, and rejected out of hand the chance that she might be jealous. Piqued would come closer to the mark. He chuckled, a low, deep sound of appreciation, as he envisioned her righteous indignation. Lord, he'd have given a monkey to see what tactics her grandfather used to prevent her from forcing her way into the house and confronting him on the spot! How it must have galled her pride!

And there, he knew, lay the real problem, the one potentially insurmountable barrier between them. Neither of them would ever give in to the other, and an acceptable compromise escaped him at the moment.

He had recovered from his initial shock of discovering that the girl he had agreed to marry was not an antidote, hopelessly on the shelf and unlikely to obtain a husband for her own sake. On due consideration, he was not now all that displeased. Her flashing brown eyes, dusky curls and slender form exactly suited his tastes. Her temperament, though, might be too close to his, for he suspected they shared a quick temper, determined pride, and an adventurous spirit. If he could bring Celia into tune with himself, instead of playing a defiant, inharmonious key, they might be able to make the marriage work.

For this, he must coax her into compliance—but he also must maintain the upper hand or lose all self-respect. She must be tamed but not broken, for he wanted none of her fire extinguished. And judging from Sir Roderick Marcombe's warning, that fire must be keeping her temper at the boiling point at the moment. He wondered if she would come up with a revenge for Thérèse, and found he looked forward to seeing what she would do.

With this reprehensible intention, he went in search of her. He heard her raised voice before he saw her, and he paused just behind the shrubbery that surrounded what his undergroom had recently been trying to turn back into a rose garden. Sir Roderick's soft voice broke across her tirade, and silence reigned for perhaps two seconds.

"How can I marry another when I love Jonathon?" he heard Celia exclaim, her voice quavering as if with restrained tears.

"I have made my decision," her grandfather informed her in a tone that brooked no opposition. "You will abide by it."

Trevor's brow lowered. This was news to him! If the silly chit really had lost her heart and there was no real objection to the young man, he would never force her to go through with the marriage arranged by her grandfather. No wonder she fought him at every turn! Why had she not come to him with her story? To his surprise, he was aware of a certain regret at the way things were turning out. Her next words, though, banished all such thoughts from his mind.

"How can you force me to marry a man who has another interest?" she demanded.

"That is enough! The matter is settled," Sir Roderick stated firmly. "You will forget Captain Edelston soon enough once you are married."

Trevor grinned as Celia gave vent to her seething anger. One fact became increasingly clear from the tone of her arguments. Lord, he doubted the little minx was any more in love with this Edelston than was her grandfather! Was this her response to Thérèse? He had to give her credit for thinking of one so quickly—one that, in fact, might have worked had she sprung it on the right man! He peered around the edge of the shrub to find that Sir Roderick had left. Celia looked about her as if she sought something to hurl after him. Then, unable to find anything suitable, she stormed off.

He had to admire her spirit, he reflected as he strolled back to the house. If only she could be induced to want this marriage, to yield to him, he sensed she could be all he would ever want in a woman, spirited and passionate. He was taken aback by the flicker of desire which this image conjured up. Restless, he went up to his room to change for dinner.

When he came down to the Gold Saloon just over an hour later, he was surprised to find Celia there before him. She had chosen to attire herself in the amber crepe lisse, a becoming gown, and he admired the charming picture she made as she perched on the edge of the wing back chair. He was not deceived for a moment by her demurely downcast eyes. He crossed to the tray of decanters and poured her a glass of the warm negus, wondering what treat she held in store for him.

"Did—did you hear that my—my *friend*—arrived early this afternoon?" she asked.

"I did indeed. I was most sorry I was not here to

receive him. I hope you enjoyed a long chat? So pleasant for you to be able to renew such an old acquaintance." He handed her the glass, his amused eyes watching her beneath half-lowered lids.

"It is much more than that!" she exclaimed dramatically, coming to her feet.

He raised polite eyebrows, letting none of his enjoyment show. "Will he do us the honor of calling again? I cannot but feel I have been derelict in my duties as a host."

Celia blinked, apparently nonplussed by his casual attitude, and he was forced to repress an almost irresistible urge to laugh. "Do you not object?" she demanded.

"Why should I?" he asked. "I have no wish to deprive you of your friends. You may continue this friendship, with my good will, as long as you are chaperoned. Just remember that you are betrothed to me now, and I expect you to behave accordingly."

"And what about your mistress?"

He raised his eyebrows again in a manner that implied she had committed a serious solecism in mentioning such a topic. She flushed, but stood her ground, defiant.

"What has that to do with what we are discussing?" he asked as if perplexed. Her response had pleased him, for it confirmed his earlier suspicion that her affections were not deeply engaged. Her pride had suffered a severe blow that morning, and it was that, not this Captain Edelston, which occupied her mind.

She turned her back on him and took several agitated steps. He caught her up easily, grasping her wrist and spinning her about to face him.

"You are as headstrong as an unbroken filly, my girl, but I have made a deal with your grandfather. I am not about to allow any silly chit to make me draw back from fulfilling my part of the bargain." He released her, and had the questionable satisfaction of seeing her run headlong from the room.

He turned back to the table and poured himself a glass of wine. He was not about to let her ride roughshod over him! If he ever gave in to her so much as a single inch, he would shortly find himself living under the cat's paw, and he had no intention of doing that. He wouldn't mind having the little hoyden, he realized, but if he married her, it must be on his terms, and his terms alone!

CHAPTER ELEVEN

Celia still seethed over what she considered to be Lord Ryde's abominable attitude when, two days later, she and Elizabeth drove into Brighton to pay the promised morning visit to Mrs. Andover and Miss Draycott. Their home stood about halfway along the Marine Parade, and to reach it they had to pass That House. Celia bit her lip, staring fixedly out to sea, refusing to allow this situation to distress her.

The ladies, it turned out, were at home, and delighted to receive their guests. For their sakes, Celia schooled her countenance into a more pleasant expression. She was really quite fond of the elderly sisters, as her mother had been, and she would not for anything offend them.

The conversation, which began with such pleasantries as the perfect weather, the balmy sea breezes, and the shockingly expensive remodeling taking place at the Royal Pavilion, soon rolled around to their hostesses' favorite topic.

"We try to hold a concert at least once a month during the off-season," Mrs. Andover, that pillar of the Brighton Music Society, told them. "Such lovely evenings as they are. We have our own musicians, of course, and more often than not we are privileged to feature a visiting *artiste.*"

"You were used to play on the pianoforte, were you not?" Miss Draycott asked Celia.

"I still do, whenever I can. I hope we shall be here for the next concert. I should enjoy it of all things!"

"But you will be, I am sure!" Mrs. Andover said brightly. "It is to be in two days' time. So busy as we have been, getting all in readiness. It is quite our greatest joy! Do say you will come!"

"Emily, my love, of course they will!" Miss Draycott put in. "Do you not remember? Lord Ryde has become one of our members! He will hardly pass up the opportunity of bringing his guests."

"We shall look forward to it," Celia promised as she rose to take her leave. Ryde again! Was she never free of hearing his name? They reached the street and entered the landaulet which their host had placed at their disposal. The man was absolutely insufferable! And the worst of him, she fumed, was the almost mesmerizing attraction he held for her. How easy it would be to forget what he really wanted and . . . She bit her lip. For a moment, she had actually forgotten. She could not marry him, even if she wished, as long as he believed Ranleigh would one day be hers.

But that was all conjecture—and of the silliest sort! She most definitely did *not* want to marry Ryde, and he would never seek her out for her own sake. As he had said, to go back on his given word would be unthinkable for him, and once that agreement was broken on her side, when Charlie appeared . . . No. Ryde would never pay court to any lady. That would be to acknowledge she held power over him. In short, the situation seemed impossible.

A lumbering farm wagon turned in front of them, momentarily blocking their way. Depressed, Celia idly scanned the few pedestrians, seeking anything to divert her troubled mind. The sight that met her eyes had exactly the opposite effect.

Just ahead of them, on the ocean side of the Parade, stood Ryde with a fashionably attired female. Long guinea-gold curls fluttered in the sea breeze from beneath her chip-straw bonnet. Pale blue skirts wrapped themselves about slender, shapely ankles as she drew her pelisse closer about herself to ward off the chill, revealing a stunning figure of full, rounded curves.

To her dismay, Celia realized her predominant emotion was jealousy. *Jealousy*, of all things! What right had the hateful Ryde to draw such an emotion from her? Furious, she looked about for an instantaneous means of showing him how little she cared. If only Jonathon were present now!

As if summoned by her need, Captain Edelston at that moment rounded the corner of the Steine and walked slowly toward them, his attention focused on the water. Their landaulet moved forward, passed Lord Ryde who did not even glance in their direction, and in a moment she was within hailing distance of her knight errant.

Jonathon!" she called, hoping her voice would carry over the rumbling of the waves. "Jonny! How wonderful to see you!"

He looked up as their coachman stopped the carriage, and a broad smile lit his handsome face. He strode immediately up to them. “Celia! Miss Westerly. How do you do? I did not expect to see you this morning.”

“We have been visiting my mamma’s friends, the Draycott sisters. You remember them, I am sure.” She peeped out of the corner of her eye, and was pleased to see that Ryde had turned slightly so that he could watch them.

“Do you sketch this morning, Captain Edelston?” Elizabeth asked shyly, indicating the large portfolio of drawing paper he carried under one arm. She kept her gaze focused on this with difficulty.

“I do.” He laughed. “Cilly will tell you that I am always sketching, when there are other, more important things to be done.”

Celia peeked back toward Ryde and noted with reprehensible smugness that he still watched them. She allowed her gaze to wander up the street in the other direction and slowly her brow furrowed.

“Jonny,” Celia interrupted him. “Do not turn around at once, but are you acquainted with those two men who are standing by the bench? They keep glancing at us in the strangest manner!”

Jonathon, with what was for him amazing casualness, turned toward the ocean, then stole a glance behind him. Immediately, the two men turned away, gesturing toward the Steine as if arguing.

“Keep running into those two.” Jonathon shrugged. “But then, Brighton’s not such a big town, after all.”

“Could they be following you?” Celia demanded.

“Lord, why would anyone want to do . . .” He broke off, staring at Celia. “. . . that,” he finished, the word coming out slow and soft.

They exchanged a long, serious glance. Did someone from the Naval Office suspect that Jonathon knew more about Charlie than he had disclosed? Were they themselves trying to locate him? And now, here was Jonathon, talking to Charlie's sister!

Out of the corner of her eye, she saw Lord Ryde pointing to the houses across the street. His companion nodded, then walked quickly toward the one where Celia had seen her the other day. Ryde watched until she was safely inside, then strolled along toward the landaulet.

Celia's present worry over Charlie was so great that she remained untouched by any feelings of triumph at detaching Ryde from his mistress. That was an accomplishment of no mean order, but she had other, more important matters to worry about. How were they to find Charlie before these men did? Could she have inadvertently placed him in danger?

In another moment, Celia was forced to drag her attention back to the immediate present. Ryde stepped up to the carriage, and even in her preoccupation she saw an opportunity too good to be missed. With an effort, she tried to appear as if no weighty matters distressed her. She raised large, limpid brown eyes to him, forced a casual, unconcerned smile of greeting to her lips and turned immediately back to Jonathon.

"Are you having an enjoyable morning?" Ryde inquired, his deep voice sending a disturbing ripple through her. If he noted her carefully displayed preference for the other man, he gave not the slightest sign.

"Most enjoyable," Celia informed him. "Now," she

added with a besotted glance at Jonathon, in case Ryde missed her meaning.

A muscle twitched at the corner of Trevor's mouth, but she could not decide if it was from irritation or amusement. He turned to Jonathon, and Celia promptly performed the introduction. The two men looked each other over carefully, and Celia was assailed by the distressing sensation that, under different circumstances, they might get along quite well.

"Captain Edelston was just about to show us some of his sketches," she told Ryde, rushing into speech to cover her uneasiness. She managed a singularly fatuous expression. "He is the most talented artist!"

Ryde raised polite eyebrows. "You are to be envied," he told Jonathon. "I cannot render a single image that even my closest friends can identify."

Jonathon grinned at him in a way that Celia secretly dubbed traitorous. "And I could not stand up for as much as two minutes with Gentleman Jackson."

"That is hardly an ability to be compared with art!" Ryde disclaimed. "I fear I am doomed to be a mere patron and appreciator."

"I do so admire a man with talent in the arts," Celia sighed, thinking it time to break up this mutual admiration. That was not something she wished to encourage. "I feel a man is incomplete if he has not a creative side to his nature."

A shadow flickered across Ryde's face, and she instantly regretted her words. She had apparently touched a nerve, perhaps a secret inner longing, and she had no desire to hurt him. That realization came somewhat as a surprise to her. She intended to fight this war to its conclusion, but she wished to do it fairly, with no underhandedness or dishonorable attacks. That was not her way, and she suspected it was not Ryde's, either.

"A concern for the arts is an admirable quality," Elizabeth said, instinctively smoothing over an awkward moment. "So—so very few are truly gifted." Here, to her dismay, her eyes strayed to Jonathon's face. "A—a man who appreciates drawing or—or music participates in his own way," she hurried on, trying to disguise her near betrayal of her feelings.

"Just so," Ryde agreed with a sudden smile that caused Elizabeth's cheeks to take on a delicate flush. "Do you return to Hastings, or have you other calls to make?" he went on, addressing Celia.

"We—we were on the point of returning," Celia admitted.

"Then, may I have the honor of escorting you?" He climbed into the landaulet without awaiting permission. "I have left my horse at the Castle Inn," he informed the driver.

Celia leaned down, extending her hand to Jonathon. "We shall see you soon, will we not?" she asked pointedly.

"With your permission," he declared promptly, raising her fingers to his lips. He released her, then extended his hand to Miss Westerly.

Elizabeth hesitated, then placed her hand in his, distressed by his kind attentions as he bowed low before her. Captain Edelston was so very considerate, so very much the gentleman! And she had to be glad it was her darling Celia that he loved. She had to be!

"We shall be pleased to see you at Hastings at any time." Trevor's voice broke into her thoughts as the two men shook hands. Jonathon thanked him, then stood back to allow the carriage to proceed on its way.

"Quite a pleasant gentleman," Ryde remarked. "A naval officer, I believe?"

"Yes, he sold his commission after he was so badly wounded at Trafalgar," Celia replied automatically, dismayed by the excellent terms the two men appeared to have established in a bare few minutes.

"We must invite him to dine with us one night soon," announced her irritating host.

They lapsed into silence. As the carriage moved up the street, Celia glanced back. Jonathon had seated himself on the bench and taken out his sketch pad. One of those two watchful men had moved up the street and was looking with considerable interest at one of the houses along the Marine Parade. The other remained where he was, but turned to direct a long, searching gaze at the occupants of the landaulet. Celia shivered uneasily.

In a few minutes the inn was reached, and Ryde left the landaulet to retrieve his horse. They set off for his estate with him riding beside them.

Celia glanced up at his enigmatic face, unable to read his thoughts. If only she could trust him! She needed the advice of someone capable, someone who could help her. If Jonathon was being followed . . . For the first time, the true gravity of the situation dawned on her and she was gripped by fear. This was no game they played. If she bungled this and got Charlie caught, he could be shot for deserting! She could not bear to lose her brother again, and in so dishonorable a manner. It would kill her grandfather, she was sure! And Ryde—would he overlook her family's disgrace and marry her anyway, just to obtain Ranleigh?

And would she be forced to accept, to be grateful that any gentleman would offer her the protection of his name?

She was getting ahead of herself! As of yet, Ryde had no inkling of this—this keg of gunpowder that might go off under them at any moment. And his very innocence of this matter was one more reason why she could never agree to a marriage with him. The thought left her depressed, so she turned to Elizabeth, rushing into speech to divert her mind.

"What would you care to do this afternoon?" she asked with feigned brightness, breaking the silence that had lasted since they left Brighton.

"I—I hadn't considered," Elizabeth replied. She sat hunched in a corner of the carriage, staring out. She raised her handkerchief, making a surreptitious dab at her eyes. "Whatever you wish. Do you have something in mind?"

What distressed Elizabeth? Celia reached out, touching her companion's arm, but received no response.

Trevor, who rode quite close to the landaulet, leaned over to speak to her. "If you would like it, Miss Marcombe, I had thought to show you about the estate. Would you join me for a ride?"

Celia looked up, vexed that now, of all times, he should at last choose to play the host.

"What—what an excellent idea!" Elizabeth exclaimed, not turning to look at them. "You will enjoy that of all things, Celia."

Under the circumstances, Celia could only give in

with a good grace. She would enjoy it, she knew, for she could use a long gallop to clear the tangled cobwebs of worry from her mind. Perhaps it would help her to think more clearly, to come up with a plan to find Charlie.

Gosson greeted them at the door with the welcome news that a cold collation had been laid out in the breakfast parlor. After refreshing themselves from this, Celia sent a message for her maid and then went up to her room to change into her habit.

Seddons arrived only a few minutes later, and with her assistance, Celia was quickly fastened into the dark green velvet dress. She allowed her maid to arrange her hussar hat over her dark curls, then picked up her gloves.

Did Lord Ryde want to race as much as she did? Celia wondered. She flushed slightly, her spirits lifting somewhat at the memory of their wild dash over the fields at Ranleigh. There had been a soaring elation they both felt, a moment when she thought she detected a kindred spirit within him. Was that what prompted him to suggest they ride again?

But the aftermath had not been entirely pleasant. Trevor had behaved in a hateful manner, making it clear the money outweighed any personal feelings he might have. But that was before he knew about Jonathon. Had the encounter startled him, made him realize that he would have to win her, perhaps—just perhaps—even that he wanted to? Although it should not have, the thought brightened her mood and she hurried down the stairs with an almost eager anticipation.

Ryde came out of the bookroom as she reached the

hall, and together they went out to the stable—a large, square cobbled yard, off of which opened boxed stalls of gray stone. Across the back stood a long stone building that housed the carriages, feed, and tack. Above this, in a second story, were living quarters to accommodate a staff of grooms and coachmen far in excess of the present number.

The overwhelming impression, even here, was one of shabbiness and neglect. The wooden doors of the majority of the stalls were splintered, hung from broken hinges, or were missing altogether. The area was clean, though, and the two horses that stood saddled and ready were the picture of health and impeccably groomed.

Trevor led her up to a small gray mare who stood peacefully with one fetlock cocked, gently swishing her tail. Instantly, Celia was on her guard. This hardly seemed an appropriate mount for her, and she strongly suspected his motives. Introducing him to Jonathon had been her retaliation for learning of his mistress. Was he now seeking revenge for Jonathon? The idea appealed to her, quite reprehensibly.

"Appearances can be deceiving," Ryde told her. He tossed her effortlessly up into the saddle, then swung up onto his own while she arranged her skirts.

"Has this animal ever been known to get out of a walk?" she asked sweetly.

Trevor's dancing eyes rested on her. "Often."

She threw him a disgusted glance, then picked up the reins to test the mare's mouth. The result was as immediate as it was startling—the mare shot backward, then sideways as Celia's weight shifted.

"I did warn you," Trevor murmured.

Celia burst out laughing. "I have never been on a horse with so light a mouth! She is a darling!" She brought the mare carefully up beside Trevor, feeling the animal's eagerness with every dancing step. "And she looked such a—a slug!"

"For a moment there, I thought you might murder me," he told her, his eyes still glinting in amusement.

"I was tempted," she admitted. "I thought . . ." She broke off. "Which way do we start?" she asked hastily to cover her near slip.

"This way, I believe. And perhaps someday you will tell me what you thought."

She threw him a fiery glance, but he was paying her no heed. His attention was concentrated on his own mount, a large, skittish bay whose sole purpose at the moment appeared to be to unseat his rider. He made several valiant attempts at this while Celia watched in growing appreciation, until he finally condescended to bear Trevor out through the arched gateway.

"Would you care for a gallop?" he asked, then barely waited for her assent. He turned the bay toward an open field and gave him his head. Thus freed, the animal sprang forward with long, eager strides.

The mare was right behind. What she lacked in length of stride she made up for in spirit, and in a moment they raced neck to neck. They continued their headlong dash across several fields, easily clearing the hedges that separated them. They turned, heading off at an angle, down a slope toward a shallow stream.

Celia had barely a glance to spare for the scenery

that flashed by. As always, she was caught up in the thrill of the ride, relishing the wind on her face, the sensation of freedom that rendered all else unimportant for the moment.

They crossed the wide stream with barely a check in stride. Water flew up, covering her skirts and face with a fine spray of fresh, chill droplets. Still together, they lurched up the steep bank on the other side. Another field, quite narrow, stretched before them, and they crossed this in record time. A high hedge loomed ahead, and Trevor angled off so that they approached a gate. They cleared this, flying, and landed on a verge on the other side. Two strides took them across the narrow lane and to the opposite verge, then they sailed easily over the fence and back onto a field.

Ahead of them stood an orderly arrangement of houses and fields. Trevor veered off.

"The next hedge!" he shouted, indicating the end of their race.

Laughing with her soaring exhilaration, Celia urged the mare up abreast of Trevor, then slightly ahead. His deep, hearty laugh rang out in response, and his bay again took the lead. They maintained this pace until the last moment, when they reined in together, as breathless as their mounts.

"Well done!" Trevor exclaimed.

"It was a wonderful run!" Celia stroked the streaming neck of the gray. The horses seemed to have enjoyed this as much as had they. She looked about. "Is this the edge of the estate?" she asked, curious.

"No, those are the tenanted farms, just over there." He urged the bay forward, and they started walking in the direction he had indicated to cool off their heated mounts.

Here, the neglect was not as noticeable, for the tenants had done their utmost to maintain their homes in some state of repair. But conditions were far from ideal. Celia drew in a deep breath, her spirits that had soared only a minute before plummeting back to earth. Without a massive input of funds, and in the near future, these shacks would defy their occupants' frantic attempts to preserve them and crumble to the ground.

"What terrible shape everything is in!" she exclaimed. "How unforgivable of your predecessor to have allowed this deterioration to take place!" She turned outraged eyes to Trevor, and was surprised to encounter his frozen features.

"It was indeed," he declared shortly.

"When will you . . ." she began, then broke off. She had been about to ask when he intended to begin repairs, but the answer was obvious. He waited only for their marriage—which could never take place. But at the moment, seeing him here in the midst of so much decay, she could almost forgive him for being willing to sell himself to salvage it. But why did the price have to include her? That was the one thing she could never forget—and even if she wished, she could not give him the money. She nipped that generous thought in the bud and, instead, deliberately added fresh fuel to the embers of her anger. He had no thought for *her*; why should *she* care what happened to him?

"It was hardly a wise move to bring me here," she informed him through tight lips, her eyes sparkling. "I doubt if anything short of selling Ranleigh could produce the enormous sums that will be necessary here!"

He looked at her, his eyes veiled. "You won't believe this, but I have no intention of touching a single penny of your grandfather's money."

"No, you'll leave that to your agents, won't you? Or do you consider the money mine? Or yours? I suppose you will also try to tell me that you have no intention of wasting it on your mistress!" She bit her lip and turned her head away. She had not meant to be betrayed into that indiscreet utterance.

"You have certainly succeeded in painting my character black, haven't you?" he said mildly. "I suppose nothing would convince you that the lady is not now, nor ever has been, my mistress?"

"What, have you been unsuccessful? Poor Lord Ryde! What a terrible blow to your pride. But then, not every woman finds your type appealing. Many of us prefer handsome men."

"Like Captain Edelston," Trevor agreed promptly, his voice shaking with something that could have been either amusement or exasperation, or possibly both.

"Why, yes! His features are a model of perfection, are they not? And so romantic!" She stole a glance at Trevor, and was irritated to find that he did not appear to be the least bit out of countenance over her rapturous description of the man she hoped he considered his rival.

She urged the mare forward with an angry nudge of her heel. Her mount broke into a canter, allowing Celia a brief escape.

A slight rustle was her only warning. A small rabbit

darted from between low shrubs and the gray mare spun, half-rearing in her sudden fright. Celia stepped down hard into her single stirrup to maintain her balance, and the leather snapped, dropping the thin, cupping metal which supported her foot—and, at the moment, her entire weight.

She gripped the pommel with her knee, but it was too late. The mare went skittering sideways at this unexpected lurch from her rider, and Celia fell.

Instinct and years of training prevailed. Celia dropped her shoulder and rolled. She landed against a straggling shrub and lay still, momentarily stunned.

"Celia!" She heard Trevor's voice, but for a moment was incapable of answering. "That damned, bloody . . ." Strong arms gripped her shoulders for a moment, then began running with gentle expertise along her legs and arms.

"I—I am quite unharmed, I assure you!" Her voice came out ragged but determined.

"Are you sure?" he demanded. "You might have been killed! When I get my hands on whoever looked over that saddle . . ." He broke off his sentence but continued his thorough examination of her bones.

She coughed and felt her breath coming more easily. "There—there is no need to manhandle me!"

Trevor let out his breath and sat back, relaxing. "Now, that sounds more like you," he said hearteningly. "Can you stand?"

"Of course." She pulled herself into a sitting position, then waited for the trees and ground to stop spinning about her in the most reckless and unmannerly fashion. "The—the mare. Is she all right?"

Trevor grinned, and sparkling lights danced in his

eyes. He rose and slowly walked the few yards to where the gray now stood, grazing quietly. She made no objection to his catching up her reins. He held these while running a hand along her legs. Satisfied, he tied her to a low branch of a tree.

"No damage there, either. It seems you were both most fortunate."

Celia nodded, discovered this simple action did not send stabbing pains through her brow or cause the scenery to dance, and decide to try standing. Trevor was instantly at her side, one hand beneath her elbow and the other firmly about her slender waist. He held her in this manner for longer than was necessary. Then, half-lifting her, he steadied her on her feet by the simple expedient of holding her against him.

"Th—thank you." She started to pull back, but his hands did not slacken their grip on her. Instead, she felt herself being drawn inexorably closer. She looked up in confusion, trying to fathom the fiery glow that lit his eyes. Once again, it seemed difficult to breathe and a dizziness assailed her that had to be the aftermath of her fall.

Somehow, his face was all that she could see. He loomed closer to her, his eyes holding hers captive, preventing her from escaping—or even wanting to. Slowly—so slowly he seemed hardly to move—his mouth sought hers, exploring with a gentle, persuasive pressure that left her helplessly clinging to him.

He raised his head at last, and she took a deep, quavering breath. A tremor shook her slender frame, and this time she had no doubts as to the cause. She opened eyes she hadn't realized she had closed, and gazed up into a smoldering expression so intense that she drew back, startled and a bit frightened.

His smile deepened . "Do you know, I just may enjoy being married to you after all," he told her.

It took a moment for the implication to settle into her befuddled mind. His meaning dawned on her at last, with a resounding crash that drove away the last, lingering sensations he had created. Furious, she pushed against him, staggering backward when he released her without protest.

"I will never marry you!" she cried. "I—I will never marry anyone but Jonathon!"

A sudden gleam of sheer enjoyment lit Trevor's eyes, and he gave her a deep, mocking bow. Celia's rage mounted. The nerve of the man, to so enjoy their contretemps! And worst of all, so did she!

She turned on her heel and made her way back to the gray mare, who stood impatiently throwing her head. She untied the reins and reached for the stirrup that she had forgotten was missing. In dismay, she began to search in the grass for it.

"Here." Chuckling softly to himself, Trevor picked up the bit of metal. "I'm afraid it will not do you much good, though. The leather was torn at the bottom. Do you think you can stay in the saddle without it?"

She turned her scathing gaze on him. "Of course I can. It was the—the suddenness with which it was no longer there that proved my downfall!"

Her unintentionally appropriate wording set off his deep, rich laughter. Her righteous indignation melted as she realized what she had said, and she herself was hard put not to succumb to a fit of the giggles. Instead, she turned her back on him and started to search for a suitable means of mounting.

"Allow me." Before she could protest, Trevor picked her up lightly and lifted her into the saddle. She was forced to cling to him while she hooked her knee over the pommel. The lack of stirrup felt odd and rather insecure, but she would never admit it to him.

"Are you all right?" he asked.

"Of course I am. You have no need to fuss about me like an old hen," she informed him.

The result was not what she had hoped, for it merely sparked his sense of the ridiculous. She was forced to endure another bout of those hateful chuckles. Fuming at him—and at herself for reacting to him—she turned the mare and began to move off slowly.

"Forgive me, Miss Marcombe, but I fear we must go in the other direction." His tone was one of humble apology but his eyes sparkled with merriment.

Again, she was forced to bite her lip. He had the most reprehensible habit of making her want to laugh when she should be extremely angry. He had had the temerity to kiss her! He had used her shockingly and was totally unrepentant. She should have protested or even slapped him for behaving in so forward a fashion. Instead, to her shame, she had wanted him to repeat his offense.

They rode back to the house in complete silence, Trevor apparently thinking it best not to try to engage her in conversation and Celia not trusting what she might choose to say to him. The return journey took considerable time since they were forced to go through gates and around any potentially hazardous areas, but at last they turned up the long drive and traversed the formal gardens.

At the front door, Trevor leaped easily to the ground and held up peremptory hands to Celia. Her difficulty lay in disentangling her knee from the pommel, not in jumping down from the saddle, but she was hardly going to point this out to Trevor. He would be quite capable of trying to help her with this delicate operation, and of uttering the most unseemly comments while doing it.

At last, though, she was safe on the gravel drive. To her surprise, Trevor swung back up on his horse.

"I'm taking them to the stable myself," he informed her briefly. "I intend to speak to a few people about this." He indicated her stirrup. Without waiting for a response, he rode through the archway that led to a stableyard.

She started up the walk to the house, then stopped abruptly. His kiss must have been his punishment for her introducing Jonathon to him. She had retaliated by announcing her intention to marry the other man. Trevor had not yet responded to her latest challenge. That meant he must be planning something especially suitable. That realization sent a thrill of excited anticipation through her—but it also worried her, and not just a little.

CHAPTER TWELVE

By the time Trevor rode out with Sir Roderick the following morning, he still had made no move of retaliation against Celia's last challenge. That fact made her rather uneasy, for she lived in the constant expectation of walking into a trap of his setting at any moment.

With his absence, though, the morning loomed ahead, safe and boring. She retired with her companion to the Blue Drawing Room, she to practice a composition by Mozart, Elizabeth to embroider. It was not long before the music, which was difficult and extremely beautiful, absorbed her totally.

She did not hear when the door opened and Gosson crossed the threshold. The butler coughed, but even this failed to get her attention. Finally, he was forced to result to less subtle means.

"Captain Edelston has called, miss," he announced in sonorous accents.

Celia stopped abruptly. "Has he? Please, show him in here."

Gosson bowed, stepped back, and in a moment Jonathon entered the room. Celia rose and hurried over to greet him, taking his hands in hers.

"How delightful of you to come! Did you guess that we should be lonely this morning?"

"What? Alone, are you? Good. Need to have a word with you." He hesitated, casting an uneasy glance at Elizabeth, who had set down her needlework and watched them with heightened color and troubled eyes. "About those men," he added in an undervoice.

Celia's eyes widened and fingers of fear clutched at her. "Have they . . .?" she broke off, distressed. "You are very right," she whispered. "We must be careful, even before my dear Elizabeth. Would you care to walk in the shrubbery?" she asked in a more normal voice. "I believe one is beginning to emerge from the weeds."

Elizabeth, when told of their plan, acquiesced with a semblance of pleasure. It was a beautiful day, she declared, much too nice to remain indoors. Collecting her embroidery, she followed them out through the French windows that led to the side of the house.

From there, it was only a short walk to a section of garden with both its paths and perimeter surrounded by high hedges. They worked their way to the center of this, where a stone bench had been set facing a Grecian-style statue in a fountain that no longer worked. It obviously had been a very pretty retreat at one time, and the attentions lavished upon it by the undergroom seemed to promise hope for the future.

Elizabeth settled herself on the bench and determinedly resumed her stitching. Celia slipped her arm through Jonathon's and led him down one of the paths. The morning sun provided a gentle warmth, but they were protected from its direct rays by a stand of yew trees just beyond the shrubbery.

"What has happened?" Celia demanded as soon as they were out of her companion's hearing.

Jonathon's blue eyes seemed to haze over as he considered. "Only one of the chaps is around now. Keep running into him everywhere I go. Then I discovered the other one is haunting the Marine Parade. I'll tell you what, Cill. There's something a trifle too smoky by half about those two. And what's more, keep thinking I've seen one of them before!"

"At the Naval Office?" Celia asked, more than half-sure of his answer.

He thought for a moment, then nodded slowly. "When I came out after asking about Charlie. There was someone hanging about in the street. Might have been the shorter of these two. Might not, too, of course."

Celia tightened her hold on his arm and, in her agitation, started walking more quickly. "Oh, Jonny, what have I started? How can we get to Charlie before they do? If only there were someone we could trust, who had connections!" She stopped suddenly. "Will you go back to Headquarters?" she asked. "Just hang around, trying to hear anything?"

He regarded her with fond exasperation. "Just what do you think I could pick up, Cill? If they're already suspicious of me they're not likely to let anything slip when I'm around, you know. Besides," he added as a clincher, "if they're following me, it's in hopes that I'll be the one to lead them to Charlie, not the other way around."

Celia started walking again. "We can't just do nothing!" she said at last.

"I suppose I could follow them for a change," Jonathon suggested with an attempt at a joke. To his dismay, Celia spun around to face him, delighted.

"But that's a wonderful idea! Perhaps you could hear them giving a report to a superior, and one of them might reveal something! Oh, please, Jonny, will you?"

He looked acutely uncomfortable, but gave his assent. Celia promptly threw herself into his arms to give him a quick hug, and he was obliged to set her carefully aside before she wrinkled the impeccable press of his olive green cutaway coat. Celia, all contrition, fell into step beside him and they continued their round of the shrubbery.

"This gives us a start, at least," she sighed. It was not much, she admitted to herself, but it was better than just waiting. And there was always a chance Jonathon really would overhear something that would be useful. If only Charlie would write!

"Jonny, you must send to your home at once and request all mail to be sent to you here," she announced, acting on the thought. "Do you realize, Charlie might have written while you've been gone?" This agreed to, Celia began to feel immeasurably better.

They turned a corner and once again came in sight of the central fountain. Elizabeth sat where they had left her, setting her precise, delicate stitches, the picture of serenity in her peaceful surroundings.

Jonathon paused, staring at her with an arrested expression in the depths of his blue eyes. "Cill," he asked suddenly, "has Miss Westerly been with you long?"

"Elizabeth? For about six months." Her mind temporarily relieved of worry over Charlie, Celia turned her attention to her beloved companion and found herself more than willing to talk about her. "She has been the greatest solace to me, Jonny, and so restful! You can have no idea. I wrote to you when my great aunt died, did I not? Poor Grandfather was quite at a loss to know what to do about me, so he wrote to all of his relations, and one of them remembered Elizabeth. She's a distant cousin, and the poor thing was apparently living in the most dreadful lodgings. She is actually a governess, but was luckily between posts."

"Why does she always dress in black?" he asked. The tone of his voice was just a bit too nonchalant, and Celia, suddenly suspicious, discovered a new and very worthy outlet for her restless energies.

"She tries to make herself look older, the poor dear," she told him warmly, setting her first tentative footsteps upon the unfamiliar path of matchmaking. "I am quite convinced that if she would only wear colors, and crop her hair in a becoming fashion, the difference in her would be startling. But she has always had to make her appearance acceptable to her employers."

"Your grandfather doesn't insist on her decking herself out like a crow, does he?" Jonathon demanded, and to Celia's secret and growing delight, she detected a note of annoyance.

"No, of course not! It is Elizabeth who insists. You see, she is far too young to be a suitable chaperone. She is only nine-and-twenty, and lives in constant dread of our being censured or of causing me harm because she is not old enough. She is the greatest dear, and so thoughtful! So, she tries to look at least forty, which she insists is a more appropriate age for a chaperone."

"What will she do when you marry?"

"That is not likely to be in the near future!" Celia informed him tartly. "Perhaps I shall eventually become an old maid, and then she may continue to live with me to bear me countenance."

"Doesn't seem much of a life," he remarked.

"She is possessed of the gentlest and sweetest disposition," Celia informed him, trying to hide her smile. "I fear I am too often a trial to her, but she is quite wonderfully understanding and sympathetic. She enjoys drawing, too. I am sure she would be thrilled to see your sketchbook some day."

During this last speech, Celia had been leading Jonathon toward the bench. Hearing their approach, Elizabeth glanced up and her soft, glowing eyes rested on Jonathon's handsome countenance. A gentle flush stole into her cheeks and she looked hurriedly back to her embroidery. It was several moments, however, before her needle found its way back into the cloth.

Jonathon remained with them a short while longer, then rose to take his leave. Celia escorted him to the stable where his horse had been taken, and watched him ride off. She stayed where she was, waiting. A few minutes later, as she had expected, a horseman passed the drive, heading in the same direction as Jonathon. Perturbed, Celia walked slowly back to the house.

There was little she could do about Charlie at the moment, so instead she turned her attention to the more pleasant prospect of romance. Considering the matter, she could not think of a couple more ideally suited to each other than Jonathon and Elizabeth. Why it had not occurred to her earlier was a mystery, except that she had been somewhat preoccupied with her own problems of late. But now, she vowed, she would do everything in her power to encourage this match.

And that presented further problems. She had to maintain her current pretense of wanting to marry Jonathon—at least until she could learn something of Charlie and tell Ryde the true disposition of Ranleigh. Until then, she had to be careful. If her grandfather guessed Jonathon was just a ruse to prevent the marriage, she would not put it beyond him to insist upon giving her at once to Ryde. And then she would have to tell the truth about Charlie, which she wanted never to do! So Elizabeth must go on believing that Jonathon and Celia loved each other.

With difficulty, she restrained the urge to confess the whole to her companion. The sight of that gentle pain in Elizabeth's sad eyes assailed her conscience. It would not be for much longer, she told herself. Soon, very soon, Jonathon must be free to pay court to Elizabeth—if he wished.

Jonathon showed concern for Elizabeth, but in him that might indicate nothing more than innate kindness. He was not exactly in the petticoat line—if she had that expression right. He had never, as far as she knew, shown her brother's proclivities for dangling after females. That Elizabeth's heart had been touched and might well be on the way to being irretrievably lost, Celia could not doubt. Jonathon, she realized, was another matter. Elizabeth might still be doomed to unrequited love—and it would be all the more grievous when she learned there was no rival who held prior claim to his affections.

Too many problems occupied her mind. Restless, she set off for a walk that took her out of what should have been the pleasure gardens and across a weed-choked field to the tree-lined bank of the stream. There, she sat on a boulder to rest and idly tossed small pebbles into the shallow, flowing waters for a very long time.

The lane should be just over the slight rise beyond the line of trees, she remembered. She rose and headed through the thicket in that direction, then paused as the sound of hoofbeats reached her. She pulled back behind an oak to hide from the approaching horsemen, for suddenly she found herself nervous at being so far from the estate without an escort.

In another moment Lord Ryde and Sir Roderick came into view. She waited until they had passed, glad for the quick action that undoubtedly saved her a lecture on impropriety from her grandfather. When the two men were safely ahead of her, she emerged from the trees and started walking along the verge in the direction they had gone. A minute later she ducked back under cover, for another horseman approached.

This one came more slowly, his hat pulled low over his face. Celia, peeking out from behind a bush, caught her breath. There was a chance she was mistaken, but she would swear it was the taller of the two men who had been following Jonathon—the one who had walked up the Marine Parade to stare into the house of Ryde's mistress. And now, he followed

Ryde. . . .

A moment later, Celia almost laughed. Another horseman cantered up the road past her—Jonathon, in dutiful pursuit of his quarry. She started to come out, then froze. Behind Jonathon, still tailing him, was the smaller man.

She shivered, and made her way back through the trees, not wanting to be on the road when the men started the return journey to Brighton. Had the situation been potentially less hazardous, it would have been comic—so many men following each other! But she felt no desire to laugh.

Why would one of them be watching Lord Ryde? She stopped suddenly as a more likely explanation dawned on her. Not Ryde, but her grandfather! Charlie's grandfather!

But what could those men hope to learn? Surely, if Charlie's family knew his whereabouts, Jonathon never would have gone to the Naval Office! So why were they being followed? And why the interest in the house on the Marine Parade?

It took Celia the better part of an hour to reach the straggling gardens surrounding the house, and by then she was more confused than ever. As she started down the path between the stable and the house she stopped abruptly, drawing back and pressing herself into the newly pruned shrubbery. Just ahead of her, entering the cobbled yard, were Ryde and the tall man—though he now appeared short and somewhat insignificant alongside Ryde's impressive stature.

Celia moved silently along the line of bushes, trying to get nearer, trying to hear what they might say. *Why* were they together? Had Ryde caught someone following him? But their manner seemed friendly. . . . She stiffened as an explanation occurred to her. Had Ryde—*could* Ryde—have done something so despicable as to hire men to follow Jonathon? Was it Ryde and not the Naval Office who had sent these men out? Was it he to whom they reported?

Relief, followed almost instantly by blind rage, flooded through her. He must be checking on her long-standing connection with Jonathon, trying to determine if there was any truth to her supposed love for him. There was no danger to Charlie; she had been worrying for nothing! Ryde would be made to pay for the hours of anxiety she had suffered!

The interview between the two men ended. The man swung onto a horse that Coxly brought around, gave a rather strange salute to Lord Ryde, then turned his mount through the archway and started down the drive. Ryde walked off toward the house, and Celia drew back, not wanting him to see her.

As soon as she could, she slipped out of the bushes and headed toward the drive, feeling like a spy herself. There, by the gate, a large black horse moved forward out of the late afternoon shadows, then started down the New Road to Brighton. Jonathon. She waited until the short man, who was still in pursuit, fell into the carefully spaced parade. What a report those two watchers would give each other when next they got together!

She went slowly into the house, then up the stairs to her room. Her greatest worry for Charlie now dismissed, she turned her thoughts to a suitable revenge on Ryde. It would be good, whatever it was, she swore. She was not going to let him get away with having Jonathon followed as if he were a common criminal!

To her dismay, the hour was more advanced than she had thought. Seddons awaited her, anxious to see her charge safely dressed for a dinner that was barely half an hour away. It was with surprise that Celia realized she was hungry, for she had been out walking and missed luncheon.

She had few thoughts for anything except righteous indignation at Ryde. Fortunately, Elizabeth came to her room as soon as she herself was ready and introduced a topic that could not help but provide a momentary diversion. The proposed concert in Brighton was scheduled for the following evening, and Ryde, as a member of the Music Society, would be sure to take them.

Celia had no idea of the program to be presented, but she looked forward with pleasure to any outing, especially a musical one. So excited was she, in fact, that it was not until after dinner, when she and Elizabeth had retired to the Drawing Room, that it occurred to her she might be able to turn the concert to her advantage.

Considerable time passed before the gentlemen joined them. Celia, who sat at the pianoforte practicing her new piece, stopped abruptly as they entered. One glance at their faces was enough to make her hesitant about requesting that Jonathon be invited to join the party. Something appeared to have put both men out considerably.

"Is anything wrong?" she asked immediately.

Ryde glanced across at her, his brow heavy. "Only that I must go to London tomorrow."

"Tomorrow?" she exclaimed. "Then you will miss the concert! Can it not be postponed?" She could hardly hope to annoy him with Jonathon's presence if he himself were not there.

"I fear not." He directed a piercing, suspicious gaze at her, but seemed satisfied. "I must be a terrible host, and desert you until the following day."

Was this the retaliation she had been waiting for since yesterday? Somehow, she suspected that Jonathon's two shadows did not count. No, this must be his next move, not to accompany her to the concert. It didn't seem adequate, though—certainly beneath his abilities. She found she was disappointed in him—unless there was more to come. Would she enter the concert hall, escorted by her grandfather, to find him there in the company of the woman he swore was not his mistress? Surely he would not dare! Not even he would bring a female of that order to such a gathering—though it was a public event. In the eyes of society it would not be an unforgivable act as it would be if the concert were private. He very well might do it! She had always felt him to be capable of the most unscrupulous behavior, and she was quite sure he was as aware as she of the state of war that existed between them.

"Does—does this mean that Elizabeth and I will not be able to attend?" she asked with feigned anxiety.

"No, your grandfather will escort you," Ryde assured her, thus confirming her suspicions. He wanted her to be there, so there must be a reason—and she greatly feared that blonde was it! Since she was alerted, she would be able to formulate a counterattack to utterly confound him.

"There really is no reason for you to go bolting off like this," Sir Roderick said in a tone that indicated this was not the first time he had expressed that opinion.

"I want to settle things with my bank manager," Ryde said curtly. He crossed to a table with several decanters and poured himself a small glass of brandy. "I don't like pushing an overdraft the way I have been."

"There is no need," Sir Roderick reminded him.

Ryde turned to face him. "We've been over this. I am going to bring the estate around on my own."

Celia looked from one to the other, frowning. What was Lord Ryde up to? He was getting a great deal of money from her grandfather—for marrying her. His journey was completely unnecessary, unless he needed an excuse to absent himself on the morrow. That must be it. Would he really have the nerve to carry out such a plan, just to infuriate her?

Preoccupied with the pressing task of finding a suitable retaliation, her fingers switched to a relatively easy piece by Bach with which she was very familiar. She continued to play until the teacart was wheeled in, then excused herself to retire as soon as she had taken a few sips from her cup.

Jonathon was, of course, the key to her plan. She suspected that Ryde did not really believe her assertion of love for Captain Edelston, but he could not be sure. Jonathon's continued presence must serve as a mildly irritating thorn in his flesh. And she would drive it in more deeply at the concert.

She went down for breakfast the next morning at a very early hour, and had the satisfaction of seeing

Ryde just leaving the house. Would he go to Brighton at once, she wondered, or did he have other things to do? In spite of its being that flamboyant female who was involved, Celia rather looked forward to seeing what Ryde had concocted for her. She was secure in the knowledge that it would be he who received the leveler, to borrow a phrase from Charlie's boxing cant.

She settled down to a hearty breakfast. Her only problem would be to contact Jonathon and inform him he was to attend the concert in her company, but even that did not worry her unduly. Even if she could not reach him, he undoubtedly would be present at the event. It would be no difficult thing for him to join her.

The door to the breakfast parlor opened, and Celia suffered a severe setback. Sir Roderick entered, supported by his valet and leaning heavily on an ebony cane. His left foot was bootless, swathed instead with thick bandages.

"Oh, no, Grandfather!" she exclaimed. "Is—is it very bad?"

"What, afraid you won't get to go to your concert?" he snapped at her. "Careful, man. No, the cushioned chair, damn you!"

His valet, long inured to his master's occasional and extremely painful attacks of gout, did not even blink at being thus addressed. He made the old man as comfortable as possible in a padded chair, then left the room to return a minute later with a cushion. This, he placed on a second chair. As Sir Roderick swore softly and steadily under his breath, the valet gingerly raised the afflicted leg and placed it gently on the pillow.

"You know your doctor has told you to drink no more than one glass of wine in an evening," Celia told him.

He merely glowered at her. "Don't you go lecturing to me, my girl. I'll do as I like, which is what I've always done."

"And so you always shall, I am sure," she replied fondly. She rose and moved across the room to drop a light kiss on his forehead, then smiled as he glared up at her. "I shall tell Gosson not to bring you any wine today."

"Don't you go meddling, girl!" Sir Roderick snapped. "And I won't be taking you to that concert!" A defensive, almost apologetic note crept into his voice.

"Of course you shall not! You shall retire to your room directly after dinner and enjoy a good book and throw things at your poor valet. Do not worry yourself. Elizabeth and I shall contrive very well."

She left him to breakfast in a solitary and grouchy state. Her first object was to warn Elizabeth of Sir Roderick's infirmity and temper. As she crossed the hall toward the stairs, Mrs. Gosson came bustling out from the back reaches of the house. Celia saw her, and paused.

"Mrs. Gosson?" she called. "My grandfather has suffered a flare-up of his gout. Could you arrange a breakfast tray for Miss Westerly? She has not come down yet."

"Certainly, miss. And we won't disturb Sir Roderick, you may be sure."

Relieved on that head, Celia started up the stairs

only to encounter Elizabeth, about to descend. She quickly informed her companion of the state of affairs, and Elizabeth gladly retired to her room to await the promised tray. Always a gentle creature, she cringed from Sir Roderick's temper at the best of times. She avoided him completely when his gout came on.

Celia went on to her own chamber, considering what to do now. Poor Ryde! She could almost pity him, to have gone to so much trouble for her discomfiture only to have her not show up. Was that what her grandfather was up to? she wondered suddenly. Was he keeping her away from the concert on purpose? Had he, too, been suspicious of Ryde's supposed reason for going to London? But his gout, she was sure, was real.

On impulse, Celia rang for Seddons, then began to unfasten her morning dress. What she needed was a good, long ride to clear her thinking. Firmly, she squashed the regret that Ryde would not be going with her for a race.

Less than twenty minutes later she sat in Elizabeth's room while her companion also changed. Today, Celia did not want to stay on the estate, but to explore the countryside. For that, she would need either a groom or her companion, possibly both.

At the stable they were in luck. Ryde's head groom had accompanied him on whatever journey he had taken, and Sir Roderick's Jem was nowhere to be seen. That left Ryde's undergroom, Ketter, who saddled the horses for them. Celia was easily able to dissuade him from joining them, for they would not go far, she declared, and he had other, very pressing duties to attend to.

They rode in silence for a long time while Celia continued to consider Ryde's plot. It really was too bad if it would be brought to naught, whether by design or accident. He was going to so much trouble just to make her angry. If only she could attend the concert, with Jonathon instead of Sir Roderick . . .

No sooner had the idea occurred to her than she determined to bring it about it. This was far better than she could have hoped! And the best of it would be that Ryde would not know why Sir Roderick was not present. All he would see would be Celia and Elizabeth, escorted by Jonathon. And there he would be—at an event he'd declared he could not attend, with a companion who was not supposed to be with him. He would be in no position to lecture her, though she strongly suspected he would manage to, anyway.

She urged her mount into a gentle canter along the verge of the road that led to Brighton, and then, at Elizabeth's suggestion, they turned down a lane they had not previously explored. It should not be difficult to leave the house that evening without her grandfather being aware of it. If he truly suffered from the gout and was not merely trying to protect her from Ryde's plot, he would retire to his room and remain there, refusing anyone admittance. Her only problem would be to obtain a coach to take them to the concert.

A lone horseman rode toward them, and she and Elizabeth reined in slightly. As he drew closer, Celia heard her companion's soft exclamation. She looked up, and to her surprise she recognized Jonathon's tall figure astride the docile black.

He saw them and waved, then drew his horse to a halt as he pulled abreast of them. "Good morning!" he called.

"Jonny, this is the most wonderful luck! I was wondering how to get in touch with you!" With Elizabeth present she could not tell him that she suspected the men who had been following him were in Ryde's employ—but the fact that Jonathon was not himself in pursuit today must mean that he had guessed the same thing. Since Charlie appeared not to stand in any danger from these men, that matter could wait until later.

"Oh, I usually come out here, most every morning," he told her promptly. There was a pointed tone to his voice which she recognized as a hint that he wished to speak to her. "Always exercise my horse out here," he finished.

She met his eyes in a quick look of understanding. He was relaxed, so it was nothing urgent.

"Well, I am glad you did so today. Jonny, there is to be a concert in Brighton tonight. I want you to take us."

"But Celia!" Elizabeth exclaimed. "Is not . . ." She broke off, remembering Sir Roderick's gout.

Jonathon frowned. "Ain't Ryde taking you? Or your grandfather?"

She explained the reasons for the unavailability of the two men. "So you see, we must miss it if you do not come to our aid! Please, Jonny, say you will?"

"Delighted, of course," he replied promptly, for civility demanded no less. "But are you sure that . . . ?"

"Oh, it will be all right! Grandfather is quite vexed

he cannot take us himself. He will be so relieved to learn we shall not have to miss it, after all! Will you be able to hire a carriage and come out to pick us up?"

He assured her on this head, then took his leave of them to make the arrangements, adding pointedly that he would see her that evening. Celia watched as he turned onto the New Road, then glanced around quickly. There was no sign of any other riders, no one who might be following him this morning. For some reason, Ryde must have called off his watchers.

Secure in that knowledge, she set about making plans for Ryde's total discomfiture that evening.

CHAPTER THIRTEEN

Celia, with Elizabeth riding just behind her, started for home. It was a relief to know that she could find Jonathon along this route almost any morning if she should need him. And he would escort them to the concert that evening, so now it would be Ryde who would receive a set-down, not she!

"I think it would be best not to discuss our plans before Grandfather," she said musingly.

"But Celia! Surely he must be told if we intend to go out for the evening!"

"He will be in his room. I doubt he will even know we are not there. We won't lie to him, of course. But the subject doesn't *have* to come up, does it?"

Elizabeth did not look convinced but she made no further protests, and Celia suspected she would do little to endanger even an illicit evening spent in Jonathon's company. This situation suited Celia quite well.

No comment was made about their morning ride. They returned to the house to find all relatively quiet, except for Sir Roderick's growling at one and all. He was induced to retire to his chamber shortly after partaking of a light nunchcon, and showed no inclination to quit his room. Peace reigned once again.

The afternoon passed too quietly for Celia and she found herself heartily bored. For a while, she allowed her mind to dwell on the anticipated offerings of the evening, but as these included the dubious honor of seeing Ryde with that woman, she soon abandoned this pursuit. Instead, she picked up her copy of *Marmion,* and spent several hours living in a very different world with the cat Andrew sleeping contentedly in her lap.

When the hour came to dress for dinner, she selected her gown with care so that she would not have to change again before going to the concert. She had best inform Gosson of their intention of going out, as soon as she went downstairs. She wanted all to appear perfectly normal before the servants so that they would not seek counsel of Sir Roderick.

As she passed her grandfather's door on her way down to the dining room, she stopped to look in on him. She knocked softly so as not to disturb him if he slept, then pushed the door slightly ajar to peep in. She ducked back instantly as a pillow connected with the jamb.

"Celia?" he demanded. "Come in here."

"Are you planning on throwing anything else at me?" she asked as she came cautiously into the room.

"Thought you were Dassett," he informed her. He sat in a large wing-back chair near the window with his foot resting on a cushioned stool. A small table nearby held a tray laden with covered dishes.

"And what has your poor valet done to annoy you this time?" she asked, smiling. It amazed her that the valet remained with anyone so difficult as her grandfather, but he had served him for many long years. Presumably, Dassett had become inured to his master's ways.

"The damned fellow refused to bring me any wine with my dinner! And he wanted to bring we gruel! *Gruel!*" he repeated, his voice dripping with scorn. "Nearly sacked him on the spot!"

"And why didn't you?" she asked promptly, her eyes sparkling with suppressed amusement.

"He threatened to quit!" He looked down at the tray, raised one of the covers, peered in, then slammed down the silver lid. "Faugh!" he exclaimed.

Celia stooped to drop a kiss on his forehead. "Do you want me to visit you later?" she asked, holding her breath.

"No, I'll take something to make me sleep and forget this pap!" He gestured in disgust at the tray, from which delicate but appetizing aromas wafted. "Go on, off with you, and hope they offer you something better for your dinner!"

That settled her last worry. No summons would come for her when she was not there to receive it. Afterward, there would be no need for stories or explanations—unless Ryde felt up to making any!

She was glad they kept country hours. She and Elizabeth sat down to dine just after six. As they were alone, she had requested that the meal be a very simple one, and they finished it with time to spare. They withdrew to the Drawing Room to await Jonathon's arrival.

He did not keep them waiting long. Celia barely had time to run through the new Mozart piece before

Gosson opened the door, bowed slightly, and informed them that Captain Edelston had arrived. The ladies gathered up their pelisses and reticules and hurried out to join him.

Jonathan had obtained a commodious closed carriage, complete with a coachman. He handed the ladies into the rear seat and seated himself facing them. Elizabeth looked a trifle disconcerted at this arrangement, for it was customary for a hired companion to ride with her back to the horses, but Jonathon would not hear of this. If it seemed odd to anyone that Jonathon should not wish to sit beside his supposed love, no one mentioned this circumstance.

He asked a polite question about the remainder of their morning ride, and it was left to Elizabeth to answer. Celia stared out the carriage window into the darkening sky, suddenly finding herself nervous. She could back out of this at any time, she knew. She could be revenged on Ryde quite easily by simply not going to the concert. But she wanted the satisfaction of turning the tables on him. She would go through with this.

They arrived outside the concert hall early enough to stroll about, watching the fashionable crowd assembling. Nowhere, she decided, did she see either of the two men who had followed Jonathon so assiduously. Ryde must have called them off. At last, her party joined those who were entering the building.

Jonathon held her back as Elizabeth preceded them through the doorway. "About those men . . ." he muttered.

Celia hushed him. "I know. I saw you all." She whispered her suspicions to him.

He shook his head as if not wanting to believe what

he heard. "Wouldn't have thought him capable of such curst, underhanded behavior. Doesn't seem like the sort of thing he'd do."

Celia glared at him. He persisted in liking Ryde! "You don't know him!" she replied firmly. "He—he can be quite odious!" She glanced ahead, saw Elizabeth watching them, and dragged Jonathon forward. They went to find seats.

To her surprise, she did not see Ryde anywhere, and she found this fact disconcerting. She craned her neck, looking about for him as Jonathon and Elizabeth seated themselves. Disturbed by his apparent absence, she started to take her place between her companions when she heard her name being called.

"Celia, my love!" Mrs. Andover hurried toward her. "So glad you could attend. It will be a delightful evening for us all. And the most wonderful thing has happened—but you, I suppose, will be one of the few Lord Ryde has permitted to know about it."

Celia looked up into the beaming face of her mother's old friend, then stood to take her hand. She introduced Jonathon, who also stood, then turned back to Mrs. Andover. "Lord Ryde has told us nothing. What wonderful thing has happened?"

"Oh!" Mrs. Andover looked somewhat disconcerted. "Perhaps I should not have said . . . but it is of no matter, for you will not repeat this to anyone." She beamed at Celia and held a conspiratorial finger to her lips. "It is Thérèse de Bourgerre," she breathed reverently. "Here, in Brighton! And all due, I am sure, to Lord Ryde—through how he contrived to bring her safely out of France I cannot imagine!"

"Thérèse de Bourgerre," Celia repeated slowly. "The

soprano? Here? I have heard her before, you must know, when she sang in London five years ago! But why did Ryde never breathe a word to me about her? Is she to sing tonight?"

"Oh, no! It is quite secret! My sister and I only learned because we were used to know her. Such a dreadful state of affairs. Napoleon, you know. She is living quite retired, but she is honoring us with her presence this evening, though I am sure she should not—even if there is some man here to protect her. She is with my sister, now." Mrs. Andover looked up as her name was called, then gave a cry of vexation. "I must rush, but do come and meet her at the interval. We are trying to hide her in the crowd." With a hurried, distracted smile, she rushed off.

A few moments later the lights dimmed, signaling the beginning of the concert. Jonathon and Celia resumed their seats, though Celia found it difficult to prepare her mind for the upcoming music. Too many questions bothered her. For one, where was Lord Ryde? Had his mistress proved too much of a distraction to him, making them late? And why had he never mentioned Thérèse de Bourgerre and his role in bringing her to England?

The members of a small chamber orchestra took their positions on the dais, then struck up their tuning notes. Most of the candles that lit the large room were extinguished and the concert began. After only a few bars of a suite by Vivaldi, Celia felt herself being drawn into the music, losing herself in the wondrous sounds.

The suite ended, and a momentary lull, followed by applause, filled the room. This died down, to be replaced by the familiar strains of Bach. Several more pieces followed, filling out the first portion of the program. Celia sat enraptured throughout, oblivious to all but the joyous notes that filled her being.

As the last strains faded away, Celia sat with her eyes closed, unaware of the lights that came on around the room, reluctant to return to present reality.

"Cill?" Jonathon's voice sounded near her ear, soft and apologetic for intruding into the private world the music had created for her.

Slowly, reluctantly, she opened her eyes to look at him. He held out a glass of punch to her and she took it, rather surprised. She must have sat withdrawn longer than she realized, unaware of his departure to obtain refreshments.

His eyes strayed past her, widened, and he stood. Celia followed the direction of his gaze and stiffened. There was no mistaking the voluptuous blonde in the diaphanous gown who walked in their direction. She had expected to see her, had counted on it, in fact. But she should have been on Lord Ryde's arm, not Miss Draycott's! And not with the shorter of Jonathon's watchers following close behind. The situation was incongruous, made no sense. She half rose, feeling confused and out of her depth. Why was Ryde not with his mistress? And what did the proper and respectable Miss Draycott have to do with a female of that sort?

These thoughts flooded Celia's mind, and it took a long minute before it dawned on her that the two women were making their way toward her. She stood slowly, her eyes drifting from the lovely, curling gold locks down to the shockingly low *décolletage* that was filled in a way that made Celia rather envious.

"Celia, my dear," Miss Draycott greeted her. "I want you to meet Mlle. de Bourgerre."

So this was the famous French singer! Celia took the dainty little hand that reached out and clasped hers. She might have known. She really might have known. And it would be just like the hateful, odious Ryde if his relationship with this—this bird of paradise, to borrow a word from Jonathon's vocabulary—was purely platonic as he had assured her! That would add the final seal on her growing sense of chagrin.

Her cheeks burned. How Trevor must have laughed at her accusations of his keeping a mistress! And how he must be enjoying the thought of her discomfiture. It was more complete than even he had planned, thanks solely to herself, unless he had anticipated her requesting Jonathon's company. There was nothing to do at the moment, though, except to behave with complete propriety.

"The pleasure is mine, I assure you," she managed.

The smile slowly faded from the lovely face before her, to be replaced by a faintly puzzled expression. "I am so pleased to meet you, Miss Marcombe," the lady said in a lovely, heavily accented voice. "But have we met before?"

"It is possible you have seen me," Celia replied before she could stop herself. "I am a guest at the home of Lord Ryde."

Something flashed in the lady's lovely green eyes, and it was a moment before Celia realized it was amusement. It vanished to be replaced by that same curious, uncertain gaze. "No, that is not it; I am quite sure—although Lord Ryde has spoken of you to me, and of your love of music. I think perhaps you remind me of someone. Forgive me, it was most rude to stare at you so."

Celia managed a polite smile that froze on her lips as a possible explanation presented itself. "Are you—were you," she corrected quickly, "acquainted with a Charles Marcombe in France?" She held her breath. If Mlle. de Bourgerre had just come from there, it was possible, just possible, that she might have seen Charlie!

The lovely brow crinkled as the lady searched her memory. "No," she said slowly. "It is not familiar, that name." She shook her head apologetically.

It had not really been worth a try, but the disappointment Celia felt was out of all proportion. "I was able to hear you sing on your last visit to England." She smiled brightly, trying to banish her depressing thoughts. "I hope I will have that honor again."

Mlle. De Bourgerre dimpled prettily. "It is most kind of you to say so," she said. "Perhaps soon I will be permitted to sing again. But these men, they say I am in danger and should not even have come tonight." She clasped Celia's hand impulsively. "When I do sing, you will come? It is most comforting to see a friend in the audience."

Celia was not proof against her charm. Nor, she discovered, was Jonathon. His greeting to the singer was warm in the extreme, as was his declared wish that she might shortly be permitted to perform once again, and that he, too, might be privileged to attend.

Elizabeth, also, was welcomed into the ranks of her

friends by the lady, who was then led on by Miss Draycott. Celia sank back into her chair. She started to cover her still flaming cheeks, then discovered the glass of punch clasped in her hand and took a revivifying sip.

This skirmish, she was forced to admit, went to Lord Ryde with all honors. She had made a complete fool of herself over this affair of Mlle. de Bourgerre! Now she felt doubly compelled to come up with a suitable retaliation—preferably one that would take the wind out of Ryde's sails as effectively as it had been done to her this night! Her mind, ever fertile, immediately went to work on this task.

The remainder of the evening was ruined for her. The interlude ended, the musicians returned to the stage, but Celia's heart no longer lay in the glorious sounds that soon filled the air. She sat back in her chair, her thoughts in a chaotic whirl, trying to sort through the tangled, disjointed jumble to find something, anything, that might truly tip Ryde the double—to again borrow one of Charlie's favorite cant phrases.

One disturbing fact stood out, practically screaming at her to take notice. Thérèse de Bourgerre was not Ryde's mistress! Now that she had met the volatile little lady, she could easily dismiss her affectionate behavior glimpsed through the window of the house on the Marine Parade. And her relief at this knowledge was overwhelming, far in extent of what it rightfully should have been!

What did she care if Ryde was keeping one or even a dozen mistresses? A great deal, she realized to her consternation. And it was not the financial drain of such an undertaking that bothered her any more.

Only one thing was important—that Ryde did not dally with another woman, that he did not take his pleasure elsewhere while seeking her in a business arrangement.

She could not concentrate, could not hit on a scheme that would prove Ryde's undoing. Nor, at the moment, did she really want to. All at once, she wanted to talk to him, learn more of his motives, of his current sentiments on any number of subjects—particularly those concerning marriage. And most of all, she wanted him to pay her court—not at her grandfather's instigation, not for the sake of Ranleigh—but just for her own sake, and her own sake alone!

A hand touched hers and she jumped, startled, to look up into Jonathon's smiling face.

"Sorry, Cill, didn't mean to scare you. The concert is over."

"It was most enjoyable, was it not, Celia?" Elizabeth stood. Both she and Jonathon seemed reluctant to leave, but the large room was now less than half full.

Celia expressed her agreement, but realized she had not actually heard a single note of the second half of the performance. They waited until there was a break in the exiting crowd, then joined the throng heading toward the doors.

Ahead of them, at one side of the hall, there seemed to be some sort of altercation taking place. Celia recognized Miss Draycott and Mrs. Andover and, taking Jonathon's arm, led him over to see if they could help.

Thérèse de Bourgerre stood in the center of the small group, with the man Celia still thought of as

Jonathon's watcher, barring her way. Neither looked pleased.

"No, miss, go that way you won't," he declared.

The lady gave a very Gallic shrug. "As you wish then, Monsieur Harding. Which way, then?"

"Back here, miss." He took Mlle. de Bourgerre's arm and took a step forward, which brought him face to face with Jonathon. He looked squarely at the tall, blond giant, and only by a flicker deep in his eye did he betray any sign of recognition. "If you will excuse me, sir?" he said, then led the lady around them.

"Oh, Celia," Miss Draycott exclaimed. "It is so silly, but her escort fears so many people going out at once. Do come out this way with us, and you can escape them as well. Was not the music delightful?"

Celia and her party fell into step beside the elderly sisters, who babbled happily about the evening's program. Nothing, it seemed, could exceed their pleasure in the music. Celia responded as best she could while they followed the others through a side exit that took them into a dark hallway.

Harding gestured for them all to wait, then walked ahead a few steps, opened a door and peered out into the darkness of the night. He seemed satisfied, for a moment later he waved for them to come forward.

"Looks clear out there." He turned to Jonathon. "Your name, sir? I'll have someone fetch your coach."

A slight smile quirked Jonathon's lips as he returned the man's bland stare and gave his name. As if he did not know it very well indeed! Celia thought. And why should this man, who had followed Jonathon, now serve as protector to Mlle. de Bourgerre? Unless, of course, he was in Ryde's service.

They waited just inside the door until the sound of horses and carriages reached them. Harding once again put out his head and spoke softly to the man Celia recognized as his partner. "Thank you, Wiggins," she heard him say as he nodded to the man. He turned to Jonathon. "Come along, then, sir. Your coach is here." He held his own party back, waiting for the others to leave.

Jonathon ushered first Celia, and then Elizabeth, through the door. Their carriage stood about twenty yards away and Celia started for it. She pulled her cloak about her as a sudden gust of cool wind rustled her skirts.

Elizabeth, walking just behind her, paused in the glow of a street light to fasten her own cloak more securely. As she bared her head to adjust the hood, the soft glow from the lamp glinted off her blond hair. A loud explosion sounded across the street and the whining hiss of a bullet sounded near Celia's ear.

Elizabeth screamed.

CHAPTER FOURTEEN

Chaos broke loose about them. Jonathon ran forward, grabbed Elizabeth, and dragged her from the light into the shadows. Another shot was fired, this time from an angle somewhere above and to their left. Elizabeth, terrified, clung to Jonathon, who shielded her with his body. A third shot, this one from directly behind them, sent them toward the carriage in a mad dash.

The vehicle rocked wildly as the startled horses backed and lurched in fright. The coachman sprang down from his box and ran to his leaders' heads, trying to steady them. Jonathon caught hold of the door and pulled it open, and in a moment, he had thrust Elizabeth to comparative safety inside and reached back for Celia.

"Stay down!" he ordered. "Don't get out, either of you!"

"What's happening?" Elizabeth wailed, her face pale with fright.

"Mlle. de Bourgerre . . . ?" Celia exclaimed, realizing suddenly what was occurring.

"Captain Edelston!" The man called Wiggins was

beside them, appearing out of the darkness like a ghost. In one hand he held a gun. He drew another from inside his voluminous coat pocket and handed it to Jonathon. "They went up the back street."

"Who are they?" Jonathon asked blankly as he took the pistol. "Why did they shoot at Miss Westerly?"

"At me?" Elizabeth squeaked, her fingers clutching desperately at Celia's arm.

"Because of your hair." Celia slipped an arm about her companion, giving her a comforting squeeze. "They must have mistaken you for Mlle. de Bourgerre."

"If you please, sir, we could use an extra man," Wiggins said, and taking Jonathon firmly by the elbow he started off.

"My hair?" Elizabeth asked. She stared after the two men until they disappeared around the corner, then turned large, frightened eyes on Celia.

"You're in no danger, now," Celia responded promptly. "They will have realized their mistake." Her arm tightened about Elizabeth's shoulders and she hugged her trembling companion. "They saw your blond hair, and they were expecting Thérèse de Bourgerre."

"Na—Napoleon's agents?" Elizabeth's voice quavered. She started forward, her hand on the door. "Captain Edelston! Is—will he be . . . ?"

"Jonny will be all right. Mr. Harding will have had men here to protect her; Jonny will come back soon." Celia spoke softly, as if reassuring a child.

Elizabeth nodded, but her gaze remained on the spot where Captain Edelston had disappeared. *"The will to do, the soul to dare,"* she quoted from Scott an awe bordering on the worshipful filling her voice.

All seemed to be quiet now outside. The coach no longer rocked and silence engulfed them, except for an occasional stamping of an uneasy hoof. The vehicle lurched slightly forward and to one side as the coachman returned to his position on the box.

Elizabeth's shivering slowed, then finally stopped, and Celia was able to relax. Her arms were stiff, a sign of her own fear that she had not had time to acknowledge. She sank back against the squabs, weak with reaction.

"He's coming!" Elizabeth, who sat peering into the darkness, was the first to discern Jonathon's limping form as he walked down the center of the street toward them.

Celia sat upright, then pushed open the door of the carriage. "Jonny? Are you all right? What has happened?"

His only reply was his ragged breathing as he leaned against the side of the carriage to rest. "They—they got a—away," he finally gasped. "No, not hurt. Just—just out of condition."

"You shouldn't run on that leg," Celia told him tartly, with a true sisterly spirit. "Now, get in here and sit down. Have you hurt your knee?"

He disclaimed any injury but was glad enough of her help to climb into the carriage. Celia settled him on the back seat next to Elizabeth, placed his booted foot up on the forward cushion next to where she sat, then leaned out and called to the driver to start. She pulled the door closed, then sat so that she faced the other two.

"We gathered they were Napoleon's agents, after Mlle. de Bourgerre," she said, giving Jonathon more time to catch his breath.

He nodded. "There were three of them that I saw, but they split off in different directions. Wiggins and Harding had two men besides me, but even the five of us couldn't find them. And there was someone else. Never got a close look at him, but someone fired before Harding got his gun out. Shot at Boney's men, not us."

"You—you were very brave," Elizabeth told him, and even in the darkness Celia could detect the adoration in her expression.

"Jonny may very well have saved your life," Celia put in promptly and was rewarded by Elizabeth's rapturous sigh and Jonathon's embarrassed demeanor.

They rode in silence for several minutes, allowing the steady, jostling pace to calm their nerves. It had been quite an adventure! It was not every day that one was shot at by French spies! And on reflection, Celia had to admit it was not an experience she would care to repeat.

"Elizabeth," she began tentatively. "I don't think we should mention this to my grandfather."

"But Celia, should we not . . . No, you are quite right. He—he would be most upset."

"I should rather think so!" Jonathon declared. "Not at all the thing—exposing you to danger."

"Did everyone leaving the concert know what was happening?" Celia asked.

Jonathon shook his head. "Didn't look like it. Well,

Boney's agents would hardly start something in the middle of a crowd! And we were at a side entrance, remember. Don't think anyone else knew what was up."

"But the gunshots?"

"Crowds make a lot of noise," Jonny said reasonably. "People may have heard something, but not realized what it meant."

Elizabeth shivered. "To think of French agents here, in England! It—it is terrible!"

"Well, we have our people in France, too," Jonathon declared in an attempt to reassure her.

It did not appear to work. Elizabeth shrank back into her corner, and silence once again claimed them. This was not broken until the carriage turned onto the drive at Hastings. At Celia's urging, Jonathon did not get out but remained where he was with his bad leg raised.

Elizabeth climbed down, then turned back. "I—I must thank you again," she murmured.

"No, nothing at all," Jonathon said hastily.

"Well, it was," Celia informed him. "But I do think if my grandfather learns anything of what happened tonight, we should merely pretend we knew nothing of it."

This was agreed to, with relief, by the others. Jonathon, Celia knew, was a quiet man who would rather not have his deeds mentioned, and Elizabeth would want to forget all, except Jonathon's heroism, as quickly as possible.

By morning, both ladies had recovered for the most part from their adventure. When they met in the breakfast parlor, the dark shadows beneath Elizabeth's eyes were the only sign that the episode had not been completely forgotten. Celia experienced an occasional thrill of remembered excitement, but aside from wondering whether Mlle. de Bourgerre was safe, she thrust the incident firmly from her mind and tried, instead, to recall the music they had heard that evening.

That, unfortunately, reminded her of her reasons for attending the concert and her subsequent discomfiture. Her spirits sank, for she felt she had fallen completely into a trap of Lord Ryde's making. While she acknowledged both his masterful tactics and total success, she did not have to like it. She felt a fool, and that stung.

Assisted by his valet, Sir Roderick entered the sunny parlor a half hour later to find both ladies sipping cups of tea while they discussed plans for the morning with an outward calm that neither actually felt. One glance at his lowering brow was enough to alert Celia that he was fully aware of at least part of their evening's entertainment. She averted her gaze, wishing she could postpone this interview until she felt more her usual self. After last night's trouncing at Ryde's ingenious hands, she did not yet feel ready to venture back into the ring.

"You have a great deal to explain, young lady," Sir Roderick said by way of greeting. "How is it you came to leave this house last night, and in the company of Captain Edelston?"

Celia swallowed, mentally picking up her cudgels. "You were unable to attend the concert, so I merely arranged for another escort," she told him, keeping her voice calm and steady. If she betrayed any sign of guilt, the old man would focus on it and then nothing she could say would exonerate her. "I have done nothing wrong, Grandfather," she continued, "except perhaps in not telling you of my intentions."

"Nothing, miss?" he demanded, his tone still fierce. "Is it nothing for you to attend a public concert in the company of a gentleman who is not in the least related to you?"

"Lord Ryde himself expressed the desire that I should attend," she responded.

"It is not your attendance that is the issue, but your choice of escort! It would have been far better had you chosen to attend alone, with only our Cousin Elizabeth to bear you company." He turned on Miss Westerly, who cringed under his ferocious glare. "I would have expected you to have more sense than to encourage her in this nonsense over Captain Edelston. I will never countenance that match, and so she well knows. I have made other arrangements for her."

Elizabeth flushed deeply in mortification. "I—I saw no harm in it, under the circumstances. I was with them every moment, so it—it was not as if there were any impropriety involved."

"Indeed," Celia broke in, coming to the defense of her trembling chaperone. "Do you accuse us of slipping out to skulk in the hedges where we would not be seen? We took every caution that there should be nothing clandestine about it! Jonathon called for us here at the house, in the presence of the servants. And both you and Ryde have told me, I do not know how many times, that you have no desire to deny me my old friends. And it was Jonathon in particular of whom we were speaking."

Sir Roderick was silent, but his color darkened dreadfully. He apparently did not trust himself to speak, though his mouth worked several times.

"There was nothing the least bit wrong," Celia said firmly. "An old friend of my family escorted my chaperone and me to a concert. There, we met and conversed with two of my mother's oldest friends. Neither of these ladies saw anything improper about our conduct. That is all there was to it." She ended on a note of finality, as if she dismissed the subject from her mind.

"Is that all there is?" her grandfather demanded.

Celia thought fast. As matters stood, the subject would be allowed to drop and the evening would have gained her nothing in her war against Ryde. Now, her only trump card lay in his learning of Jonathon's presence. Somehow, her grandfather must be induced to tell him.

She allowed her shoulders to slump. "That—that is all you will permit," she said softly. She raised large, soulful eyes, then lowered them quickly as she encountered her grandfather's watchful gaze.

"I have made my decision for your own good," Sir Roderick declared, and for a moment Celia thought she detected a defensive note creeping into his voice. No trace of it showed in his cold, stern face, though.

"Yes, Grandfather," she murmured. She caught her voice on a rather artistic sob and kept her gaze focused on her plate.

"We won't speak of this again," Sir Roderick declared. He hobbled to the sideboard, took a plate, then began filling it from the various dishes.

Celia stole a glance at him, but could glean no hint of his intentions from his stiff bearing. She sighed, then took another bite of roll. Would he tell Ryde? If not, she would have to find a way of bringing the subject up without appearing anxious to discuss it. Still puzzling over the problem, she retired at last to the garden with a book she had no real expectation of reading.

She was joined shortly by Elizabeth, who set her nervous fingers to work on her embroidery. They sat silently for some time before her companion at last spoke.

"I—I fear your grandfather may now be too angry to listen to Captain Edelston's suit." She turned her gentle blue eyes toward Celia, then reached out to touch her hand in sympathy. "Do not despair, Celia dear. When—when he grows to know him, becomes more accustomed to seeing him, he cannot help but be won over by his manners and charm."

Celia choked back a most unladylike snort of disbelief. The only things her grandfather admired were courage and strength of will. While Jonathon might possess the former, the latter was sadly lacking in him. He must always be pronounced a good, agreeable fellow, but he hardly possessed the determination to inspire Sir Roderick with a profound respect.

"It would perhaps be best if we do not press the subject at the moment," Celia agreed diplomatically. "It is more important right now for Ryde to give way to Jonathon. Once he has withdrawn his own offer for me, Grandfather will be at a loss and probably quite glad to give me to one whose affection is of so long a standing, and who is undeniably a gentleman."

Elizabeth nodded wisely, taking this at face value. "Then it is Lord Ryde we must concentrate on," she said in her soft, tender voice. "Oh, surely he cannot persist when he knows his addresses are repugnant to you!"

That was not strictly true, but Celia felt it best not to correct her chaperone's erroneous view. "I would believe anything possible of a man who would marry for money!" she declared with lofty disdain.

This seemed to leave Elizabeth with little to say. She resumed work on her embroidery and Celia sat silently watching her while her mind returned to the problem at hand.

It would be best, she decided, if she were not around when Ryde returned to Hastings. This would give him ample time to inquire into her activities. He must be quite eager to see how she enjoyed the concert—and the truth about his relationship with Mlle. de Bourgerre. It would probably irritate him to have to wait to personally view her chagrin. But she, he would discover, would be so taken up with Jonathon that she would not have a thought to spare for her misinterpretation of his relationship with the beautiful singer.

The purpose of his journey to London—if that was indeed where he had gone—still puzzled her. Had it to do with Thérèse and his past mysterious journeys into France? She must betray no sign of interest, evince no curiosity whatsoever. She made some swift calculations, and determined that he could not possibly return until the early afternoon. Therefore, she and Elizabeth would ride out—in the company of a groom, so there could be no comment—for a very lengthy, leisurely ramble through the countryside.

In one way, Celia's calculations were correct. At just after two o'clock, Lord Ryde turned off the New Road and onto the neatly raked drive. His thoughts, though, were far from the concert he had missed. He was tired and worried, and his preoccupation lay along very different lines.

His journey home, following as it did hard on the heels of the one to London the previous day, left him more drained than he cared to admit. While his errand in certain government circles was completed without a hitch, his own business had been neither easy nor pleasant. His bank manager proved to be irritatingly skeptical, and it had taken every ounce of his persuasive abilities to bring the arrangments to even a halfway satisfactory conclusion.

He was taking a considerable gamble with the estate, as his bank manager pointed out in endless detail. In the end, however, Ryde had won out. In his pocket, safely confined in a cloth bag, he carried the rolls of flimsies that had been advanced to him to cover the cost of seed and hire of laborers to produce the first crop grown at Hastings in several years. But the spring was already well advanced and the early planting season long gone. It was more than likely already too late in the year to make this desperate attempt, which meant he stood to lose the time, the crop—and the investment. Everything he possessed that was not entailed stood as his pledge to the bank. The odds were heavily against him.

Word of his engagement to the Marcombe heiress would have solved his problem. The bank would have been only too happy to advance massive sums to a man on the verge of so profitable an alliance. But he could profit from this circumstance no more than he could touch her money itself. He would bring himself about on his own, he swore, and realized his determination for this had grown since he had made Celia's lively acquaintance. Aside from his personal revulsion at relying on his bride's funds, Celia had made her own scornful opinion of such a course abundantly clear.

Celia would become his wife only on his own terms. His pride demanded this. He must be financially independent of her, and she must bow to his will, truly wanting to help rather than hinder him. The first condition, he realized—with his first flash of humor that day—seemed almost as impossible as did the last.

He drew the curricle up in front of the old stone house and swung down. The door opened almost immediately and Gosson came forth to welcome him. Wrenn, Ryde's valet, hurried out in the butler's wake and took charge of his valise, and the groom drove the carriage around to the stable. Ryde was left to enter the house.

Upon inquiry, he learned that Celia and Elizabeth had ridden out some time earlier and were not expected back until quite late. A slight, lopsided smile twisted his lips. The hour of his return must have been anticipated. Celia lost no time in renewing her passive hostilities. She was certainly a determined adversary. The lines of his mouth tightened once again, for this was not a trait he wanted in the lady who would share his life and difficulties.

Dear God, why had he ever agreed to a marriage that threatened to cause him nothing but domestic unrest? The girl was a beauty and had certainly captured his interest, but it was nothing that would not have been satisfied with a flirtation. He enjoyed their duels—until he recalled that this constant state of strife might be his fate for life. He wondered if her pride and fiery temper would ever mature into a companionable liveliness, and experienced a disturbing longing.

He found Sir Roderick dozing peacefully in the bookroom, an open copy of the *London Times* spread out on his lap. Adolphus, who lay sprawled comfortably on the hearth rug, rose at once and bounded forward to greet his master, his tail wagging ecstatically. Trevor stooped to silence the dog's delighted noises. These must have penetrated Sir Roderick's slumber, for less than a minute after Ryde entered the room, the elderly gentleman stirred, opened his eyes, and glared at his host.

"So, you've come back, have you? How did you fare?"

"Well enough, sir," he replied. With Adolphus happily at his heels, he crossed to his desk, unlocked the bottom drawer, and removed the bag with its wad of softs from his pocket.

"So you got the money, did you? You're really going through with the planting?"

Ryde nodded. "I am. I'm not giving up without a fight."

"Fool!" his doting godfather declared, but there was a measure of respect in his tone.

Ryde smiled grimly. "Very possibly, sir, but there is more at stake here than Hastings."

Sir Roderick snorted. "She's a proud, difficult chit. You'll suit each other very well."

"Has anything interesting happened while I've been gone?" he asked, allowing the man's comment to pass unanswered.

Sir Roderick hesitated, and immediately Ryde became aware of something odd, a tenseness in the atmosphere. So, Celia had not been idle in his absence, he guessed shrewdly. In spite of this fresh evidence that she still fought him, he felt a spark of interest stir, lightening his mood. As troublesome as she might be at times, she could also be entertaining. He would not push for explanations, he decided. It would be more diverting to allow his guests to reveal their mysteries in their own time.

Apparently, no more was to be learned from Sir Roderick at the moment. Instead, they discussed the business that had taken him to London, the strategems employed to obtain the funds, and the uses to which it would be put. Sir Roderick, who had stoutly disapproved of his intentions to borrow money from the bank, now entered wholeheartedly into the plans for spending it. This fact further stirred Ryde's curiosity, making him wonder what topic it was the man wished to avoid.

Ryde did not have the opportunity of observing his guests together until they gathered in the Gold Saloon before dinner. He was the first to arrive, which put him in the advantageous position of being able to watch each one individually as they joined him. Their demeanor was sufficient to convince him he had been correct in his guess. Something had indeed happened, and he was sure that not all of those present concurred with the wish to keep him in the dark.

His suspicious gaze drifted to each of his guests. Miss Westerly, always reticent, seemed even quieter than usual. "Chastened" might be the best description. Sir Roderick appeared stiffer than normal and more than once directed a quelling gaze at his granddaughter's flushed countenance. Celia herself could best be described as defiant. Her eyes flashed as they encountered his, and he admired the effect.

While they waited for dinner to be announced, she cast Sir Roderick several glances that Ryde could not quite fathom. What on earth had she been up to in his absence? he wondered, intrigued. Or perhaps the more entertaining question might be how long it would take him to find out.

Gosson at last announced that the meal was served, and Ryde stood and offered his arm to Celia. As she rose from her chair, she peeked up at him through her lashes, a delightful trick that nevertheless bore no trace of flirting. She was up to something, the little minx. His only regret was that the joke would probably be sprung on him, not shared with him.

The meal itself was strained. None of his guests

appeared anxious to talk, which left the burden of conversation on Ryde. As he did not yet know what had occurred, he could not be sure what topic would be safe. He chose to confine himself to the merest commonplaces about the weather, which he uttered with the blandest of smiles. Twice, he caught Celia biting her lower lip, her eyes alight with suppressed mirth as if she realized his predicament and enjoyed it too much to have any intention of helping.

By the time the ladies withdrew from the dining room, Ryde could barely restrain himself from demanding an immediate answer from Sir Roderick. Impatiently, he waited while Gosson cleared the table and brought out the brandy and snuff jars.

At last, the butler left the gentlemen on their own. Ryde poured himself a glass, passed the decanter on to his godfather, and settled back to hear the worst.

"Well?" he asked after Sir Roderick had taken a sip of the amber liquid. "What has been going on?"

"Nothing," Sir Roderick declared firmly. "What makes you think something has occurred?"

"Just a suspicion. I must apologize if I am wrong. Do you care to come with me to Brighton tomorrow while I arrange for seed?"

The conversation slipped safely into farming details, but Ryde was not fooled. So, Sir Roderick was anxious to keep whatever had happened quiet. That meant Celia would undoubtedly be equally anxious to tell him. That knowledge afforded him a certain measure of amusement.

He glanced at his godfather, who appeared somewhat ill at ease. It would be cruel to tease him further on the subject, but his curiosity was getting the better of him. As soon as he reasonably could, he suggested that they join the ladies. This did not seem to particularly please Sir Roderick either, but he made no outward protest. He merely drained his glass and came to his feet.

As they entered the Drawing Room, the soft strains of the Mozart piece reached them. Celia must learn quickly, Ryde noted, for he recognized a far more polished version of what she had attempted for the first time only a couple of days before.

As the door closed behind the men, Celia broke off, her eyes darting toward them. Ryde forced back a smile at the clear disappointment and chagrin in her face as she noted his own carefully blank expression. Just what was it the silly chit had hoped her grandfather would reveal to him?

"Please, don't allow us to interrupt you," he urged. "Keep playing." He seated himself on the sofa and turned his attention to Miss Westerly, smiling at her in an encouraging manner and asking if she had enjoyed her ride that afternoon.

Elizabeth, who was unaware that the sole purpose of their ride had been to keep them from Ryde's company for as long as possible, was able to reply with what was, for her, an unusual enthusiasm. It had been a slow, meandering journey of exploration, exactly suited to her tastes, and she rhapsodized with a clear conscience over the delightful vistas they had glimpsed.

Ryde settled back, prepared to enjoy the evening. Out of the corner of his eye, he could see Celia's growing frustration. She bent over the instrument, frowning, and her fingers ran over the keys with an unaccustomed inaccuracy. This continued for about twenty minutes, when she stopped abruptly.

"It is quite warm in here," she announced. "I believe I will walk in the garden." With only a quick glance at Ryde, and none at all at the other occupants of the room, she crossed to the long French windows and let herself out onto the walkway that led to the shrubbery.

Ryde waited patiently, allowing the hands of the mantel clock to advance ten minutes. That should allow enough time for her obviously simmering temper to have reached the boiling point, he decided. She would be ready to come to daggers drawing with him the moment he appeared.

Lazily, he stood and followed her. The moon, almost a perfect round as it neared its fullest, rode high in the sky, bathing the garden in a surprisingly bright light. He would be able to see her face clearly, and the prospect pleased him. Gone completely was the depression he had suffered earlier in the day.

He found her at last, seated on the bench in the middle of the garden and gazing up at the canopy of stars. She looked around quickly at the sounds of his approach, and gave an affecting start that might have been interpreted as nervousness. Ryde attributed it to dramatic ability, and his almost gleeful anticipation grew.

"Grandfather has told you All!" she declared by way of greeting. Her tragic tones would have made an actress as accomplished as Sarah Siddons green with envy. She rose, and regarded him for a moment as if gauging the effect of her speech. Apparently, it failed to satisfy her. "I shall continue to see Jonathon!" she pronounced next.

The soft light of the moon glinted on a sparkling tear that ran slowly from her eye and down her cheek. Another followed a moment later, and she allowed both to fall unhindered.

"I'm sorry," Ryde confessed with an air of apology. He really had to admire such a consummate performance. "I am afraid your grandfather has said nothing to me. But please, do not keep me in the dark," he encouraged her cheerfully. "Is there anything I should know?"

Celia sniffed, though the look she threw at him was rife with suspicion. "Grandfather was not able to take us to the concert last night," she informed him. "So Jonathon acted as our escort!"

"Quite right," he approved on the instant. "I could not feel it proper for two females to have attended a public event without the support of some gentleman. I must extend my thanks to him when next we meet." Was that all she had been up to? It might well be enough, though, to set Sir Roderick off in a towering rage.

"Grandfather does not agree with you," Celia informed him, permitting herself another delicate sniff.

Ryde controlled the amused twitching of his lip and, instead, raised a polite eyebrow. "I have no desire to deprive you of such an old friend," he assured her. "The outing appears quite unexceptionable. I shall reassure Sir Roderick on that head, if you like."

"Jonathon is far more than a friend to me!" Celia

announced, her eyes shining in the moonlight. Her chin quivered slightly, though he suspected this was more from an innate sense of artistic melodrama than defiance.

In spite of this belief, Ryde felt himself torn between a strong appreciation of her tactics and a strange, unfamiliar sensation he suddenly realized was anger. To let her know she had succeeded in irritating him was unthinkable! It was bad enough that he knew it himself. His counterattack had best come immediately.

Without thoroughly thinking through his spur of the moment reprisal, he took a step closer to her. The force of his penetrating gaze drew her reluctant eyes to his, and he held her like that, powerless to look away, until her breath seemed to come deeper and quicker. Her slender form began to tremble and she swayed slightly toward him as if she no longer had the strength or wish to withstand him.

To his surprise, an answering flicker of desire leaped through him, startling in its force. She was lovely, almost unbearably so, bathed in moonlight, captive in his power. The impulse to kiss her was almost irresistible.

But resist it he must! Here he stood, so close to victory, teetering on the brink of surrender. He allowed his gaze to wander from her gleaming dark curls to the low-cut neckline of her gauze gown, from her slender waist down to her tiny, slippered feet. In every yielding line of her bearing he felt the power he might—he must!—one day have over her.

What a ridiculous line of tripe he was feeding

himself! His victory would be no less complete if he kissed her—because he wished to, of course, and not because he could not help himself!

A scraping on the gravel prevented him from putting this plan into action. Gosson appeared, his manner deeply perturbed.

"My lord," he began. "It is a Mr. Harding!" The butler almost wrung his hands in consternation. "Something is dreadfully amiss. He requires instant speech with you, says it is most urgent. . . ."

"That it is, my lord." Harding, one arm resting interestingly in a sling, pushed passed the distressed butler. He hesitated, his eyes narrowing as his gaze fell on Celia. He relaxed as he recognized her. "Evening, Miss Marcombe." He nodded briefly to her before turning back to Ryde. "They've made two attempts on Mam'selle de Bourgerre, sir. Tonight's nearly succeeded, and they did get someone else. If you could come at once, I'd be most grateful."

CHAPTER FIFTEEN

Lord Ryde muttered an expletive under his breath, too soft for Celia to catch. "Is Mlle. de Bourgerre all right?" he demanded.

Harding nodding. "Yes, m'lord, for the moment. I've left several of my men guarding her house. But that gentleman who was shot, he's in a bad state. Best come at once if you want to see him."

Ryde's brow lowered. "I have no real authority . . ." he began.

"Begging your pardon, m'lord," his visitor broke in, "but it's Mam'selle as we really need some help with. Worked herself into quite a state, she has. Won't leave his side, and you know what that means, what with the meeting set for the morning and all."

Ryde nodded and turned to Gosson, who hovered just behind Harding. "Send Coxly to saddle my horse. And Miss Marcombe . . . "

"You'd best hurry, my lord." Celia, forgetting their differences in the face of a crisis, stepped forward, just touching his arm. Her large brown eyes lifted to his, clear and sparkingly alive. "You will be needed there."

He took her hand, raising her fingers quickly to his

lips. "Convey my apologies to your grandfather, please."

With Harding hurrying in his wake, Ryde strode rapidly down the garden path and around the corner leading to the stableyard. There, he found a whirl of activity as his own horse and a fresh mount for Harding were saddled.

"What happened?" Ryde asked tensely as they waited, impatient.

Harding appeared distinctly uncomfortable. "Can't say for sure, m'lord. Mam'selle had invited Wiggins and myself to take tea with her. Then, there was some shooting outside. Wiggins took Mam'selle to an upstairs room and I ran out. No one in sight; then, I heard Mam'selle scream. Left my men searching the street and ran back in. She said there was someone moving about in the next room so we went in and found a man unconscious. Bleeding like a pig, he was, m'lord, with a shot through his ribs that may kill him yet."

"A French agent?"

"No, m'lord. Seems the lady knew him. Threw herself down beside him and starting crying, calling him by some strange Frenchy name. She wasn't making much sense, but I think this fellow was her courier, the one who got shot in France."

"Either he dragged himself a long way, or he makes rather a habit of getting in the way of bullets," Ryde said dryly. "You did right in coming for me. I'll be glad of a chance to talk to him."

He turned as running footsteps crunched across the gravel, and Wrenn, his valet, entered the yard bearing his hat, gloves and greatcoat. Ryde donned them quickly, then took the reins of one of the horses led up by the grooms.

They accomplished the journey to the town quickly, too intent on reaching their destination to waste time in speech. In less than twenty minutes, they entered Brighton where they were forced to check their speed and proceed at a more decorous pace. At last, they dismounted before the house on the Marine Parade.

One of Harding's men ran forward out of the shadows to take their horses' heads. Ryde mounted the few steps to the door, which was opened for him as he reached it. He passed into the house, stripping off his gloves and coat as he went. These he tossed over a table in the narrow entry hall, then turned to Harding who was just behind him.

"Do you have guards all around the house?" he asked.

"Yes, m'lord. No one else will be slipping in all quiet-like on the upper floors."

Ryde started up the stairs. At the top, he was met by Wiggins who escorted him down a short passage and opened a door to one of the bedrooms. A single candle cast a pale glow over the room, making it difficult to discern either furnishings or occupants.

Thérèse de Bourgerre looked up, startled, from where she sat in a chair beside the raised bed in which lay a shadowy figure. She sprang up at once, rushing toward Ryde with her hands outstretched. "Trevor, *mon cher,* you must help him! He lies so very still!"

"Has a doctor been sent for?" He set her gently aside and strode up to the bed, taking the man's hand and feeling for the weak, erratic pulse.

"*Mais oui!* On the instant, when I could convince

these so stupid men that he is not an assassin. He has but only just left."

Ryde looked down at the almost lifeless figure beneath the coverlet. Strips of cloth bound a wound on the man's forehead, and shining glints of mahogany in his dark brown hair showed where the blood had not been completely washed away. The face was gaunt and pale, but Ryde gained the impression of a young man, perhaps his own age of thirty, with the clean-cut features of a gentleman.

"Will he live?" he asked at last.

"The doctor, he—he would not say." Her voice broke on a sob, which she valiantly fought down. "He—he is in much danger, but the bullet is out of his side." She sank back down into the chair, then covered one of the man's cold, still hands with her own.

"Who is he? *Le Maniganceur?*"

Thérèse nodded a wordless assent. The light from the candle glistened on the tears that slipped unheeded down her cheeks.

"How did he get here? What happened in France?"

"I . . ." She broke off, took a deep, ragged breath, then continued in a steadier voice. "I do not know. All I know is that he is here, and in such a state!"

Ryde let it drop. Answers would have to wait until the man could tell his own story—providing he recovered. In the meantime, there was little he could do.

"Tell me what happened tonight," he directed her.

Thérèse pulled herself together with a visible effort, then told a story almost exactly the same as Harding's. She had seen no one and was not sure from which direction the attack came.

"But it did not seem to be directed at the house,"

she said slowly, her lovely brow wrinkling in an effort to remember. "It—it is possible that it was *mon Maniganceur* whom they sought and not me this time."

"I can well imagine they would like you both." Ryde paced the length of the room, then crossed to the window to peer out. The houses on the street were all connected, so any attack would have to come from the rear or the front—or from above. He opened the sash and leaned out, peering upward into the starry night. That must have been how *Le Maniganceur* entered the house, descending from the roof by a rope. A question to Thérèse confirmed this guess. A rope had been found—and removed.

"He was lucky he made it through the window before collapsing," Ryde murmured, looking down the three stories to the pavement below. He turned back to the room. "Did no one, in the neighboring houses, hear the commotion?"

"That I do not know," Thérèse replied, and it was obvious that she also did not care. Her whole concern was for the man who lay so still and pale in the bed.

"Do you still feel safe here?" he asked.

Thérèse shrugged. "There are guards; you do all that you can."

"I would feel better if you came back out to Hastings," he told her, his voice level.

"Non!" She spun to face him. "I will not leave him!"

Ryde almost smiled. "No, not yet. But as soon as he is well enough to travel, I shall take you both out there."

Therese appeared to accept this. "But what of your visitors?"

He considered. He had best send them away, get

them safely out of the danger that surely would be drawn to his home. To his surprise, he was not as anxious as he ought, to be rid of Celia's presence. Well, the decision could wait for a couple of days.

"We will see," he finally said. "Is there anything I can do for you tonight?"

"Non. I shall sit with him."

"You received my message about the meeting tomorrow?" he asked. "I have arranged for Harding and Wiggins to take you in a coach. It will be daylight, so there should be no trouble."

She raised large, determined eyes to him. "I will not leave him."

He had been warned, and so he was prepared. "Thérèse, you know how important your information is. Do you want this," he gestured to the man, "to have been for nothing?"

"Could—could it not wait until the next day?" she asked, torn between duty and her longing to remain.

"The men cannot stay." He gave her a crooked smile. "There is a war on, Thérèse, as you may have noticed. There are other matters, equally urgent, that need their attention."

"Oui," she whispered.

"You must not let *Le Maniganceur* down, Thérèse," Trevor continued persuadingly. "You will stay with him tonight and you will be gone only a few short hours tomorrow. And there will be guards here at all times. He will be all right."

She nodded reluctantly. "I will go—for the sake of *mon Maniganceur.* Will you be there also?"

"I will." He took her hand, kissing it lightly. "If there is nothing more I can do, I shall take my leave of you. Until tomorrow, then."

Leaving Thérèse to turn her full attention to the inert form of *Le Maniganceur,* he went out into the hall. Wiggins was there, just beyond the door, slouched in a chair but with a serviceable-looking horse pistol clutched firmly in one hand. Ryde nodded to him and made his way downstairs.

Harding came down the passage from the kitchens as Ryde was about to let himself out the front door. Together, the two men made a complete tour of the outside premises, conferring with the guards and checking the precautions that had been taken. When Ryde at last swung himself into his saddle, he was convinced that he had done all that he possibly could.

The hour was considerably advanced when he at last rode up the drive at Hastings. To his surprise, a light burned in the window of the Gold Saloon. Gosson must be waiting up for him, he thought with a slight smile. And it would not surprise him if he found Wrenn trying to stay awake in a chair in his dressing room, determined to help him prepare for bed.

Coxly was on the alert, and came down the stairs from his quarters in the stables as soon as the shod hooves struck the first of the cobblestones. Years in Lord Ryde's service had taught him not to ask questions. Instead, he merely directed a searching glance at his master to assure himself that he did not seem either injured or unduly perturbed. Satisfied, he turned his attention to the horse.

Trevor let himself into the house, finding that the door had been left on the latch for him. Gosson was not in sight, nor did he come hurrying from the back reaches. Must have fallen asleep, Ryde reflected. He would lock up himself.

The door to the Gold Saloon stood slightly ajar, and a wavering glow indicated a candle that had reached the guttering stage. He entered the room, then paused just over the threshold. It was not Gosson who had tried to wait up, but Celia. She sat curled up on the sofa, one arm draped across her knees, her head resting against the back.

He came forward, his features relaxing into a smile. She was dressed in a very pretty negligee of pale pink muslin, fastened high at the neck and hanging loosely about her slender form. Only a very shapely leg pulled the material tight. A cap of matching muslin and lace confined most of her dark brown curls.

In repose, her features were classically pretty, though lacking the constant animation that gave the piquant face so much character. His brow lowered slightly as he studied the straight little nose, the line of cheekbone and jaw. It was almost as if he saw them for the first time, yet found them hauntingly familiar. He had never seen her asleep before.

She stirred, her head moved sideways, and her long lashes fluttered as her eyes opened. It took a moment for her to focus, then she sat up straight.

"When did you get back? Is Mlle. de Bourgerre all right?"

"She is completely unharmed. And I just got back, a moment ago."

"I—I am glad. Tell me what happened." She gestured to a spot on the sofa beside her, obligingly sliding over to make room for him.

He shook his head, declining her offer. "I had best

go up to bed. It has been a rather long day for me."

"Will you not tell me, then?" Celia asked, her voice strangely tight.

"No." He hesitated, reading the emotions that flashed across her expressive countenance. "I do not want you involved," he explained more gently.

"Can I not help?" she asked.

Her eyes glistened in her growing temper. While he admired the effect, he was not about to expose her to danger. He shook his head. "No. The less you know about all of this, the better it will be."

"For who?" she demanded. "You? Is Mlle. de Bourgerre the only female allowed to play your games?"

"I already have to worry about her being shot; I do not want you exposed as well," he snapped back, weariness robbing him of discretion.

"No, that's for Elizabeth!" she threw back at him, forgetting he did not know about that aspect of their escapade at the concert.

"What are you talking about," he demanded.

Celia bit her lip, but knew she must tell him. "You heard that someone tried to shoot Mlle. de Bourgerre as she left the concert?" she asked slowly.

"Yes, but I was not aware that you knew of that episode."

"Elizabeth, Jonathon and I—we—we were talking to her, and Mr. Harding escorted us out by the back entrance when we were ready to leave. Elizabeth and I went out first, and—and someone shot at her, thinking she was Mademoiselle."

Ryde spoke one word softly that caused Celia's eyes to fly open wide. "Why the devil did no one tell me?"

he exploded.

"We—we thought it unnecessary; you have enough on your mind. And they—the assassins—realized their mistake quickly enough, with no real harm done."

"That settles it. You must return to Ranleigh until this business is over."

"Can we not stay and be of some assistance?"

"This is no place for you or your grandfather. And if they mistook Miss Westerly for Thérèse once . . . "

"You think they may do it again?" Celia asked quickly as he broke off. "You intend to bring her back here, to this house, do you not?"

"Celia, are you at all familiar with the concept of doing what you are told without arguing?" he asked, exasperated.

"Only if the orders make sense. Do you not see?" She stood, walking up to him in her eagerness. "We might be able to help you!"

"Would Miss Westerly be delighted to place herself in jeopardy?"

"Oh!" she exclaimed in disgust. "You *will* not see. You think I would only get in your way. Why is it that only men are allowed to have great adventures? Why cannot I?"

He placed gentle hands on her shoulders. "This is not a game, Celia. It is deadly serious. Deadly." He repeated the word, hoping it would make an impression on her.

"Do you think I am a coward, then?"

"What if something happened to you? What of Sir Roderick? Your brother has already given his life for his country; there is no need for you to be anxious to do the same."

She looked down, suddenly trembling, unable to answer. The candle, which was now little more than a pool of wax in the bottom of its holder, sputtered and wavered. Celia groped about in the near-darkness, found another one that lay ready on the table, and lit it from the first, just as it gave out. Stronger light filled the area as she fitted the new taper into position.

"Does Sir Roderick know about Miss Westerly's adventure?" he asked.

Celia kept her back turned to him. "No," she admitted.

"It is for the best, Celia," he said firmly. He came up behind her and placed his hands on her shoulders again. For a moment, she leaned back against him; then she pulled away.

"You treat me as a child, as you have from—from the moment we met! I want to be a part of this. I must! You do not understand!"

"There is no need. We have plenty of men; Thérèse is as safe as anyone can make her for the present."

"Will—will the French agents know she is here? Or will you keep up the pretense that she is at the house in the Marine Parade?"

"Celia, forget about it," he snapped. "It does not concern you. Tomorrow, or the next day, you will bring your visit to a close and return to Ranleigh. No," he stopped her as she began to protest. "I have made up my mind." His voice took on a sterner note. "I will not be disobeyed in this or any other matter. Now, go up to bed. The matter is closed."

Celia's eyes blazed in fury at him. Then, without another word, she turned and ran from the room. He watched her go, troubled, but knowing he had made the only choice possible. If she would but think, just once, she must see why he could not trust her! She was too volatile, her temper too ready to flare, and he could count on her to act on impulse without due consideration. She was just too young and flighty to be a suitable wife for him. He closed his eyes as the pulse at his temple throbbed with penetrating force. *Damn and damn and damn . . .*

CHAPTER SIXTEEN

After tossing fitfully for the better portion of the night, Celia rose early and wrapped a shawl about her shoulders against the morning chill. Her head ached so unbearably she could barely think, but she knew—had known since the night before—what she must do. Somehow, she must convince Lord Ryde to permit her to stay, to take some role in the drama that raged about them. It was up to her to atone for Charlie's cowardice, no matter the personal cost. Her pride would allow no less.

She waited by her window, staring out over the back garden where late spring blooms raised their determined heads. The grounds looked less gloomy than they had when she arrived, not so very long ago. Somewhere below her, a bird set up a melodic trill and was answered by another, closer by.

As soon as the hour seemed advanced enough for the servants to be stirring, she rang for Seddons and drew her riding habit from the clothes cupboard. What she needed was a good, long gallop to clear her head, and then she would tackle Ryde and tell him she insisted on remaining. He would see she was not to be dismissed lightly.

She dressed quickly and hurried down the stairs. Apparently, her summons to Seddons had alerted the staff, for an array of rolls and beverages was already set out on the sideboard in the breakfast parlor. She poured herself a cup of tea, drank only a few sips, then put a roll in a napkin to eat on her way to the stable.

To her surprise, both Coxly and Ketter were already in the yard, grooming horses. Ketter went immediately to saddle the gray mare, but Coxly directed a piercing look at her before turning back to the animal who stood patiently waiting.

Idly, Celia glanced about the yard. The door to the carriage house stood ajar, and Ryde's curricle was not in its accustomed position. Frowning, she turned back to the head groom.

"Has Lord Ryde driven out already?" she asked.

"Yes, miss." He paused in his combing of the large bay's tail to turn politely to her. "Into Brighton, he said, to see about some farming equipment and seed." He returned his attention to the horse's tangled hair, pointedly putting an end to the conversation.

Probably he had gone back to see Thérèse, Celia thought, with a flash of irritation. There was a female he admired, who he championed, who was a part of the exciting life he enjoyed living. Why could he not allow one more girl to share in this adventure? Did he doubt her mettle? She must show him—or perhaps herself—that not all Marcombes ran in the face of danger.

Within a few minutes, Ketter led the mare up to her and assisted her into the saddle. With a word of thanks, Celia turned her mount out of the yard and down the drive at a walk. She had no clear idea of where she wished to go, only that she wanted a long, undisturbed run. On impulse, she started down the New Road toward the lane where she had met Jonathon once before.

In the distance, a horseman approached, trotting easily, but she paid him no heed, lost as she was in her plans to convince Ryde to let her help. The rider was almost upon her before his voice, calling her name, penetrated her abstracted thoughts.

"Cill!" he exclaimed. "Really, Cill, have you gone deaf?"

"Jonny! I am so sorry!" She reined in beside him, forcing a smile to her lips.

"Called you five times!" he complained.

"Oh, Jonny, do ride with me. Which way are you heading?"

"No direction in particular. Just giving him some exercise." He patted the gelding's shining black neck. "Along the lane, I suppose." He gestured back the way she had come.

She turned, surprised, realizing she must have passed the lane only a short time ago, never even noticing it. She moved the mare into position beside Jonathon and they walked together along the road, then turned onto the narrow way.

"Everything all right?" Jonathon asked after a bit. "You look a bit down this morning."

"Just restless. Worried about Charlie, I suppose."

"Well, at least we know those two men weren't after him. It was probably all a hum and no one is interested in his whereabouts at all."

"*I* am." Celia sighed. "If the government isn't hunting him for us, then we must do something ourselves."

Jonathon stared blankly at her. "What?"

She shook her head, unable to think of a single plan. The only one that presented itself she dismissed out of hand. She could not apply to Ryde for assistance. If she did that, she would have to tell him the truth—or would she? She could try the story of a possible memory loss, of Charlie wandering somewhere on the Continent. Surely Ryde had enough connections for discreet inquiries to be made!

But if any man could discern the fatal truth, she was sure it was Ryde. No, she could not tell him of her brother's continued existence until she had Charlie safely home—until they were all letter-perfect in their stories of how he came to leave Trafalgar.

She looked about, seeking another topic of conversation, anything to divert her mind. She found it in Jonathon himself. "You look unusually fine this morning," she informed him. "Is that a new way of tying your neckcloth?"

He beamed at her. "Like it? Took me the better part of a month to perfect it. Called the Waterfall."

"Well, I must say, it makes you look all the crack." She regarded him with a sisterly fondness, noting other changes in his appearance. The points of his shirt collar, normally of only moderate height and stiffness, now reached well above his chin. Not precisely dandyish, she decided, for he could move his head with ease, but he no longer looked a country squire. The touch of town bronze, added to his classically handsome features, would be enough to turn the head and heart of many of a young lady.

"Miss Westerly is not with you this morning?" he asked. "Really, Cill, not the thing for you to be careering off about the countryside without an escort, you know."

"I thought it best to go alone this morning," Celia replied, ignoring his reproof. "I wanted a gallop, and Elizabeth does not enjoy that, the poor dear. She much prefers to keep to a sedate canter, and that would never do for me."

"Sensible of her," Jonathon approved. "Don't see how anyone can keep up with that neck-or-nothing style of yours."

"Well, you need not, at any rate," she smiled. "I will be quite all right. Do you know, it is a shame Elizabeth did not come with me after all, for then you two could have kept each other company while I indulged myself with a run."

He was silent for a moment. "Rather a nice female, Miss Westerly," he pronounced. "Easy to talk to. Tell you what, Cill, you're lucky to have her for a companion."

"Very lucky," Celia agreed, encouraging him in this vein. "She is possessed of the—the gentlest and sweetest nature. She would make an excellent wife for a man who loved country living and could overlook her lack of dowry."

Jonathon blinked, apparently considering Elizabeth as a marriageable young woman for the first time. Celia watched him, wondering if she had said enough to fix the idea in his occasionally porous mind. Better take it slowly, she decided.

"Well, I shall leave you, now." She held out her hand to him.

Jonathon regarded her with a certain reluctance. "Let me come with you, Cill. Delighted to bear you company," he added, lying manfully. No more than Elizabeth, did he enjoy the wicked pace Celia could set.

"It is not at all necessary, but thank you." She pressed her lips together to keep from betraying her amusement.

He shook his head. "Wouldn't feel right letting you go off on your own."

She relented, but secretly wondered how soon he would regret his gallantry. Urging the mare into a canter, she felt the eager energy beneath her. She eased off her hold on the horse's mouth, keeping her in check just enough to permit Jonathon to stay abreast. This was not the wild, hell-for-leather ride for which she had yearned, but it would do well enough.

What she lost in speed, she made up for in distance. They left the lane and cut across the hills, staying clear of planted fields but occasionally cutting across pastures. Three times they reined down to a walk to rest their mounts, and each time, Celia's restlessness drove her to charge on, leaving Jonathon to make a valiant attempt to catch up with her.

At last, they crested a hillock and found themselves coming down on a road. Celia slowed and glanced up at the sky, surprised to see the sun riding so high. They must have been riding for hours! Her throat felt it, too, and she would have been glad of a glass of water. Her mare's sides heaved as the sweat streamed down the glossy dark gray neck.

"We'll have to cool them," she called to Jonathon as he rode down to join her.

"Us, too," he agreed. "Not sure how far we've come, but there ought to be an inn back there somewhere, nearer the Brighton road."

"It sounds wonderful. The horses should be cool enough for a drink by then, with luck." They started walking in companionable silence.

Over half an hour passed before the inn came into view. By then, the horses had recovered from their exercise and needed only water before being ready to continue. Celia, though, wanted something more, and immediately bespoke lemonade. Jumping lightly to the ground, she handed her mount over to an ostler.

They crossed the threshold to be met by a bowing landlord, who informed them at great length that he deeply regretted not being able to offer them a private parlor. This, he feared, had been bespoken by the gentlemen from London who were presently in residence. He ventured to suggest that the common room, being at the moment empty, might suit their needs.

Celia glanced at Jonathon, reading the silent relief in his face. A private parlor, while quite comfortable, would be shockingly indiscreet under the circumstances—investing their pleasure ride with all the trappings of a clandestine assignation.

She settled herself in a corner where she could look out over the inn's yard. In a few minutes, the landlord himself carried over her lemonade, a giant tankard of ale for Jonathon, and a plate of cakes. She selected a small pastry from the latter, realizing suddenly that she was ravenous, having had nothing but the roll for breakfast.

Jonathon lounged back and took a long draught of ale, then reached over absently and picked up a large pastry which he consumed in three bites. He selected another, which quickly followed the first. "Good idea, coming here," he remarked.

Celia rose and strolled idly to the window. On the whole, her gallop had raised her spirits considerably. She felt ready to tackle anything now. Her only regret was that it had not been Ryde who accompanied her.

Heavy, booted footsteps descended the staircase behind her, then ceased abruptly. Celia glanced over her shoulder, then spun about as she recognized Ryde's tall, commanding figure. He might have appeared in answer to her thoughts! Her eyes widened in pleasure which vanished abruptly as two minor details struck her. What was Ryde doing here, in a country inn, when he was supposedly transacting farming business in Brighton? And why was he approaching her with his brow darkened in murderous fury?

It was this second problem that took precedence. His rapid scrutiny of the room could not have failed to detect Jonathon, and she realized with disturbing clarity how this must appear. This time, Elizabeth was not there to bear them countenance.

Ignoring Jonathon, Ryde strode up to her and sketched her the briefest of mocking bows. "What brings you to this inn?" he demanded.

To confess the truth—that they had ridden too far

and stopped to rest—would perhaps have been the most prudent. But in reaction to the suppressed anger in his voice, her defiance rose like the hackles on a dog so that she could almost feel the prickling along the back of her neck. Without thinking, she matched his supercilious tone.

"I might ask you the same. I understood you had urgent business in Brighton this morning."

His dark eyes narrowed to slits that sent a shiver of fear mixed with excitement through her. "My movements are no concern of yours," he said softly. "Your own, however, leave much to be desired." He lowered himself onto the settle that stood near the window, a move calculated to put her at a disadvantage, as she remained standing like a reprimanded schoolroom miss. With studied casualness, he drew his snuff box from his pocket and took a small pinch. For several minutes his attention appeared totally involved with this action.

Celia remained on her feet before him, trying to control the nervous quaking that threatened to overcome her. Her rebellion had been short-lived and her temper, for once, threatened to desert her just when she needed it most. If she were not careful, she told herself in disgust, she would be reduced to a tearful heap, at his mercy!

He raised his eyes to her again, and this time there was only icy politeness in his voice. "It really is not quite the thing for you to be at an inn with only a gentleman for escort."

That stung, for she knew him to be correct. With her embarrassment, though, came a return of her fighting spirit. She opened her own eyes wide in feigned innocence. "But surely," she asked sweetly, "it would have been far worse if I had come alone, would it not?"

"Your behavior, as you know perfectly well, minx, is outrageous!" he was goaded into retorting.

"Oh, she'll come to no harm with me." Jonathon's voice sounded behind her, making her jump. "Taking care of Cill is rather a habit of mine."

His presence and support gave her confidence, and she took a deep breath. With the arrival of relief troops, she now felt herself prepared to charge into the next skirmish with her foe.

Ryde forestalled her. "Then, I am surprised you have so little regard for her reputation!" he snapped back.

Jonathon drew himself up, his own expression darkening at this insult, and Celia intervened quickly. "What business is it of yours?" she demanded.

"As my affianced wife . . . " Ryde began, but Celia interrupted.

"I am no such thing!" she exclaimed, prudence giving way before her unruly temper. "And if you think, for even one moment, that I would consider marriage with you . . . !"

"Oh, be quiet, Cill!" Jonathon broke into her tirade in a most un-loverlike manner. "Don't create a scene in public!"

She sniffed, but he ignored her and turned instead to Ryde. "I encountered her out riding, alone, and indulged her urge to go for a long gallop. We went farther than we intended, so we stopped to rest the horses. That is all there is to it."

An angry muscle twitched at the corner of Ryde's

mouth as he regarded the classically handsome countenance before him, but the matter-of-fact way in which the man spoke mollified him somewhat.

Celia's surprised glance darted from one man to the other. Was that jealousy on Lord Ryde's part? With a flash of inspiration, it occurred to her what a marvelous opportunity this might have been to goad him farther, to convince him to draw back from this impossible marriage! And Jonathon had bungled it!

But it was enough to bring her to her senses, to remind her she must keep Ryde at a distance. With a pang of regret, she abandoned her hopes to persuade Ryde to trust her with his secret business. Charlie's affairs were of greater import, and to protect him she must keep Ryde as the enemy—and she had best not forget it again.

"So now you know why *we* are here," she snapped at him. "I repeat, what brings you to this inn?"

He opened his mouth to reply, but Celia's sudden gasp stopped him. There, coming down the stairs he had not long ago descended, was Thŕeèse de Bourgerre, uncommonly alluring in a diaphanous gown of peach crepe that molded itself to her admirable figure as she moved. Her hair, a thick mass of golden curls, formed a halo about her lovely oval face, creating the image of a delicate angel that her revealingly low decolletage belied.

"How dare you!" The words escaped Celia in a long, soft, furious whisper. She spun back to face Ryde, conscious suddenly of an anger with him that bordered on the unreasonable. "How dare you object to my being in a public place with an old friend, when you have been meeting *her!* So, she is not your mistress, is she? Is that all your fine words and promises are worth?" Though she seethed with indignation, miraculously she kept her voice low. "Now I need have no hesitation in telling you that this was precisely my intention in coming here with my beloved Jonathon! If you can have an assignation with—with *her,* then I can meet the man I love! It is only fair!"

Ryde's dark eyes flashed and Celia, with sudden fear, realized she had gone too far. He grabbed her shoulders, shook her, then turned her about. Mlle. de Bourgerre had reached the bottom of the stairs, but she was no longer alone. Three gentleman had joined her, and their age, their dress, their very bearing proclaimed their importance. It did not take Ryde's words, hissed in her ear, to identify them as members of His Majesty's Government.

Celia felt herself going limp in his grasp. The attack on Mlle. de Bourgerre the night before, the previous one where Elizabeth had been the mistaken target, Ryde's mysterious journey to London—it was only natural that the Government would be anxious to question the young woman in secret. It was the obvious explanation. *Why* had she been so ready to make a fool of herself, accusing Ryde of something she did not really believe?

Her cheeks burned hotly in mortification at having allowed her tongue to run away with her, at hurling those ridiculous accusations at Ryde . . . and at implying that she herself was involved in a relationship, with Jonathon, that was as shocking as it was untrue.

"You have not seen any of these people this morning," Ryde's voice sounded again near her ear, but she realized he addressed Jonathon.

The other man nodded slowly. "Celia, I think we had best leave."

"*You* had," Trevor agreed. "I still have business to attend to with Miss Marcombe."

"Yes, Jonathon. I will be all right." Celia's pride came to her rescue. She straightened up slightly and shook off Ryde's hands that still rested on her shoulders. "As Lord Ryde said, he and I have a few *business* matters to discuss."

Jonathon hesitated, looking from one to the other, and came to a decision. "I will call on you in the morning, Celia." He turned on his heel and left the inn.

"I believe our discussion might best take place in private," Ryde said softly. Angry glints still lit his eyes. He excused himself to her and crossed over to join the group by the stairs. They spoke for several minutes, so quietly that Celia could not catch a word. Then he took Mlle. de Bourgerre's hand, kissed it lightly, and led her to the door.

Through the window, Celia watched with sinking spirits as Jonathon rode out of the yard. He had barely cleared the arched gateway when a closed carriage swept passed him and pulled up in the yard directly before the inn. The man called Wiggins jumped out, then let down the step and assisted Thérèse into the vehicle. He climbed up after her, replaced the step, and the equipage started out to the lane.

Without another word, Ryde returned to Celia, took her by the arm and propelled her out of the inn.

He called for his curricle, and when it arrived, directed that Celia's gray mare should be tied to the back.

"Get in," he ordered her curtly.

He made no move to assist her, but she obeyed immediately. Their earlier battles had been enjoyable. This one, she feared, might not be. She had said a number of very unwise things, and, knowing the nature of his business, she knew her own motives to be petty in comparison. It had not been fear for Charlie that had prompted her outburst, but a raging, unreasoning emotion she suspected might be jealousy. For once, she was unsure of her ability to come off the better in their encounter.

Ryde swung up into the seat and immediately gave his horses the office. He drove out of the yard in silence and they proceeded down the lane for approximately a mile before he spoke.

"Your behavior has been abominable," he pronounced through clenched teeth.

"You already said that," she replied before she could stop herself.

The horses checked as Ryde's hands clenched at the reins, then continued. Celia almost blurted out a barbed comment about driving when angry, but caught herself just in time. She did not need to add any fuel to his already blazing temper, no matter how great the temptation.

"I will do you the honor of believing Captain Edelston's version of your presence at the inn rather than your own."

Relief swept through her, leaving her weaker than she could have expected. Did it truly matter to her that much what he thought of her? The idea raised unnerving possibilities.

"I—I was wrong to speak so slightingly of Mlle. de Bourgerre," Celia admitted in a small voice, offering her own olive branch.

"For all I know," Ryde said reflectively, "you might be right about her. But not where I am concerned."

That brought a choke of laughter from Celia, which she tried to turn into an unconvincing cough. She steadied herself. "You must admit, to look at her . . ." she began.

He nodded. "There is every chance that that is how she obtained the information our government is so anxious to get hold of," came his damping reply.

She turned to look at him, wondering just what role he played in all of this. A new, and far from pleasant, thought occurred to her. He must never learn the truth about Charlie! A man as deeply involved in the affairs of the war as was Ryde would never protect a deserter. Ryde might deeply regret the course of action, but he would feel he had no other choice than to turn Charlie over to the proper authorities for questioning—and subsequent punishment.

Anger welled within her at this projected despicable behavior. In her eyes, Charlie's life meant more than the security of the nation. Ryde, it seemed, might prove her greatest danger.

"What—what exactly is your involvement in all this?" she asked at last.

"Nothing that need concern you," he replied promptly.

That answer was exasperating in the extreme. "Oh, why can't you trust me?" she exclaimed.

"I might say the same to you," he replied. "You have not been completely honest with me, have you?"

Fear gripped her. Just how much did he know? Had he been told of Jonathon's questions at the Naval Office? Did he suspect?

They drove on in silence for several long minutes. At last, Ryde spoke, his eyes straight ahead. "What exactly is your relationship with Captain Edelston?"

Relief left her weak once again. This lasted for approximately two seconds before anger surged through her, directed at Ryde for the fear he had unknowingly caused her. Suddenly, she wanted to cause him as much pain as he had inflicted on her. Without stopping to consider the effect of her words, she burst into speech.

"We have been betrothed since I was a child. He swore to my brother on his deathbed that he would wed me. We have always loved each other!" It was almost the truth, though misleading in the extreme. He had certainly promised to look after her. It lent a note of veracity to her voice as the fateful words rang out.

Ryde's jaw clenched tightly and he pulled his horses up, stopping them in the middle of the lane. He turned to fix her with piercing regard. His eyes held hers as they demanded the truth, her secrets, an answer from her very soul. Without looking away, he thrust the reins beneath his leg to hold them. His hands came up to her shoulders again, forcing her with gentle firmness to face him fully.

She trembled beneath his touch in sudden nervousness. His response to her declaration had been greater than she expected, and suddenly she feared the consequences. One of his strong hands moved slowly from her shoulder up to her neck, encircling it, with his thumb resting on the rapidly beating pulse at the base of her throat. When he drew her closer, she dared not protest.

His lips descended on hers gently, almost tenderly. She had not expected that, preparing herself instead for a punishing force. To encounter the opposite dismantled her defenses. In another moment, she abandoned her attempt to analyze his tactics and succumbed to the teasing pressure of his mouth.

Who moved closer to whom was a matter of complete indifference to her. She only knew that she was pressed tightly against his broad, muscled chest, his arms firmly about her with a pressure that threatened to leave her bruised. Her own hesitant hand crept up across the lapel of his coat toward his collar, then up to touch the thick dark curls at the back of his head.

She was not imprisoned but cradled in his embrace. He ended the kiss, followed it with another brief, feathery touch, then claimed her lips fully once more. Nothing mattered except that they should remain like this forever, adrift in this sea of wondrous sensations that enveloped her.

"You belong to me." The words were both a command and a caress. "Don't ever forget that. You are mine and mine alone."

He moved his head back and Celia opened her eyes, gazing up into his. Conscious, rational thought didn't stand a chance. His mysterious dark eyes glowed with a burning desire, and she knew he had spoken the truth. If he wanted her, she was his for the taking.

But she couldn't be. With an agonizing wrench, she started to pull back. Charlie stood between them. Charlie, who would one day inherit Ranleigh. She could never marry Ryde while he still expected it to be hers.

"Celia?" His voice was soft, an enveloping touch that made her want to cry out with the pain it caused. Somehow, she had to keep him at a distance . . . .

Ryde stiffened abruptly, cast a searching look up the lane ahead of them, then grabbed up his reins. "Did you hear something?" he demanded.

"Hear?" Celia repeated, shaking her head. "I—no." She had been aware of nothing but Ryde himself and the aching confusion of conflicting desires that assailed her.

He urged his team into a canter. "I thought I heard a shot."

"Thérèse!" Celia exclaimed, at once alert to the imminent danger. She clutched the side of the curricle as it bounded forward along the rutted dirt road.

They rounded a bend and almost crashed into the overturned carriage that lay directly in their path, blocking the lane. Ryde's team reared and lunged, and for a minute his sole concern was bringing them back under control while Celia hung on desperately to keep from being thrown out. Somehow, they avoided a collision, and Ryde brought his team to a halt beside the other vehicle.

The coachman lay face down in the road, and it only took one horrified glance for Celia to realize he was dead. Someone groaned, and she turned to see Wiggins dragging himself out of a ditch.

"My lord!" the man exclaimed, rising to his knees.

He gestured toward the rolling hills across the road, then collapsed forward on his face.

Above them, just reaching the first crest, two horsemen dashed madly away. One of them carried something before him on his saddle, something bulky, like a person wrapped and muffled in a cloak. Someone like Thérèse de Bourgerre.

CHAPTER SEVENTEEN

Lord Ryde swore violently. He grabbed a pistol from beneath the seat, thrust the ribbons into Celia's hands, and jumped down from the curricle. She caught the strips of leather just in time to stop the horses as they bounded forward.

"Can't chase them in this!" he exclaimed. He looked about and caught sight of Celia's forgotten mare tied to the rear of his carriage. Without a word, he strode toward the horse and jerked free the reins. With one toe of his shining Hessians shoved into the tiny stirrup, he swung into the sidesaddle.

The raised ridge on the saddle's right side caught his leg, and there was no stirrup there to help his balance. The only available stirrup had been adjusted for Celia's meager inches, and he found his knee almost level with the horse's withers. He had no choice. He hooked his other knee over the pommel that stuck up before him and dug his heel into the mare's ribs.

The response was instantaneous. Despite her exercise of the morning, the little gray was full of spirit and took off with a leap that nearly unseated Ryde. He clung to his precarious perch with grim determination as the mare crossed the lane in two strides, jumped the ditch, and took off at a gallop up the hill.

Celia stared after him, stunned for a moment by the rapid and terrifying events. She saw Ryde teetering dangerously on the sidesaddle but somehow staying with his mount. It would be two men, armed with pistols and dangerous, against just him! He was at a disadvantage in every way. . . .

A low moan from beside the road claimed her attention. Wiggins . . . she had to do something! Her frightened gaze scanned the front of the curricle. There was a bar that stuck out. . . . She tied the reins in a clumsy knot about it to hold the team's heads, then sprang down to the ground.

Wiggins rolled to his side and gripped his shoulder near the neck. Blood covered his coat and pooled on the ground where he lay. Celia fought down a wave of nausea and knelt beside him, uncertain what to do next. She would have to stop his bleeding, but how?

Wiggins's eyes opened briefly. "My—my neckcloth," he gasped, then collapsed again.

Was he choking? Her inexperienced fingers tore at the clean white cloth, freeing it from about his neck. The material was thick and soft . . . she folded it into a pad. While she struggled with his coat, the man regained consciousness.

"Mam'selle . . . ?" he began, trying to rise.

"Stay where you are," Celia directed. "Ryde has gone after them."

"Armed," he managed to whisper. "Waiting for us round a corner. Never expected an attack . . . in daylight." He took the makeshift pad from her and pressed it against his chest. "Harding?" he asked.

She looked about, and her heart seemed to stop. There was no one but the coachman. . . . "Was—was he driving?" she breathed, horrified. It couldn't be! She *knew* Harding, and people she knew just didn't lie dead in the middle of the road! But she couldn't see the man's face. . . .

"Inside." Wiggins rolled over onto his back, still clutching the wadded cloth just below his collarbone.

Celia ran to the overturned coach and stood on tiptoe, trying to peer inside. "Harding?" she called.

A ragged breath sounded from within, and she heard a groggy response. Relief flooded through her.

A bloody head appeared at the upper window. Celia struggled with the door and managed to pull it open. With her aid, Harding crawled free of the wreckage and staggered over to Wiggins. There, his knees buckled and he dropped to the ground.

The men could take care of each other until she could get help. But Ryde . . . She scanned the area, seeking a weapon. A huge horse pistol lay on the ground near the dead coachman. Trying not to look at him, Celia ran over and picked up the heavy piece. Ryde was out there somewhere alone, two against one, and they held a hostage!

She ran back to the curricle. Her hands shook as she untied the reins. They had gone up that hill . . . . She could see the fleeing horses in the distance with Ryde closing the gap between them! They must know he chased them.

She urged the horses forward, searching for a break in the ditch and hedges that lined the lane. The curricle lurched unevenly. Ryde's pair were unnerved by the commotion and the unfamiliar, inexperienced hands on their mouths. On their own, they broke into a canter, and Celia clutched at the reins to keep them from being pulled from her trembling fingers.

She found the gap she looked for. Abruptly, she pulled the horses up and tugged them to the other side of the road. They spun immediately, and for a split second started back the way they had come. The curricle rocked wildly, trying to turn on one wheel, then steadied as she jerked the horses back on course. Amazingly, they headed for the gap. Then, with a terrifying, shuddering pitch that nearly threw her from the seat, they were across the ditch and galloping madly up the hill on the other side.

The riders were nowhere in sight. Fear for Ryde raced through her and she shook the ribbons, hoping to urge the pair onward but only frightening them more. The horse on the left reared while the other danced wildly. Celia lost a rein, dove frantically to retrieve it, and found herself on her knees, leaning against the front board. Tears filled her eyes, half-blinding her, but somehow they moved forward again without the curricle overturning.

They crested the top of the hill, jostled and rattled as they pelted down the other side, then bounced drunkenly as they crossed a dry, rock-lined creek-bed. Starting up the next hillock, Celia clung desperately to the reins, trying to keep the spirited pair under control.

As she reached the top, an unwelcome sight met

her frightened eyes. Part way up the next slope, two men on foot circled each other warily, then suddenly closed violently. Another man lay sprawled on the ground beside a muffled heap that remained frighteningly still.

Heedless of the danger, Celia set the curricle hurtling down, her only thought to help Ryde. The ground beneath her leveled as they reached the bottom and dashed for the stream that seemed to grow in size the closer they came. The horses balked, then plunged forward. The wheels caught on rocks, the curricle teetered crazily to one side, then fell over, throwing Celia into the swiftly flowing stream.

She landed in water almost two feet deep, enough to cushion her from the rocks. The horses reared and danced, trying to free themselves from the shafts, and Celia instinctively rolled to safety. She rose on her hands and knees, her wide eyes on the combatants above.

A loud, broken-off exclamation reached her as a blow connected neatly with Ryde's chin. Ryde staggered backward, caught his balance, ducked the next jab, and came in with one of his own to his opponent's stomach.

Celia scrambled to her feet. The curricle was firmly wedged, and the horses, apparently sensing their entrapment, had settled somewhat. Caught on the corner of the seat nearest her, barely above water level, was the horse pistol. Celia splashed over, seized it and waded to the other side.

She started up the slope, trying to run, stumbling over the sodden skirt of her habit as it wrapped itself about her legs. She fell, dropped the gun and nearly screamed. Miraculously, it did not go off. Was it even loaded? She had no idea. She had never so much as touched a gun before. Gingerly, she picked it up by the butt and ran as best she could.

The men were now less than a hundred yards away. Twiggy branches from low shrubs reached out, dragging at her dripping skirt as if trying to pull her down, but at last she drew near the struggling figures.

A husky man circled Ryde slowly, his body hunched over, his eyes never leaving his opponent. Suddenly he sprang, his hands closing about Ryde's neck, and both men went down, rolling. They came to a stop with the heavier man on top.

Celia raised the horse pistol with shaking hands. Making a wild guess about the firing mechanism, she aimed the unwieldy gun at the two men. It was too heavy; it waved dangerously—and at which of them was it pointing? Ryde gave a tremendous heave, tossed the other man off, then fell against him with the force of his effort. Now, he was on top—and if Celia pulled the trigger at this moment . . . Dear God, which of them would she hit?

She bit her lip, watching the two men with horrified fascination. The husky man let out a gurgling sound, brought up his arms from beneath Ryde's, and threw him off. Breathing heavily, he dragged himself to his feet, then dove on top of Ryde once again. A half-strangled sound escaped Ryde as the air was driven from his lungs.

If she couldn't use one end of the gun, she would use the other. Celia transferred her grip to the barrel, wielding it with both hands as she waded in to the struggle. Ryde's opponent was on top, so she swung down with all her strength.

But at that moment, Ryde threw off his attacker and rolled with him. The butt of Celia's gun came down on the point of Ryde's shoulder and he let out a yowl of pain. His brief glance at her spoke volumes as she stood there, the pistol dangling from one hand while the other flew to her mouth in dismay.

Ryde ducked a swift punishing jab and tried to regain his footing. This time, his opponent pinned him more easily, for Celia's blow had left Ryde's right arm momentarily useless. Massive hands closed firmly about Ryde's throat, and Celia came at them again, determined to atone for her mistake. She took no chances, aimed carefully and brought the butt down on the back of the man's head with a sickening thud.

He sprawled across Ryde and the deadly grip of his powerful hands slackened. With an effort, Ryde shoved the man off and dragged himself away.

"I—I see your—your aim . . . improves with . . . practice," he managed between gasps for breath. Unsteadily, he pulled himself to his feet and stood swaying.

Celia stared at the recumbent figure with horrified eyes. A wave of nausea swept through her and the gun dropped from her nerveless fingers.

"Is—is he dead?" she asked.

Ryde dropped to one knee at the man's side and felt for the pulse at his neck. "No. But if you hit him half as hard as you did me, it will be a miracle if his skull isn't crushed."

A shudder ran through Celia's slender frame, leaving her shivering. Large tears ran down her cheeks and a sob escaped her. Trevor rose swiftly and gathered her into his arms. He held her there tightly until her shaking at last subsided.

"I—I *hate* females who cry!" she managed.

A deep, rumbling chuckle was his only reply. He transferred his hands to her shoulders, holding her off slightly as his critical gaze moved over her.

"Good God, girl, what have you been doing?" he demanded.

She lowered her eyes to stare in dismay at the condition of her riding habit. The cloth that was not covered by blood and mud had been shredded by her encounters with the rocks and shrubs. She dared not think how her face and hair must look.

"I . . ." She shook her head, unable to think clearly.

A low moan came from behind them. Trevor released Celia abruptly and strode quickly over to the figure wrapped in a black blanket and tied with ropes. Celia ran after him, keeping her eyes firmly away from the man who lay sprawled on the grass. They both went to work on the knots and pulled Thérèse de Bourgerre free from the smothering folds of thick wool.

She took a deep, ragged breath as her head came into the open. Her huge blue eyes flew to Ryde's frowning face and she sighed with relief.

"Ah, *merci, merci, mon cher* Trevor!" She threw herself into his arms. "And Mademoiselle Marcombe!" With a shaking hand, she swept crushed golden ringlets back from her eyes and looked about her. "They are dead, those men?"

"One is. We'll have the other for questioning." Ryde examined one of the lengths of rope, then stood and walked over to the man who still lay unconscious, leaving Celia and Thérèse regarding each other.

"Are you all right?" Celia asked, uncertainly. The young woman looked uncommonly pale, though that was not particularly surprising under the circumstances.

"Oui. They hit me, and I do not remember anything until I found myself tied, and I screamed." She raised a hand to feel tentatively along the side of her head, wincing as her fingers encountered a large lump hidden beneath the disordered curls.

Trevor came back with the gray mare. "You ladies have my profound respect," he declared. "How do you ever stay in such a ridiculous saddle?"

"It is only because you are unaccustomed to it," Celia assured him promptly. "It is supposed to be a much safer way of riding than astride."

"Safer be damned," came Ryde's disgusted reply. "I nearly went off I don't know how many times!"

Celia forced down an hysterical giggle, a reaction to the events of the morning. "You didn't, though. You caught those men, and I must say, I don't know how you did it."

Vraiment? You did it alone?" Therese demanded, turning wide, admiring eyes on Lord Ryde.

"I only arrived just at the very end," Celia told her.

"How did you get here so quickly?" Ryde asked suddenly. "I had your horse."

"I—I drove your curricle." Her voice sounded small, even to herself.

"You what?" He looked about, and for the first time saw the overturned equipage lying in the stream below. Fortunately, words failed him.

"Nom d'un nom d'un nom," Thérèse murmured.

"There are easier ways of securing your team so they will not run off when you leave them." Ryde's tone was surprisingly mild.

"I never pretended I knew how to drive," Celia retorted with what dignity she could muster.

"You didn't have to demonstrate it quite so dramatically!"

"You will not squabble!" Thérèse interrupted them. "You came to my assistance, Mademoiselle Marcombe, and for that I am truly grateful."

"So am I," Ryde said unexpectedly. He took Celia's muddy, scratched hand and raised it to his lips.

Their eyes met, and a wealth of sensation flooded through her, leaving her weak and confused. "Do—do you forgive me for hitting you?" she asked, suddenly nervous, trying to fill the silence that enveloped them.

"I do," he said softly. "I know of few ladies who would have dared to help."

"Or done it more inaccurately," she agreed promptly, on a bantering note, afraid to let the conversation turn serious until she had time to sort out her tangled emotions.

"What of my escort?" Thérèse asked suddenly. "Messieurs Harding and Wiggins?"

Ryde swore softly. "We'd best get back."

"They are both injured, but I think they will be all right," Celia spoke up quickly.

"Did you help them, too?" Ryde asked, a lurking smile lighting his dark eyes.

Celia's cheeks warmed with deepening color, for there was no mistaking the admiration in his voice. Well, she had wanted him to notice her, not be indifferent, but everything was happening too rapidly. She needed time . . . .

Ryde looked from the dead man to the one he had bound, then glanced about for their mounts. He handed the reins of the gray mare to Celia and went in pursuit of the other two horses. He caught them with surprisingly little trouble and led the animals back.

While Thérèse held the reins of all three horses, Ryde lifted the dead man and heaved him up toward his saddle. Celia hesitated, loathe to touch a body, but the sight of Ryde's struggles overcame her squeamishness. With only an inward shaking, she caught at the man's coat from the other side of the horse and pulled him up so that he would not slide off. Ryde secured him with a rope while Celia turned away, feeling unsteady and ill.

Strong hands clasped her shoulders and she jumped, then sank back into the firm support of Ryde's arms.

"Brave girl," he murmured against her hair. "Come on, the next will be easier."

He was right. The man might still be unconscious, but at least he was alive. In only a few more minutes, he, also, was safely tied to his saddle.

They led the animals down the slope to where the wreckage of the curricle awaited them. Ryde walked slowly about it, talking soothingly to his horses the whole time. Not one sarcastic remark escaped his lips, and Celia found herself admiring his reticence.

They could leave the damaged curricle and walk the distance back to the lane, but they did not know what the situation would be when they arrived there. It was possible another vehicle might have come along and that rescue for the injured men was already on its way. It was equally possible that everything was exactly as Celia had left it, and they would need safe transport for Wiggins, at the very least.

"We'd better get it upright," Ryde decided, regarding the vehicle with resignation.

His first act was to unharness the spirited bays who had waited with amazing patience. He led them to a group of trees about fifty yards upstream and tied them to stout branches, then turned his attention to his once-immaculate carriage.

It might be a lightly built racing curricle, but it proved beyond the powers of Trevor alone to right it. After watching his efforts for a few minutes, Celia and Thérèse took the horses with their burdens to join Trevor's bays and returned to his aid. The three of them, together, at last returned the vehicle to an upright position.

Ryde walked about it, slowly, examining what he could see of the lower carriage and axles. One wheel stood at a crooked angle. He subjected this to a thorough scrutiny, but at last pronounced it provisionally able to bear passengers.

It took almost half an hour to maneuver the curricle back onto dry ground and reharness the unwilling horses to the shaft. By this time, the husky man had regained consciousness, but after a few initial struggles he subsided once again. The horses were tied to the back of the carriage and Thérèse was assisted into the vehicle. Ryde turned to Celia, who held the gray mare she had elected to ride.

He looked down at her in a manner she could not

fully decipher but that left her unaccountably breathless. She gazed back, trapped by the dark pools of his eyes, unable to look away. For a long moment, the essence of the man filled her, leaving her awed and wondering at the selfless bravery and honor that was so very fundamental to him.

Here was a man deserving of devotion, one whom she would willingly follow anywhere . . . .

She looked down abruptly, swallowing hard. She could do nothing of the kind as long as Ranleigh stood between them. She was a cheat, for even if his regard had animated toward her, he still believed that Sir Roderick's estate would one day be his. And she could not tell him the truth, not yet—no matter how much she longed to! She had just witnessed his fearless and unquestioning response to duty. What would be his reaction to Charlie's despicable behavior? A deep, painful shame filled her at the thought of her brother's cowardice—a cowardice she must always share. She could never follow what she was sure would be Ryde's unalterable course of action—to turn him in so that the government might learn what they could.

And no matter what story she and Jonathon concocted, no matter what glib alibi Charlie would produce, no matter who else believed them, Ryde would not. He would know—and not forgive. Misery, as cruel and as sharp as a dagger, drove into her heart. Ryde could never esteem the sister of one who had betrayed his country by deserting in her hour of need.

A strong finger touched under her chin and forced

her face back up. Trevor's brow was creased, but with concern, not anger. He lowered his head, gently kissing her tear-filled eyes.

"It's almost over, my little Celia," he said softly. "Be strong just a little longer."

It was almost too much to bear. With difficulty, she restrained herself from stepping into his sheltering arms. That haven was not for her.

"I—I promise I will never drive your curricle again," she said with a determined brightness that sounded false to her ears.

"I will give you lessons," he promised. His shoulders shook slightly with an amusement that began to replace his receding tension. "And teach you to use a gun. If you are going to make a habit of fighting French spies, you might as well be prepared."

"I hope it is not one of your normal entertainments for your house guests." She turned from him and began to fiddle unnecessarily with her saddle.

"It is one I tried very hard not to involve you in," he admitted with a rueful smile. "I dare not think what your grandfather will say to me for returning you to him like this."

Celia glanced down at her ruined habit. "It is a small price to pay for saving Mlle. de Bourgerre. But do you wish to tell Grandfather the truth?"

"Part of it, I shall have to. Until this matter is settled, you will be safer away from here. I cannot doubt he will take you back to Ranleigh on the instant."

Celia nodded, mute, trying hard to be glad. It was for the best, she knew, for if she stayed near him . . . A pain, agonizing in its intensity, filled her. She turned to look fully up into his disturbing eyes and finally admitted the truth to herself. She loved him, desperately. And there was no hope of ever becoming his wife.

CHAPTER EIGHTEEN

It seemed incredible to Celia that barely an hour had passed since she and Ryde first came upon the overturned coach. She led the way back, riding the mare, with Thérèse and Ryde following in the damaged curricle. The two horses, each with its human burden, walked quietly behind the vehicle.

Celia emerged onto the road to find that help was already there in the form of an elderly country squire and his wife, both of whom accepted unquestioningly the quickly concocted story of highwaymen. Sir Peter and Lady Tunbridge were only too delighted to place their commodious landau at the disposal of the injured men. The disheveled appearance of the trio, their arrival from between a gap in the hedges—even the two men tied to the backs of their horses—caused no more than a shriek from Lady Tunbridge and a rapid blink from her stolid spouse. Their only comment was a sincere wish to read an account of the whole in their paper on the morrow.

To Mlle. de Bourgerre's consternation, Ryde insisted that she accompany Harding and Wiggins back to the inn and remain there until he could arrange for a new guard for her. The lady protested, tears in her eyes, but Ryde turned a deaf ear on her pleas to return to her home. The house on Marine Parade, he insisted, was not likely to concern her enemies when it was known she was not there. Celia, trying very hard to appear not to listen, wondered why she would not then be safe there—and why her house concerned her so. Suddenly unbearably weary, she found herself unequal to the task of puzzling this out.

With the injured men carefully lifted into the landau, the procession started back toward the inn. The commotion their arrival caused in the yard brought the landlord running. Never before had he been called upon to deal with such a situation, for highwaymen, he swore, were unheard of in such a quiet location. The arrival on the scene of the gentlemen from London, however, provided the explanation as far as the innkeeper was concerned. Here, he avowed, were likely targets for any cutpurse or footpad, just asking for trouble as they were with all their fobs and fine rings.

One of these gentlemen, whom Ryde referred to as Pembroke, took instant charge. Within minutes, the establishment's two ostlers were commandeered and sent running for horses, one to seek a doctor, the other to carry a sealed message to London. Harding and Wiggins were made as comfortable as possible in one of the rooms upstairs, and the man Celia had hit on the head was placed in a cellar with Pembroke's own valet standing guard over him with a pistol.

While all of this took place, Thérèse and Celia were escorted upstairs to a room occupied by one of the gentlemen, who assured Mlle. de Bourgerre that he was quite honored to place this apartment at her disposal. His man, he added, would remove his trappings at the earliest opportunity. A chambermaid appeared bearing a pitcher of hot water, and the two ladies set about the almost impossible task of making themselves more presentable.

By the time Celia descended the stairs, her habit had received a stiff brushing. Stains and rents might remain, but she had the satisfaction of knowing that the caked-on mud no longer lingered. Her dusky curls were once again hidden demurely beneath her beaver, and her hands and face were clean of all except scratches.

Ryde, who was deep in conversation with two of the dignitaries, broke off at sight of her. As soon as he could, he took leave of his companions and joined Celia to escort her to the waiting curricle.

Once again, he tied the reins of the gray mare to the back of the now dilapidated vehicle. The strain and adventures of the morning showed in the deep lines carved in his face, but he smiled as he turned to hand Celia up to the seat. She went without a word, too exhausted to do more than climb up and sink back gratefully against the mud-streaked cushions.

The relatively short journey to Hastings was accomplished in complete silence. Ryde kept the horses to a walk, for he did not want to risk breaking the bent wheel. Celia closed her eyes, wondering how long it would be before she had the strength to open them again. The gentle, uneven rocking of the carriage soothed her, and a pleasant lassitude crept through her aching muscles.

She stirred as the curricle turned, and she heard

the familiar crunch of gravel as they passed through the gate to the estate and proceeded up the long drive. Instead of letting her out before the stately old house, Ryde turned onto the side path that led to the stableyard.

"My servants are to be trusted completely." He spoke for the first time since leaving the inn.

"You seem to inspire loyalty," Celia replied softly, then hoped he had not heard her.

His dark eyes rested on her for a moment before returning to his horses. "You have had a very trying morning. Go up to your room and lie down for awhile. I will make all the explanations necessary. Do not worry. No one will question you."

She gave him a feeble smile of gratitude. If ever she got into a scrape, she would want him on her side, helping her out. But she *was* in trouble, and could not seek his comforting assistance. Tears of exhaustion rose to her eyes and she quickly averted her face.

In another moment, she froze. Sir Roderick Marcombe stood in the center of the cobbled yard with not only his own groom but both of Ryde's before him. The three grooms looked considerably chastened, and every line of the elderly man's bearing bespoke raging temper. At the sound of the curricle's approach, he spun about.

He stared hard for a moment at the two occupants of the vehicle, then strode forward as it came to a stop. "Good gad, what happened to you?" he demanded. "Did you overturn? Celia, are you all right?"

She did not trust herself to answer. If she spoke, she would burst into sobs, and that she could not bear. It was with relief that she heard Ryde's calm, steady voice.

"She is unharmed, but will be better for some quiet. Something happened, as you can guess. If you will come with me to the bookroom, I will tell you about it." He swung down, turned a bland face to his appalled grooms, and came around to assist Celia. His fingers closed over hers tightly, and she looked up to meet a reassuring smile in the depths of his eyes.

Sir Roderick hesitated, relief at Celia's safety taking the form of a resurgence of his anger. "Where the devil did you get off to this morning?" he demanded. "These fools say you rode out right after breakfast, with no one to accompany you!"

"I—I am sorry if you were alarmed, Grandfather. I—I met up with Ryde, and—but he will explain." She gave them both a shaky smile, then stood on tiptoe to plant a soft kiss on her grandfather's wrinkled cheek. Her legs seemed strangely unwilling to support her as she walked toward the house.

"What have you been doing?" she heard Sir Roderick demand. "Never known you to overturn a curricle. Cow-handed thing for you to be doing, especially with my Celia with you."

"As a matter of fact, I didn't," came Ryde's amused answer. "It was Celia. She may be able to ride anything with four feet, but no one ever taught her to drive!"

Celia felt the burbling of an hysterical giggle rising within her and almost ran for the door. She darted through it, came face to face with Mrs. Gosson who stared at her in open-mouthed horror, and bolted up the stairs to the safety of her own chamber. Closing the door firmly behind her, she sank down onto the bed. When her trembling subsided somewhat, she unfastened her habit and allowed it to drop on the floor.

She shivered. She felt chilled all over . . . . She badly needed a bath—even her chemise was stained and dirty from her fall in the stream. Shakily, she crossed to the door and tugged at the bell pull.

It was the dark-haired girl, Jane, who eventually answered her call. She bore a bundle of sticks and small logs, and with only one wide-eyed glance at Celia, scurried over to the hearth and began laying a fire.

"If you please, miss, Gosson will bring you a bath." The girl hesitated, then crossed to the wardrobe and opened it, peering uncertainly inside.

Celia joined her and drew out a dressing gown. Jane assisted her into this, then hurried to answer the firm rap on the door. A deep voice rumbled softly, and Jane stepped back to clear the way for Gosson and Wrenn who carried a large, heavy tub. After setting this down before the fire, they retreated from the room with Jane scurrying in their wake.

Seddons arrived only minutes later, pushing a teacart on which had been placed several large pitchers filled with hot water. These she poured into the waiting tub. Next, she drew a tiny bottle from the capacious pocket of her apron. The contents of this she emptied into the steaming water, and the delicious fragrance of violets filled the air. While Celia discarded the rest of her disheveled clothing, Seddons arranged a screen to reflect the fire's heat back to the bath.

Celia sank down into the steaming tub, wincing as

the hot water stung her numerous scratches. Every muscle ached! She shifted her position slightly before leaning back to relax.

By now, Ryde must have told her grandfather the whole. That meant it would be only a matter of hours before they would all depart. The thought had to please her. She could never allow herself to give in to the abject misery that threatened to possess her. Ryde was a man worthy of devotion and respect—and if she remained near him, her heart would betray her and he would surely see the love she could never acknowledge. For now, it was not only the possession of Ranleigh, but Charlie as well, that stood irrevocably between them.

She emerged from the bath to wrap herself in soft warm towels, then don fresh undergarments and chemise. Jane arrived bearing a belated luncheon tray, and Celia was surprised to discover how very hungry she was. She finished the meal, then fought off an almost overwhelming desire to go to sleep. She was not such a poor creature as that! Hers had been a relatively minor role in the drama of the morning. It only went to prove she was not in the least a suitable bride for a man of Ryde's stamp, and this opinion depressed her even more.

To her surprise, no urgent, angry message came from Sir Roderick. Perhaps that meant their departure would be postponed until the morrow, and she could have one last evening with Ryde. Once they left, she knew she could never come back. To do so would be to seal her fate, for it would be tantamount to accepting their marriage. And that was the one thing she wanted but could never have.

When she finally descended the stairs, she found no one in either the Gold Saloon or the Drawing Room. She ventured farther and discovered Elizabeth sitting in the garden, her copy of *Marmion* open in her lap and the cat Andrew at her side. The bright, eager eyes her companion turned on her proved that she already knew at least part of the tale, and it was to Elizabeth's credit that she did not immediately bombard her with questions.

"My dear Celia, what a terrible time you must have had!" she exclaimed. *"A blazoned shield, in battle won, Ne'er guarded heart so bold."*

Celia managed a feeble smile. "I did not exactly have a shield, and my heart was far from bold. I was shaking so disgracefully I could hardly move."

"Lord Ryde said he might not have succeeded had you not come to his aid."

"Then he exaggerates, Celia replied, and tried to hide her pleasure at these words. "I hardly did a thing. It was he who was brave." Her smile slipped awry. *"Far may we search before we find A heart so manly and so kind,"* she murmured, borrowing Elizabeth's habit of quoting Scott. She sat down abruptly, scooping up the hefty cat and cradling him for comfort.

Elizabeth tilted her head slightly, regarding Celia through narrowed eyes. "He—he is a remarkable man. I gather this is not the first time he has been involved in such danger, that it is all a part of that shooting when—when Captain Edelston saved my life."

Celia closed her eyes, fighting off the urge to tell Elizabeth the truth. At least one of them should be happy! Since she could not marry the man she loved, she would see to it that Elizabeth did! But not yet. She must still maintain the fiction of her engagement to Jonathon, for she might still need to fall back upon it.

"What—what has my grandfather decided?" she asked, trying to divert Elizabeth.

"About what?" her companion asked blankly.

Had he not announced his intentions to depart, then? Curious, Celia took her leave of Elizabeth and went in search of Sir Roderick.

She discovered him at last, once more closeted in the bookroom with Ryde. Uncertain whether or not to interrupt them, she peeped cautiously in at the door and was surprised to see their relaxed attitude. Adolphus, sprawled at Ryde's feet, thumped his tail by way of greeting but did not bother to rise.

Trevor looked up. He had apparently found time to change as well. He now appeared as disconcertingly arresting as ever, precise to a pin and with an air of nonchalant elegance. He might have spent the morning at his club in London instead of haring over the hillsides and engaging in bouts of fisticuffs with French agents. And now, he sat at his ease, smiling a welcome, wrenching her heart.

"Come in, Celia. Have you rested?" he asked.

She nodded, for a moment not trusting herself to speak. "Yes. I—I feel much more the thing, now."

Sir Roderick turned his frowning gaze on her. "You are not to venture off the estate again without an escort," he ordered.

She lowered her head. "No, Grandfather. I shall pledge to behave myself exactly as you would wish."

"At least for the rest of the day," Ryde murmured.

That forced a reluctant smile from her, but she found it easy to suppress.

"Minx," her grandfather muttered, but he no longer seemed overly upset. "Now, Ryde tells me that the Prince of Wales has just arrived at the Pavilion, and that we shall be invited to an afternoon gathering there. Will you like that?"

"Yes, of all things! But . . . " She turned uncertain eyes to Lord Ryde.

"It seems I am not to be deprived of your company yet, after all."

Not going? She managed a shaky smile for his benefit, but felt his eyes boring into her. How could she continue to see him, day after day, and not betray her wayward love? And why did she have to succumb to the one man who could see through any story she created to protect Charlie—the one man who would undoubtedly put duty before marriage ties, and turn in the brother of his affianced wife? If he loved her—if only he loved her!—she might convince him to let Charlie go free. But how could such a man as Ryde ever esteem or honor the sister of a deserter?

"We—we are to stay?" she asked him at last, floundering to fill the gap.

He nodded, his brow still furrowed. "As long as Mlle. de Bourgerre is still believed to be at her house in the Marine Parade, there should be no danger here. If you leave suddenly, it will only cast suspicion on this house. As you see, I use you both abominably. But it is your grandfather's suggestion."

Celia swallowed. "He is quite right. Your plans will be much safer if nothing changes here. We shall stay, and behave as normal."

Ryde nodded, still not completely pleased. "I shall try to keep you out of harm's way in the future." He stood. "You must excuse me now. I have some unfinished business in Brighton."

"You go to Mlle. de Bourgerre's house?" Celia asked quickly.

"That, and purely mundane estate matters. There is not a plow fit to use in the barns." He hesitated a moment. "There is a chance I may not be able to return until quite late tonight." With that, he sketched her a quick bow and left the room.

His words proved true. By the time they sat down to dinner that evening, he had not yet come back. Celia sat up quite late in the Drawing Room, trying hard to concentrate on the piece by Mozart but finding it increasingly difficult to keep her eyes open. She gave up at last, wondering if Ryde intended to wait until he knew the household would be asleep before smuggling Thérèse back in.

She must have been far more tired than she was willing to admit, for it was late the following morning when a rustling about her chamber finally penetrated her sleep-fogged mind. Her eyes opened as the heavy curtains were drawn back from about the bed. Seddons stood before her, holding a tray of chocolate and rolls. She set it down on the small bedside table.

Several minutes passed before Celia felt awake enough to sit up and take a sip from the cup. "What time is it?" she asked.

"Just after ten o'clock, miss." Seddons opened the cupboard and drew out the morning gown of pale yellow jaconet.

"Ten? You should have called me sooner!"

"My orders were to let you sleep, miss, and sleep is what you needed. Now, your grandfather and his lordship have just come in from riding. If you hurry a bit, you may join them in the breakfast parlor."

Celia did hurry. She wanted to see Ryde, to know that all had gone well, that Thérèse was safe. She entered the parlor less than thirty minutes later to find the two gentlemen just finishing what appeared to have been a substantial meal. Elizabeth, always an early riser, was nowhere to be seen.

"Did all go well?" she asked by way of greeting.

Ryde nodded. "Quite satisfactory. Most of the farm equipment was delivered first thing this morning, and we shall start work at once."

His eyes held hers, a lurking smile in their depths that answered the more important questions. Thérèse must be at this moment safe in one of the upstairs rooms. It hurt a bit that he did not speak openly of the matter, but she knew it was for the best. She crossed to the buffet and took a small serving of eggs and another roll.

"I think our best chance lies in the grains," Ryde commented.

Celia turned to stare at him, then realized this last remark had been a continuation of an interrupted discussion with her grandfather.

"You'll do as you like," Sir Roderick informed him testily.

"I usually do," Ryde admitted with a broad smile that caused the old man to emit a short bark of laughter. "But I have spoken to the tenants and the managers of the neighboring estates, and they almost all agree we may be able to pull this off."

"You're being damnably stubborn about it," Sir Roderick informed him. "Why not just take the money and have done with all this risk?"

Ryde cast a quick, sideways glance at Celia, who sat looking from one man to the other. He shook his head. "You know my feelings about that, sir."

Sir Roderick glared at his godson. "I do! And your pride will be the ruin of you."

Celia took a tentative bite of the eggs, found they were good, and took another. That was all very well and good, but *she* did not know his feelings about whatever "that" was. Presumably it was the money her grandfather offered.

Her head came up slowly and she stared at Ryde, her fork poised in midair. Had he—*could he*—actually have refused her grandfather's offer of money? Was he really trying to bring the estate about on his own? He had told her that once, but she had not believed him. But now . . .

Oh, how disgustingly typical of him to behave so nobly! The men continued to discuss the estate and Celia listened in growing dismay. It would be difficult to save it, she gathered—nearly impossible. But Ryde, as Sir Roderick had once told her, was a very capable man. If anyone could pull Hastings together single-handedly, it would be he. It took a man, in every sense of the word, to refuse help for a scruple and face up to such a herculean task.

Why must everything he did cause her to love him more and more? Why could she not hate him again? If only she could be at his side every weary, troublesome step of the way! A new thought struck her, and for one glorious moment her heart sang. Ranleigh did not matter to him! He would not care if she came to him penniless . . . if he loved her.

Was that what caused him to reject the money! A desire to win her respect? No, it was more likely the need—for the sake of his own pride—to save himself rather than sell himself. He was not one to touch a penny of his wife's money.

And Ranleigh was not the only thing that stood between them. She could never escape the looming menace of Charlie's discovery and denouncement. No, she could never marry Ryde, never risk exposing him to the scandal that hung over the Marcombe name like the Sword of Damocles.

Lord Ryde took his leave of them to return to the fields, and Sir Roderick followed him out shortly thereafter. Celia sat for some time sipping her tea. If Ryde were indeed beginning to like the idea of marriage . . . Well, she would have to make him change his mind again. This decision hurt terribly, but there was no other choice.

Restless, she went upstairs. As she started down the hall toward her room, the gentle shutting of a door down a side corridor caused her to pause. Mlle. de Bourgerre must be moving about, hopelessly bored with being confined to a single room.

On impulse, Celia turned down the passage. The sound had come from some distance . . . . She hesitated at one of the doors, listening for any indication of someone within. Silence greeted her, so she tried the next door.

Here, the results were not quite what she had hoped for. The soft, musical lilt of Thérèse's voice reached her, but just as she was about to knock, a deeper, masculine voice answered. So, Ryde had not gone directly to the fields but had stopped to check on his secret guest. Celia bit her lip, turning away. Mlle. de Bourgerre was quite beautiful, a gifted singer, incredibly brave . . . and Ryde shared in her dangerous life. How eminently well-matched they were.

Celia retraced her steps slowly. A marriage between them would not be out of the question. The de Bourgerres were an ancient and noble French family, though now living in exile in Italy. Her virtue might have been compromised in the service of England, but a man of honor might be persuaded to overlook this for the sake of the lady's courage. Yes, it would be quite ideal if Ryde would offer her marriage.

Depressed, Celia went in search of Elizabeth, and found her kneeling on the floor of her room. Before her lay the most becoming of her few gowns, and in her hands she held paper, pins and shears. The completed pattern for the skirt lay on the bed, and she concentrated now on the bodice and sleeves.

Andrew crouched at her side, the tip of his ridiculous black and white tail twitching as he watched her intently. Elizabeth smoothed out a sheet of paper on her dress and the cat pounced on top of it, batting at the edges. Celia swooped down on the animal and scooped him up before he could do any real damage.

"Thank you," Elizabeth sighed as she replaced the sheet that had gone flying with the cat's assistance.

"Why have you not put him out?" Celia asked as she rubbed Andrew under the chin.

"I tried." Elizabeth gave her a crooked smile. "But he would scratch at the door so, and his meows sounded so piteous . . . ."

"And softhearted creature that you are, you let him bamboozle you," Celia finished. She sank to the floor beside Elizabeth and, with the cat confined on her lap within the circle of her arm, held the shoulder of the gown. Elizabeth made a delicate adjustment to the position of the paper and then, with the shears, trimmed it to fit. At last, the young woman sat back.

"That ought to do it. Thank you, my dear."

"You should have allowed the seamstress to make this up for you." Celia reached up to the chair where the soft, cocoa brown material lay. "It is high time you wore something other than black."

"Your chaperone much be beyond reproach," Elizabeth reminded her. "I am not really old enough to protect either of us from unseemly gossip."

"I must prefer having you as just a companion and friend," Celia sighed. "Then you could wear what you like, and not try to make yourself look an old crone, which you are not! But I suppose Grandfather would feel obliged to replace you with some fun-hating old harridan, and that I could not put up with—besides missing you dreadfully."

"Well, I believe the brown will be acceptable, as long as I only wear it when we are alone. It is such a pretty color."

Celia curled her legs under her, then leaned back on one hand. Andrew draped himself over her knees and regarded the pile of papers through now sleepy eyes. Nine-and-twenty was not that old! It was certainly too young for Elizabeth to consider herself an—an ape-leader, hopelessly on the shelf! Jonathon had not thought this of her, and he had only seen her in her strict chaperone guise. Elizabeth might not dare hope for it yet, but as soon as Celia could arrange it, she would marry Jonathon. And then, together, they would throw out every dark, unbecoming gown she possessed and replace them with the soft colors that would set off her fair complexion.

Elizabeth turned back from the closet where she hung the dress she had copied and turned her attention to the material. Celia, to Andrew's annoyance, obligingly took one end of the fabric and helped to shake it out. They laid it carefully on the floor and smoothed out the wrinkles.

"I met Jonathon while I was out riding yesterday, before all the trouble started," Celia said casually, though she watched her companion's face closely. She was rewarded by the sight of soft color suffusing the pale cheeks. The gray eyes remained lowered, concentrating on the smooth placement of the pattern.

"Did you?" Elizabeth asked carefully. "I trust he was well?"

"And as kind as always. He asked after you." Celia forced back a smile as the other lady's color deepened.

"He probably was not pleased to see you riding alone," Elizabeth said softly, her voice heavy with constraint.

Celia bit her lip. She had not meant to cause her beloved Elizabeth pain. She would tell her, she vowed, as soon as she could. Captain Edelston—although not a notoriously fast mover and not usually inclined toward the petticoat line—had shown signs of awakening interest.

By the time the gong sounded to dress for dinner, Elizabeth's new dress had been cut out. Celia laid aside the pieces of the skirt that she had pinned for seaming and rose from the floor.

"Will you not wear your gray gown and the blue shawl this evening?" she begged her companion. "I—I don't want you to look so very severe." It sounded a paltry excuse in her own ears, but the woman needed to be coaxed out of her unattractive shell and learn that she still possessed the power to blossom.

Reluctantly, Elizabeth agreed and Celia went to her own room feeling that at least she had done something for someone that day. And now for Lord Ryde. She forced down a pang that clawed at her heart. She must give Ryde a disgust of her, cause him to draw back from the marriage agreement, leave him free to pursue a woman more worthy than herself. It would not be easy, for his deep sense of honor would hold him to his course, no matter how distasteful it might be for him. A gentleman did not draw back from an engagement. His pride, she was sure, would be the key.

And her own pride. What price that? She felt it stir, sensed her reluctance to follow this course—and also the necessity. For ironically, it was her pride that demanded she free Ryde and uphold the honor of the Marcombes by not dragging him down with her family.

Dressed in the simple gown made from the sea green gauze purchased at Layton and Shear's, Celia left her room some time before the dinner gong sounded. She decided to stop by Mlle. de Bourgerre's room for just a moment. Hopefully, some of that woman's courage would rub off.

She made her way through the corridors and stopped at Thérèse's door. Again, there was the sound of voices—the lady's light tones, and the deeper, masculine ones answering in a low rumble. Celia turned and headed for the stairs. So Ryde was with her once again. Perhaps it would not be as hard as she feared to make him withdraw his offer. This thought had to be a relief to her, but her spirits did not rise.

She entered the Gold Saloon and stopped short. Lord Ryde stood by the mantelpiece, staring down into the flickering blaze. Celia crossed to the sofa, barely reaching it before her knees buckled beneath her. If Ryde were here, who was the gentleman with Thérèse? Should she ask? Or would this just be another subject he would refuse to discuss?

After a minute, Ryde looked up and seemed surprised to see her. "I didn't hear you come in," he commented. He crossed over and took the chair opposite her. "Did you spend a pleasant day?"

Her reply was interrupted by the arrival of Elizabeth, and she had the pleasure of seeing how well her chaperone looked in the softer, gentler colors. Sir Roderick arrived next, followed almost immediately by Gosson, who announced that dinner was served.

Ryde rose and offered Celia his arm. "I am sorry I was occupied most of the day. Were you able to keep busy?"

"Yes, thank you," she responded demurely. Her fingers rested lightly on the smooth sleeve of his coat and she kept her eyes lowered. He was making it so difficult to fight him, but she had to, for his own good!

"Now, why do I suspect you are up to something?" he murmured so that only she could hear.

She forced a laugh that broke on a sob, but he did

not seem to notice. His deep, rich chuckle sounded, and his other hand reached out to cover hers briefly.

"Confess, minx. What are you plotting?" he demanded softly.

"What—what a shocking thing to accuse me of! What makes you think I am up to something?"

"You are too quiet," he replied promptly, "too—too well behaved."

"What a monster you make me out to be!" She tried to give him a saucy smile that failed miserably. "I assure you, I am not one to tie my garter in public! My occasional indiscretions are quite—quite unintentional."

They had entered the dining room by this time, and they fell silent as he helped her to her seat. Sir Roderick and Elizabeth caught them up, and for a time their conversation could be abandoned. Several times, though, Celia sensed Ryde's frowning gaze resting on her while they dined. Once, she glanced up, met his eyes, and managed a quick, tremulous smile before turning her attention back to the others.

The meal ended at last and Celia and Elizabeth made their way to the Drawing Room where they settled to their usual pastimes. While Celia concentrated on the Mozart piece that was beginning to sound almost perfect to her, Elizabeth set neat stitches into the hem of a handkerchief.

The gentlemen joined them sooner than she expected. As Sir Roderick took a seat near the hearth, Ryde rang for Gosson. When the man arrived, Ryde sent him for the chessboard.

Celia paused in her playing. "Do you not usually play in your bookroom?" she asked, surprised.

"I find musical accompaniment stimulates the mind. I stand in need of all the help I can get when I play your grandfather," Ryde explained. His tone was casual, as if to deny the intention of any compliment to her skill on the pianoforte. She also sensed no trace of his sharing a joke with her.

Puzzled, she looked up at him to again find his eyes resting on her. What was he about? He turned away, took the chair opposite Sir Roderick, then looked over at Elizabeth.

"Have you enough light?" he asked. "I can have Gosson bring you another branch of candles, if you wish." Elizabeth shyly disclaimed any such need, and thanked him for his kindness.

The chess set arrived and was placed on a table between the two men. Once the pieces were in position and the game begun, neither of the players had a thought to spare for anything else. Celia played on at the pianoforte, trying different compositions, wondering if either Ryde or her grandfather were aware of anything other than the moves of their chess pieces.

She peeked over at them under the cover of changing the music on the stand. Ryde sat in profile to her, bending forward to study the board. One strong, tanned hand stretched out, hesitated, then selected a pawn and moved it forward.

That was what she felt like, she realized, annoyed. She was just a pawn, in the midst of a dangerous game. This tangled web might not be initially of her weaving, but it was time she withdrew from the ranks of the pawns and took control.

Tomorrow, she vowed, she would throw down a gauntlet that Lord Ryde could not ignore and that would not please him in the least. She struggled with her unhappiness and tried to think purely noble thoughts, but found it depressingly difficult. She gave up and instead struck the opening chords of a familiar piece by Bach, trying to lose herself in the complexity of the notes.

CHAPTER NINETEEN

The next day provided little opportunity for Celia to put her plan into action. Lord Ryde remained preoccupied with the plowing and planting, Sir Roderick accompanied him when he rode out, and Celia found herself alone much of the time—prey to the depression that seeped through her.

In desperation, she spent the morning with Elizabeth, working on the new brown dress, carefully stitching a hem that would not be too noticeable if her stitches were messy. This occupation kept her hands busy but left her mind free to wander down the murky paths of hopeless frustration.

She knotted her thread, then regarded its meandering passage through the fabric with dissatisfaction. "They won't be seen here, will they?" she asked.

Elizabeth looked up and smiled. "Not in the least." She took the skirt from Celia and examined the hem. "Well, it is not likely to come down, is it?"

Celia's apologetic reply was cut off by a gentle rap on the door, followed almost immediately by the entrance of Gosson.

"If you please, miss, Captain Edelston has called. He is awaiting you in the Gold Saloon."

"Thank you, Gosson." Celia stood and shook out her narrow skirts. "Elizabeth?" She looked at her companion and surprised a soft flush on the woman's cheeks. Celia turned away at once and made a great show of putting away the sewing things, giving Elizabeth a chance to recover her countenance. She could only hope, for the sake of her beloved companion, that Jonathon was similarly afflicted.

Captain Edelston stood as they entered the room, then came forward with his hand extended. Elizabeth, her eyes lowered, murmured a greeting before withdrawing discreetly to a chair out of hearing. She sat staring out the window, her delicate color heightened.

"Is Miss Westerly well?" Jonathon asked softly as he drew up a chair beside Celia.

"I fear our deception troubles her." Celia folded her hands demurely in her lap.

"She knows the truth, then?" Jonathon asked quickly. "And it does not please her?"

"She does not know the truth," Celia replied firmly. "And that is what does not please her."

Jonathon's eyes opened wide, an arrested expression in their clear, innocent blue depths. He turned the full force of his gaze on Elizabeth.

"Jonny," Celia sighed, exasperated. "Do not stare so! You will put her to the blush!"

"Should we not tell her?" He sounded uncertain.

"Not yet. Not until we hear from Charlie. I—I may

still have need of you."

Jonathon shook his head, melancholy replacing the eagerness of a moment before. "Don't know what to do next, Cill. Asking questions didn't get us anywhere. And it's been well over a year since I've had a letter from him. How do we go about looking on our own?"

Celia fought down a most unusual but almost irresistible urge to burst into tears. Charlie might be dead, for all they knew! And if he were, would they ever hear of it? Had he succeeded in losing his identity so effectively that no one would ever find a trace of him? Afraid to love and unable to marry . . . Would she be forced to wait indefinitely for word that might never come? There was not a single thing she could do except wait—and hope that Charlie, if he were alive, would eventually send another letter, one that would give them some clue as to where to resume their search.

There seemed little more to say that morning. Jonathon took his leave shortly, and Celia, escaping Elizabeth's worried frown, slipped out into the garden to think. Beaten and dispirited, that was what she was—a weak, feckless, ineffectual female! But not even insults could rally her sagging morale. She longed to run to Ryde, lay her troubles at his feet, tell him about Charlie, turn it all over to his capable hands. But she could not. She sank onto a bench, staring blindly at the statue in the fountain before her. *Oh, what a tangled web we weave . . .*

Instead of seeking Ryde's aid, she had to steel herself for a fight with him, a fight she doubted her ability to carry off with the necessary effectiveness.

And the sooner she got on with it, the better. Every day she remained in his home made the thought of leaving that much harder to bear. She gave herself a mental shake. Enough of this nonsense! The very next time she saw him, she would have to make him angry.

The scraping of boots on the gravel reached her, and within a moment, the barely solidifying mortar of her resolve had crumbled. Lord Ryde rounded the corner of the shrubs with Adolphus trotting at his heels. Perversely, he appeared more attractive to her than ever. The dirt that streaked his coat and buckskins bore silent testimony to his morning labors in the fields, enhancing his aura of sheer masculine power. A repressed air of energy and excitement hung about him, revealed in the brilliance of his dark, compelling eyes.

But his eyes clouded as they rested on her and his brow snapped down. "Good God, girl, what has happened?" he demanded.

"Not a thing! You—you find me unwell, that is all." She forced a combative note into her voice, hoping to goad him into leading the argument. Dolph sat by her feet and laid his head in her lap, his large, soulful eyes looking up at her. Absently, and much to his delight, she pulled gently on his ears.

"A most inconvenient moment for me to disturb you," Ryde said pleasantly, but he subjected her face to a minute scrutiny.

She colored slightly beneath this gaze and a flicker of spirit rekindled within her. "As you say," she agreed.

A sparkle, quickly suppressed, gleamed in his eyes. "But then, we are agreed that I have very little regard for your convenience, are we not?" he asked, quite affably.

A quick choke of outraged laughter escaped her. "We most assuredly are!" she snapped at him. "Of all the abominable, odious . . ."

He held up a hand, stopping her. "If you intend to enumerate my other faults, would you mind if I sit down first? I have a distinct feeling this is going to take some time."

"Please do." She moved over on the bench to make room for him, all too aware that his closeness played havoc with her composure. "But I fear we have not the time for so extensive a list unless you have nothing else to do for the remainder of the day."

The glint in his eyes returned, awarding her the point, and this time the smile remained. "I know you shall be desolated to hear I can only remain a few minutes."

"Quite inconsolable," she agreed, and told herself she could not allow this to be the truth. Dolph, momentarily satisfied, wandered off to give the shrubbery a thorough sniff and she felt suddenly bereft of support.

"I have not spent much time with you," he said bluntly. "I fear I have been a terrible host."

"Oh, there is no need to change your ways. I am quite accustomed to it, I assure you," she responded as brightly as she could.

Something of her distress must have penetrated his joking mood for his eyes narrowed slightly. *"And by each courteous word and deed To cheer her strove in vain,"* he quoted softly from *Marmion*. "Have I offended you?" he added abruptly.

She averted her face. "We have been at daggers

drawn since we met, my lord. Why should you expect it to be different now?"

"I had thought we were well on our way to an understanding." A curious note crept into his voice, and Celia peeked sideways at him to catch him watching her with an intensity that was unsettling. He drew a deep breath, then let it out slowly. "You are not one to share your secrets, are you?" he said.

She looked up, startled, for he might have been reading her mind. "What—what do you mean, my lord?"

"Only that you surprise me," came the enigmatic reply. All trace of amusement left him, and he continued to study her every feature. "I could wish that you would trust me," he said at last.

"You do not exactly trust me, either." She stood, staring down at him with something akin to fear, anxious to escape from him. The conversation had not gone the way she expected and she found herself more confused than ever. What did he mean? What did he guess? Did he suspect anything about Charlie? Just how clumsy had Jonathon been that day he visited the Naval Office? Had that man Harding, or any of Ryde's other acquaintances in government circles, spoken the dreaded words that Charlie might be alive—a deserter, hiding somewhere on the Continent?

With a murmured excuse, Celia took her leave of him. Her own room was the one sure refuge, so she hurried there, wanting only to be alone. Again, as she made her way down the corridors, she heard the soft opening and shutting of doors in the distance, a murmur of voices that indicated the presence of at least two people—unseen and, for the most part, unknown. How could he speak of trust, when there was so much she did not know or understand about him and the life he pursued?

When Elizabeth knocked on her door some time later, Celia lay on her bed with the curtains drawn, her copy of *Marmion* open but unread beside her. It took little persuasion on Elizabeth's part to convince her to take dinner in her chamber that evening. It proved more difficult for Celia to convince Elizabeth that she would prefer to be alone, but at last she persuaded her companion to dine downstairs with the gentlemen and then remain in the Drawing Room to pour tea.

Celia turned back to her book as the door closed behind Elizabeth. *All lonely sat and wept the weary hour.* The line seemed to spring up at her. How appropriate and how depressing, she reflected with a sigh.

Shortly after the dinner gong sounded, Seddons arrived bearing a dinner tray which, to Celia's dismay, contained a bowl of Mrs. Gosson's special herbal broth. Declining her maid's offers of burnt feathers, pastilles and hot bricks, she applied herself obediently to the steaming bowl, found it excellent, and finished it under her maid's approving eye.

With renewed requests that she not be disturbed, Celia sent Seddons off to her own meal, then crossed to the window to stare out across the shadowed gardens into the darkening sky. Now, in the gathering dusk, the details of neglect were smoothed over so that only impressions and silhouettes remained—a mirrored promise of the beauty that loving care would one day create. Now that she knew she could not remain—that the hand that would work the transformation would not be hers—Hastings appeared more beautiful and welcoming to her than ever. As did its master.

There lay her biggest problem. She had to anger Lord Ryde. She considered a moment, then decided that the surest way to invoke his enmity would be to strike at his pride. He would never take to wife a vixenish little hoyden who defied and disgraced him at every turn. So that was what she must do.

Only the thought of Charlie's dishonor kept her firm in her resolve. She passed a sleepless night, prey to her unhappiness, and rose in the morning looking every bit as ill as she had pretended to be. Seddons, carrying in her mistress's morning cup of chocolate, tried to persuade her to return to bed and allow a doctor to be summoned. Celia remained adamant, though, and shortly thereafter descended the stairs to the breakfast parlor.

Ryde, to her dismay, was the only person in the room. He looked up as she entered and his heavy brow lowered in concern.

"Are you sure you should be up?" he asked quickly. He stood and came toward her, placing a solicitous hand beneath her elbow and leading her to the table.

For a moment, she allowed herself to revel in the sheer pleasure of his touch, then pulled away. "I am not in the least invalidish." With difficulty, she forced an argumentative note into her voice. "There is nothing amiss with me that a good, long gallop will not cure."

Ryde frowned, suddenly serious. "You will oblige me by remaining on the estate this day."

"I am not as feeble as that! I doubt there is a horse in your stable that could throw me, even if I am not feeling quite the thing."

"It has nothing to do with—with the way you feel. I do not want you to go beyond the gates of Hastings."

Her heart sank. Here, being handed to her upon a salver, was the opportunity she needed to anger Ryde. As much as her very soul cried out against it, she could not let this slip away. "Why?" she demanded, managing to sound belligerent.

"Do not ask me questions you know I cannot answer." His tone remained gentle but there was also a hint of steel that sent a shiver through her.

"And do not order me about! You have no . . ." She broke off as the door opened.

Gosson stood on the threshold, bowing slightly. "Your curricle has been brought around, my lord."

"Thank you." Ryde waited until Gosson withdrew, then grasped Celia firmly by the shoulders. "Just once, my girl, do as you are told." His fingers pressed into her tender flesh for a moment, then he released her and strode quickly from the room.

Celia stood there, trembling, fighting down a desire to run after him and throw herself into his strong arms. He had given her a direct order and she had no choice but to disobey. He must have had a reason. . . . She closed her mind to that line of thought. Whatever that reason might be, it was of less importance than the mess Charlie had made. Lord Ryde must be made to renounce the idea of marriage before she betrayed her love for him.

She turned to the sideboard, poured a cup of tea, and carried this to the table. As she started to sip it, the door opened and Elizabeth and Sir Roderick came in together.

"Ah, Celia. Feeling better?" her grandfather asked at once.

"Yes, thank you. But I would like some fresh air."

"Pity Ryde had to leave early. He might have driven you into Brighton with him." Sir Roderick filled his plate and carried it back to the table.

So her grandfather was unaware of Ryde's orders! That made it all so much easier. She gave a weak smile of greeting to Elizabeth, who took the seat beside her.

"You are not planning on riding, are you?" her companion asked in concern.

"No, I thought a drive might be quite pleasant. Just a gentle airing, you know. Grandfather, do you think we might go into Brighton? I—I would like to visit the lending library."

It was settled with surprising ease, and half an hour later Sir Roderick handed Elizabeth and Celia into the landaulet for the five-mile drive. Celia sank back against the squabs, fighting to keep her resolution firm. Barely a week ago she would have defied Lord Ryde with a ready will and the joy of battle surging through her. Was this what love did to one? Undermined the spirit and left one weak and listless? She had never been so—so stupidly missish in her life!

"Celia!" Elizabeth leaned over and touched her arm. "Are you sure you want to do this?"

Celia's eyes flew to her companion's worried face. For a dreadful moment, she thought Elizabeth had divined her purpose. But she read nothing in her expression but honest concern.

"Are you quite sure you should not be keeping to your bed today?" Elizabeth persisted.

"Nonsense!" Sir Roderick shook his head. "Do her good to get out a bit. Never saw the point in you females lying about in darkened rooms with salts and burned feathers and all that nonsense. Noxious fumes! No wonder you are always swooning and having the vapors."

"Yes, Grandfather," Celia agreed with meekness, though for a moment she experienced a slight lightening of her depression. "Will you be coming with us to Donaldson's Circulating Library?"

"No. I am going to Ragget's Club for a quiet game of piquet."

"Thereby closing yourself in a dark room filled with the smell of brandy, snuff and cigarillos?" Celia murmured.

Sir Roderick's brown eyes almost twinkled at her. "Ah, but those are pungent odors, not noxious."

They left the carriage at the Castle Inn and walked the short distance to the library. Sir Roderick saw the ladies safely within the door, then departed for the peaceful sanctuary of the club with promises to meet them for luncheon at the inn.

Once inside the library, Celia allowed Elizabeth to lead the way from room to room, scanning the shelves with an eager delight. Celia followed more slowly, finding it hard to concentrate on the titles. She was not in the mood to select a book. It had only been an excuse to defy Ryde, and she was finding little pleasure in that activity. Fidgety, she turned her attention to the paintings on the walls, then to the posters announcing upcoming events. There was to be a concert and a poetry reading and . . .

"Elizabeth!" she called softly. "Do come and see!"

Her companion turned to peer over her shoulder at the notice. "A masked ball?" She sounded dubious. "Really, Celia, I do not think Cousin Roderick would approve."

"But Elizabeth! It would be of all things such fun! Do you not think Lord Ryde would take us?"

"It would not do at all in London," Elizabeth demurred.

"But this is not London! I know the public masked balls there are quite vulgar, but surely not here! Why, I make no doubt it would be the most select gathering. Since the Prince of Wales has now arrived, all the *ton* are following. Only see how many more Fashionables there are about town today."

Elizabeth glanced about the room as if gauging the accuracy of Celia's last statement. Suddenly she paused, her eyes resting on a plump, matronly woman who had just entered the room. "Is that not Mrs. Andover?" she asked. "Yes, for there is Miss Draycott as well." She raised a tentative hand in greeting, and gave a small sigh of relief as the two women saw them and came over.

"How lovely to see you!" Miss Draycott hurried forward and kissed Celia's cheek. "Come, do sit with us for a moment and we shall enjoy a comfortable coze." She led the way to a cluster of padded chairs set in the center of the room for just such a purpose.

"Have you seen the announcement of the poetry reading?" Mrs. Andover settled herself on a small sofa and patted the place beside her invitingly. "Will you be able to attend?"

"I will have to tell my grandfather and Lord Ryde about it," Celia replied with a noticeable lack of enthusiasm. "And the masquerade ball, of course."

Miss Draycott and Mrs. Andover exchanged a quick glance. "Oh, no, my dear," Miss Draycott exclaimed. "*Not* the masked ball. They are not at all the thing, you know."

Celia frowned. "But I thought that here . . . Well, it could not be as bad as if it were in London."

"There is something about wearing a mask and not being recognized that seems to promote the most shocking behavior in normally quite well-behaved gentlemen," explained Miss Draycott in repressive tones.

"They—they positively ogle the females in the most dreadful manner," Mrs. Andover agreed. "It is not the place for a lady."

If that were so, it would be exactly the sort of event to which Lord Ryde would refuse to escort her. There was a good chance he would even forbid her to attend—if she handled it properly. That meant, of course, that she must make arrangements at the earliest opportunity for Jonathon to take her. That should make Lord Ryde doubly furious. Once she made her opposition to him so abundantly clear, he would be sure to have nothing further to do with her. Now, if only that thought could give her the pleasure it must!

By the time Celia's wandering mind returned to the conversation, the others were discussing the upcoming concert. She joined in, for she looked forward to any musical event, but was not displeased when her mother's old friends announced that they must be getting on their way.

Elizabeth resumed her exploration of the shelves, and Celia, once she was sure that her companion was safely occupied, slipped into the foyer and borrowed pen, ink, and paper. She wrote a quick note to Jonathon, putting forth her scheme and emphasizing the necessity for such a questionable outing. She sealed this with a wafer, then arranged for its delivery to Jonathon's lodgings.

This accomplished, she strolled into the next room and selected a volume at random. Elizabeth, with three slender books clasped in her hands, came in search of her and the two ladies signed for their books. Paying the small subscription fee, they made their way out into the street.

Celia consulted the watch that she carried in her reticule. "It is still well before noon," she remarked. "Would you care to stroll about the streets and look at the Polite World, or shall we walk through the Promenade Grove? It should be quite empty at this time of the morning."

"The Grove, by all means," Elizabeth decided. "But let us walk the long way around."

They turned their steps up the Steine in the direction of the Pavilion, passing it and continuing on toward the New Road. Here, they turned and proceeded along to the North Street, which eventually led them to the southwest side of the Pavilion and their destination. As they expected, only a few other people strolled among the meandering pathways or sat on the benches placed at irregular intervals.

They were resting on one of these when booted footsteps approached, then stopped before them. Celia looked up quickly.

"Jonny! Oh, I am so glad to see you."

He bowed deeply before them and his large blue eyes rested on Elizabeth's softly flushed countenance for a moment too long before he recalled himself and raised Celia's fingers to his lips. "What brings you into Brighton?" he asked.

"Donaldson's," Celia explained, indicating the book she carried. "Come, you may escort us back to the Castle Inn, unless you have anything else to do?" She ended on a querying note.

He immediately disclaimed any prior engagements and turned to accompany them back through the Grove. Celia, her arm firmly through his, paused several times on the pretense of admiring the formal flower beds and at last managed to get a slight distance away from Elizabeth. In a hurried undertone, she told Jonathon about the masquerade and her determination to attend. His reaction mirrored that of her mother's friends, but she overruled his objections and extracted from him a promise to pick her up secretly, two nights hence, in the lane beyond Hastings.

That matter settled, they left the Grove and crossed the Steine, heading toward the Castle Inn. As they entered the yard, the front door of the hostelry opened and Lord Ryde, accompanied by two elderly and very distinguished gentlemen, emerged. Ryde stopped short, seeing her, and even across the distance between them she could see his dark brow glowering.

Icy fingers gripped her stomach. How she hated that expression, dreaded the blistering set-down that seemed to hover on his tightened lips! But that was exactly the mood into which she needed to goad him. She had to be pleased—*must* be pleased—for only her defiance could make him despise her enough to go back on his given word to marry her. She closed her eyes tightly to hold back annoying, burning tears, then moved forward on Jonathon's arm with forced casualness.

She was safe for now. She kept repeating that thought, holding onto it for support as if to a tree in a raging wind. Ryde would not ring a peal over her head in public. That would wait until they were alone. It was agony! How long could she keep up her courage, pretend that every stinging glance or biting word meant nothing to her, when in reality she knew they would tear her apart?

"Lord Ryde appears to be displeased about something." Elizabeth turned worried eyes on Celia. "Do you suppose his meeting has not gone well?"

Jonathon coughed. "Best not to meddle in his affairs, you know," was all he said.

Ryde parted company with his companions, and the men returned to the inn. He made directly toward Celia, and mentally she braced herself for the encounter. The anger had disappeared from his face, replaced by a total blandness that did not deceive her in the least. After the battle that plainly loomed ahead, she would be well on her way to destroying any regard or affection he might have felt for her. She could almost hate Charlie for making this necessary.

Ryde bowed slightly to Elizabeth, then nodded a greeting to Jonathon. "Miss Marcombe, might I have a word with you? It will only take a moment." His voice remained calm but a brooding, determined gleam lit his dark eyes.

She took a deep breath, then stepped into the fray. "Why, you can say anything you like before Elizabeth and Jonathon," she replied, knowing full well that this response would only fan his smoldering temper into full flame.

"Nevertheless." He took her elbow in a firm grip. "Please excuse us for a moment."

Restraining the impulse to cast a quick, frightened glance over her shoulder at her erstwhile protectors, Celia allowed herself to be led a short distance away. She had to brave this through, she reminded herself. Ryde would come to hate her, and it was better that he should do so now rather than after she married him. When her family's disgrace came . . . but she had been over her reasons so many times already. The nobility of her motives did little to lessen the ache that possessed her heart.

"Will you continually defy me?" Ryde demanded in a savage undervoice. Celia looked slowly up into his face and was surprised to see a set smile on his features. Anyone watching them would assume this was a perfectly friendly conversation, not the heated exchange that actually took place.

"I have told you before, I shall continue to see Jonathon!" Celia declared in tragic accents while she matched his fixed smile with one of her own.

"This has nothing to do with Captain Edelston, as well you know!" His grip tightened painfully on her arm, causing her to wince. "I made a simple request that you remain on the estate today!"

"You ordered me! I am not a servant, to be ordered about!"

"You are a spoiled child who would be better for a spanking!" came the instant reply.

"You wouldn't dare!" she breathed, but knew, full well, that this man would dare anything. She fought down the surge of admiration for him that swelled within her.

"You will not disobey me again," he said softly in a voice that brooked no argument.

In truth, Celia doubted for a moment her ability to do so. Only her desperation drove her on. "I will continue to do as I please."

"Did it never occur to you that I might have had a good reason?" he demanded. Still, his voice was low and the smile never wavered. "That I might have your safety in mind?"

"Then you will have the goodness to tell me the truth and not expect me to cower before highhanded decrees." She turned away, but found herself trapped in the viselike grip of his fingers.

"Of course," he said in normal tones. "I will now escort you home." He released her and offered an arm which she had little choice but to take.

"There is no need." She allowed him to lead her back toward Elizabeth and Jonathon. His other hand came up to cover hers in warning, and she explained without thinking. "My—my grandfather will be joining us here in a few minutes."

Ryde stared down at her, surprised. "Sir Roderick? Is he in Brighton?"

"At—Ragget's, I believe he said."

"Was he your reason for disobeying my expressed wishes?" Ryde asked in an altered voice.

"No, my lord. I have already told you my feelings

concerning your—your wishes." She bit off the last word as if with distaste, then risked a glance up at his furious profile. How she longed to make light of this episode, to allow a note of banter to enter into their argument, making it the game it always had been before.

He was once again composed, his features miraculously relaxed, by the time they joined the other two. He turned to Jonathon. "Are you enjoying your stay?" he asked quite affably.

"Yes," Jonathon admitted. "Much prefer the quiet to all the racket of London, you know."

"I will be escorting my guests to one of Prinny's little entertainments, a musical afternoon at the Pavilion, the day after tomorrow. Would you care to make up one of our party?" Ryde asked.

Jonathon hesitated, obviously surprised by this unexpected invitation, then accepted with apparent pleasure. "Delighted. I mean—well, delighted. Not likely to be invited to an affair there myself, you know. Not one of the Prince's crowd."

"Nor am I." Ryde's expression held a wealth of understanding. "We will call for you."

As they arranged the details, Sir Roderick strolled up to join them. His disapproving gaze rested on Jonathon for a moment, but seemed to relax somewhat at the obviously easy terms on which the other two men stood. He accepted without comment both the news of the invitation to the Pavilion and the inclusion of Jonathon in their party. His piercing brown eyes moved from one man to the other, and Celia shivered, wondering just how much of the situation he guessed.

Jonathon, somewhat uneasy under Sir Roderick's continued regard, took his leave of them. Ryde watched him walk away, then turned back to Celia.

"And now, I believe I am going to escort you back to Hastings," he said softly.

CHAPTER TWENTY

The return journey was postponed while Lord Ryde entertained his guests at luncheon in a private parlor at the Castle Inn. Not even Celia could fault his manners or attentions to any of them, and not so much as one more word did he utter on the subject of her illicit trip into Brighton. It was as if the incident had never occurred.

The meal finished, Ryde sent for the landaulet and his curricle. He assisted the others into the large carriage, then climbed into the newly repaired vehicle and led the procession along the Steine to the New Road and on to Hastings. Once at the house, he remained only long enough to exchange his more formal attire for buckskins and riding coat before he called for his horse to be saddled and rode out to inspect the progress of the planting.

Celia did not have a chance to see him again until dinner, when she made the most of her opportunity.

Studying his firm profile covertly while carrying on the most superficial conversation with Elizabeth, she came to the conclusion that he was both very tired and disturbed. Deep lines etched their way from the corners of his eyes down toward his mouth, giving him a harsh, almost saturnine appearance. He spoke little, and more than once Celia caught his dark, troubled eyes resting on her with an expression that might have been puzzlement and certainly was not pleasure.

How she longed to smooth back his thickly waving hair, to kiss the spot where it curled away from his forehead, to smooth the worry from his brow and see those dancing, teasing glints light up his mysterious eyes. She dragged her gaze away from him. Every moment she remained near him it became increasingly difficult not to betray her love. And if things went ill for him on the estate, did she have the heart to pursue her own, cruel rejection of him?

It was only cruel if he cared for her, and she had no proof that he did! She repeated that, over and over, but it did little good. She felt a traitor, turning on him when he most needed her support. . . . She stopped herself. That line of thought took her nowhere except into deeper misery. Her course of action was the best for him, in the long run. Only his pride was involved where she was concerned. He had sworn to marry her and it must be an irritation to him, nothing more, that he could not win her over. But soon, he would no longer want to.

Throughout the following day, Ryde remained cordial but strangely elusive, excusing himself from any opportunity of conversation with her. It was almost as if he deliberately prevented them from coming to the point of drawing daggers. It was not a situation that she could allow to continue. The morrow offered two splendid possibilities, and she determined to make the best use of both of them. The gathering at the Pavilion took place that afternoon and the masquerade ball that night. She would do something so shocking that it would give Ryde a disgust of her, enough to overcome his pride and cause him to break his word about marriage.

Here, her courage wavered. Could she actually bring herself to do anything at the Pavilion that would embarrass him? She greatly feared not. Although Ryde was not a member of the Carlton House set, he did move in political circles. She could not chance ruining him in the eyes of the Cabinet Ministers and government officials with whom he worked his secret business.

Whatever she did, it would have to be discreet so that no one but Ryde would ever know of it. Perhaps if he merely saw her potential for scandalous actions it would be enough to give him pause. If he contemplated a political career, his wife would have to be both trustworthy and beyond reproach. Perhaps she could prove to him that she possessed neither virtue, without openly causing a scene that might injure him.

And she would deal what she hoped would be the final blow that night. Her resolution threatened to desert her, but she reminded herself once again that she had to go through with this. Her attendance at the masquerade—following, as it would, hard on the heels of whatever she did at the Pavilion—should be sufficient to give him a disgust of her.

First, she had to get him to refuse to take her himself, then forbid her to attend with Jonathon. It should not be too difficult.

As soon as she was dressed the next morning, she went downstairs in search of Ryde. She reached the hall just as he came out of his bookroom. He looked up and smiled at her as if no anger or resentment stood between them. Repressing the wish that this were true, she went at once to join him.

"I understand there is to be a masquerade ball in Brighton this evening, my lord," she said immediately, forcing her own hand. "Will you take me?"

"Absolutely not," he replied with prompt affability. "What are you thinking of, minx? That is no sort of entertainment for a lady."

"You are being absurd. If you mean to be disobliging, I shall ask Jonathon. He is a gentleman upon whom one can depend. He quite delights in lending me his aid."

"In being wrapped about your finger, you mean." Ryde's heavy brow snapped down and he grasped Celia's arm. "Now listen to me, vixen. You are not to attend that ball in Edelston's company! Do you understand?"

"Jealous, my lord?" Her tone was one of innocent surprise, but inwardly she quaked. She had experienced his anger before and only her desperate need to bring their betrothal to an end steeled her to face it again.

Lord Ryde's lip curled. "You are a spoiled, disobedient child, my girl, but before I am done you will learn to obey me. Is that understood?" He drew her up against himself and his nearness sent a quivering through her that she fought to control. "You can quit throwing Edelston at my head, minx. I have kissed you, remember? You have no more intention of marrying him than I do, and we both know it."

"Do we? I—I may have been taken in by you for a brief moment, but you are as nothing compared to the—the solid worth and constancy of Jonathon's love!"

The smoldering light in his eyes was her only warning. Before she could protest, she was clasped firmly in his embrace and lifted almost off her feet as his lips found hers. She clung to him, helpless against the wave of sensation that swept over her.

He released her and she came crashing back to earth. "Let us have no more of that nonsense," he informed her. "I have already told you that you are mine. And you *will* learn to obey."

"Will I, my lord?" she demanded. She could almost feel the angry sparks glinting in her eyes. Or were they tears of distress? "We shall see, will we not?"

She turned on her heel and walked down the hall to the breakfast parlor with what dignity she could muster.

To her relief, no one was inside. She had little appetite, but nibbled at a roll to give herself something to do. She had gotten what she wanted—to an extent. Ryde had forbidden her to attend the ball, but did he have to kiss her? Her attitude and words might defy him, but when his lips touched hers all subterfuge melted away, leaving only a love that was becoming increasingly difficult to deny. Knowing only that she must avoid him for a while, she sought the privacy of her room.

It was almost time for luncheon before Celia realized that the house seemed strangely quiet. On impulse, she slipped down the hall where she had heard the voices before. She listened at each door, but no sounds came from within. Turning the knobs, she discovered that several of the rooms in this wing were empty, merely storehouses for broken furniture that had yet to be repaired or replaced. Two doors, though, were locked.

Where were Mlle. de Bourgerre and the mysterious man? And why, after she had taken such an active role in these affairs, could Ryde not have the decency to inform her when something occurred? The least he could have done was tell her that his secret visitors were gone and the house was no longer in imminent danger of being attacked by French agents!

Here was another opportunity to annoy him! She would demand an explanation, thus meddling in affairs he considered to be strictly his own. She hurried down the stairs, encountered Gosson, and asked him where his master was to be found. Upon being directed to the bookroom, she crossed to this door and raised her hand to tap on it, but paused. Beyond it, deep and rather muffled, she could make out her grandfather's voice.

". . . without any delay!" Sir Roderick was saying, his tone urgent. "I want to see her safely wed and under your control before she does something outrageous! You have seen what she is like."

Celia stiffened. Listening to them might be shocking conduct, but for once she unhesitatingly allowed her curiosity to overcome her sense of propriety. This subject was of too much importance to her!

"I have," Ryde's low, rumbling voice agreed. "And I would rather not marry her immediately."

Celia's head came up, for these last words surprised her—and left her somewhat chagrined. Her plan was working, it seemed. He no longer desired to marry her!

"I do not want to force Celia against her will," Ryde went on, clarifying his previous comment and unknowingly causing her heart to lurch at this unexpected consideration. But was it her feelings, or his own, of which he thought?

"This nonsense has gone far enough!" Sir Roderick declared. A slight clinking sound followed, as if he set a glass down hard on a tray.

"Celia's wishes must be considered," came the reply, though outside the door she could not be sure whether or not she detected an amused tremor in Ryde's voice. "I will not have her forced," he repeated. "There is time enough."

A sudden harsh scraping, as of a chair being pushed back, reached her, and she darted away from the door. She had no desire to be caught listening to such an interesting conversation. With a quick glance about to assure herself that none of the servants had seen her, she slipped out the front door and headed toward a garden that was now almost worthy of the name.

She strolled along the paths between the straggly shrubs, mentally pulling an occasional weed or watching an imaginary flower come into bloom. Why was he showing her such consideration? Her suddenly fluttering heart kept her moving, too restive to sit quietly on one of the benches. Was he indeed thinking of her—or was this a graceful way to back down, to get out of an agreement of which he no longer wanted any part? The idea hurt, but it was what she must bring about.

Oh, if ever she saw her despicable brother again, she would tell him, in no uncertain terms, what she thought of his behavior—and of his putting such an insurmountable obstacle in the way of her happiness!

All too soon, it was time to dress for the afternoon party. With Seddons's assistance, Celia donned the becoming yellow muslin, then sat quietly before the mirror while her maid arranged her hair in a halo of dusky curls.

To Celia's dismay, Elizabeth chose to wear the severest of her dresses, an unrelieved black with a high neck and long sleeves. When she protested, her companion merely shook her head with firm resolve.

"I am your chaperone," Elizabeth asserted. "At a party such as this, with so many notables present, you must be beyond reproach."

"But you needn't look such a—such a crow! Jonathon will not like it!" she exclaimed before she could stop herself.

"You are quite wrong," Elizabeth said softly, averting her face in an attempt to hide the dull flush that crept into her cheeks. "Captain Edelston's only concern is for you. He will be glad that the proprieties will be observed so—so properly."

Celia bit back her retort. Jonathon would not be pleased, and he would quite rightly blame her for Elizabeth's severe appearance. This was hardly nurturing the cause of romance between the two—but then, it would all be over soon. Ryde would renounce her utterly; she would tell Elizabeth the truth, and Jonathon would be free to court the lady so perfectly suited to his temperament and heart.

They went downstairs together to the Gold Saloon and Celia stopped short just over the threshold. Ryde, magnificent in a blue coat, buff pantaloons, and a sash that indicated services to the Crown, turned from his contemplation of the fire. His eyes moved slowly over her and a strange expression flickered in their depths.

She struggled against the ripple of pleasure that his gaze created in her. It would be so easy to bask in his admiration, to flirt with him, see the smoldering glow in his eyes turn to blazing fire. Instead, she gave him the briefest of greetings and seated herself beside Elizabeth where she concentrated her attention on the shawl her companion drew from her workbag.

Sir Roderick had barely entered the room when Gosson announced the arrival of the carriage. To Celia's consternation, she found that she must sit close beside Ryde on the journey, both loving and dreading every jostling bump that thrust her against him. Profound relief filled her as they drew up at last before the Old Ship, and Ryde himself stepped down to arrange for a message to be sent up to Captain Edelston.

Celia waited inside the carriage, rehearsing the role she was determined to play. She had to pretend a preference for Jonathon's company that would insult her supposed fiancé. She must avoid Ryde, deny herself the pleasure of sitting at his side throughout the musical performances, and, most importantly, not allow him to present her to anyone of any importance.

If, as she greatly feared, he intended to take this opportunity to introduce her as his prospective bride, she must not give him the chance. And then . . . but she still had no clear idea of what she should do to give him a disgust of her. She could only hope for the inspiration and resolution to seize any opportunity that presented itself.

When the carriage door opened to admit Jonathon, she was prepared. She forced to her lips a bright smile, stood out at odd variance with her unnatural pallor. Fortunately, in the shadowed interior of the coach, this was scarcely noticeable.

"Jonny! Why, you are—all the crack! Is that the right expression?"

"Oh, as fine as fivepence," he responded promptly. He took the seat beside Celia as she moved over to make room for him, then turned to greet Sir Roderick, miraculously not appearing to notice that gentleman's stiffness of bearing and curt nod. When he turned to Elizabeth, his expression betrayed his disapproval of her austere appearance.

Ryde seemed not to notice the alteration in their seating arrangements. He took the seat beside Elizabeth, addressed a casual remark to Jonathon concerning the expected entertainments for the afternoon, and the two men beguiled the short journey to the Pavilion with the most commonplace small talk.

They were handed down from the carriage beneath the domed Indian canopy of the porte-cochère. At this point, Lord Ryde took the lead and offered his arm to Celia. She could hardly cause a scene by rejecting him, so she accepted his escort into the Octagon Hall, the small eight-sided antechamber with floor-length windows. She paused as her wide eyes took in the predominantly Chinese furnishings and décor.

This room led into the Entrance Hall, where the Chinese influence was somewhat muted by the cool green and gray tones predominating there. Celia barely had a chance to glance about before a footman stepped forward to take her shawl, and Ryde led her through the small, low opening into the Corridor.

Here she stopped, momentarily rooted to the spot, for nothing could have prepared her for the shock of this long, wide hallway which was alive with reds, pinks, amber and blue. The room was lit by a multitude of flickering candle lanterns and oil lamps that glittered back from their reflected images in the numerous mirrors. The preceding rooms might have hinted at the Chinese theme, but here it overwhelmed the visitor. Celia stared about in disbelief as Ryde guided her down the Corridor. Even the mantel clock was Oriental, fashioned of white marble and ormolu in the shape of a Chinese pagoda. Six cabinets of beechwood, carved and painted to resemble bamboo with red silk panels, lined the walls.

"Do you like it?" Ryde murmured near her ear.

A shaky giggle broke from Celia. "Did—did the Prince decorate this himself?" she asked.

"Have a care in what you say to him. He left it in the hands of the firm of Crace, but it is all to his order. He is quite proud of it."

"I—I will keep that in mind."

There was little time for more. A liveried servant came forward, bowing, and guided them to the South Drawing Room. He announced their names, then stepped back to allow them to enter the large room.

Here, the other guests had gathered this afternoon instead of in the Corridor, and Celia was able to slip away from Ryde's side and join her grandfather where he stood with Elizabeth and Jonathon just inside the doorway.

"It is quite a large apartment, is it not?" she asked Sir Roderick out of a need to say something, anything, to block Ryde from her mind. Even here, amongst these notables, his was a presence that commanded attention.

Sir Roderick snorted. "At least you aren't overpowered by all that Chinese nonsense in here. I've heard he's got plans to build on a music room. Can you imagine what that will be like?"

Ryde returned to them at that moment and led them around to the far side of the room where there stood a man of such magnificence that Celia knew she beheld none other than the Prince of Wales. No consideration for his impressive girth constrained his opulent taste in coats, and his waistcoat was both beautiful and awesome to behold. Lines of dissipation marred his once handsome countenance, but his expression was affable as he greeted each of his guests with a condescension that spoke of an easy good humor rather than pride or haughtiness.

Celia, upon being presented to him, sank into a deep cursty. He looked upon her with a kindly eye, for he was inclined to admire a pretty young lady, and welcomed her to his little party. She thanked him, blushed at the interested manner in which his gaze moved over her, then stepped quickly aside to allow her grandfather and Jonathon to take her place.

"Is he everything that you expected?" Ryde asked

softly as he led her away.

"He is certainly everything that one would expect of a prince," Celia replied with diplomatic aplomb.

Ryde chuckled softly. "He is certainly that. And ruthless, as well, when it suits him."

"You do not like him?" She turned to stare up at Ryde.

"Let us say that I am not one of his close friends. Now, who else would you like to meet?" He looked about the room. "I had not expected such a crowd this afternoon."

The Drawing Room was indeed filling rapidly. Celia recognized several acknowledged leaders of the *ton* who had been pointed out to her in London, but none with whom she was personally acquainted. Just ahead of her, Sir Roderick was hailed by an old friend, and within a very short time he was persuaded to slip off to one of the card rooms in search of an entertainment that for him held more allure than did music.

Elizabeth retired to a seat near the wall amidst several elderly ladies whose propriety of dress and bearing proclaimed their status as chaperones. Celia could not like it, but knew any attempt at remonstration would fall on deaf ears. For all her sober attitude, Elizabeth was enjoying herself in this select gathering. She was quite content to merely observe—indeed, would have felt uncomfortable and out of place if she were suddenly called upon to play a more active role and mingle with the guests.

Jonathon hovered near Celia's elbow. In spite of his own fashionable air, Celia sensed his discomfort with his surroundings. The Pavilion, even the exalted company, were not to his taste. She was willing to bet that if offered the least excuse, Jonathon would quickly desert her and, like her grandfather, seek the solace of the card rooms. It was with relief that he recognized an old friend from naval days and, with a murmured excuse to Celia, bolted toward a group of young bucks with all the air of a fox going to ground.

The first group of musicians took their place at the far end of the room, and the guests sought their seats. Ryde guided Celia to Elizabeth's side, then excused himself for a moment. Celia next glimpsed him in conversation with an elderly gentleman who looked vaguely familiar to her; then, the two of them left the room together.

By the time the third piece of music ended, Ryde had still not returned. The musicians rose, their portion of the program apparently at an end. The guests broke up into small groups once again, and Celia and Elizabeth followed several people into the next room where a long table was set up with punch bowls. A footman poured them glasses, and they retreated into a corner where they stood sipping their punch.

Ryde's continued absence irritated Celia. He had escorted her to this party; the very least he could do would be to remain by her side. How could she display a carefully cultivated indifference to him if he were not there?

People seemed to be wandering freely from room to room. Emboldened by their example, Celia slipped away from her companion, bent on exploration. How often would she have the opportunity to see what was, to all intents and purposes, a palace? The Pavilion was certainly not something to miss. Her taste might not run to the opulent oriental, but such a garish display could only delight her sense of the ridiculous. Curious to see to what lengths the theme had been carried, she began peeking into each of the rooms that were open.

Without realizing it, she wandered from the state apartments into the private. She opened a door, peeped in, and discovered she was in an empty library. She returned to the hall, passed under a stairway, then tried another door. She had it open before she realized there were people within this room.

Thérèse de Bourgerre stood near the head of a table around which seven men sat. Slightly to one side, was another man, with a bandage that half-covered his dark brown hair. He sat slumped in his chair, and, at the moment, was the cynosure of all eyes. The man Harding stood beside him, as if his guard or jailer.

". . . if it had not been for that man!" Thérèse declared in dramatic accents. She waved an expressive arm in the direction of the wounded man.

Celia, curious, peered at him. As she watched, his head came up slightly. Her throat went dry and a dizzying numbness crept over her. His tousled dark hair, the line of nose and jaw—even after almost five years, all were as familiar to her as if she stared in a mirror.

Blood rushed to her head, then drained away, leaving her trembling and faint. An anguished gasp escaped her lips and she took a hesitant step forward. It was too terrible to believe, the worst of her nightmares coming true. It was over, all over, and only disgrace and shame lay ahead. She shook her head, trying to deny the evidence of her eyes.

"Charlie!" she cried, unable to prevent his name from escaping her lips.

CHAPTER TWENTY-ONE

A stunned silence enveloped the room. All eyes turned to stare at Celia, who stood helplessly rooted to the spot, staring at her long-missing brother in shock and with something akin to pure panic in her face.

"Charlie!" she repeated, her voice hoarse with emotion.

"Get her out of here!" Her brother leaned weakly back in his chair, but his voice carried clearly.

Someone rose and came forward, grasping Celia by the shoulders and turning her about. Strong hands propelled her out of the room and the door was closed firmly behind them.

"Get a grip on yourself!" It was Ryde's voice that issued the command.

Celia, her eyes blinded with tears, tried to focus on his expression but failed. "How did he come here?" she finally managed to gasp.

Ryde did not answer. He forced her down the passage, back to the empty library into which she had looked such a short time before. "I brought him," he declared as soon as they were safely within the room.

His hands remained gripping her shoulders, virtually all that held her on her feet.

"You . . . !" She stared at him in horror tinged with a dawning revulsion. "You turned him in! How could you?" Her clenched fists beat furiously against his broad chest. "How could you? Dear God, do you want Ranleigh so much? Could you not spare him for the sake of one who has been a father to you?" Tears streamed down her cheeks and she tried to pull away, loathing his traitorous touch.

"Celia!" His sharp exclamation commanded her attention, but she ignored him.

"Was there a bounty for him?" she demanded. "Did you get your thirty pieces of silver?" She broke into uncontrolled sobs as the fears of the last weeks solidified into reality.

"Celia!" he repeated. He shook her until she cried out. "Be quiet, you little idiot! The only person placing him in danger is you! What the devil do you mean by barging in on a meeting of that nature? Are you determined the whole world should know who he is? Keeping his identity secret is his only chance for survival, and here you go blurting out his name!"

"But they—they have him!" she wailed. "It won't matter to them who he is. They—they'll execute him, anyway!" She fell to her knees, her legs no longer able to hold her up as shuddering sobs engulfed her.

Ryde grasped her elbows and dragged her back to her feet, where he was forced to support her. "Stop blathering such nonsense!" he ordered. "The French don't have him. We do! Now, strive for some sense, for once. They will only get him if fools like you shout his name everywhere!"

She stared at him through eyes half-blinded with tears, trying to make sense out of his words. "But . . ."

"But nothing. Good God, Celia." Holding her with one hand, he ran the other through his disordered locks. His eyes blazed with anger at her. "We've gone through one hell of a lot of trouble to help him. Just once, girl, think of someone other than yourself! Don't give him away!" He released her abruptly, turning away and taking several agitated steps.

"What—what will happen to him now?" she asked in a very small voice.

"Well, thanks to you they now know who he is." He took a deep breath, trying to control his explosive emotions. "With luck, we can hush it up. Those men wouldn't be in there if they weren't discreet, and Thérèse won't expose him. He'll just quietly appear. Jokes about a loss of memory and premature reports of his death should do the trick."

She shook her head, not believing her ears. "You would help a deserter," she finally said.

He looked over his shoulder at her. "Deserter? What are you talking about?"

Fortunately, there was a chair nearby, for she could no longer stand. She sank into it, her head in a whirl.

"Oh, my God!" he said softly and reverently. "Celia! Look at me! You knew what he was doing!" His harsh voice made his words a statement, not a question.

"No! I—I thought him dead. Then—then Jonny told me, when we met in London, that Charlie hadn't been killed, that he was alive, that he . . ." She broke off, unable to continue.

"That he what?" Ryde strode up to her and forcibly raised her chin. "What did Edelston tell you? How much does he know of this business?"

"That—that Charlie deserted!" she whispered, barely able to bring herself to say the words. "He—he didn't want me to know the truth, said I had no idea how terrible it was in battle. But when it came to Grandfather's breaking the entail—well, Jonny had to tell me! Charlie's body had never been found; there might have been questions asked, and—and the truth might have come out!"

"He told you your brother deserted?" Ryde demanded explosively.

Celia nodded, unable to control her voice to speak.

"Of all the idiotic sapskulls! But I suppose it is really your brother's fault. He could hardly be expected to entrust the truth with anyone so addlepated as Edelston!"

She sat back. "But . . . what is this about?" she begged.

He sank down on one knee beside her. "Celia, listen to me. This is your brother's life at stake. You must never, *never*, repeat a word of this. Do you understand? I am going to tell you, just so that you know how serious this actually is. Charles did not desert. He left Trafalgar so mysteriously on the orders of the Government."

"But . . ." Celia shook her head, suddenly out of her depth. "Mlle. de Bourgerre was denouncing him! She . . ."

"She was praising him. What you heard was the tail end of her story of how she was rescued from Napoleon's gaol by a man known only to her as *Le Maniganceur*—until you supplied another name."

"*Le*—I don't understand." Celia stared blankly at

Ryde for a moment. "Are you telling me my brother is a—an *agent?* A British agent?"

"That, my girl, is exactly what I am trying to tell you."

"Charlie? Why, *why,* did he let us think he was dead?"

"He will have to tell you that himself. But since it was his life he was playing with, I don't imagine he fancied trusting anyone with the secret. Either that, or Edelston gained the wrong impression and decided to spare you what he thought was the truth."

Celia's mind seethed with the turmoil of her thoughts. It would have been just like Jonathon—particularly if he had been heavily sedated after being wounded—to have gotten it all wrong. And no wonder Jonathon's casual inquiries in the Naval Office had created such a stir! An agent, whose work was of the utmost secrecy, might have been exposed at any moment. . . .

"Oh, could someone not have told me? Or Grandfather?" she cried. "To let us believe him dead . . ."

"No one knew, except his superior. The story about his death was put about to protect him."

"But you knew." She stared at him, her eyes widening. "Are—are you . . . ?"

"His superior? No, I am not. My involvement is of a less—less formal nature, let us say."

"Did Mlle. de Bourgerre tell you who he really was?" she asked suddenly.

"No. Not even she knew. He used the code name to protect himself."

"Then how did you know?" she demanded.

"I didn't, exactly. I guessed. I never actually met

him when I was in France, or if I did, he was in disguise. I saw him for the first time at Thérèse's house on the Marine Parade. Do you remember that night Harding came to the garden and said a man had been shot? That was Charlie. I didn't realize who he was at first because, like you, I believed he was dead. But there was something familiar about him, and after looking at you again, I realized what it was. I think I was sure in less than a day after I brought him to Hastings."

"To Hastings! Do you mean to tell me that Charlie—*Charlie*—was the man . . . Charlie has been in the same house with me all this time and you did not see fit to tell me?"

"Well, his identity was his secret, after all. If he did not want to reveal who he was, it was hardly my place to do so."

"Did he know Grandfather and I were staying in your house?"

"I imagine Thérèse told him. Your names, at least. She would have had no idea of the relationship, of course."

"But you knew!" She had pulled somewhat away from Ryde during the course of this exchange, and now threw his hands off her shoulders. "You—you unspeakable cur!" Blazing anger replaced her chaotic fears. She was seething with indignation. "Allowing me to worry myself to the point of distraction over Charlie, thinking he might be captured and shot at any moment, and all the time you knew the truth! You odious, unprincipled . . . !"

At that, Ryde's deep chuckle rumbled forth. "I was not to know what you thought. If you will remember, you did not choose to honor me with your confidence."

It was too much for Celia's shattered nerves. Without stopping to think, she struck out at him and had the satisfaction of feeling the palm of her hand strike his cheek with a gratifying sting.

He brought his hand up to cover the reddened patch of skin. "Do you feel better now?" he asked.

"Yes!" To her dismay, she hovered on the brink of tears again. With a valiant effort she swallowed and regained some measure of control.

"Is this why you fought so hard against our marriage?" he asked abruptly. "Because your brother was really alive? Why did you not tell me the truth?"

"I couldn't! Had he been a deserter, you would have felt it your duty to turn him in!"

"Is that what you truly think of me?" he demanded.

"Oh, I don't know what to think!" She turned away to stare blindly at the shelves of books that lined the room. "I have lived in constant dread of his exposure, and it was all for nothing."

The deep rumbling of his chuckle sounded once again, causing her temper to flare. She felt a fool, exhausted by her turbulent emotions, and there had been no reason for any of her distress! And most unforgivable of all, Ryde had known the truth! At any time during these last couple of days he could have told her, but he had chosen not to! She was of so little concern to him that he had not cared how she suffered! That she could not forget! Tears spilled down her cheeks.

"I want to go home!" she managed to say.

He hesitated. "I still have work here this afternoon."

That broke the last shred of her control. "Oh, I would not want to take you away from your precious government officials. I have no need of you! Jonathon will take me home. He—he may not always understand everything quite properly, but at least he has my interests at heart. I can trust Jonny!"

"Don't be a fool. I'll take you myself."

"There is no need to go to any trouble! Jonathon will be only too happy to take care of me!"

Ryde's color darkened and his lips tightened into a firm line. "There is no call to disturb him." He crossed to a desk, sat down, and pulled out a sheet of paper.

Celia watched him writing for a moment, then turned and slipped silently out the door. She had no wish to be closed into a carriage alone with him for the journey back to Hastings. In a few minutes, she found herself back in the Corridor where two footmen stood on duty. One of these she sent to summon the carriage and the other she entrusted with a message to Jonathon.

She went into the Octagon Hall to wait. The minutes passed while the coachman was found and the vehicle brought round, and she caught herself throwing nervous glances over her shoulder. At any moment, Ryde might appear, and she was too distressed to see him again so soon.

Hurried footsteps approached, then paused in the doorway behind her. She did not need to turn her head to know who stood there, whose glinting eyes bored into her. She stiffened but did not otherwise acknowledge his presence.

"Have you already sent for the coach?" Ryde's deep voice sounded just behind her, his tone one of studied casualness.

"Yes," she replied through gritted teeth.

"Good. Then it should be here at any minute. I have explained your headache to your grandfather, but I saw no need to disturb Miss Westerly. Captain Edelston promised me he would bear her company until I returned."

"How considerate of you," she declared with heavy sarcasm. Still, she did not look at him.

A silence fell between them, thick and impenetrable, broken only after they had entered the carriage and it started forward.

"Does my grandfather know about Charlie?" she asked stiffly.

"I will have to speak to your brother first, but I hope to tell Sir Roderick tonight."

"When will you permit *me* to see my brother?"

"It is not in my hands. He is still very weak, you must realize. He and Thérèse will both spend the night at the Pavilion; then, I believe he is to be taken to London in the morning."

Celia lapsed into an impotent seething. She had quite a few things she wished to say to her brother—and a great many questions to ask him. Four and a half years of mourning, and over a month of acute worry and fear, lay between them. He had a great deal to answer for.

But it was not truly his fault, if Jonathon had indeed garbled his message to her. Tears of confusion burned her eyes and she raised a hand to surreptitiously wipe them away. It was all too much to take in at once. In one moment, Charlie had been transformed from a traitor to a hero. It left her lost, unable to think clearly.

Her mind was still in a disordered jumble when they turned onto the drive at Hastings. Ryde saw her safely into the house where he paused in the hall.

"I must go back now, but I still have a few things to say to you," he told her.

"Have you?" she asked coldly, her pride coming to her assistance.

Her response did not please him. "I have," he replied coldly. "I shall speak to you when I get back." Without another word, he went out to the waiting carriage for the return journey to the Pavilion.

Did he really believe she would just sit there, meekly awaiting another rakedown? Or did he mean to formally break their ridiculous engagement? She mounted the stairs to her room, too upset to think clearly. She needed time to assimilate all that had happened. Right now, she was just too confused. Charlie . . . And Ryde's cruel, biting words . . .

Oh, God, he had made it abundantly clear what a low opinion he held of her! How bitterly he must have regretted agreeing to marry her once he discovered what a selfish, thoughtless, irresponsible termagant she was—and how glad he must be that Charlie's resurrection meant that he could break the agreement with all honor. Tears filled her eyes and spilled down her cheeks once more. She could not face him again that day!

And Jonny! She had to tell Jonny that Charlie was safe, for he was almost as worried as she! But when . . . With a sense of shock, she remembered the masquerade ball that night—in only a few hours time, in fact. Would Jonathon still come as he had promised? Suddenly she wanted to go, desperately. She would escape this house, escape Ryde, seek Jonathon's soothing if somewhat vacuous company. Explaining the situation so that his vague intelligence could assimilate it would help clarify it in her own mind.

She sat in her room, staring out the window, trying to regain some measure of calm. Time must have passed, for she heard the others return. Her only action was to bolt her door so that no one could disturb her. She sat on the bed, waiting, and soon she heard the sound of heavy footsteps coming down the long hall. A peremptory rapping on the wooden door beat out a demand for admittance.

She didn't move; just sat there, biting her lip until it bled, willing Ryde to go away. Instead, she heard the knob turn. The door held fast, barring his entrance, and she breathed a sigh of relief. Softer footfalls and the rustling of skirts announced that someone had joined him.

"Does she not answer?" She heard Elizabeth's gentle voice.

"No," came Ryde's curt reply.

"Perhaps she has taken something to make her sleep. Why not speak to her later?" Elizabeth suggested.

"I must go out tonight and I do not want this to wait." Impatience sounded in his voice and he knocked again.

"It seems you have no choice. I will not have her bothered, my lord." To Celia's surprise, there was a note of determination in her companion's voice.

"Miss Westerly," he began, but Elizabeth cut him off.

"Let her rest, my lord." Her words were a definite order. "If she has taken laudanum, it will be some time before she can hear you, anyway."

With a soft oath that Celia could not make out through the heavy door, Ryde strode off. Celia leaned back on the bed, too emotionally drained to move any more.

CHAPTER TWENTY-TWO

Jonathon reined in the pair of job-horses that were harnessed to the rented curricle and reviewed his plan for the seventh time. He would go up to the house and inquire after Celia's health. Her leaving the Pavilion so abruptly provided him with an excellent excuse. If possible, he would even talk to her. That way he would know whether or not she still wished to attend that damned silly masquerade. No sense sitting out by the shrubbery in the cold breeze for half the night if she wasn't going to show!

Sure of his course of action, he turned the horses onto the gravel and started up the drive. He was met in the stable by a surprised Coxly, who took the equipage in charge while Jonathon gathered his courage and approached the house.

"Is Lord Ryde at home?" he asked when Gosson opened the front door to him. The butler bowed, said that he would ascertain, and would the Captain care to wait a moment?

He was left cooling his heels in the hall. Idly, he wandered into the Gold Saloon, stopping as he saw that the room was occupied. Elizabeth, seated by the fireplace, was engaged in setting stitches in a tiny square of cloth.

She glanced up as the door opened, then dropped her needlework into her lap. "Captain Edelston!" she exclaimed.

Encouraged, he came farther into the room. "Came to see how Celia is. Worried when she left like she did. Well, one just doesn't walk away from a party given by Prinny without good reason! Is she feeling better now?"

"I have no idea. She did not answer when I knocked on her door, so I hope she is asleep. Oh, pray be seated. I am so glad you have come!" she ended impulsively.

"Are you?" A sudden hopeful smile quirked up the corners of his mouth and he drew a chair close to hers. In the face of so promising an opening, discretion flew to the winds. No time like the present, he decided. "Always delighted to see you, of course," he declared. "In fact, quite a pleasure. Don't expect a cove to be witty or forever mouthing flowery phrases. Comfortable sort of female." He beamed at her.

Elizabeth flushed deeply. "I did not . . . Captain Edelston, it is Celia!"

"Celia?" His mind, rarely up to dealing with more than one momentous issue at a time, drew a blank. "What the devil has she to say to anything?"

"But . . . you called to see how she goes on, and I very much fear she is in desperate need of your assistance!"

"Is she?" To Elizabeth's surprised eye, he appeared somewhat taken aback. "What's amiss?" he asked.

"It is Lord Ryde!" Here, Elizabeth's voice dropped to a conspiratorial whisper. She threw a frightened glance at the door, but it was firmly closed. "He was in the most dreadful temper this afternoon when we returned from the party. I—I believe Celia might have locked herself in her room to hide from him."

"Doesn't sound like Cilly," Jonathon caviled. "Game as a pebble! Always ready to show her colors and sport her canvas."

"Not today. They have been arguing of late, not bantering as they were used to do. He—he may have threatened her!" She swallowed and forced herself to go on, trying nobly to ignore the pain her words caused her. "I have been going over every possible solution in my mind, and there is only one that will do the trick. You must defy convention and marry her at once! When you have her safely wed, there will be nothing Lord Ryde can do to harm her."

"Marry that hellcat?" Jonathon exclaimed. "Now really, Miss Westerly, I'd have thought you'd have more know in your cock-loft than to make any such addlepated suggestion. Marry Cilly?"

Elizabeth sank back in her chair, her eyes wide. "But—but you are engaged to her! You have wanted to marry her this age! Oh, Captain Edelston, I had never thought *you* to be inconstant!" Tears filled her eyes at so traitorous an act. "Could I have been so deceived in your character?" she ended in a whisper, distressed to detect feet of clay on a golden idol. Captain Edelston, who had come to embody every romantic, heroic quality in her daydreams . . . Her knight errant, instead of dashing bravely into battle to save his lady fair, seemed on the verge of just shrugging and walking away . . .

Jonathon leaned over and grasped both her hands between his. "Nothing of the sort, Miss Westerly. It was all a sham, so she wouldn't have to marry Ryde! Never any question of our getting leg-shackled. Lord, could you really see me a tenant-for-life with Celia? What a merry dance she would lead me! Always been very fond of her, but dash it all, that's going too far!"

Unconsciously, Elizabeth's hands turned within his grasp and clung to his. "But you promised her brother . . ." She gazed up into his handsome face, longing for his tarnished image to shine once more. She shook her head slowly, too confused to be able to assimilate what this all meant.

"Only told Charlie I'd look after her. Lord, he wasn't such a nodcock! Some things you just don't ask a fellow, and tying up with a spitfire like Celia is one of them!" He looked down at their locked hands and rubbed his thumb gently along her wrist. "Prefer a quieter sort of female," he explained, his tone almost apologetic.

Elizabeth's eyes widened, but as Gosson chose that moment to enter the room she was prevented from uttering any of the questions that jostled in her mind. She pulled her hands free and averted her face to hide her heightened color.

The elderly butler bowed slightly to them. "His lordship is preparing to go out for the evening, but if you would care to wait, Captain Edelston, he will be down in a few minutes."

"Just came to see if Miss Celia was feeling more the

thing," Jonathon told him hurriedly. "Miss Westerly can tell me that."

Gosson's gaze took in the gentle flush on Miss Westerly's cheeks and the embarrassed air that hung about Captain Edelston. "Very good, sir." Permitting himself a prim smile, Gosson retired from the room. When he had closed the door securely, a sentimental sigh escaped him, for he was of a romantic disposition. He liked Miss Westerly, and Captain Edelston seemed to him an excellent young gentleman, if a trifle bacon-brained. He saw no need to mention his presence to Sir Roderick.

"Captain Edelston," Elizabeth began carefully as soon as they were once again alone, "We—we must consider how best to help Celia."

"Best not to interfere. If I know Cill, she's playing a deep game. She's a downy one, don't you worry. Not likely to wind up at fiddlestick's end."

Elizabeth, although not quite certain what Jonathon's mysterious words implied, could not be easy. "I fear this has gone beyond a game. She has been most sincerely unhappy!"

"Poor Cill," he agreed. He was silent for several moments. Abruptly, he stood and took a quick, restless turn about the room. "Got a snug little house near Bath," he announced suddenly. "Not as big as this one, but comfortable. No long drafty halls or endless staircases. Few hundred acres to go with it," he added. The expression he turned on her resembled that of a hopeful puppy.

"You—you would marry her to see her safe?" Elizabeth breathed, torn between an almost worshipful admiration of a man who would make such a sacrifice and a misery she tried hard not to acknowledge.

"Not Cill." Jonathon shook his head firmly. "You!"

Elizabeth felt the blood draining from her cheeks. She could not have heard him aright! Handsome blond giants did not drop the handkerchief to drab little companions long past the first blush of youth. He should be addressing himself to a beautiful young girl like Celia. . . . She found she was shaking her head in her disbelief.

"Am I making a mull of it?" Jonathon asked, anxious. "Thing is, never offered for a female before. Don't know how to go about it." He regarded her expectantly, as if waiting for her to give him instructions.

She rose, agitated. "Captain Edelston, I—I fear you are making a mistake!"

"I am? Should I have asked Sir Roderick's permission to pay my addresses to you? Thing is, Celia don't want him to know yet that our engagement was all a fudge."

"No! That is . . . Oh, you cannot *truly* wish to marry me!" Elizabeth wrung her hands. It was too cruel! Here was everything she had ever dreamed of . . . a man who, in her eyes, embodied perfection . . . all she could ever desire. . . . Enchanted things did not happen to her! All her life she had known that hers would be the drear lot of a spinster bound to genteel servitude. She did not dare to hope. . . .

Jonathon grasped her cold, shaking hands in a firm grip and raised them to his lips. She lifted eyes full of wonder to his godlike countenance, oblivious of the tears that slipped down her cheeks. He reached out with a tentative finger and wiped them away.

"Jonathon?" The whispered name came out as a question.

He beamed at her. "That's the ticket. Been wondering when you'd use my name." His smile went slightly awry and a strange light came into his eyes. "Been wondering when I'd get to try this, too," he murmured. He gathered her unprotesting form into his arms and his lips brushed her cheek. On the second attempt, he found her mouth.

"Now," he went on when he finally let her go. "When will you marry me?"

Elizabeth rested her head against the broad chest so conveniently at hand. "I—I cannot!" she cried out on a sob.

"What? Now, really, Elizabeth!" He raised her chin with one hand so that he could look into her face. "Not at all the thing, you know, to go kissing a fellow if you don't want to marry him!"

"I do! But—but I cannot! Oh, how could you ask me to leave Celia at such a time, when she is in such trouble?" Reluctantly, she disentangled herself from the haven of his arms.

"Take her with us, if you like," he suggested.

Elizabeth shook her head. "She belongs at Ranleigh, and she must be brought out properly in London and given a chance to find someone she can love as much as I . . ." She broke off in consternation, realizing what she had been about to say.

"As much as you love me?" he asked with that hopeful little boy look that melted her heart. "I did mention that, didn't I? That I love you? Do, you know. Have for some time, now. Just didn't know how to go about telling you."

Elizabeth gave a choking laugh that turned into a sob. "Oh, Jonny, what are we to do? I cannot marry you while Celia needs me!"

"You can still chaperone her when she goes to London," he said reasonably. "Be even better, for you'll be a married lady. Give you both more consequence."

"You do not understand! When Cousin Roderick realizes Celia only pretended to be in love with you to avoid marrying Lord Ryde, he will be so angry he will force her to marry him at once! And I could never forgive myself if that were to happen."

Jonathon sank down into his chair, for it seemed to him exactly the sort of thing that would happen. His expression of dismay was so comical that Elizabeth would have laughed had she herself not been so distressed. "We're really in the suds, aren't we?" he said at last.

"I—I fear we are. You do see that we cannot marry?"

"Not while Celia can be forced to marry Ryde," he agreed. "And it will be over two years before she comes of age!" he added glumly. He looked up to see her tear-filled eyes and stood promptly so that he could pull her back into his arms. "It won't be that bad, love. Something'll happen. She's trying pretty hard to put Ryde off, isn't she?"

Elizabeth nodded, her face somewhere in the vicinity of his coat lapel. "If she can once get him to draw back, then perhaps we . . . ?"

"Don't breathe a word of this, but she's up to something tonight. Got me to agree to take her to that damned masquerade ball. Don't know what she hopes to gain by it. But tell you what, you wait up, and we'll talk about it when I bring her back."

Elizabeth agreed to this readily, only too willing to see him once more that night. Jonathon checked the clock, decided it was time to meet Celia, and kissed Elizabeth once more for good measure.

CHAPTER TWENTY-THREE

Celia must have fallen asleep, for when she stirred nd sat up on her bed the room was in complete arkness. Remembrance of the day's events flooded ack to her and she groaned aloud. Groping on the edside table, she found a candle and lighter, and oon, a warm glow filled the room. According to the rmolu clock on the mantelpiece it was almost eight clock.

She wanted to see Jonathon. . . . With luck, he ould soon be outside the gate, waiting for her. She o longer cared about the ball, but she desperately eeded to talk to her oldest friend—and keep out of yde's way that night.

It took over half an hour to attire herself in an vening gown suitable for a ball, but at last she eeked around the edge of her barely opened door. he hall was deserted, though she could hear the unds of movement below stairs. The soft crepe of er evening dress rustled slightly as she slipped out id closed the door behind her. As silently as possie, she made her way through the halls to the back airs.

The servants were busy elsewhere. She made safely to the back door, pulled the bolt which wa mercifully well-oiled, and glided out into the gathe ing dusk. Hurrying, she kept close to the shrubber walking on the damp grass verge beside the gravele path. Her feet in their light slippers were drenche but it could not be helped. She dared not make ar noise, dared not be caught until after she had sorte through this tangled, confusing mess.

She emerged from the long drive onto the roa There was no sign of Jonathon! For one dreadf moment she wondered if his courage had failed hi and he had decided not to come. He could not— would not—do that to her! She needed his quie stolid presence.

The darkness closed in about her. Somewhere i the distance came the sound of an approaching hor and she started forward in relief. A single horse, ar no sound of a bouncing vehicle . . . She ducked ba into the bushes, gathering her cloak closely about h to hide the paleness of her gown. In another minute lone rider trotted past, never casting so much as glance at the gate to Hastings.

Celia remained behind the bush, nervous, countir the minutes as they marched slowly by. More soun reached her, but they came from behind her, down th drive! She could hear the hoofbeats of at least tw horses and the rattle of a light carriage. Did Ryde out? She held her breath, waiting, hoping above ho that he would not see her crouching there.

A curricle pulled abreast of her, turned carefull and drew up beside the road just beyond the gate. Sh let out a deep sigh of relief, for even in the di maining light she recognized Jonathon.

She emerged from the bushes, startling the horses .d sending them dancing. Jonathon struggled with em for a moment, brought them under control, and ld them firmly while Celia scrambled up onto the at beside him.

"Oh, Jonny, you haven't failed me!" she cried as she rew her arms about him in relief. "But what were u doing up near the house? Ryde or my grandfa- er might have seen you!"

"Dash it all, Cill!" He disentangled himself from her d steadied his sidling horses again. "Went to ask w you went on. Had to know if you were really k, didn't I?"

"Of course. That was most intelligent of you," she d him admiringly, soothing his ruffled feathers.

"You are all right, aren't you?" He set the team gging down the road. As soon as they were moving oothly, he spared a glance for Celia's worry-lined e. "Dash it all, Cill, you don't look at all the thing! u sure you should be going out? Why did you leave Pavilion so early?"

"I had a very good reason, I assure you. And I am right. At least, I am not ill. Jonny, can you nember exactly what Charlie told you that night he t?"

Jonathon frowned, a sure sign that he taxed his ntal abilities to their not too distant limit. At last shook his head. "Not exactly, Cill. They'd given me danum; don't think I was too clear in my head. re I'd remember if he said where he was going, ough. Sorry, but I've no idea how we are to find n."

"We already have. Hush, Jonny! Don't holler li that! You will scare the horses again. Now, you a not to breathe a word of this to anyone!"

"Well, really, Cill! That's coming it too strong, aft all those years I kept mum about it!" He modulat his tones a bit. "Now, what the devil do you mea Has he turned up?"

Celia told him a somewhat edited version of h story and had the dubious satisfaction of seeing l chagrined expression. "An agent, is he?" Jonath asked at last. He shook his head slowly. "Could swe he didn't say anything about that. Then all's right a tight? Charlie can come home without being shot

"The only people likely to shoot him are Fren agents. And me! Oh, to think of all the trouble he h caused! I don't know whether I shall hug him strangle him! And he has been right here, in Ryd house, for days! He could have told me at any time shall have a few things to say to him when next I s him, you may be sure!"

Jonathon drove on with a bemused expression his handsome face. "Charlie, an agent! Never thoug it of him."

"I gathered," Celia said dryly.

"Just like that Wilton chappy in that poem of Scot you're always reading. Back from the dead and pro ing himself a hero." Jonathon shook his head.

They were silent for several minutes. "Did y bring me a domino and loo mask?" she asked su denly.

"In a box, under the seat." He hesitated a momer "Been wondering," he began, conversationally. "Y were going to this ball to infuriate Ryde, weren't yo 'hat I mean is, no need for it now, is there? He on't want to marry you now that he knows he won't :t Ranleigh."

"Oh, I don't care about the ball!" she snapped at m. "I just want to avoid him, and I wanted to tell ›u about Charlie! And you are quite right. Ryde ›esn't want to marry me any more. I saw to that."

"You did?" he asked. "Knew you could pull it off. ›ld Elizabeth you was a knowing one. Well, shall I ke you home, now?"

"No! I told you, I—I don't want to take the chance seeing Ryde."

"Is he being disagreeable?" Jonathon demanded. ›ut you don't have to worry. He's going out tonight, o."

"Let us go on," she decided. "I don't want to just sit my room tonight. I need diversion."

Jonathon gave a deprecating cough. "You sure, ll? Not at all the thing, you know, these public balls. ell, what I mean is, a gentleman may go for his nusement, but not a lady!"

"You won't refuse to take me, will you?" she be-eched him. "I—I need to be in company tonight."

"Now look here, Cill, it's about time you told me ıat you're up to. Something dashed havey-cavey ing on, and you can't tell me otherwise. With ıarlie safe, and Ryde no longer forcing you into arriage, seems like you should be happy! What's 'ong?"

"I'm being stupidly missish!" she exclaimed in dis-st with herself. "Oh, Jonny, I did everything I could ink of to make Ryde hate me, and now that he does ." She broke off, unable to control her voice any longer.

"You don't want him to?" he finished with surpri ing gentleness. "Lord, Cill, have you gone and falle in love with him?"

She nodded mutely and he let out a long breat "What a pickle you've landed yourself in! Thoug you weren't entirely indifferent to him, but yo couldn't marry him with Charlie missing. And no . . ."

"Is this what is known as steering oneself to poi nonplus?" she asked with a halfhearted attempt at h usual humor.

Only silence answered her. They tooled along f some time before Jonathon spoke again.

"You know, Cill, maybe if you went to him, tell hi why you acted like you did, might change his mi again," he suggested.

"You want me to go down on my knees and b him to marry me?" she demanded, a flicker of pri returning to her. "And what if he never really want to?"

"There is that, of course," Jonathon responded m rosely, and Celia sank back into gloom.

As they pulled up before the inn where the ball w to take place, Celia rallied somewhat and pulled t loo mask on over her curls. Once this was arranged her satisfaction, she exchanged her heavy cloak for t concealing folds of the flimsy domino.

As Jonathon led her into the large ballroom, s experienced a slight raising of her spirits. Here, least, she would not be free to indulge in depressi reflections. Music, laughter, costumes and brilliant colored dominoes filled the hall. Checking to ma re her mask was still in place, she caught her cort's arm and dragged him onto the crowded floor, termined to lose herself in the gaiety for at least a tle while. With Jonathon manfully keeping up with r on his stiff leg, they swung into the swirling steps a waltz which she secretly knew she had no busi-ss dancing.

"The maskers quaint, the pageant bright, The revel loud d long," she quoted in Jonathon's ear, trying to pture the lively mood of the crowd about them.

He frowned at her. "Not going to quote poetry at e all night, are you?" he demanded.

"Elizabeth is very fond of poetry," Celia informed m baldly.

"Is she? Daresay I'll grow to like it, I suppose."

For the first time that night, Celia felt a trifle tter. She would miss her companion, but that lady's ppiness must come first.

The musicians ended the piece. As they struck up other tune, Jonathon firmly led her from the floor vard a group of chairs, trying to force a way ough the jostling throng. From the accents she ıld hear in the momentary lull, Celia realized that company was far from select. Quite vulgar, in t.

A buck in a resplendent purple domino ogled her enly through a quizzing glass. Her chin tilted up as gave him a scathing glance from head to toe, signed to depress any pretensions. Far from being ashed, his smile broadened and he started to bear vn on her. Blushing furiously, she grabbed nathon's arm and pulled him in the opposite direc-n.

They found chairs, but Celia soon began to regr her decision to come. The music was gay and th revelers certainly enjoyed themselves, but she was n at her ease. In spite of her pride, in spite of h earlier words to Jonathon, all she wanted at th moment was a chance to see Ryde—to tell him wh she had behaved as she did. Even if he did not lo her, she must prevent his hating her as he did! S would go home and sit in the Saloon until he r turned, and she would speak to him. Perhaps, if s behaved with the utmost propriety until her grandf ther took her back to Ranleigh, Ryde would forgi her. . . . Suddenly, it was of the utmost importance her that he never learn of her attendance at th masquerade.

"Jonny!" She tugged at his arm. "I think we shou leave!"

He nodded. "Best thing to do. Not at all the sort place you should be. Besides, Elizabeth will be wa ing up for us."

"She will? Did you tell her what we were doing Celia demanded.

"That's right. Told her you had a plan to ma Ryde back down. Come to think of it, now that won't want you anymore, nothing to stop us, there?"

"Stop us from what?" she asked, wholly at sea

"Not you. Elizabeth and me. Says she won't mar me until you're safe from Ryde."

Celia blinked. "You asked her? Tonight? W didn't you tell me?"

"Keep you voice down, Cill! Yes, I asked her, b she says she can't while you still need her."

"What—what utter nonsense! As if I would stand in the way! Did you not tell her so?"

Jonathon looked uncomfortable. "Well, there was your grandfather to consider."

"Well, it—it doesn't matter any more. Let us go and tell her at once. Oh, Jonny, I am so happy for you both." She threw her arms about his neck, subjecting him to a thorough hug.

She let go of him and stood looking down at her costume. Her domino had fallen open to reveal her white gown with its distinctive blue Vandykes. She pulled the black folds of cloth closed, and then turned to follow Jonathon through the crowd toward the door.

And she stopped dead. Just ahead, bearing down upon them with a purposeful stride that thrust the merrymakers apart, came an unmistakable figure, the one person she least wanted to see. There was no doubt Ryde had recognized her, probably from that glimpse of her gown. Deep furrows creased his dark brow, and with a sinking heart she realized he must have witnessed—and not enjoyed in the least—the sight of her in Jonathon's arms. Instinctively, she drew close against her escort's side for protection; then, too late, realized this was a mistake.

With one hand at the neck of Celia's domino and the other at Jonathon's, Ryde pulled them apart. He released Celia, and the fingers of that hand clenched into a punishing fist that rose and hesitated in midair, prevented from crashing into Jonathon's chin only by a summoning of massive will power. The impropriety of initiating a bout of fisticuffs in the middle of a ballroom must be the only thing that restrained him, for his expression was murderous in the extreme.

"You . . ." He broke off, the violence of his feelings for once leaving him bereft of words. With a muttered phrase that shocked Celia, he released his opponent and turned on her instead.

She stared at him in horror. This was the second time that day she had faced his rage, and the first time was as nothing compared to this. Never, even in her worst nightmares, could she have imagined the raw fury that set his muscular frame trembling with his effort to control it. She shrank back but he continued to advance until he overtook her.

Iron-strong fingers gripped her shoulders and he started to shake her. Jonathon latched onto his arm, momentarily pulling him from her, but Ryde, without so much as a glance over his shoulder, threw him off and grasped Celia once again.

"Like it or not, you are going to marry me, my girl," he hissed. "If I ever catch you with Edelston again, I'll kill him! And then you! Is that understood? And believe me, I will take the greatest of pleasure in doing it!"

Jonathon stepped back, staring at the pair. Celia turned to him, her expression a mixture of fear and chagrin at his desertion.

"I am taking you home, now," Ryde informed her, then broke off, his expression arrested.

"Do not worry about me, *mon cher.*"

Celia's startled gaze flew to the petite figure disguised from head to toe in the muffling folds of a red domino. Only delicately tinted lips, curved in a smile, could be discerned of her face.

"You brought *her!*" Celia gasped as outrage, chagrin, and blinding pain vied within her for supremacy.

"I did." His tone was icily cold. "I promised Thérèse some time ago that I would take her. Unlike you, my spoiled brat, she has been cooped up for weeks, unable to go out. A masked ball was the only entertainment safe for her."

"I will be all right," Thérèse assured him.

Ryde hesitated. "Edelston," he said at last. "You will escort Mlle. de Bourgerre back to the Pavilion. Harding is waiting just inside the door. And take this." He drew a gun from inside his coat and handed it to Jonathon. "You shouldn't need it."

Here was anger indeed, if he entrusted his charge to another! Celia, not daring to cross him, submitted with surprising meekness as he transferred his grip to her elbow and propelled her forcibly out of the ballroom. Half dragging and half pushing her, he thrust her out of the inn and sent for his waiting curricle. In the steadily pulsing pressure of his fingers on her arms, Celia felt his temper reaching and passing the boiling point while he waited. She tried to pull free, but it made no impression on him whatever.

"You are hurting me," she said at last.

The viselike grip relaxed somewhat but he did not release her. "I'm not done with you yet, my girl," he muttered softly.

The curricle pulled up and his groom swung down, offering him the reins. Ryde ignored him as he almost threw Celia up into the seat and climbed up after her. He took the ribbons, gave the horses the office, and left Coxly to swing up behind as best he could.

They took off at a breakneck pace. Celia clung to

the seat to prevent being thrown out as they made the turns to reach the New Road, and hung on as Ryde urged his pair into a reckless gallop. She had barely a thought to spare for the hapless groom on his precarious perch.

In record time, they turned up the gravel drive. Ryde barely checked their headlong progress until they made the last turning into the stableyard. He pulled the horses to a stop on the cobbled stones and jumped down. Coxly was beside him in a moment, taking the reins as Ryde turned and dragged Celia from the seat.

"My lord!" Celia protested.

"Be quiet!" he told her through gritted teeth. "I have a great deal to say to you, and for once you are going to listen!" Still pulling her, he entered the long carriage house and proceeded to the far end where there was a single, empty box stall in which straw and benchs were stored.

He shoved her inside and glared down at her, his presence menacing in the extreme. "Now what the devil do you mean by behaving like a common lightskirt?"

"I . . ." She stared blankly at him.

"Throwing yourself into a man's arms in public! A man expects more decorous behavior of his mistress, let alone a lady!"

"I—it wasn't what you think!" she cried.

"It better not have been!" He grabbed her arm, sat down on one of the benches and hauled her over his lap. With the air of one goaded beyond endurance, he proceeded to spank her. She cried out with fury rather than fear, yet he kept on with unseemly relish. He released her so suddenly that she fell to the straw on the floor. She struggled to her feet as he rose.

"How dare you!" she whispered, her eyes glinting daggers and her bosom heaving with her indignation.

"I told you I'd not be defied again, my girl. You can be thankful I treated you as the child you are instead of the prime article you pretend to be." He took a deep breath, his pent-up frustrations now somewhat relieved. His eyes rested on her, his expression almost tortured. As if unable to help himself, he gathered her firmly in his arms and kissed her until she gasped for breath. He let her go abruptly, turned on his heel and stormed out of the stable.

CHAPTER TWENTY-FOUR

Celia dropped down onto the straw, too weak to stand. The raw emotions of the last hour filled her. Never had she been more frightened in all her life! But worse, far worse, he had humiliated her! His anger alone she could have withstood—even, perhaps, respected. But spanking! And then, as if he had not insulted her enough, he had kissed her like the—the *prime article* he had called her!

If any lingering hopes had remained that he might hold her in any esteem or regard, they were shattered now. He had proved, beyond any doubt, of what little account she was to him.

And she loved him. . . . The overwhelming strength of her feelings shattered about her, tearing at her soul with the jagged edges of their remains. By her incautious temper, her ill-judged actions and her foolish pride, she had completely destroyed any chance she might have had for happiness. The misery of this knowledge threw her into the very depths of despair, and tears came again, not angry but hopeless.

She had no idea how long she stayed like that. Tota

darkness surrounded her when at last she stirred. She pulled herself to her feet, stumbled out of the stall and along the aisle inside the low stone building—toward the rectangle of grayness that indicated a doorway. She had no idea what time it was and found she did not really care. Nothing mattered. . . .

What was she to do now? She could not bear the thought of seeing Ryde again. If only she could run away, escape from his house.

She shivered in the cool night air. The domino must have fallen off in the stall and her cloak remained in Jonathon's rented curricle. It seemed incongruous that she could be aware of physical discomfort when her entire world had collapsed about her!

A scrunching in the gravel along the drive finally penetrated the shroud of misery that enveloped her. Footsteps, approaching steadily . . . She crossed the cobbled yard to hide in the shrubbery, not wanting to be seen.

Through the straggly branches she could make out the figure of a tall man who limped slightly as he walked. Jonathon! Unbelievably, miraculously, help had come! She emerged from her hiding place and ran to meet him.

"Oh, Jonny!" Her voice caught on a sob as she threw herself into his arms and, for once, she did not have to draw on her acting ability for melodrama. "You did come!"

"Well, of course I did. Said I would, didn't I? Just had to see Mademoiselle to safety. Leaves for the country tomorrow, so that's all right and tight. But what are you doing out here?"

"It is all over!" Celia exclaimed. "You must take me away from here! I cannot remain!"

"What happened?" he demanded.

"He . . . It doesn't matter. You must take me away."

He patted her shoulder soothingly. "Well, you know, Cill. Been thinking about it. Only acted like that because he was jealous. Plain as a pikestaff. Turned absolutely green when he looked at me."

Celia lowered her head, shaking it. "No. It was his pride, and—and I have disgraced him utterly. He will never forgive me, or—or I him."

Jonathon shook his head. "Doesn't seem right, Cill. You're in love with him."

"Rather foolish of me, isn't it?" She forced a watery smile. "It will all be called off now, anyway, as soon as he tells Grandfather about Charlie. I just cannot bear to wait."

Jonathon looked up at the house. "All right, Cill. You just leave it all to me. Got an idea."

She eyed him with little hope. Jonathon's plans, as a rule, were notorious nonstarters.

"You go up to your room, now, and pack a bag. Nothing much, mind. Just a few essentials. I want to see Elizabeth."

"What are we going to do?" she asked, unable to think clearly for herself.

"Take you to my mother," he said promptly. "Give me about half an hour, then meet me at the back door. All right?"

She nodded, barely able to believe that Jonathon had actually come up with a viable suggestion. Still in a state of numbness, she led the way around to the back of the house. She found the door, tugged at it vith frantic fingers, but it would not budge. It was olted from the inside. She was locked out! Helpless ears started once again, telling her more surely than nything else how completely demoralized she was.

"Let's try the front, Cill," he said. "Elizabeth said he would wait up, remember?"

She stared at him, still not used to practical sugges-ions emerging from this source. She followed him round to the front, and up the steps.

She moved past him, grasped the handle and pulled n it, almost falling as the door gave way easily and wung noiselessly open. She stared at it for a moment n relief. They went in and Celia conscientiously olted it.

Elizabeth emerged from the doorway of the Gold aloon. "Celia?" she called softly.

Celia looked across at her companion, opened her nouth and found herself unable to speak. Leaving onathon to explain, she ran to where a lamp burned t the foot of the stairs, lit one of the candles that tood at its side, and mounted the steps as fast as she ould.

Safe at last in her room, she dragged off the gown nd discarded it across the arm of a chair. She would eed to wear a comfortable dress and take a change of ndergarments. . . . She had not seen Mrs. Edelston or almost two years. How would that lady react to eing awakened in the early hours of the morning to earn she was to have the dubious pleasure of an nexpected visitor? And Mrs. Edelston herself was taying with friends! Any plan of Jonathon's would ot hold water, Celia thought savagely, but what else ould she do? She could not stay here!

She sank down onto her bed, lowering her face into her hands. She could not indulge herself in tears again, not yet! She was becoming little more than a watering pot! But Ryde's furious eyes . . . How much she loved him, and how much he hated her!

Another, terrible, thought struck her. What if Ryde discovered Jonathon in the house after his earlier threats? What if he caught them escaping together?

With shaking hands, she pulled on a traveling gown and selected a warm pelisse. Only one small bandbox remained in her room, and she thrust her hairbrushes and a few other necessities into this.

A soft tap sounded on her door and she froze, but it was Elizabeth who slipped into her room. Her glowing countenance and trembling smile were enough to tell Celia that Jonathon had convinced her not to sacrifice herself.

"Oh, Elizabeth, I am so glad for you," Celia exclaimed before her companion could speak. She enveloped Elizabeth in a warm embrace. To her shame, she was forced to fight down a pang of jealousy for one who had found happiness.

"Are—are you sure?" Elizabeth asked, obviously not yet able to believe that her heart's dream had come true. "I—I will not leave while you still need me."

"Jonathon will have something to say to that," Celia told her. She turned away, looking hastily about the room, trying to hide the tears that again threatened. "Is—is he ready?"

"You are to meet him by the back door, just inside the Long Hall," Elizabeth told her. "You will be safe with his mother before morning."

Celia looked up at her companion, half in hope, alf in despair. She had the oddest sensation for a noment that something was not quite right.

Elizabeth blushed. "It is the best thing for you, Celia," she asserted earnestly. "The—the house will be n chaos tomorrow, with everyone wondering what has ecome of you. In the confusion, I will pack our hings and follow. Now, sit down and rest for a noment. I—I will go and make sure your way is lear." She almost scurried from the room.

She acted like a frightened rabbit! Poor Elizabeth, he was not suited to any form of intrigue. Celia lmost smiled. Elizabeth was so straightforward, so oodhearted; it must upset her terribly to be part of ıch an unseemly escapade. And the morrow, when ir Roderick and Lord Ryde's tempers exploded . . . ! lo wonder the poor creature was nervous.

Elizabeth returned in a moment. "Oh, Celia," she xclaimed. "I—it is for the best," she repeated, claspg her charge's hands. "Go now. He—he should be eady for you."

Celia picked up her bandbox and slipped silently om her room. The hall was dark and the carpet ercifully muffled her footsteps. For a moment, she ished she had brought a candle, but she did not dare sk discovery, not so close to making her escape. She lt her way carefully along the now familiar passages, and down the several short flights of steps. How e would miss this deplorable wreck of a house! And e neglected fields and farms . . . and Lord Ryde. ıt her pride would not permit her to remain and allow in her misbegotten love, awaiting the moment hen Ryde would formally cancel the agreement with her grandfather.

At last, she approached the main section of th house and the back stairs. Gripping the banister, sh cautiously descended the steep, narrow stairway. A the bottom, she started down the Long Hall.

"Cill?" Jonathon stepped out of the shadows. "Yo ready?"

"Yes," she whispered. She didn't know whether t be glad or unhappy. But she had to go! She looke about, nervous, half expecting Lord Ryde to loom u from out of nowhere.

"Come on, Cill. Don't worry so." He picked up th bandbox, knocking it against the wall. In Celia terrified state the bumping seemed to echo througho the empty hall.

"Do be careful, Jonny!" she begged. "If . . ." Sh broke off with an audible gasp.

A door opposite them swung open. Celia spu about, her eyes wide with fear. There, by the light a branched candelabrum, stood Ryde, weavin slightly. A long-stemmed glass was clasped loosely in hand that was none too steady. Celia raised her ey to his face and felt the blood drain from her ow Never, in all of her life, had she seen such a mixture hatred and rage, and it left her weak and shaking wi terror.

"So, thought you'd run off together, did you?" h demanded with a slight slurring of his words that d nothing to diminish the menace lurking in them.

Celia shivered, cold fear clutching at her heart. Sh had experienced a taste of his temper already th night, and if ever a man had looked murderous . .

"Swore I'd kill you, Edelston, and I meant it!" H

tepped back into the room, and to Celia's amaze-
nent, Jonathon followed.

"Jonny!" Celia's voice came out in a squeak. "He—
e means it!"

Jonathon threw her a glance she could not quite
athom in the poorly lit hall. "Matter of honor, Cill. A
nan doesn't run from something like this."

He disappeared into the room. Celia ran after the
wo men, not able to believe what was happening.

Lord Ryde strode to the fireplace where a pair of
ncient dueling swords hung crossed on the wall. He
rew these down and flipped one expertly across to
onathon.

"Light more candles!" he ordered Celia.

"You'd better," Jonathon added grimly.

Her hands trembling, she complied. Her knowledge
f duels was limited to the pages of novels, but,
omehow, she had envisioned seconds, a doctor, meet-
igs at dawn. But that did not take into consideration
temper and pride as wild as Ryde's! Nothing but
istant blood would satisfy him, and it was all her
ult! How could she ever have involved Jonny in
omething like this? If he was hurt, she could never
rgive herself!

They must have light. . . . She looked about, then
oved the candelabrum to a table that Ryde had
oved to one side. Jonathon was pushing chairs out
the center of the room, clearing an area large
nough for their deadly work. Celia glanced from one
an to the other, sick with horror, reading a deadly
tent in the faces of both.

Clutching the back of a chair for support, she
atched with terror-widened eyes as the two men met

in a brief salute. They separated, then lunged forwar with grim determination. A ringing clang sang out a steel met steel, followed by a slithering hiss as th blades slid along each other. Jonathon retreated a ste with Ryde in pursuit, and the light from the flickerin candles danced along the flashing foils.

The resounding clash of swords filled the roo along with the stamp of firm, controlled footfalls a the two men parried and thrust, advanced, lunged and retreated. Ryde seemed to be forcing Jonatho steadily into the defensive, and Celia held her breat fearing a fatal thrust at any moment.

The blades locked suddenly and there was a spli second of stillness, then the hideous *sotto voce* shriek c sliding steel as the two men broke apart. Jonatho lunged at once, unexpectedly, and caught Ryde off hi stride. Jonathon's foil slid upward and Celi screamed.

Ryde gave a strangled cry, staggered backward an fell against a chair, his right hand clutching his le shoulder. Jonathon, breathing hard, dropped hi sword.

Celia screamed again. Without realizing she ha moved, she was beside Ryde, falling on her knees ne to his prostrate form. He was still, deathly white b the flickering glow of the candles.

"Oh, my love," she sobbed, cradling his head in h arms. Not Jonathon, but Ryde had paid the price her hateful pride! Why had she been such a fool? shattering sob racked her body and her tears f unheeded as she caressed his beloved cheek and for head. "Oh, my love, what have I done?"

Ryde's eyes opened slowly. "Celia," he murmure

Iis right arm went unsteadily about her, pulling her own against him. "One last kiss, my beautiful, dored Celia."

This was not the moment for deception or pride. he hugged as much of him as she safely could, illing him to hear, to understand. "I love you, revor," she declared hoarsely, then repeated it, over nd over. It seemed so inadequate, and too late to ake up for the irrevocable harm she had done.

She choked on a sob of remorse as he pulled her ead down. Her lips sought his and she felt their armth, the pressure that never failed to draw a ngling response from her. He shifted beneath her, tting up, and his other arm crept about her and athered her close.

She held him tightly, kissing him fiercely, releasing very pent-up fear and emotion that raged within her, rateful for the burning ardor of his response, the elcome strength of his comforting arms. . . .

"Forgot were hatred, wrongs, and fears," he quoted from *armion* shakily. *"The plaintive voice alone she hears, Sees t the dying man."*

She sat bolt upright, thrusting him away so that she uld stare down at the clean, untorn fabric of his fine wn shirt. There was not so much as a ruffle out of ace! No blood, no wound met her gaze of growing itrage. She raised shocked eyes to his laughing face.

"You see, my darling Celia, your love has healed e."

"How—how dare you!" she exclaimed. "You—you cked me!" She tried to scramble to her feet but he lled her firmly back down.

"You are quite right, my love. An odious, hateful

trick. But what could I? We are both too proud for our own good, you know. And when your friend Edelston told me to what extremes my temper had driven you, I had to take desperate action."

"You mean *Jonny* betrayed me?" she demanded. She looked about, but the miscreant was no longer in the room.

"He took me to task pretty firmly, my darling. Told me in no uncertain terms what a precious pair of fools we were acting, and that it was obvious to all the world that we loved each other but were both too proud to admit it."

"The only thing you love is humiliating me!" she declared hotly.

"Now, is that a challenge to prove you wrong?" he murmured. Then, the smile faded from his eyes as they rested on her distressed countenance. "No, my love. I do not. And I have bitterly regretted my words and actions of this day. The misery, the hatred in your eyes has haunted me! I have called myself every vile name I could think of, but it could do nothing to remedy the situation. I knew I had given you a disgust of me."

"I—I thought it was the other way around," she said in a very small voice.

"No." His lips twisted into a wry smile. "My damnable pride and violent temper. What would you have done had I gone back to the stable and begged you to be my wife?"

She hesitated. She had been so angry . . . . "Probably thrown something at you," she admitted candidly.

"And now?" His voice was soft, persuasive.

"I—I haven't heard you ask me anything, now."

He leaned forward, pulling her closer, but she jerked her face away so that he kissed the base of her throat instead. "I had to force you to overcome your pride, my love, and surrender to me." There was an implicit note of apology in his words. "And now that you have . . ."

His lips moved up her throat and she trembled. Her anger began to dissipate under the strength of the emotions he created in her.

"Your grandfather was quite right, you know," he told her between soft, nuzzling kisses. "We are perfectly suited to each other. Would you not enjoy working with me to fix up Hastings?"

"There—there is no need for this marriage now, my lord," she told him. "The—the bargain with my grandfather is no longer valid. Ranleigh will go to Charlie, and—and there will be very little dowry."

"Damn Charlie, damn Ranleigh, and damn that ridiculous bargain," he said affably, his lips brushing the smooth skin of her neck. "Will you marry me, my penniless darling?"

His lips had reached her chin, and in spite of her determination not to, she lowered her head a fraction, enough for her mouth to find his.

"Oh, my beloved Celia," he murmured against her cheek when he could speak again. "My darling love."

So their war was over and done with. She might have surrendered first, but here were the words of love she had waited so long to hear. She had won—though she doubted Lord Ryde would ever admit it. But what did that matter? She had discovered a woman's most valuable weapon—the art of surrendering to get one's own way. A surge of elation swept through her.

"You haven't answered me, yet," he chided her tenderly. "Will you forgive my deception?"

She studied his face. The dark, mysterious pools of his eyes glowed in the flickering candlelight, revealing an intensity of emotion equal to her own. Certainty filled her, giving her confidence.

"If you ever have the audacity to spank me again," she began threateningly.

"I wouldn't dare," he assured her promptly. "Celia, my love, I am still waiting. You will marry me, won't you?"

There was only one possible answer. Unhesitatingly, she slid her arms about him, drawing him near, her lips seeking his.

The creak of the door opening caused her to jump. Trevor muttered something under his breath, but kept his arms firmly about her.

Jonathon stuck his head around the corner and observed their intimate position with a certain satisfaction. "You've settled everything then, have you?" he asked cheerfully. "Didn't hear anything breaking in here, so figured you must have."

Trevor sighed. "Be a good fellow and take yourself off, will you, Edelston?"

"Jonny!" Celia stopped him in sudden suspicion and his grinning face reappeared. "Does Elizabeth know about this?"

"Of course. You don't think I'd keep any more secrets from her, do you? Not after the May game we've played with her all this time!"

"An example we will do well to follow," Trevor commented as the door closed at last. "And now, my love, to get back to more important matters . . ." He pulled her even closer, and his lips sought hers once more. For a very long time, there was no need for further words between them.

THRILLING GOTHIC SUSPENSE
By Zebra Books

SAPPHIRE LEGACY (1979, $2.95)
by Beverly C. Warren
Forced into a loveless marriage with the aging Lord Charles Cambourne, Catherine was grateful for his undemanding kindness and the heirloom sapphires he draped around her neck. But Charles could not live forever, and someone wanted to make sure the young bride would never escape the deadly *Sapphire Legacy*.

THE SHADOWS OF FIELDCREST MANOR (1919, $2.50)
by Casey Stevens
Alleda had no recollection of who she was when she awoke at Fieldcrest Manor. But unraveling the past was imperative, because slowly but surely Dr. Devean was taking control of her mind . . .

SHADOWTIDE (1695, $2.95)
Dianne Price
Jenna had no choice but to accept Brennan Savage's mysterious marriage proposal. And as flickering candlelight lured her up the spiral staircase of Savage Lighthouse, Jenna could only pray her fate did not lie upon the jagged rocks and thundering ocean far below.

THE TERRORS OF PENHARRIS MANOR (2167, $3.95)
Erin J. Brown
When the handsome Gideon Penharris rode off moments after his marriage to innocent Morwenna, leaving her to travel alone to his distant Cornwall estate, the deserted bride didn't know if she could ever believe in Gideon again. Then little accidents started plaguing her with increasing danger and she realized she would have to find her absent mate . . . or lose her sanity and fall prey to THE TERRORS OF PENHARRIS MANOR.

Available wherever paperbacks are sold, or order direct from the Publisher. Send cover price plus 50¢ per copy for mailing and handling to Zebra Books, Dept. 2281, 475 Park Avenue South, New York, N.Y. 10016. Residents of New York, New Jersey and Pennsylvania must include sales tax. DO NOT SEND CASH.

"There's only one way I can go ahead with helping my father,"

Zack said. "You'll have to marry me."

"Is my whole life to be sacrificed to your pride?" Lara asked.

Zack shrugged. "Take it or leave it."

Lara knew marriage to Zack would be risky business. With all his old hatreds and resentments so close to the surface, there was a good chance she'd be hurt.

Without intending it, she let her gaze flicker over his hard midsection, then dart lower. He was so utterly desirable, so neatly and beautifully made. Though revenge, not love, was his motive, he could be hers if she said the word. Already a little of her shyness, her indignation at his effrontery had faded. There was only one possible decision she could make.

"All right," she said, coming to terms with it. "I'll marry you whenever you say."

Dear Reader,

It's March—and spring is just around the corner. We all know spring is the season of love, but at Silhouette Romance, every season is romantic, and every month we offer six heartwarming stories that capture the laughter, the tears, the sheer joy of falling in love. This month is no exception!

Honey, I'm Home by Rena McKay is a delightful reminder that even the most dashing hero is a little boy at heart, and Lindsay Longford's *Pete's Dragon* will reaffirm your belief in the healing power of love . . . and make-believe. The intense passion of Suzanne Carey's *Navajo Wedding* will keep you spellbound, the sizzling *Two To Tango* by Kristina Logan will quite simply make you want to dance, and Linda Varner's *As Sweet as Candy* will utterly charm you.

No month is complete without our special WRITTEN IN THE STARS selection. This month we have the exciting, challenging Pisces man in Anne Peters's *Storky Jones Is Back in Town.*

Throughout the year we'll be publishing stories of love by all your favorite Silhouette Romance authors—Diana Palmer, Suzanne Carey, Annette Broadrick, Brittany Young and many, many more. The Silhouette Romance authors and editors love to hear from readers, and we'd love to hear from *you!*

Happy Reading!

Valerie Susan Hayward
Senior Editor

SUZANNE CAREY

Navajo Wedding

Published by Silhouette Books New York

America's Publisher of Contemporary Romance

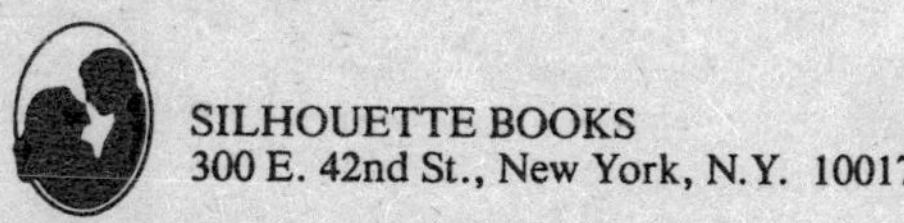
SILHOUETTE BOOKS
300 E. 42nd St., New York, N.Y. 10017

NAVAJO WEDDING

ISBN: 0-373-08855-8

First Silhouette Books printing March 1992

Printed in the U.S.A.

Books by Suzanne Carey

Silhouette Romance

A Most Convenient Marriage #633
Run, Isabella #682
Virgin Territory #736
The Baby Contract #777
Home for Thanksgiving #825
Navajo Wedding #855

Silhouette Desire

Kiss and Tell #4
Passion's Portrait #69
Mountain Memory #92
Leave Me Never #126
Counterparts #176
Angel in His Arms #206
Confess to Apollo #268
Love Medicine #310
Any Pirate in a Storm #368

Silhouette Intimate Moments

Never Say Goodbye #330
Strangers When We Meet #392

SUZANNE CAREY

is a former reporter and magazine editor who prefers to write romance novels because they add to the sum total of love in the world.

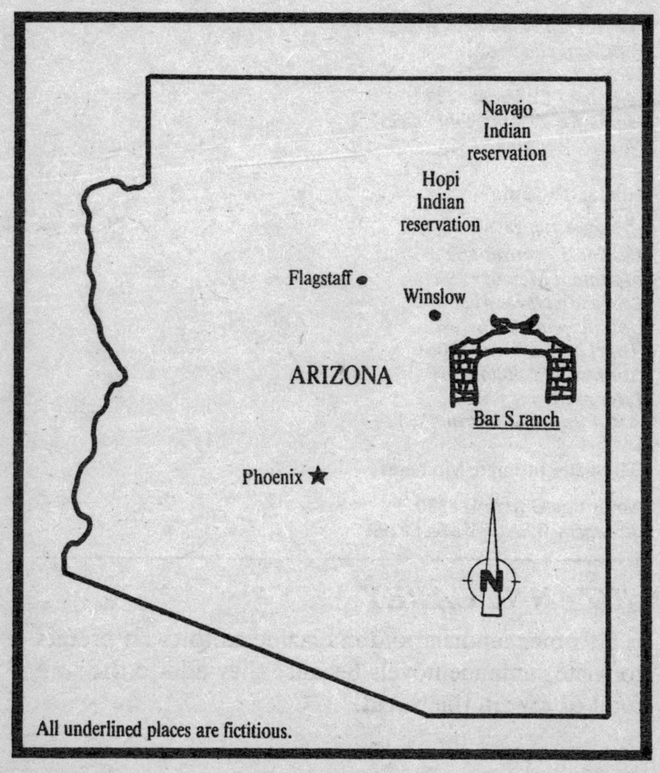

Navajo
Indian
reservation
Hopi
Indian
reservation
Flagstaff
Winslow
ARIZONA
Bar S ranch
Phoenix
N
All underlined places are fictitious.

Chapter One

Heads turned as Lara Stone walked into former governor Matthias Burney's palatial adobe-style residence just outside Phoenix. She was an hour late. The party she'd promised to attend was already in full swing—an exuberant crush of important people, bustling, white-jacketed waiters and the usual mariachis, playing their hearts out for hire. The party was designed to boost the political coffers of Jake Tynan, a candidate for the U.S. Senate.

By now conversation had been pumped up to full volume by the free flow of alcohol. The splashing of a copper-and-tile fountain that dominated the entryway was all but obliterated by the din, as were a few whispered comments that rippled among the guests. Lara didn't appear to notice she was getting any special attention. The daughter and only heir of millionaire rancher, hotel owner and political kingmaker Woody Stone, she was more or less used to it.

With a smile for the Burneys' butler, whom she'd known for years, she surrendered her swingy faille jacket and surveyed the crowd. The move bared shoulders as smooth as cream. Their only adornment was the pair of thin rhinestone straps that held up her dress, a slim, abbreviated column of black silk crepe. Its fit was pure class, a subtle compliment rather than a bold delineation of her curves. At twenty-five, with her finishing-school carriage and shoulder-length, Scandinavian-blond hair, she was the kind of woman who would attract attention even if it weren't for the money and power she'd wield someday.

Yet she wasn't beautiful in a classic sense. Her mouth was slightly too generous for that, her nose a shade too bony despite its aquiline refinement. Watching her with a narrowed, speculative gaze, Zack Silverheels decided it was her air of tough-minded innocence that fascinated him most.

Little Lara had grown up and then some. He'd known that, of course—seen her photograph in the *Arizonan*'s society pages the last time he was in town. In his opinion it hadn't done her justice. He didn't know whether to hate her or imagine himself taking her to bed.

The woman she'd become contrasted sharply with the image of her he'd carried around for two decades, that of a tow-headed child who'd held out chubby arms to him and asked to be lifted off her pony. At the age of five, Lara Melody Stone had been the first member of her sex to repose any trust in bad boy Zack, the seventeen-year-old despair of his father and all his father's friends.

I wonder how much she knows of men, he thought. If she's anything like Lily, her air of innocence is a fraud. Fascinated, he watched as Matt Burney's wife detached herself from a group of friends and greeted Lara with a fond embrace. Seconds later a handsome, graying man made a production of kissing her hand. A somewhat younger man brought her a drink. Accepting it, Lara accompanied him into the vast living room with its oversized adobe fireplace. The two of them paused several times to chat with people they knew.

Zack followed. Becoming aware of his gaze, she turned and stared straight at him. Gray eyes probed the black ones with the look of Native America about them. *Who are you?* hers asked. *Should we know each other?*

He inclined his head, giving her the sketchiest of salutes. Sooty with mascara, her lashes lowered a fraction, but not before he'd detected the telltale widening of her pupils. So she likes dangerous men, he thought. And recognizes one when he flirts with her. She's Lily Stone's daughter, no mistake.

Suppressing a little shudder at the oddly pleasant notion he was stalking her, Lara looked away. Who was this dark-haired man with coppery skin she'd surprised in the act of undressing her soul? She was certain she'd never seen him before. Yet there was something familiar about him, something so implicitly *known* she almost wondered if they'd met.

"Do you know who that man is?" she asked her male companion.

Scott Thackery frowned. "I didn't catch his name. I understand he's some kind of developer. From California."

Joining them, Scott's mother, Myrtle, overheard the exchange. "Stands to reason," she chimed in. "They're literally taking over the place. How's Woody, anyway?"

Lara focused on the problem that had consumed most of her time and energy for the past few days. "His latest test results are fairly good," she said, exaggerating a little. "He's still in remission... though for how long, we don't know. They're talking bone-marrow transplant... checking the national registry. Dr. Gooding may have some news for me when I see him tomorrow afternoon."

"What're the odds of finding an unrelated donor?" Scott asked.

"Only about one in 20,000, I'm afraid. Naturally I had my blood tested, anyway. And it was definitely off the mark. But I refuse to be disheartened by statistics. Woody's always been lucky. Maybe his luck will hold."

Myrtle responded with a hug and warm words of encouragement. It was no secret she and her husband, Judge Ben Thackery, wished Lara and Scott would get together.

Lara didn't explain that if the donor registry failed to turn up anyone, she had a last-ditch ace up her sleeve. She doubted the Thackerys would approve. But their reaction to what she planned would be mild compared to Woody's if he ever found out. She didn't plan to tell him. With his life on the line, she'd do whatever she had to do.

Conversation turned to the price of beef cattle and Jake Tynan's Senate bid as they strolled out to the patio. As Myrtle and Scott disputed the candidate's chances, Lara sipped sparingly at her martini and took in the familiar scene. A dance combo was setting up in the mariachi's place. Strings of artificial lights cascaded through the date palms. The surface of the Olympic-size pool was fractured with brilliance like one in a David Hockney painting. Glassware clinked, the sound punctuated by undulations of laughter. Somewhere a cactus was in prolific bloom. The sky was spiked with stars.

"When are we going to have some time alone?" Scott asked as his mother moved off to speak with friends. "It's diabolical the way you've avoided me the past few months."

Though Lara's mouth curved, she didn't melt. She wasn't in love with Scott. Or anyone else, for that matter. The man hadn't appeared who could make her yearn for something more than her single, virginal state.

"I assure you... there isn't anything diabolical about it," she replied. "Woody and his business affairs have kept me hopping. With him back in the hospital for tests, I have to oversee our ranching interests and the hotels pretty much by myself. As for his purchase of Club Cochise..."

Everyone in Phoenix's business community knew Woody Stone hoped to add the once glorious resort in the foothills of the Sierra Estrella to his hotel chain. With negotiations thrust into her lap, Lara was finding them increasingly burdensome. The Gila Bend tribal council owned part of the land and wanted some say-so in any transfer of the leasehold. Meanwhile, representatives for the seller, a Las Vegas based conglomerate, were dragging their feet. Rumor had it another buyer had emerged.

Deliberately she set the problem aside. I won't think about business or Woody's illness anymore this evening, she promised herself. I need a break. Just then the stranger she'd traded glances with wandered outside.

Almost immediately he was detained by Ned Carpentier, Jake Tynan's campaign chairman, and Lara had a chance to study him. Tall and lean, with coppery skin and hair like onyx-black silk, he clearly had Indian blood. From the look of him, it was probably Navajo. Though he appeared to have inherited that tribe's pride and rangy elegance, he seemed to lack its traditional modesty and reserve.

If I had to guess, I'd say he's a *mestizo,* a half-breed, she thought, noting the vaguely Anglo cast of his features. And rich. Without an impressive net worth, he wouldn't have been invited to the party. Nor would Ned have buttonholed him. It's a fund-raiser, after all.

She had to admit his mixed heritage had blessed him with a splendid physique. Broad-shouldered and narrow of waist, he had hips as straight and lean as an arrow shaft, the kind that made a man seem half a god on horseback. Instinctively she pictured him that way, in dusty wrangler's duds and well-worn boots, despite his snowy shirt and impeccable evening clothes.

Afraid he'd catch her staring, she switched her attention back to Scott. The musicians were taking their places. There'd be dancing at the far end of the pool.

"May I have the honor?" a deep, soft-spoken voice murmured at Lara's elbow as the lead musician announced the first set.

She turned, knowing exactly what face, what eyes to expect.

"As a matter of fact, Miss Stone and I..." Scott began defensively.

Lara silenced him with a glance. "I don't believe we know each other," she told her would-be partner.

A muscle quirked beside Zack's mouth. "I'm a visitor here. Since Phoenix is famous for its hospitality..."

He'd count her a snob if she refused to dance with him. And she'd regret the lost opportunity. "My home's up north, in Coconino County," she said, handing her drink to Scott. "But I don't mind defending Phoenix's reputation."

Leaving her longtime beau staring after them in frustration, they walked toward the open area near the bandstand. As he guided her with a light touch at the small of her back, Zack wondered if the tingle of contact he felt was mutual. If so, he guessed, she probably wouldn't acknowledge it. An obvious Thoroughbred despite her heritage, Lara Stone would shy easily and prove difficult to break.

Part of him longed to give it a try. Her acceptance would ease the nagging sense of rejection that still plagued him after so many years. At the same time it would bring him into closer contact with his nemesis. And he wasn't certain he wanted to disrupt his life to that extent.

He refused to deny himself a taste. The set opened with a sensuous, slow-moving number. Flashing her a smile that didn't betray his thoughts, he held out his arms.

A bit tentative as she stepped into them, Lara felt she was abandoning the known coordinates of her world. As a lover or an enemy, she believed, her dark-haired partner would be both accomplished and difficult to predict. Allowing him to take her right hand in his left and press strong fingers against the base of her spine, she inhaled his clean, erotic scent. She couldn't suppress a shiver of response as he drew her closer and leaned his cheek against her hair.

How light she is, Zack thought. How unexpectedly fragile. Though she was Woody Stone's daughter—Lily's child—he became aware of a wholly spontaneous desire to nurture and protect. She isn't a kid any longer, he reminded himself. She's a grown woman, with less right than most to claim his protection. And perhaps it was fortunate that was the case. Her delicate perfume and the brush of her bosom against his chest were making him want the kind of congress with her he knew her father would deplore.

Deciding to go with the flow, he pulled her closer still. As they danced, surrounded by the upper crust of Phoenix society, he imagined them lying naked together on rumpled sheets. His thoughts more heated by the moment as he pictured the contrast between her fair skin and his darker complexion, he let his hand slide downward to her buttocks. It had been a long time since he'd wanted a woman so much.

Instantly Lara knew she was out of her depth. This man, who might be an unsavory character or worse, was making her feel things she'd only read about. Rather than shrinking from the hard evidence of his need, she longed to know it more intimately. What on earth was she *thinking* of?

Yet as he led her faultlessly to the music, she didn't stop a second time to consider what kind of spectacle they were making of themselves. Or anticipate the gossip they would set in motion. Instead, she found herself trusting him. The moth in her was eager for the flame.

She came partway to her senses at the number's end. But she didn't pull away from him. Seconds spun out, ephemeral as cobwebs, as he continued to hold her. They'd ended some distance from where Scott was standing, on the far side of the pool beneath the overhanging canopy of an exceptionally large palm. Zack took a backward step.

"Umm, hadn't we better look for my friend?" Lara asked unsteadily as the combo switched over to a more energetic tune. "He'll be wondering what's become of us."

Zack had little doubt her irritated beau could pinpoint their exact location with the efficiency of radar. "All in good time," he promised, drawing her deeper into shadow so that her body screened him from the other guests.

"But..."

"A lady doesn't leave her partner in the lurch."

It was clear from her puzzled expression she didn't understand. With a flicker of irony, he explained. "I'm sure I needn't tell you that the feelings we stirred up just now can cause certain physiological changes in the human body. Unfortunately a man can't hide them as readily as a woman. If you'll give me a moment..."

He was using her as a shield! Lara's cheeks flamed in her embarrassment. Attempting to wrench free, she realized she wasn't going anywhere. No gentleman, it seemed, he gripped her wrists with unyielding fingers.

Ned Carpentier chose that moment to silence the musicians and introduce their host. "Ladies and gentlemen, Carolyn and I would like to welcome you to our home," Matt Burney said, taking the podium in his stead. "In a moment it'll be my very great pleasure to introduce the man of the hour in Arizona politics...*and* the next six years in the U.S. Senate...Jake Tynan!" There was an enthusiastic round of applause. "But first—" Matt grinned "—I hope you've all brought your checkbooks."

With her back turned to Zack and her wrists still imprisoned in his grip, Lara realized he didn't plan to let go of her without a fuss—whether or not the evidence of his desire had subsided. Her only option was to appear unruffled and cooperate.

Abruptly her resistance ceased. To his chagrin Zack found he was holding her with more force than he'd intended. Experimentally he dropped his hands. His attraction to her deepened when she didn't make a point of chafing at her wrists, or walking away from him. Instead she raked back her curtain of hair and went on listening to Matt Burney's speech. You have to hand it to her, Zack thought in admiration. Lara Stone can stand on her own two feet.

Jake Tynan was up next and there was a lot of clapping and cheering throughout his remarks. He'd almost finished when a portly man standing near the outdoor buffet began to gasp for breath. His panic-stricken *aaaaauuugh* as he coughed and clutched at his throat quickly became terrifying.

"Oh, no!" Lara exclaimed. "Burt Dinsmore... he's turning blue!"

By now several people were slapping the choking man on the back, trying to dislodge whatever particle of food had stuck in his trachea. Before Lara realized what he was about, Zack had sprinted to his side. A murmur went up as he applied the Heimlich maneuver and got Burt Dinsmore breathing again.

Relieved, the assembled guests gave him a round of applause. He shook his head slightly, rejecting it. Touched by his unexpected modesty, Lara revised her opinion of him. "Who *is* he, anyway?" she asked a middle-aged woman who was craning her neck for a better view.

A state senator's wife whom Lara knew slightly, the woman gave her an amused look. "I don't know if you don't," she replied. "*You* danced with him. He certainly is a hunk."

Out of the corner of her eye, Lara saw Scott advancing in her direction. The last thing she wanted at that moment was to field a barrage of questions from him. Operating solely on instinct, she met her dark-haired dancing partner halfway. "My compliments on some quick thinking," she said, holding out her hand to him. "As well as my gratitude for making this evening a more pleasant one."

After the way he'd embarrassed her, Zack hadn't expected thanks or praise. He took her slender fingers in his.

"You're leaving?" he asked, the beginnings of a frown drawing his dark brows together.

She nodded. "It's been a long day."

Tomorrow would be even longer for her if the business deal he'd concluded that afternoon had any effect on her state of mind. Surprisingly he wasn't disposed to gloat. Instead he wanted to see more of her—pretend she wasn't who she was.

"Let me drive you home," he offered.

A thrill of anticipation raced through her. "Thanks, but there's no need," she answered. "I came in my own car."

Zack shrugged. "My chauffeur can follow us."

She felt brushed by the wings of fate. From the moment she'd set eyes on him, she'd been inexorably drawn to this part-Indian, part-Anglo stranger who looked so handsome yet dangerous in his evening clothes. Added to that rapport was her own view of herself as a risk taker. Plus the odd feeling she had of trusting him. "All right," she conceded. "Give me a minute to powder my nose."

Lara didn't manage to buttonhole Ned Carpentier as she'd been hoping to. But she did bump into his secretary on her way back from the powder room. "Maybe *you* can tell me, Nancy," she said with a distinct feeling of relief. "Who's the dark-haired, good-looking man who saved Burt Dinsmore's bacon a little while ago? Ned must have invited him."

The secretary thought a moment. "His name's on the tip of my tongue but I can't seem to come up with it at the moment," she admitted finally, shaking her head. "I remember thinking it was a little offbeat."

A short time later the hired parking attendant was delivering Lara's cream-colored Mercedes convertible to the Burneys' front door, and Zack was helping her into the passenger seat. A black limousine pulled in smoothly behind them as they started up the drive. Zack had put the top down and a soft breeze disarranged their hair.

"Where to?" he said, throwing her a covert, appreciative look.

"The Wickham Hotel. We...er, own it."

The corners of his mouth turned down slightly, hinting at suppressed mirth. "You and a partner?"

"My father, actually."

Zack knew full well what Woody Stone's holdings were and Lara's place in the scheme of things. He didn't comment. Grateful that he seemed unimpressed, she leaned back and closed her eyes.

His expert driving brought them to the hotel's portico in just under forty minutes—record time, though he hadn't seemed to rush. "May I see you to your room?" he asked as the doorman summoned an attendant from the garage.

Because of the way the Stone family quarters in the Wickham were laid out, Lara usually didn't invite relative strangers upstairs. Instinct told her it would be all right in this case. "If you like," she assented.

A private elevator whisked them up to the penthouse floor. Instead of a hallway—safe, anonymous, with a door to close once the formalities of saying good-night had been observed—it opened directly into the foyer of the owners' suite. From there it was just a few steps into a vast, open living area with a magnificent wall of windows. Beyond lay a sweeping panorama of city lights.

Zack tried without much success to soft-pedal his curiosity. "Mind if I take a closer look?" he asked.

She could hardly refuse. "Please... be my guest," she answered, dropping her jacket on a chair. "May I offer you a drink?"

He crossed the thick carpet to the windows. "Thanks, no. The view from here is intoxicating enough."

For some reason Lara got the distinct impression his presence in the Stone family suite had a hidden significance for him. Whatever it was, it appeared to have evoked a melancholy mood.

So this is Woody Stone's perspective on Phoenix, Zack thought, shoving his hands into his trouser pockets as he checked out Camelback Mountain and the urban sprawl at its feet, transformed to a matador's suit-of-lights by darkness and electricity. At the age of thirty-seven, he was a powerful, wealthy man as a result of his own efforts. Yet somehow, as he stood figuratively in Woody's shoes, nothing he'd been or done since he was seventeen seemed to be worth a damn. Without Woodrow Wilson Stone's absolution, he'd always be a shirtless, hell-raising, part-Indian boy in the deepest part of himself.

He felt rather than saw Lara approach. "I still don't know your name," she observed in a low voice.

Zack shook off his reverie. "Are labels that important to you?" he asked. "Where's your sense of adventure?"

You know who *I* am, she thought. Before she could rephrase her question, he grasped her chin with strong, tan fingers. "You're right," he admitted. "I've heard of Woody Stone and his daughter, Lara. But then, hasn't everyone?"

With the inevitability of a thunderstorm sweeping from mesa to canyon, he took possession of her mouth. Sighing, she accepted her fate. Her unconditional surrender had him hot in seconds. Just as he'd guessed, Lily Stone's daughter was sensuality itself behind the elegant persona she wore like a designer dress. He longed to pull her down on the carpet, make love to her at the city's brink.

Not yet, a voice inside him whispered. If you take your time, let things unfold in their natural order, your revenge will be doubly sweet. He contented himself with rubbing his thumbs over her hardening buds through the silk of her bodice. The liberty wrung a half-smothered cry of pleasure from her lips.

She all but stumbled when he released her, as if the ground had shifted suddenly beneath her feet. As he looked down at her, Zack's eyes were too knowing for comfort. "Sorry," he said, his tone more mocking than he'd intended, "I hate to kiss and run. But I have an early plane to catch."

Did he think that if he'd been willing to stay, she'd have welcomed it? Her eyes blazing in denial, Lara saw him to the door. Yet as the elevator made its whispered descent, she couldn't help wondering if she'd see him again.

She was almost ready for bed when the phone rang. Not the private line, but the extension from the hotel desk. Was it her stranger? Snatching up the receiver, she managed a shaky hello.

The Hispanic accents of Frank Ortiz, the Wickham's night manager, met her ear. "Sorry to disturb you, Miss Stone," he said. "But Sally Hinkel from the *Monitor* is on the line. She says it's urgent."

Lara had seen the gossip columnist, who wrote for one of the area's less reputable publications, at the Burneys' party and deliberately avoided her. The after-hours call was probably a fishing expedition. No doubt Sally would demand the name of her mysterious dancing partner.

Sorry I can't help you, Lara thought dryly. I don't know it myself. Unfortunately, as Woody's stand-in during his hospitalization, she couldn't afford to miss a trick. She knew Sally had given him some interesting and extremely useful tidbits of information in the past.

"Okay," she conceded. "I'll take the call."

As it turned out, Sally had some truly stunning news to impart. "I was just wonderin'," the columnist drawled, dropping the bomb of a lifetime with her usual saccharine finesse, "how come you left the Burneys' party with Zack Silverheels, your daddy's love child?"

Chapter Two

Lara could think of only one reason to count her blessings when she arrived at hematologist Dr. Jerry Gooding's office the following afternoon. Zack Silverheels *wasn't* her brother. Or for that matter, a blood relative of any kind. Had the opposite been true, she felt certain she wouldn't have been able to live with herself.

Outwardly calm as she took a chair, she was steaming for a number of reasons, not the least of which was her deliberate deception at the hands of the man who'd kissed her with such passionate intensity the night before.

By itself the fact that Woody had a son hadn't come as a surprise. Like most everyone else, she'd heard the story of how Woody's youthful fling with a Navajo girl had resulted in an illegitimate pregnancy, prompting his father to bribe the girl's parents and hustle her back to the reservation.

She'd even met the progeny of that venture in sowing wild oats shortly after her fifth birthday, when she and her mother, the former Lily Burkett, had come to live at the Bar-S following the latter's marriage to Woodrow Stone. By then Woody's father had died and seventeen-year-old Zack had been in residence for several years.

Lara remembered him in flashes: a tawny, arrogant youth with slim hips and broad shoulders who'd lost his mother to influenza and seemed to feel scant gratitude for the generosity of the man who'd sired him.

Like most such yarns of its type, the story didn't end there. Everyone agreed that when Zack had appeared on the scene, all the girls his age at the district school, not to mention quite a few of their mothers, had fallen for him in a big way. Very quickly he'd acquired a reputation as a Don Juan that put Woody's laurels in the shade.

Even as a relative youngster, Lara guessed to her annoyance, Zack hadn't been overly concerned with the sensitivities of women who succumbed to his appeal. Legend had it that when Marcy Suger, a former self-styled temptress and the wife of Woody's longtime foreman, Hank, had out-and-out propositioned him, Zack had lured her to Indian Wells and left her stranded there in her underwear.

Woody had laughed whenever he'd recounted the story, though he'd always hastened to add he'd meted out a just punishment. What he hadn't been able to laugh off, *or* forgive and forget, had been Zack's reported attempt to seduce Lily. There'd been a terrible row in which Woody had wielded a horsewhip. From various third parties, Lara had gleaned the same telling footnote: Zack hadn't offered any defense.

For a short time afterward, the only child of Woody's loins had lived on the reservation with the Tsosies, his mother's people. Perhaps in an oblique attempt to connect him with his father, who'd been christened in honor of a U.S. president, Margaret Tsosie had named her son Zackary Taylor Stone. After Woody had disowned him, Zack apparently had found his surname—and the homage paid by the name Taylor to a white man's political hierarchy—intolerable. It was then, or so the story went, that he'd begun to call himself Silverheels.

At the age of eighteen, after joining the Navy to see the world, he'd made the assumed name legally his. By law he'd been required to publish the change in a newspaper of record. Someone who knew both father and son had sent a clipping to Woody Stone.

Now and then Woody had mentioned Zack over the years. But he'd never expressed a wish to see him or mend the rift. To Lara's knowledge, the old hostility and male rivalry he felt for his son were still alive and well. The only positive note she'd been able to discern had been a certain veiled pride that Zack had done well for himself, parlaying an unexpected wizardry with circuits into his own company, then selling it at a huge profit to go into the resort business on the West Coast.

There hadn't been any reason for Lara to suspect that Zack was connected with RD Developments, Inc., the firm that, roughly twenty-four hours earlier, had bought Club Cochise out from under them. To her dismay she'd found out he was. She wanted to wring his handsome neck. Her neat kidskin pumps still dusty from a futile visit to the property that morning in hope of meeting with the owners' representative, she recrossed her legs and thought with fury of the news that had greeted her there.

"I'm sorry, Miss Stone, but we've struck a deal with another party," the corporate executive who'd flown in from Las Vegas had told her, forestalling any attempt on her part to sweeten the pot. "The buyer, I might add, has the tribal council's full approval. I've asked our comptroller to cut a check covering your earnest money. You should be receiving it in a few days."

Something about the man's mention of the tribal council had rung a warning bell. From her cellular phone, Lara had called Stone Enterprises's Phoenix office and demanded a full inquiry into RD Developments and its chief operating officer. Her mood had been little short of murderous when Woody's director of research had rung back twenty minutes later to say what she'd been hoping he wouldn't—that the man in charge of Rainbow Dancer Developments was none other than Zack Silverheels. Zack was also the major stockholder.

"It's a multi-million-dollar company, very well capitalized, with headquarters in Los Angeles," the research director had told her, keeping his voice expressionless. "Holdings include Rancho Santa Anna near Mexico City, Dancing God Retreat overlooking California's Big Sur, and the firm's most recent acquisition—except for Club Cochise, of course—the Spirit Mask Inn, situated on a particularly scenic headland along the Oregon coast."

The property outside Phoenix, the research director had added, was Zack's first venture in Arizona, the state of his birth.

Lara didn't doubt revenge was her erstwhile dancing partner's primary motive. Her knuckles white from the anger she felt as she gripped the arms of her chair in Dr. Gooding's waiting room, she was convinced Zack had gone into the resort business for the sole purpose of beating Woody at his own game. Making a play for her had just been icing on the cake.

What had he expected Woody to do on that terrible day so long ago...*thank* him for trying to seduce his wife? He had one hell of a nerve!

Regrettably his carefully plotted vengeance posed several thorny problems for her. First and foremost was the necessity of admitting to Woody she'd flubbed the negotiations for a property he dearly wanted. Yet, unpleasant as that prospect was, the enmity Zack still felt for his father was likely to have an even more far-reaching effect.

Though she'd kept her thoughts to herself from the first mention of a bone-marrow transplant to halt the devastation by Woody's leukemia, she'd considered seeking out his estranged son and begging him to be a donor if his marrow matched. Now that she'd met him, she believed Zack would laugh in her face. Maybe the registry had turned up someone. She could only hope.

One glance at Dr. Gooding's face, when his nurse showed her into the inner sanctum, told her that hope was misplaced. "I'm afraid I have bad news for you, Miss Stone," the balding, bespectacled physician said. "We were unable to find a viable donor for your father. However, I wouldn't give up yet. We still have a few tricks up our sleeve. Since Woody's currently in remission, he may be eligible for an autologous transplant. In other words, if further testing shows him to be completely free of cancer cells at this juncture, we can harvest a portion of his own marrow, purge it and try to regraft."

Lara frowned. "That sounds rather complicated."

Dr. Gooding took off his glasses and rubbed the bridge of his nose. "Any type of transplant involves considerable risk. The autologous procedure works very well in some instances. But..." He shrugged perceptibly.

"The so-called allogenic graft from a relative or other closely matched donor would be better."

"In Woody's case, yes. From his past history, I doubt if the probability of finding sufficient cancer-free cells in his marrow is very great."

A small silence echoed in the comfortable room, fraught with dire possibilities. Pride is a small price to pay, with Woody's life hanging in the balance, Lara thought. And it's the only thing keeping me from approaching Zack.

"There might be another alternative," she said.

Dr. Gooding wasn't as enthusiastic as Lara had hoped when she told him of Zack's existence. "The likelihood of finding a successful parent-child match isn't as great as it would be between siblings," he said. "Of course, it wouldn't hurt to have Woody's son tested. The odds *are* somewhat better than they'd be with regard to the general population."

Woody was seated in an armchair beside his hospital bed, wearing his oldest bathrobe and reading the *Arizonan*'s business pages when Lara walked into his room. If she'd hoped to keep the Club Cochise fiasco from him, she'd have realized at once it would be impossible. Woody kept up with everything that interested him. And now that they'd been notified, news of the club's sale would probably be released to the press forthwith.

Painful as owning up to her failure would be, she'd never have considered doing anything else—even if Woody could be kept in the dark. He'd cherished her like his own child and, in the process, taught her a few things. One of them was to take her lumps when she had them coming.

I can't tell him the whole truth, she thought regretfully, bestowing an affectionate kiss on his leathery cheek. Not if I want him to get well. If he found out Zack was behind our loss of the Club Cochise property, he might put two and two together—surmise we've been in contact and guess what I have in mind.

Despite Dr. Gooding's reality indoctrination, she was stubbornly determined Zack Silverheels would submit to a blood test. Maybe it was wishful thinking on her part. But she had a strong feeling he could provide the break they'd been praying for.

"Tell me you love me, Daddy Bear," she coaxed, giving Woody her most winning smile. "I need a shot in the arm."

He grinned back, the crinkles that surrounded his faded blue eyes deepening with pleasure at the sight of her. "You know I do, gal," he said. "As for shots, I get enough of them around here for both of us. What happened? Did the Club Cochise deal go sour?"

Lara tried not to stare. At times, Woody bordered on the psychic. Unless she wanted an explosion, she'd better not let thoughts of Zack sneak into her head.

"As a matter of fact, it did," she admitted. "Apparently some California outfit with a big bankroll cozied up to the powers that be at Gila Bend."

To her relief Woody didn't suspect any skullduggery beyond sharp business practice, the sort of thing he was thoroughly capable of himself. Nor was he as angry as she'd expected him to be. "I'm right sorry to hear it, sugar," he replied. "Our only consolation is that the other fella probably got stung."

Lara shook her head. Zack was no patsy, and somehow she doubted it. "I know how much you wanted that resort, Woody," she commiserated. "I should have done a better job."

"Hell, baby..." He squeezed her hand with big, rawboned fingers and flashed his grin again. "You did your best. I know that. No matter how hard you try, some things don't go your way. That's just how this old world is."

* * *

Woody Stone would get a new lease on life if Zack could provide the wherewithal—one to two pints of fat, blood and closely matched bone marrow amounting to less than five percent of the immunity-producing matrix found in the average human body. Lara didn't plan to take no for an answer.

In her view Woody had given her life—or rather a life—just as surely as if he'd fathered her. Without him she'd have been an orphan since she was eight years old. Perhaps fortunately her real father had left for parts unknown before her birth, and Woody had become her only parent after Lily's death in a car accident. He'd been a good one. Now she had a chance to repay him. If Zack had the match Woody needed, she'd damn well see to it he cooperated—at whatever cost to herself.

As she hailed a taxi outside Los Angeles International Airport shortly before 6:00 p.m. the following afternoon, Lara felt a few stirrings of guilt about misrepresenting herself to Zack's secretary on the phone. But only a few. Every word she'd told the woman had been the literal truth.

"I'm an old friend of Zack's...from his boyhood days in Arizona," she'd said. "I'll be in L.A. tomorrow evening and I'd like to surprise him. Do you suppose we could set something up without being too specific... say around 6:30 p.m.?"

An obvious gem, the secretary had expressed her pleasure that Zack would have an unexpected visitor. "Leave it to me, Miss Stone," she replied with a smile in her voice. "I can be vague with the best of them."

It was already dusk when the cabbie dropped Lara off in front of a tall steel-and-plate-glass office building. Glancing at the directory beside a bank of elevators in the lobby, she saw that RD Developments, Inc., had offices on the eighteenth floor. This is it, she thought, smoothing her hair and pushing the Up button. If you want his cooperation, you'll have to be both persuasive and persistent. Any resentment you might feel over the way he's treated you or Woody, you'll keep strictly to yourself.

Walking into the reception area of Zack's suite was like entering a treasure trove. From what Lara could see, the Native American art objects he'd amassed rivaled the Museum of Northern Arizona's priceless collection of hand-woven rugs, Kachina dolls and pottery. Beige linen walls and indirect lighting set off each piece to maximum advantage.

"They're lovely, aren't they?" Zack's secretary said.

To Lara's surprise, the woman—gray-haired, about fifty, with the dramatic flair of an artist—was still at her station. "Yes...yes they are," she replied, holding out her hand. "I'm Lara Stone. Did you..."

"Tell him about the surprise?" The secretary smiled. "No, indeed. I'll leave that to you." Punching a button on her intercom, she informed Zack his 6:30 p.m. appointment was waiting.

Lara felt her nervousness mount at his brusque, somewhat preoccupied instructions to "send 'em in." She'd be at a distinct disadvantage, begging favors, and she hated that. But she'd be damned if she'd turn tail and run. Graciously thanking the secretary for her help, she walked through the door indicated.

Seated at a desk that consisted of heavy plate glass supported by what appeared to be several large stone slabs, Zack was reading and initialing a contract. He didn't glance up for a moment.

When he did, his eyes narrowed in surprise and speculation. Instead of an anonymous caller eager to sell him something or solicit a charitable contribution, he found himself face to face with the slim, Scandinavian blonde who'd succeeded to his birthright and haunted his every waking thought for the past two days.

In her plum-colored linen suit and antique silver jewelry, Lara was every bit as decorative and cosseted looking as he remembered. Today, French braiding swept her hair back from her temples. A minimum of makeup gave her a more businesslike air. Zack sensed immediately she'd come hat in hand, a supplicant. And that she disliked the necessity. Probably she wanted him to rescind his takeover of Club Cochise. If she thought he'd cave in just because she showed up in Los Angeles and asked nicely, she had surprise in store.

"Lara Stone, as I live and breathe," he said, casually inspecting her feminine curves. "What's this about? I'm flattered you followed me all the way to Los Angeles."

She didn't rise to the bait. "Mind if I have a seat?"

They were on his turf now. And he'd bested her by making off with the property Woody wanted. He could afford to be magnanimous. "Be my guest," he said, echoing the words she'd spoken at the Wickham when he'd asked to see her view.

Lara sat gracefully in one of two dove-gray tub chairs facing him, placing her briefcase on the floor beside her. She didn't say a word.

"Let's not beat around the bush," Zack prompted. "I won't bite. That is, unless you want me to. Are you here on business? Or do you have something else in mind?"

Unbidden and unwanted, the yearning that had hurtled through her like a torrent at Zack's kiss came back in a rush. Her emotions on the verge of betraying her, Lara struggled to keep a firm grip on herself.

"Actually, it's business," she said.

"If it's about Club Cochise..."

"It's not. I realize you're the new owner. My visit has nothing to do with that."

Apparently it was to be a whole new ball game. He couldn't discern a hint of the upcoming pitch in her eyes. "Is this about Woody?" he asked, calling his quirkier instincts into play. He assumed she knew most of the story, though probably not the truth about his part in it.

Lara's expression confirmed his guess was on target. "As you may or may not be aware," she said, "Woody Stone—*your father*—has been ill. He has leukemia...."

Something closed in Zack's face. He'd heard about Woody's illness. And made up his mind not to care. "Hold it right there," he told her. "Woody Stone *isn't* my father. He happens to be the man who sired me at the age of seventeen in the back seat of a broken-down Chevy. But that's all. Being someone's father is lot more complicated than that."

So is being someone's son, Lara longed to retort. Woody gave you a home just as soon as circumstances allowed. And you repaid him by trying to seduce his wife! It wasn't the first time since learning Zack's identity that she'd wanted to die of shame. To think her mother had been forced to endure the pressure of his cataclysmic mouth—feel the same pleasure-giving hands on her breasts that Lara had enjoyed so much. Furious at herself, she vowed to root out the attraction she felt for Zack Silverheels if it was the last thing she ever did.

"How do you know?" she responded, allowing only the faintest ripple of her feelings to surface. "Have you ever fathered a child?"

Zack gave her an appraising look. "Not to my knowledge," he answered, the corners of his mouth turning down with suppressed humor. "Though it's entirely possible, I suppose."

Unable to stop herself, Lara blushed. Was there no end to the man's capacity for embarrassing her? She had no intention of discussing his sexual escapades the way two strangers might talk about the weather.

Typically he pounced on her discomfort. "Can I get you something cold to drink?" he asked. "Or turn on the air-conditioning? You seem . . ."

"I'm fine." She spoke without rancor, though keeping her cool in the face of his sarcasm was one of the toughest challenges she'd ever had to face. "Would you mind if we returned to the subject at hand?"

"Not at all." He folded his arms across his chest.

No neophyte at reading body language, thanks to the many business meetings she'd attended in Woody's place, Lara realized she'd have an uphill fight. In the end she'd probably lose.

"Woody needs a bone-marrow transplant if he's to survive beyond his current remission," she said tenaciously, cutting through the preliminaries in the hope she'd gain points for a direct approach. "We've tried to find a donor through the national registry without success. And, though I'd be happy to donate, genetically I'm ineligible. As Woody's only close relative, you're our last hope."

It was Zack's turn to be incredulous. The man who'd treated him like a charity case, then horsewhipped him and cast him out, actually expected his help? With effort he managed to contain himself. "If Woody thinks I'll come to his rescue now," he said, "he's sorely mistaken."

"Woody doesn't know anything about this," Lara replied.

"Then . . . this scheme to have me save the day, so to speak, is your own invention?"

She nodded.

"I have to hand it to you, Miss Stone. You're a strong-minded woman. I doubt if peddling religious medals to the devil would give you pause. But . . . admiration aside . . . my answer's still the same—a firm and unequivocal *no.*"

For several seconds they stared at each other across the gleaming expanse of his desk. Lara didn't budge. "I don't plan on going anywhere," she said, "until you change your mind."

Despite her spirited response when he'd used her as a shield at the Burneys' party, Zack hadn't expected her to dig in her heels to that extent. Instead of turning on the tears or pleading, apparently she'd just wait him out. Lily Stone's daughter was no pushover.

"I could have you bodily evicted," he observed.

Lara shrugged. "I don't think you'd do that."

For the second time since she'd mentioned Woody's leukemia and asked for his help, the ghost of a smile twitched at Zack's lips. He was actually beginning to enjoy himself.

"No," he agreed. "I don't suppose I would. That being the case, what shall we do to pass the time? My workday's about finished. And I was on the verge of fixing myself a drink. May I get you one?"

Chapter Three

Zack's bar turned out to be in the luxury apartment he maintained next door to the headquarters of his resort development and management firm. Like his office it boasted a stunning view of Los Angeles, dreaming now under a purple and magenta haze as a mediocre sunset made its last bid for glory.

But that was where the similarity ended. His private quarters, dominated by a sweeping, primeval fireplace of white adobe that recalled the ceremonial fire pits of his Indian ancestors, had a personal flair and warmth the low-key, mostly dove-gray and smoke office lacked.

A small pile of wood and kindling had been laid ready on the hearth, which was flush with the floor's gleaming, putty-colored tiles. When Zack touched a match to it, reflected flames skittered away over the tiles to lick a Navajo rug in the prized Two Gray Hills design with light.

Above the hearth was a so-called sleeping shelf, supported by a smooth, rounded beam that was in reality the peeled and seasoned trunk of a small tree. It was sparely ornamented with an Apache basket and two small but perfect San Ildefonso pots, shiny black on mat black, richly carved and burnished.

More art objects and countless books lined the burlap-covered walls. Strewn with hand-woven pillows and throws in shades of tan and burnt-orange alpaca, a conversation pit in chocolate-brown leather was positioned to take advantage of the fire's warmth. The seating arrangement was the most inviting Lara had ever seen.

"Take off your shoes and make yourself comfortable," Zack said, obviously undismayed by her stubborn presence. "I'm having Scotch. But I can fix you a martini if you'd like."

As usual, the Los Angeles weather had turned cooler once night had fallen. "Scotch is fine," she murmured, kicking off her pumps and causing the couch's butter-soft leather to creak slightly as she curled up in one corner and pulled one of the burnt-orange throws over her knees. "Don't overdo it, though."

Zack's working costume had been a handsomely tailored gray sharkskin suit, white shirt and crimson tie. Loosening the tie, he exchanged his suit jacket for a gray cashmere pullover, which lay folded and ready on a nearby table.

He fixed their drinks without comment, pausing before sitting opposite her to switch on the stereo. Softly the strains of an aria from the little-known opera *La Wally* filled the room. Lara couldn't hide her surprise.

"What did you expect, a war chant?" he asked, crossing his legs and leaning back against the cushions.

For the first time since her arrival, her composure faltered. "I'm not sure," she admitted.

Downing a swallow of his Scotch, he took pity on her. "When I was in the Navy, I spent some time in Italy," he explained. "Over there, opera's like pop music. I grew to appreciate it, along with *pasta e fagioli* and Roman architecture."

She didn't answer, wary of putting her thoughts into words. Zack's track record with Woody, not to mention his treatment of her, forbade much sympathy or admiration for him. Yet she couldn't help but approve of his exquisite taste. Or feel a grudging respect for the cultivated, powerful man the once untutored, rebellious boy had become.

Apparently at some point he'd decided to give himself all the things his birth and family situation had denied him. Though so far she hadn't seen one about, she had a hunch that these days a manservant built his fires, laid his pullovers ready and turned down his bed. He'd paid his own way and she couldn't blame him for demanding the best—she blamed him though for refusing to help someone he owed the most basic loyalty.

"A penny for your thoughts," Zack said.

There in the firelight, with the outside world dissolving into mirage, he was even better looking than she remembered—a man in a million, with high cheekbones and coal-black hair, Woody's arrogant nose and mouth. Instead of overcoming her attraction for him the way she'd intended, Lara could feel it growing by the moment. With a little jolt she forced herself to remember the purpose of her visit.

"I was thinking that a man who lives as well as you do ought to give something back," she said, keeping her thoughts about his allure strictly to herself. "Even if you're holding a grudge against Woody, he gave you life.

He tried to make a home for you as soon as he could. With all your success, you can afford to be generous."

"No," Zack said, taking care not to let her see the turmoil of emotion her plea had evoked.

A small silence rested between them. I won't give up, Lara thought. I'll keep on hounding him until he says yes.

"I brought some pictures," she told him, reaching for the briefcase that lay beside her pumps. "I thought maybe you'd like to see them. Naturally they were loose in boxes rather than stuck, orderly fashion, into albums. You know how Woody is..."

Her stab at reestablishing tolerance via a reference to Woody's foibles appeared to pass unheeded. "They won't change my mind," Zack warned.

"Would you like to look at them, anyway?"

He hesitated. Damn, but this cool, utterly desirable woman knew how to hit below the belt. Leafing through snapshots of the two years or so he'd spent at the Bar-S would be like inviting old insecurities to surface. Still, he couldn't deny his curiosity. He possessed few photographs to connect him to his youth.

"I suppose it wouldn't hurt," he conceded at last.

Withdrawing a small manila envelope, Lara unbent the clasp. She didn't let her tremor of excitement show when Zack picked up his drink and moved closer to her so that they were almost touching.

"Here's one I rather like," she said, switching on the lamp beside her and passing him a photograph of a man in early middle age, a boy of about fifteen and a fractious-looking horse. The man was Woody. The boy, Zack, was holding the horse's bridle. Already his muscular shoulders and narrow, form-fitting jeans hinted at the lean but powerful build he would take for granted someday.

Frowning, Zack held the photograph to the light. "This is Deviltry, the first horse I broke after coming to the Bar-S," he said after a moment. "He was hell on hooves, and Woody ordered me to stay away from him. He didn't know about all the experience I'd had with horses on the reservation..."

"Woody told me once how impressed he was with your skill," Lara said. "He called it witchcraft. Said it had something to do with the way you used your hands."

Zack hardened his heart against the belated praise. When the chips were down, Woody Stone had believed the worst of him. "Let's see what else you've got," he said.

One by one she handed the photographs to him—a series of artless, awkwardly posed vignettes of a past she hadn't shared or barely remembered. Marcy Suger was in one of them with her husband, Hank, and Lara caught the barely perceptible downturn at the corners of Zack's mouth.

"That incident with Marcy must have been pretty funny," she acknowledged, "though I guess it got you in a whole lot of trouble."

Zack nodded. "I lost my driving privileges. And got sent to bed without supper for a week."

At least that was better than being horsewhipped, Lara thought. Though she understood and sympathized with Woody's outrage when his wife of less than a year had come crying to him, she'd always cringed a little at its expression. She wondered now if the scars were still visible on the coppery skin beneath Zack's shirt.

"Here's one of us together," she said, changing the subject. "From the looks of things, you were helping me learn to ride a pony."

The snapshot, which captured a towheaded, chubby Lara at the age of five, reactivated the memory that had assailed him at the Burneys' party. For some reason it made him feel protective of the woman she'd become in ways he didn't choose to contemplate. He could picture himself making love to the attractive Miss Stone in living color and erotic detail. But he didn't want to care about her.

"You were a cute little kid in those days," he said. "What happened, anyway?"

Caught off guard, Lara laughed heartily. The delightful sound made his nerve endings tingle. "Advancing age," she retorted, a dimple flashing beside her mouth. "Eventually it overtakes us all."

Was she insinuating that, at thirty-seven, he was too old for her? Though he'd decided against having an affair with Lara Stone when he'd stepped back from their embrace in Woody's suite at the Wickham, Zack began to waver. Twelve years' difference in their ages was hardly insurmountable. If she thought so, he was damn well capable of changing her mind. He felt his manhood stir as he pictured himself dragging her moaning and shuddering to the brink of paradise.

Despite her lack of carnal experience, Lara felt the change in his mood at once. A sudden charge of electricity seemed to permeate the air. As he regarded her without speaking, Zack's eyes were as black and unfathomable as jet.

Refusing to dwell on an imagined scenario in which he rested one hand on her knee and lowered his forest fire of a mouth to hers, Lara attempted to disperse the sudden tension between them. "Some of these photographs are doubles," she said. "Or near enough. You may keep them if you'd like."

Zack shook his head. "Under the circumstances, I wouldn't feel right about taking them."

"Have one, then. Or several. It's your past, too. You've every right."

Her generosity threatened to undermine his defenses as no argument ever could. I'm not going to do what she wants no matter what she says or does, he thought. But maybe I could accept her offer. What she said about it being my past, too, is the literal truth.

"Okay, if you're sure," he said.

Casually going through the pile of snapshots, he avoided choosing the one of himself and Woody with the horse he'd broken, though for some reason he wanted it most of all. "I'll take this one of me and Hank in the Jeep and the one of you on your pony," he added, "if you don't mind."

Maybe she'd picked up some of Woody's psychic ability over the years. Or maybe Zack simply had that effect on her. In any event she could almost read his thoughts.

"Please...take the one of Deviltry, too," she urged. "I want you to have it."

She'd mentioned the horse, not his father. Yet he couldn't help but feel a little suspicious of her motives. Lara Stone wouldn't be human if she didn't hope he'd take a private look now and then at Woody's face beneath the battered, shapeless cowboy hat and allow himself some compassion for the man whose very existence hung in the balance.

"Why that one, particularly?" he asked.

"Because it documents one of your indigenous talents. And earliest accomplishments. From where I sit, I'd say that horse was well named."

To every appearance, she was sincere.

Zack realized that mere possession of the snapshot would be a vivid reminder of feelings he'd rather forget. No one had ever made him feel as vulnerable, as despised as Woody had. Yet, conversely, he longed to relive the pride that had consumed him when he'd ridden Deviltry up to the corral gate and his Anglo father's mouth had dropped open in astonishment.

If he took the picture, he vowed, he'd use it to keep his resentment alive. Each time he looked at it, he'd recall the bitter day he'd stripped down as far as his jeans, preparatory to taking a shower, and Woody had come bursting into his room.

He shrugged. "If you insist."

His CD player had an automatic changer, and in unexpected contrast to the lush soprano of Eva Marton, the mellow, earthy tones of Bobby Blue Bland met their ears. More my speed, isn't it? Zack asked Lara silently. As an art form, the blues is better suited than opera to the common man.

A second later he admitted she didn't deserve the slam. To date, he couldn't fault her treatment of him. Yet he didn't like dealing from his weakest suit. He needed to reestablish his position as Woody Stone's bad boy before she gained any further ground.

"Still hanging in there on the picket line, Miss Stone?" he inquired, reaching across her lap to place the snapshots on an end table and deliberately brushing against her in the process. "It's almost dinnertime."

She nodded, retreating under the alpaca throw. With Zack so disturbingly near—Zack *touching* her—she needed to erect some kind of barrier.

He grinned despite himself. "No doubt you carry a toothbrush in that briefcase."

The realization she might end up spending the night at his apartment in order to make good on her threat brought a flicker of uncertainty to Lara's eyes. "As a matter of fact, I do."

"I'll bet you were one hell of a camper as a Girl Scout. Did you ever let any Boy Scouts come along?"

Having set out to conquer his merciless baiting with equanimity, she couldn't react defensively. "Not on your life," she answered, smiling sweetly back at him.

Zack was beginning to realize what kind of fighter he had on his hands. From recent experience he knew how quickly Lara's soft, gray eyes could blaze up in anger. And how capably she could deal with that sometimes difficult emotion. That evening, it seemed, no amount of teasing could prod her into losing her cool.

He found to his amusement that he liked her and wanted her to stay. He was attracted to her, sure—more than a little hot for her willowy but voluptuous body. But that wasn't his only motivation for wanting to spend time with her. More than any woman he'd ever met, Lara Stone challenged him. He'd always enjoyed a battle of wits.

"How about a bite of supper, then?" he said. "I don't know about you, but I'm getting hungry. My houseman and cook, Giorgio Fukita, always prepares more than adequate portions."

Lara debated whether to accept. Though she believed she'd dictated the terms of their confrontation up to that point, she sensed that the longer she remained in his apartment, the more likely Zack was to get the upper hand. One thing was certain: if she planned to stay, it wouldn't serve any purpose for her to starve while he ate his fill.

"All right...I accept your invitation," she said. "If you don't mind my asking, what nationality is your houseman? Italian? Or Japanese?"

With a faintly sardonic smile, Zack stood and helped her to her feet. "Actually both," he said, imprisoning her hand in his a moment longer than necessary. "Like me, he's a half-breed . . . at home in disparate worlds."

The kitchen was small and functional, a model of efficiency done up in stainless steel, white tile and glass blocks. Giorgio had left dinner warming in the oven. According to Zack, the delicious-looking concoction was Zuni green chili stew. The oven also contained a pan of freshly made corn bread.

"You can take the boy out of the Southwest but you can't take away his taste for mutton, hominy and chili peppers," he remarked, getting two ceramic plates and a pair of matching mugs out of the cupboard. "I'm having coffee with my dinner, and I take it black. Will that do for you, as well?"

Lara assured him coffee would be great. In the living room her most irresponsible self had wanted him to go on holding her hand forever. Another Scotch and there's no telling what might happen to my inhibitions, she thought as they carried their food into the dining room. Despite everything I know about him, just being around Zack Silverheels is enough to make me feel things I've never felt before.

The dining room contained a sturdy table, matching chairs and buffet in Taos-style bleached ash. Over the buffet, on a wall of used bricks that contrasted effectively with its soft, dense texture, hung one of the most beautiful Indian rugs Lara had ever seen. It was every bit as striking as the most costly tapestry or oil painting.

Zack's dark eyes followed her gaze. "That's a *Storm Pattern,*" he said. "From the Gray Mountain area of the Navajo Reservation."

"And that figure? The one whose body is elongated and bent around the corners to form a border on three sides?"

"He's a Rainbow Dancer, a stylized representation of one of the *Yei,* or Indian gods. They turn up in sand paintings and jewelry, too."

"As well as in the name of your company."

"Yes."

He didn't explain further. The casserole, which Lara noted also contained juniper berries, onions and strips of green pepper, was both spicy and delicious. However, hungry as she was, she ate her meal as slowly as possible. Unsure of what was to follow, she couldn't think of a way to work the conversation around to Woody again without disrupting their truce.

Whatever I say, it probably won't have much effect, she thought. A moment later, as she sipped her strong, aromatic coffee, she ordered herself to stop taking a defeatist stance. She'd walked into Zack's office less than two hours earlier and, compared with the depth of her commitment to Woody, the time she'd spent thus far trying to convince Zack to help him was minuscule.

After dinner, once they'd rinsed and stacked their dishes in the kitchen sink, Zack informed her he planned to watch a PBS documentary about coastal conservation in Oregon and Washington State. "We have properties in both areas," he said. "You're welcome to watch with me if you're interested."

"Just for the record," Lara remarked as they went back into the living room, "have you changed your mind about helping Woody yet? Initially it wouldn't involve anything more than a simple blood test, you know. There's a strong probability your marrow wouldn't match."

With my luck it would, Zack thought. And then there'd be hell to pay. "I'm afraid the answer is still no," he said. "Care for an after-dinner drink?"

Amply fed and more tired from the tensions of the past two days than she'd thought possible despite the energizing effect of the coffee and Zack's company, Lara declined. At the rate things were going, she admitted, she'd soon be too relaxed to go looking for a hotel. Well, if it came to that, she was prepared to camp out in his living room.

"I didn't sleep very well last night," she said, nestling back under his alpaca throw with every air of feeling at home. "No doubt that was partly from worrying about Woody and partly gnashing my teeth over the Club Cochise deal. If you don't mind, I'll rest a few more minutes on your couch."

Zack couldn't deny he liked her style. Frank about the distress his one-upmanship had caused her, she'd offhandedly consigned it to the past and refused to worry about it any further. Giving her a covert look of approval, Zack poured himself a cognac and switched on the television set, which was housed in a cabinet with pierced tin doors beside the fireplace. After adding several more pieces of wood to the fire, he settled back into what was probably his favorite spot in the leather-covered conversation pit, perhaps an arm's length away from her.

Though she fought against it, Lara's eyes started to close the minute Zack's program got under way. In spite of her determination to get what she'd come for and the anger she'd originally felt, it was incredibly comfortable to curl up there in his company—to drift in the low sounds from the television set and the unique aroma of the piñon logs that burned in his fireplace.

Zack might be the accomplished womanizer who at seventeen had tried to seduce her mother; the hard-as-nails businessman who'd deliberately trumped their bid in order to get back at Woody; the son who wouldn't lift a finger to save his father's life. Yet, incredibly, she *liked* him. She was too sleepy to resolve the paradox.

Some time later he was shaking her by the shoulders. "Miss Stone . . . Lara . . . wake up," he demanded in the deep, faintly rough voice that had begun to weave itself into her dreams. "It's quarter to eleven . . . not the most auspicious hour to cruise around L.A. looking for a hotel. I really think you ought to stay here. I have an extra bed . . ."

He was offering her his hospitality. And not suggesting they sleep together.

"If you need something to sleep in," he added, "you can borrow one of my shirts."

About to confess she had a nightgown in her briefcase along with her toothbrush, Lara held her tongue. The thought of sleeping in an article of Zack's clothing was too delicious to resist. "Yes, please," she answered drowsily, getting to her feet.

"*Yes, please* what?"

"Yes, I'd like to stay. And borrow a shirt if you wouldn't mind."

Zack considered the idea of her sleeping in one of his shirts sexy, too. He thought how much he'd like to see her in it, preferably with most of the buttons unbuttoned. They were standing very close, and it was all he could do not to skim her tempting breasts and narrow waist with his fingertips, think about trying his luck. The mental image of loving Lara Stone to distraction had been distracting him all night.

Why not have a go at it? he asked himself. Your body's aching for her. And, if she's anything like Lily, she'll welcome you with open arms. He'd tasted Lara's passion, her sensuality, at the Wickham and backed away. Now he wondered if he'd made a mistake.

Something stayed his hand. Maybe he didn't want to live up to his reputation in her eyes. Or owe her something he couldn't repay. The last thing he wanted was to find himself obligated to help Woody. Nothing could make him feel more used, more victimized.

"C'mon," he said, lightly touching her arm. "I'll show you to your room. And point you toward the facilities."

Chapter Four

Filtering through an overlay of smog, the first rays of what passed for sunlight in Los Angeles stole into the small guest bedroom where Lara slept. Nestled beneath a lofty quilt in Zack's shirt and her bikini panties, she didn't wake. Instead, murmuring something unintelligible that sprang directly from her subconscious, she snuggled deeper, hugging one of the pillows to her chest.

In her dream, sunlight was streaming down at ten billion watts or so, though there were dust motes, too, in the air. She was in the old corral at the Bar-S, astride Deviltry, riding in the pillion position behind Zack as he schooled his conquest.

Her arms were entwined about Zack's waist, her cheek resting between his shoulder blades against the rough chambray of his shirt. They were riding bareback, and as they gripped Deviltry's sides, their blue-jean-clad thighs and knees fit together like spoons. Every jounce of the sleek, dark animal as Zack eased his pace into a trot caused them to make renewed bodily contact.

"That's it, boy," Zack whispered to the horse, who was still wild in spirit, though compliant to his touch. Lara could feel his pleasure at the colt's obedience.

Abruptly she became aware of Woody's presence. He was leaning over the corral fence, a battered hat shading his eyes from view. "Two of a kind," he muttered, continuing to watch them as he shook his head.

Thoroughly immersed in her dream state, Lara didn't hear a discreet rap at her bedroom door. Or soft footsteps crossing the carpet. She was startled awake by a slight movement beside her bed. Blinking, she found herself staring into the impassive dark eyes of Zack's houseman, Giorgio, who'd brought coffee on a tray.

"Good morning, Miss Stone," the servant greeted her, with no more interest in his voice than if it were a common occurrence for him to find strange women in his employer's guest room.

Probably the more usual routine is to find them in Zack's bed, Lara thought, waking up a little more and dragging the coverlet up to her chin. *No doubt Giorgio has concluded I'm a charity case.*

The houseman waited as if for instructions from her. "Would you like to sit up and have me prop the tray over your lap?" he asked finally when she didn't give him any. "Or shall I leave it there, on the table by the window?"

"Leave it, please...."

With a minimum of fuss, Giorgio did as asked. "By the way," he said deferentially, "Mr. Silverheels has asked me to inform you he'll be leaving for Oregon in an hour or so. He hopes you'll be able to join him at the breakfast table long enough to say goodbye."

A brisk wind of exigency swept the remaining cobwebs from Lara's head. Unless she took quick action, Zack would win their stand-off by default. About to throw off the covers, she realized it wouldn't be easy to mount an offensive in lacy underpants and Zack's rumpled shirt.

"Quick, Giorgio," she begged, reaching for her briefcase and extracting a hairbrush, "bring me one of Mr. Silverheels's robes."

When she appeared in the dining room a few minutes later, Lara was swathed from neck to calf in oversized midnight-blue terry cloth. Her hair was neatly brushed and the robe's generous tie was wrapped twice about her waist. She'd even washed her face and applied a dab of lipstick.

With his back to the city's sun-drenched smog, Zack put down his newspaper and gave her an appraising look. Darkly handsome in an Italian-made charcoal suit, purple tie and silver cuff links, he'd been reading the business section.

"Sit down...have some more coffee," he offered casually. "Giorgio's making a fresh pot."

"No, thank you." Declining to take a seat, Lara stood there glowering at him.

He shrugged. "I take it the bed wasn't to your liking."

"It was fine."

"Then, what..."

"You're *leaving*. And it isn't fair."

Zack was silent a moment. "It so happens I have out-of-town business to transact."

"I'll just bet!" Aware she sounded childish and unreasonable, Lara didn't care. "I came here with the express purpose of sticking around until you changed your mind about Woody," she accused. "I even told you so. And you've responded by cutting the ground out from under me!"

Mildly Zack pointed out he'd committed to the Oregon trip a full week before her arrival. She was an uninvited guest. He was under no obligation to change his plans.

"I've done my best to be a gracious host," he said. "But my life *is* my own. You're welcome to stay until I return on Friday since, in a way...you're family. But I warn you...when I do, my answer will be the same."

Unaware of the incongruous picture she made, Lara rested one hand combatively on her hip. "What else can I expect," she retorted, "if you won't give me a chance to argue Woody's case?"

Zack regarded her thoughtfully for a moment. With Lara asleep in his apartment just a few paces down the hall, he'd spent a particularly restless night. Again and again he'd considered going to her room and making love to her. And each time he'd rejected the notion. From an emotional standpoint, he believed, it would be risky for them to get involved.

But maybe the game they'd been playing wasn't over yet.

"If you're dead set on haranguing me," he said, arriving at a spur-of-the-moment decision, "you're welcome to come along. But you'll have to be quick. Ask Giorgio to press your suit."

Lara was stunned by the sudden invitation. Already out on a limb where Woody was concerned, by spending the night under Zack's roof, she hadn't bargained on taking off with him for some new and unfamiliar destination. To do so, she guessed, would wrest all control of the situation from her grasp.

Yet apparently it was the best offer she was going to get. Meanwhile her determination to recruit Zack's help for Woody, if his bone marrow matched, had grown stronger in the face of his refusal.

"All right," she conceded. "Give me half an hour."

Forty-five minutes later they were boarding Zack's corporate jet: a silver Lear with the name *Rainbow Dancer* and one of the curious Navajo symbols Lara had commented on the day before, stenciled on its side in red. Her plum linen suit restored to bandbox freshness by Giorgio's expert hand, she could feel Zack's gaze on her as she preceded him up a short flight of portable metal steps.

The Lear's passenger cabin was richly appointed, with roomy leather seats and elegant fittings. Zack motioned her to a place across the aisle from him. "If you don't mind," he said, "we'll have the talk you want after I meet with my general contractor this afternoon. Right now, I need to go over some plans."

Convinced his invitation to accompany him was a sign that he was weakening, Lara was the soul of cooperation. "As you pointed out," she said, "the chance to plead Woody's case is a privilege, not a right. I'm at your disposal."

With only a slight delay, they were aloft. By the time they'd reached Santa Barbara, they'd outrun the smoggy inversion that hung over Los Angeles. The weather was sparkling clear.

Glancing up from his work, Zack mentioned that he'd instructed their pilot to follow the coastline at a fairly low altitude. "You should be able to pick out a landmark or two along the way," he told her with a smile.

Though she'd flown more times than she could count, Lara had never seen anything quite so beautiful as the California coast from the air on that crisp fall day. A deep ultramarine blue with its horizons dissolving in the mist, the mighty Pacific swept endlessly to shore, spending itself in breakers against jagged rocks and the sandy half-moons of hidden coves. Pleased with her ability to spot them, she located the vehicle-assembly building at Vandenberg Air Force Base as well as the famous bridge over Bixby Creek and Esalen Institute along Big Sur. At one point she made Zack come and look out the window on her side of the plane, certain she'd spied a pod of migrating whales.

They were as far north as Santa Cruz when she remembered Woody's doctors didn't know where she was. What if something goes wrong and they have to get in touch with me? she thought.

"I need to call the hospital just as soon as we reach Newport," she noted a trifle anxiously.

Zack glanced up from the pile of schematic drawings he'd spread over his tray table. "You can call right now," he answered, scribbling a number where she could be reached at the Spirit Mask Inn on a notepad for her convenience. "There's a phone in the cabinet in front of you."

A limousine with the inn's name and logo—a tiny spirit mask typical of those created by the Indians of the Pacific Northwest for ceremonial use—was waiting for them at a small private airstrip outside Newport. From the moment Lara had walked into Zack's Los Angeles office to plead Woody's case, she'd maintained that her involvement with him was strictly one-dimensional. Yet she couldn't help feeling they were a couple, of sorts, as he helped her into the limo's back seat.

It was obvious that's what the chauffeur thought. Once or twice she caught him watching them in the rearview mirror with curiosity and approval in his eyes.

As they set out on the short drive north to Otter Crest, the craggy peninsula where the inn was situated, Zack told her about the renovations he'd undertaken. Encouraged by her interest, he went on to describe his personal business philosophy.

"When I got out of circuits and into resorts, a far more humanistic enterprise, I realized I had an opportunity to do something constructive for my people," he said. "Spirit Mask is a good example of how I've used my good fortune. Though I've kept on most of the previous help, gradually...through attrition and creating new jobs...I've added Native Americans to the staff, many of whom might otherwise be unemployed.

"Everyone who's on the payroll for at least six months can invest in RD Developments at well below the market value of our stock. For many of my Native American employees, it's the first time they've owned part of a successful business. And it's a revelation to them. I've found that people of every race and ethnic group will work harder and do a better job if they share in the profits that result from their efforts..."

Zack broke off in mid-discourse as they passed a roadside vendor's display of kites. Being with Lara had revived his sense of playfulness, and acting on impulse, he instructed their driver to turn around.

Before she realized what was happening, they were parked on the grassy verge and he was helping her from the car. "You'll probably think I'm headed for my second childhood, but I've been wanting someone to go kite flying with ever since we acquired the Otter Crest property," he said, inviting her to choose from the colorful display. "You just got elected."

Charmed by his spontaneity, Lara found it difficult to believe he didn't have a dozen women eager to keep him company no matter what pursuit he had in mind. "I'm not exactly equipped for this sort of thing," she warned with a little shake of her head. "It's one thing to borrow your shirt to sleep in. But I doubt if your spare tennis shoes will fit."

Zack grinned, the tension of his hectic schedule easing out of his neck and shoulders. "Not to worry," he replied. "Even with renovations under way, we have everything from clay-court tennis to a first-class restaurant at Spirit Mask. You'll find whatever you need in our gift shop."

In Lara's opinion, the gaudier a kite, the better. The three-inch heels of her pumps sinking into soft, damp earth, she surveyed the possibilities, finally holding up her choice for Zack's inspection. Shaped like a giant condor, the kite she'd selected had spreading wings in ombré stripes of vivid color.

"I was hoping you'd like that one," Zack admitted, getting out his wallet. "See how its wings curve? It's a rainbow dancer of sorts."

Getting their purchase into the limo without bending the wings in question called for ingenuity and a certain amount of teamwork. Once they'd succeeded, Lara realized its bulky shape would force them to sit closer together.

As they rounded a hairpin turn that offered a magnificent vista of waves crashing against the rocks below, Zack's thigh inadvertently pressed against hers—hard, muscular, almost primitive in its allure. Tantalized despite her resolve to keep things on a friendly but not-too-intimate basis, she tried not to imagine what it would be like to make love to him.

No one had ever prompted her to think such thoughts before. At some point between where they were now and her initial awareness of Zack at the Burneys' party, she realized, she'd become a different woman—one closely attuned to subtleties and open to suggestion. A woman focused on a particular man.

No, *please,* she thought, casting a surreptitious glance in his direction. Don't let him be the one. Caring for Zack would be the ultimate disloyalty to Woody. Yet once they reached the striking redwood-and-stone inn perched on its oceanfront spit of land and he invited her to accompany him on an inspection tour, she was more than happy to remain at his side.

As they roved guest rooms, public areas and kitchen pantries, Lara got better acquainted with Zack's taste and eye for detail. She found herself making mental notes on a half dozen innovations that could be put to good use at several hotels owned and operated by Stone Enterprises.

When at last they'd finished, Zack pointed her in the direction of the gift shop before ducking into his manager's office to make a few phone calls. "Why not pick up a bathing suit while you're at it?" he suggested. "You may need it. Don't forget to tell the salesgirl it's on the house."

Ready with her spur-of-the-moment wardrobe some twenty minutes later, Lara learned from Zack that the general contractor's ten-year-old son had fallen out of a tree and been rushed to a local emergency room. "It's nothing serious," he remarked as he led her to his private suite. "As I understand it, a broken collarbone... typical boy stuff. But naturally his dad wanted to go with him. Don and I will meet over dinner this evening, if that's okay with you. In the meantime we'll have the afternoon to ourselves."

Hoping Zack's suite had more than one bedroom if she was expected to spend the night there with him, Lara forgot her concern when he ushered her out onto a balcony overlooking the Pacific. The one-hundred-and-eighty-degree view from his railing was breathtaking. She felt invigorated, just drawing the damp, salt-charged air into her lungs.

"I believe we could fly our kite right here," she said, her eyes alight as she unconsciously asserted joint ownership.

She was so much warmer and down-to-earth than he'd expected, so lively and full of enthusiasm. Zack wanted to hug her on the spot. Right, he told himself with a touch of asperity. And you know where that would lead. Whether or not she's anything like her mother, getting physically involved with her would be a mistake.

Of all the women in the world, he knew, Lara Stone was the least available to him. His suspicion that if he ever made love to her he wouldn't be able to get enough only made the situation a more impossible one.

"I don't doubt it," he answered, a rueful smile playing about his mouth. "But I know a better place."

Lara changed to her new slacks, matching top and tennis shoes in Zack's guest bath. She was waiting on the balcony when he emerged in faded jeans and an old sweater he apparently kept on the premises. Announcing it would be "a little cool out on the point," he lent her another of his sweaters, a heather-gray raglan that had seen better days. On her, it was distinctly oversized.

What a place this would be for a honeymoon! she thought as she walked at Zack's side down a soft dirt track that led away from the inn between moss-covered trees and a lush undergrowth of ferns. And what a fabulous man he'd be to honeymoon with, if real life didn't beckon just around the corner! She'd never met anyone who exuded more sensuality and raw sex appeal.

Wry, handsome and unpredictable, Zack had a tender heart, she was convinced, if only she could reach it. His philosophy as an employer told her that. Ditto the way his intelligent and likeable secretary doted on him.

At the same time he was a loner with dimensions she couldn't begin to contemplate. There was his Indian heritage, which she experienced both as a source of pride to him and a barrier erected to keep her out. In addition she guessed that however many women he'd known, none of them had been truly special to him. He probably hadn't let anyone get close enough.

Perhaps the aloof quality she sensed stemmed from being disowned by his father a scant two years after his mother's death. At the age of seventeen, Zack had been forced to make his way in the world without parental support. He'd had to put the past behind him and land on his feet. It was enough to make a loner of anyone.

From his characteristic response each time she mentioned the possibility of his helping Woody, she had a feeling Zack saw himself as the injured party in their dispute. And that didn't make sense. If he wasn't guilty of trying to seduce his father's wife, why hadn't he defended himself? Why had Lily said such terrible things about him?

She wouldn't get an answer from the trees, with their emerald, moss-grown trunks. Or the waves, which beat a louder rhythm with every step they took. Certainly not from Zack, unless she wanted to reopen old wounds and consign Woody's chances to the scrap heap. She'd just have to sit on her questions and wait.

They emerged on the point to be buffeted by a stiff breeze off the water. "The prow of a continent," Lara murmured, not altogether certain what she meant.

Immediately Zack took exception to the remark, confirming her musings of a few moments before. "From my admittedly skewed perspective," he answered, "the continent's 'prow' would have to be the land bridge over the Bering Strait, now submerged, whereby my ancestors crossed from Siberia to the new world. If it weren't for their restlessness, their curiosity, I wouldn't be standing here with you today."

Did he feel his Anglo heritage half as keenly? Or had he turned his back on it along with Woody? Again Lara didn't dare ask. She only knew she wished he wouldn't, because she was part of it. Though they could never be more than friends, and that only in a limited sense, she didn't want to feel so separate from him.

"Here goes," Zack announced, breaking into her thoughts. "The condor's maiden flight."

His black hair whipped by unruly gusts, he played out the double line, introducing their kite to the air's capricious currents. At first it scaled them in fits and starts, threatening several times to self-destruct. Following a few adjustments by Zack, however, it caught hold with a vengeance, forcing them to scramble after it over the rocks until they could bring it under control. An incredibly short time later, it was a rainbow-hued speck high above their heads.

"If we let it go, do you think it might turn up on a beach in Japan?" Lara asked, sitting on a smooth, flat stone and hugging her knees.

Zack dropped down beside her. "More likely Portland or the Cascades, if the prevailing weather patterns have anything to do with it," he said. "Shall I release it so you can see what direction it takes?"

"No, don't. I like sitting here, watching it soar. It's as if we could touch the sky..."

Her use of the joint pronoun made Zack feel extraordinarily close to her, as if some sort of bond had been established between them. As they lounged on their sun-warmed rock, dreaming into the blue and watching their kite execute an endless series of dips and turns, he opened up for the first time in years—telling the barely remembered child turned desirable, compelling woman about his dirt-scrabble existence on the reservation before his mother's death.

"Oddly enough, though we were very poor, those were among the happiest years of my life," he admitted. "My uncle Charley Tsosie, who passed on a while back, used to tend a medium-sized flock of sheep... some his, some belonging to my mother. I helped out evenings, weekends, in the summertime so she could spend her time at the loom.

"It was Charley who put me on my first horse when I was barely able to walk, and later showed me how to break one. Charley and my great-uncle Henry, our local medicine man, taught me the ways of Diné, the People, and the importance of living in harmony with the universe."

By contrast Woody showed up late, too hamstrung by pride and guilt to teach you anything, Lara thought with sudden insight. How you must have mistrusted him, after his apparent neglect of your mother! And how it must have rankled when Lily and I arrived on the scene—two good-for-nothing outsiders who were treated like royalty, with everything you'd been denied for so many years handed to them as a matter of course.

"What do you mean, 'in harmony'?" she asked, steering clear of the mine field that was his and Woody's brief but stormy past. "Must a person live the simple life of a Navajo sheepherder to achieve a state of grace?"

Zack's mouth curved. "Not necessarily, though it helps."

"Then..."

"The key is maintaining perspective...flowing with the rhythms of nature rather than flying in their face. Traditionally Navajos believe that illness and evil result when a spirit is out of balance with the forces that nurture it. The aim of a cure, or of justice, if you will, is to restore the natural balance. It sounds easy. But in practice, it's not such a simple thing."

About to suggest that burying the hatchet where Woody was concerned might restore one kind of balance to his life, Lara held her tongue. Such things weren't easy, he'd said, and he had cause to know. During their brief time together, she'd begun to realize there might be more to the circumstances of his banishment from the Bar-S than most people thought.

Though her attraction to him deepened as they talked, she was back on her guard a few minutes later when he reeled in their kite and suggested a session in his hot tub.

"I always have a soak when I'm here," he said, offering her his hand as they picked their way over the rocks and returned to the path. "It calms my city nerves."

Offhandedly he added that they'd have a chance to finish discussing Woody's problem if she liked.

Lara's misgivings only increased when she learned the tub's location—in his bedroom, facing the sliding glass doors that led to his private balcony. Noting her apparent discomfort, Zack couldn't believe it was genuine. But he was willing to play along. "Nothing will happen," he promised, "unless we want it to."

Considering the way she'd begun to feel about him, Lara regarded the assurance as a shaky one. He's probably telling the truth—for now, she thought. But when we get into the tub together, it might be a different story. To make matters worse, she didn't trust herself.

Zack was a magnificent specimen of hard-bodied masculinity in his black swimming trunks, when she joined him a few minutes later. One look at the gleaming copper skin of his torso and her pulse was racing. Yet he seemed to take his own extraordinary looks for granted. For his part he was clearly fascinated with the turquoise bikini Lara had selected and those parts of her anatomy it didn't leave to the imagination.

Wondering what had possessed her to choose such a brief suit, she slid quickly into the tub and sank into a froth of bubbles up to her chin. Zack joined her, his amusement plain. As they watched the slow pyrotechnics of a Pacific sunset, he was relaxed and amiable. But he didn't budge from his previous position. His answer to her eloquent plea on Woody's behalf was still no.

Against all logic Lara felt encouraged. Since their arrival in Oregon, Zack had seemed a little less angry over the past, a bit more approachable. With continued gentle pressure, she believed, she might be able to change his mind.

She wasn't expecting his kiss. Nor did it seem planned. When he reached across her to adjust the tub's temperature, she tried to move out of his way and he drew back to let her. Seconds later she was in his arms.

They'd already shared one passionate kiss in the Stone family suite at the Wickham, and the memory of it was fresh in both their minds. That evening they were a thousand miles from the spot where it had taken place—alone together on Zack's turf. With Lara wet as a mermaid and three-quarters naked in his embrace, he couldn't think clearly. His self-control disintegrating, he took possession of her mouth.

To Lara his kiss felt as inevitable as an avalanche. Parting her lips at the bold seeking of his tongue, she slid her hands upward over muscle and sinew to explore the powerful shape of his shoulders.

Her response kindled a fire that, if they allowed it to burn unchecked, could consume them both. This time, Zack vowed, he wouldn't stop at a quick brush of his thumbs over her nipples to make a point. He'd have it all—her wild gasps of pleasure as he drew her to the brink, the sweet annihilating ecstasy of losing himself in her depths.

They were on their knees, her lower body crushed tightly to his. With a wave of déjà vu that recalled her experience at the Burneys' party, she couldn't help but be aware of his engorged need. Each more heated than the last, his kisses were devouring her neck and shoulders.

She moaned when, with expert fingers, he undid the string ties that secured her bikini top. Recognizing acquiescence, not protest, he removed it and let it fall. His eyes meeting hers for a fraction of a second, he lifted her creamy fullness to lush heights and began to tease her nipples to taut readiness.

Never had Lara allowed a man to caress her so intimately. Never, by look or gesture, had one called forth such cataclysms of desire. In seconds she was ready for anything he might suggest. Half-coherent snatches of thought insisted that what they were doing was insane, given their situation and her strong feeling that lovemaking should be part of a lifetime commitment. Yet at some primitive level, without proof of any kind, she was convinced what she felt was right.

The longing Zack was evoking became almost unbearable when he took one sensitized peak into his mouth. She thought she'd die of delirium as he traced concentric circles about it with his tongue, then sucked her firmly, avidly, as if to draw all the sweetness from her body.

Abandoning her unspoken reservations and about to jettison her principles for all time, Lara was brought up short when suddenly Zack let her go. Though his dark eyes continued to smolder and he was obviously still aroused, she knew with absolute certainty he wouldn't take her.

The question burst from her despite her natural reticence. "What's wrong?" *Don't you want me?* she longed to fling at him. *Don't I measure up?*

As if goaded by thoughts she hadn't shared, Zack caressed her wet nipples lightly with his fingertips, then dropped his hands. "If and when we make love," he said, "I want you to take full responsibility for your part in it. That's why I'm giving you a couple of hours to think things over... and make up your mind."

Chapter Five

No promises, Zack seemed to be telling her. And no regrets. If we become lovers, it'll be because that's what we both want. It'll have absolutely no effect on whether or not I'll help Woody.

Holding her gaze for a moment as if to make sure she'd understood, he got out of the tub and extended his hands to her. Strongly conscious of her partial nakedness, Lara took them. A moment later he was wrapping her in a thick, white towel.

Smiling that half smile of his, he handed her the wet scrap of her bikini top. In that select company, apparently, he wasn't the least embarrassed that the outline of his desire was still visible through the fabric of his swimming trunks.

What a paradox the man was! He'd nearly seduced her and now his every gesture made her feel cherished, almost loved. Yet he'd pulled no punches about the risk she'd be taking. She had to admit that knowing the choice was hers fired her imagination.

Zack was watching her as if he wished he could read her mind. "If you're not completely incensed with me by now," he said at last, tilting her chin upward with one finger, "I'd like to ask a favor. As I mentioned earlier, I'll be meeting with Don Larson, my general contractor, over dinner tonight. I'd be honored if you'd join us... as my official hostess."

Lara looked at him in surprise. "I thought you were planning to talk business..."

"I am... afterward. I prefer to be sociable over food."

Partly to wear down his resistance for Woody's sake but also because she wanted to be with him, she said yes. Her head full of erotic notions and more aware of her body's hunger than she'd ever been in her life, she showered, shampooed and dressed in her plum skirt, pumps and a marvelous sweater she'd bought to go with them in the inn's gift shop.

Hand knit of plum, magenta and brown angora, the sweater featured an oversize "cuff" neckline randomly lit with paillettes in softly matching shades. Pushed down below the points of her shoulders, it framed her face and hair like the setting of a cameo.

Zack's dark eyes glowed with admiration when she appeared. "You look exceptionally lovely tonight," he said in a husky voice, resting one hand possessively at her waist. "But then, you already know that, I suppose."

Thought of what had almost been, and what might be later, crackled between them as they started down the stairs. Imagining herself delirious with passion as she and Zack moved together in his big bed, Lara almost missed the bottom step.

Don Larson, a tall, bluff man, was waiting for them at a reserved table between the fireplace and the windows in the inn's oceanfront dining room. Zack wasn't surprised by his reaction when they walked in. Though he dated occasionally, none of his business contacts in Oregon had ever seen him with a woman. With Lara on his arm, he guessed he'd be starting at the top in their estimation.

As he'd expected, by the time their drinks arrived, his contractor friend was thoroughly impressed by her style and intelligence. Basking in the reflected glow, Zack ordered for them from the inn's new menu, which featured several Native American specialties of the Pacific Northwest—smoked salmon and red caviar with buckskin bread, spinach salad and roast pheasant stuffed with wild rice, fruit and nuts.

As they talked, the subject of the conversation ranging from hotel construction to politics to questions of art and philosophy, Zack's respect for Lara grew. Never hasty to voice her sentiments, and more given to questions than hard-and-fast statements, she made a number of lively and penetrating observations, more than holding her own with her two male companions.

Maybe her mother *was* an alluring alley cat and her real father a ne'er-do-well who fled the scene before she was born, Zack thought. But that didn't stop her from turning out first-rate. It crossed his mind that as the world measured such things, she was probably too good for him despite his millions. But that didn't matter a damn. Or stop him from wanting her. Meeting her eyes as Don Larson inveighed against post-modern architecture, he was barely able to bank the fires of his excitement about what the night might bring.

Like him Lara had only one question in her mind. Far from certain she'd let Zack make love to her, she'd discovered that just contemplating the possibility could push her past reason into an abyss of longing. His willingness to let her decide was a powerful aphrodisiac.

Finally the tension of sitting across the table from him, trading glances and thinking wildly libidinous thoughts, became too much for her. She excused herself to powder her nose.

In her absence Zack's friend and business associate offered his unsolicited advice. "Hang on to that one, Silverheels," he said. "She's one of the smartest, classiest and . . . hell, why not say so? . . . sexiest women I've met."

Zack smiled, accepting the tribute. Why shouldn't she be sexy? he thought. She comes by it honestly. Much as he'd disliked Lily, he had to give credit where credit was due. If Lara was anything like her, and they made love that night, he didn't have the slightest doubt the entire inn would go up in flames.

The next moment he was annoyed with himself for being unfair to her. Just because, once her cool persona was set aside, Lara burned with a wattage that would have put Lily's to shame didn't mean she was amoral or treacherous. Or that he had any right to take advantage of her.

As if conjured by his thought, Lara chose that moment to return to the table. Restless enough to require a change of scene, Zack suggested they have their after-dinner coffee in the bar.

The Spirit Mask's bar, which Zack had decided not to alter, ran along one side of a cavernous lounge that was dominated by a massive stone fireplace. As they slid onto bar stools, there was a flicker of movement on a high shelf at one side of the chimney.

"It's a raccoon!" Lara exclaimed, spotting bright eyes and a small, furry mask.

Quietly Zack restrained her from jumping to her feet. "She and her babies are regular visitors here," he told her with a smile. "Stay put and watch what happens."

As he spoke, a waitress appeared with a bowl of whipped cream. Plainly wary of humans, but expectant, too, the raccoon scurried out of a small opening with a swinging door that had been cut in the wall beside the chimney, and watched through a window.

Once the waitress had placed the bowl on the shelf and retreated a safe distance, the raccoon returned. She was followed in due course by two cautious youngsters. Lara watched, delighted, as the small forest creatures devoured their treat as part of what appeared to be an established routine.

When at last their coffee had been drunk and the raccoons had returned to their wooded hillside, Zack confided that he and Don Larson would need roughly an hour and a half to talk about progress on the renovation and several change orders he had in mind. They planned to meet in the manager's office. Would Lara mind waiting for him in his suite? He handed her a key.

"Of course... I'd be happy to," she whispered.

Zack's fingers had closed over hers as he'd placed the key in her palm, and just perceptibly they tightened. "I'll be with you as soon as I can," he promised. "Don't go anywhere."

Alone for the first time in his comfortably decorated but impersonal home away from home, Lara made a quick inspection tour. As she'd thought, there was only one bedroom, with the enormous king-size bed she'd seen earlier.

At least there were no telltale negligees in the closets. Still mulling over the question that had consumed her all evening, she returned to the living room where someone had lit a piñon-wood fire in the small freestanding fireplace.

Beyond the partly open sliding glass doors to the balcony, in a night dark as pitch, breakers continued to crash against the rocks. Mesmerized by them and by her thoughts, she didn't switch on a lamp. By now she was all but certain what her answer would be, though God knew she couldn't justify it. Goose bumps feathering over her skin, she curled up on the couch to wait.

Zack's meeting took longer than he'd expected. He could feel himself growing impatient with the task at hand, even while the better part of him cautioned he should give Lara ample time to think. Considering his nonexistent relationship with Woody and all the bad blood there was between them, it wasn't difficult to conclude he and Lara were wrong for each other.

By the time he let himself into his suite, Lara was fast asleep, curled up on her side with her cheek resting on one of his throw pillows. About to wake her, he stayed his hand. Lying there in what was left of the firelight, she looked so young. Almost virginal.

Despite his craving for her, which had only intensified, and the belief he nurtured that she had more than a few scalps on her belt, she reminded him of the little girl whose picture—along with Woody's—he now carried in his billfold. You can't do this, he told himself after a moment.

Lara stirred with the first rays of sunlight on the breakers to find a quilt covering her and a bed pillow tucked beneath her head. At first she thought Zack had decided not to wake her and gone to sleep in the next room.

Then she saw his note. A plain white envelope addressed with her name, it was propped on an end table, against the lamp. She tore it open with shaking fingers.

"Had to leave unexpectedly," he'd scribbled in his distinctive hand. "The *Rainbow Dancer* should be back in Newport by the time you wake. Phone the desk to make arrangements for a driver. Todd—that's my pilot—will fly you back to Phoenix. Or wherever you want to go."

There was no goodbye. No mention of the fact that they might have become lovers. Least of all any reference to the opportunity he'd promised her to "harangue" him further about Woody's case. He hadn't even signed his name.

She'd been left in the lurch—just like Marcy Suger! The only difference was that she'd been dumped in Oregon, not Indian Wells. And Zack hadn't taken everything but her underwear.

Humiliated and angrier with him by the minute, Lara crumpled the note and threw it across the room along with several pillows. Zack had cheated her. Deprived her of the opportunity to help Woody. Abandoned her after mesmerizing her to the extent that she'd been ready to make love to him. She'd wring his good-looking neck if it was the last thing she ever did!

Punching the number pads on the phone's push-button dial as fiercely as if she were shaking her fist in his face, she placed a call to Los Angeles. But Zack wasn't there. Or if he was, his secretary wouldn't admit it.

"All right," Lara said, trying to remain calm and only partially succeeding. "Tell me where he is, then. We have some unfinished business to transact."

Genuine regret softened the secretary's tone. "I'm sorry, but I can't do that, Miss Stone," she answered. "Mr. Silverheels's whereabouts are his personal business."

It might be weeks before she got hold of him. Meanwhile Woody was due to be released from the hospital soon if they couldn't find a donor. His remission wouldn't last forever. Without a transplant his future looked bleak. Maybe Zack's bone marrow wouldn't have matched, Lara thought. I know the odds were against it. But at least we'd have done everything we could.

Grinding her teeth in frustration, she stripped off her wrinkled skirt and stuffed it, along with the sweater, suit jacket and heels into a plastic shopping bag she found in Zack's guest closet. Dressing in her slacks, top and tennis shoes and scornfully ignoring the incongruity of carrying a briefcase with that getup, she summoned the limousine driver to take her to the airstrip.

In San Francisco Zack had spent the night at a hotel. By the time Lara woke, he was boarding a commercial jet to Albuquerque, New Mexico. A shadow beard darkened his jaw and there were dark smudges beneath his eyes from lack of sleep. Even so, several of the stewardesses glanced at him with more than casual interest.

A short time later he was in a rental car, burning up the highway between Albuquerque and the tiny settlement of Teec Nos Pos, Arizona. From there, after visiting a great-great-aunt who was well into her eighties, he planned to head south on U.S. 191, then west on one of the Navajo reservation's rutted secondary roads to the hogans of his cousins, Jimmy and Buck Tsosie, and his great-uncle Henry.

Living in the Anglo world and making a success of himself was one thing—a kind of triumph or vindication. Letting himself care about an Anglo woman enough to let her off the hook was quite another. When that woman was Lara, daughter of Lily Stone and apologist for his nemesis, the misstep was one of grievous proportions. He was desperate for Jimmy's stoic calm, Buck's wisdom and Henry's healing presence. At the moment he needed them more than he needed food or rest.

None of Lara's subsequent attempts to reach Zack in Los Angeles yielded a return call. Though her anger at him became more entrenched with each passing day, she had to push it down and smile sweetly for Woody's sake. She wanted to scream when Scott Thackery called to remind her she'd promised to be his date for a charity benefit on Saturday. In her infatuation with Zack and subsequent fury at him, she'd totally forgotten. She could hardly renege at that late date. Both she and Scott were on the committee. They were expected to say a few words.

Dressed in her slinkiest evening gown on the off chance Zack might turn up, Lara drew a host of admiring glances. But it was wasted effort in her opinion, because Zack wasn't there to see it. To make matters worse, Scott proposed again and she had to let him down gently without ruining their friendship. It was a relief just to go home to the Wickham and crawl into bed.

The following Monday she was drinking coffee in the hospital cafeteria while Woody underwent the second to last in a series of tests. As she scanned the *Arizonan*'s editorial page, she heard someone mention Club Cochise. Focusing on the conversation, which was taking place at the next table, she learned Zack had returned to the Phoenix area. Apparently, with the help of a team of experts and the advice of tribal leaders from Gila Bend, he was assessing the deterioration of the once-grand resort and deciding what steps to take.

Since he'd abandoned her at Spirit Mask, Lara's fury and resentment toward Zack had simmered just below the surface. Now they boiled over again. By God, she'd see justice done! Flinging her paper aside, she raced up to Woody's floor and buttonholed the head nurse.

"Something's come up and I have to leave," she announced. "I won't be here to accompany my father back to his room when his test is completed. Will you please see that someone else takes care of it? And tell him I'll return as soon as I can?"

Barely waiting for the woman's nod of comprehension, Lara hurried back downstairs to the hematology lab. It was nearly 3:00 p.m. Kevin Deering, a young technician who'd frequently drawn blood from Woody, was about to go off duty.

"Kevin...*hello!*" she greeted him, slightly out of breath. "I need a very big favor."

When he heard what she wanted, Kevin shook his head. "I'm sorry, Miss Stone," he said. "I'd like to help. But what you're proposing is really offbeat. I could get myself in a whole lot of trouble by going along with it."

Lara controlled the urge to push him too hard. "I know it is," she soothed. "And I know where you're coming from. But this may be my father's only chance. Please... could we talk with your supervisor?"

Each year the hospital received a hefty donation from Stone Enterprises, and Lara wasn't above pointing that out to the lab director. After what seemed like endless hesitation on his part, followed by consultation with his superior over the phone, he reluctantly okayed her scheme.

Grounds people and maintenance workers were swarming over the Club Cochise property when Lara and Kevin drove up to the entrance in her convertible. The gatekeeper wouldn't let them pass. "Sorry, miss," he explained. "But we're in the process of renovation. Club Cochise is temporarily closed to the public."

Lara hadn't gone to that length simply to fail. "You don't understand," she insisted, glancing toward her companion, who was still wearing his lab coat. "It's a medical emergency."

The gatekeeper raised bushy eyebrows. "Why didn't you say so?" he asked, releasing the red-and-white-striped bar that blocked access to the drive and allowing them to proceed.

Zack was meeting in temporary office quarters with a team of architects and an older man who was clearly a tribal elder when Lara paused in the open doorway to assess the situation. As darkly handsome as ever, he'd donned jeans, a blue cotton work shirt and Navajo jewelry—the first she'd seen him wear. Upset though she was, she couldn't help but think the change was significant.

Or remember how much she'd wanted him.

Damn him, she thought. I still do. Taking a deep breath, she strode into the room. Kevin followed a bit hesitantly, carrying his lab equipment.

Heads turned. Zack stared at her in amazement.

"Is this what I think it is?" he asked after a moment.

Lara wasn't the type to swear in public. But this time she was really hot. "You're damn right it is," she answered. "You walked out on me under circumstances I'd be too embarrassed to relate in present company. And you owe me one. I plan to collect."

Impassive throughout her tirade, the elderly Indian from Gila Bend didn't blink. But the architects looked a little confused and apprehensive. Kevin was clearly ill at ease.

Lara didn't flinch as Zack inspected her from head to toe. It wasn't easy. He knew what she looked like in nothing but a wet bikini bottom, and she had a fair idea he was remembering that.

Despite her anger or perhaps because of it, Zack found her irresistible. He'd tried to root it out and he'd almost convinced himself that he'd succeeded. But it seemed the attraction between them was stronger than he was. Seeing her again was like being hit by a freight train. Or a Mack truck.

He couldn't let her guess how much it affected him. "A blood test to determine compatibility?" he inquired, the ghost of a smile tugging at the corners of his mouth.

She nodded, not trusting herself to answer.

"You're getting married?" one of the architects concluded—a bit thickly, Lara thought. There didn't seem to be much doubt in his mind that, if his guess was correct, it would be a shotgun wedding.

She gave him a withering look.

Thinking things over, Zack was forced to concede she had a point. She'd never understand why he'd left her that way. And he didn't know how to explain. At the moment she didn't want explanations. What she wanted was for him to take a simple blood test. Compliance wouldn't commit him to anything.

With a shrug, he rolled up his sleeve.

A few days later the test results were back. Awash in hope, but terribly afraid, too, that the odds against a viable match would be borne out, Lara presented herself in Dr. Gooding's office.

"You'll be happy to learn, young lady, that your hunch was correct," he said with a smile. "We have compatibility. In the committee's judgment, the match is close enough to proceed. You mentioned the prospective donor is your father's natural son. And part Navajo. Does Woody have Indian blood, too?"

Overjoyed, yet in a sense more worried than ever, Lara admitted that he did—two generations back on his mother's side.

"It's possible that factor made all the difference," the hematologist said. "As we discussed earlier, with the exception of identical twins, siblings provide the best match, because they draw on the same gene pool. With parents and offspring, it's a far more iffy proposition. Yet the odds are a little better if the donor and recipient have the same ethnic background. My next question's a practical one. When can Mr. Silverheels come to the hospital so the donation process can get under way?"

That, thought Lara ruefully, is anybody's guess. Though Dr. Gooding didn't know it, she faced a monumental task of persuasion, one at which she was all too likely to fail. "I'm...not sure," she said at last. "I'll have to talk with him. Please don't say anything to Woody about this yet."

Mulling over her approach to Zack, she realized he'd probably have a difficult time donating his bone marrow to Woody out of the goodness of his heart. To do so, she guessed, would destroy his pride.

Whatever had taken place the day Lily Stone had come running to her husband and accused his son of trying to seduce her, Zack clearly felt he'd been wronged. If Lara were ever to enlist his aid, she'd have to find some way of striking a bargain with him. It would require all her negotiating skill, given her ambivalent feelings about him. Driving to the Wickham, she squared her shoulders and picked up the phone.

Chapter Six

Thrown off balance by Lara's sudden appearance at Club Cochise, Zack's emotions had gone into a tailspin. Part of him longed to call her. Or turn up on her doorstep. Thoughts of driving her to the point of rapture with his lovemaking kept running through his head. If she was half as hot as he'd become to recapture missed opportunity, they had the makings of a torrid affair.

The Zack who'd fled to the reservation insisted she wasn't for him. She was an Anglo. Lily's child. And Woody's daughter—if not by blood, then by commitment. If she let him take her, it would be because of what he could do for Woody. *No,* the part that wanted her argued. She knew that wasn't an issue. And she'd have let you make love to her, anyway.

In the complex maze of his feelings, one fact stood out. Nobody but Lara could ease the ache he felt.

He planned to let someone try.

Earlier that afternoon, as he'd leafed through a copy of the *Monitor* while eating his lunch beside the pool, Lara's name had leaped at him from the page.

"What's next for cattle and hotel heiress Lara Melody Stone?" gossip columnist Sally Hinkel had written. "The dear child simply has too many 'playthings' (read admirers). After a very private out-of-state sojourn with a dark-eyed millionaire, our pet has collected another proposal of marriage from the son of a wealthy and prominent judge. Rumor has it she's waiting to see the size of the rock before passing judgment."

In the hot tub at Spirit Mask, Lara had simply been using him! She'd been involved with someone else all along—a man more suited, no doubt, to her white, Anglo-Saxon Protestant background and refined taste. Accidently knocking over his iced tea so that the glass shattered on the pool decking, Zack jumped to his feet and stalked into this office for his "little black book." It had been quite a while since he'd seen the good-looking redhead whose name he quickly located under the *M*s. But he didn't doubt that she would remember him.

As it had turned out, TV weather forecaster Kathie McMurtree remembered Zack very well. Penciling in the changes he wanted for the pool area on an architect's rendering shortly after 6:00 p.m., he tried to tell himself a night in Kathie's arms would solve everything. She'd ease the fire in his gut that was an undeniable tribute to another woman, the sexy but mercenary daughter of the cheap little tramp who'd cost him his father's friendship.

Don't be a fool, he told himself bitterly. Woody's defection wasn't all Lily's fault. He never trusted you. Or wanted you around. He was just salving his conscience when he brought you home to the Bar-S to live. As for Lara, you ought to have your head examined for letting her off the hook. If you'd taken her to bed—spent the night making repeated love to her—you'd have gotten her out of your system.

In Zack's experience there were two kinds of women in the world: the good ones like his mother, who usually ended up as victims, and the sexy, confident ones like Lily and her daughter, who sapped a man's judgment and led him down the garden path. Any notion he'd had that Lara was a rare combination of virtue and sensuality was just so much moonshine and cobwebs.

He answered the phone on the second ring.

"Hi," Lara said hesitantly. "We need to talk."

Against all odds, the blood test had come back positive. His bone marrow matched Woody's. Zack knew it as surely as he was sitting there. A feeling of power came over him, coupled with the gut-wrenching sensation of being trapped. I'm really in for it now, he thought.

"What about?" he asked.

"Could I come out to Club Cochise?"

He'd been about to jump into the shower and get ready for his date. But he could always phone Kathie. Say he'd been detained. Or cancel out altogether.

It would take Lara forty-five minutes to an hour to reach his doorstep whether she was phoning from the Wickham or the hospital. "Sure...come if you want," he said. "I'll alert the gatekeeper to pass you through."

For several moments after he put down the phone, Zack simply stared at the wall. Then he picked up the phone again and dialed Kathie's number. "Something's come up and I can't make it tonight after all," he told her. "Hope you understand. Rain check?"

Though she was obviously disappointed, Kathie assured him she understood. Telling her goodbye, he extracted the snapshots of Woody and Lara from his billfold. Except for his cousins on the reservation, the woman he craved and the father who'd rejected him were the closest thing he had to family. Something in him yearned for their acceptance.

Stifling such thoughts as indicative of weakness, he vowed to take Lara down a peg or two and get the revenge against Woody he'd always wanted.

But how?

The first stages of an idea forming in his head, he placed another call. "Hello...Joe Twelve Crows?" he asked when a man answered. "Zack Silverheels. I know it's short notice. But if you'd like to interview for that position at Club Cochise, I have an hour free this evening. Good. Shall we say 7:00 p.m.? In the former spa area?"

As promised, Lara was expected. Phoning from his kiosk, the gatekeeper summoned one of Zack's night security people. She was slightly taken aback when the guard escorted her to the resort's shuttered health facility instead of the office she remembered. "Mr. Silverheels is interviewing a prospective employee," the man reassured her. "He said for you to go right in."

Though it was well lit and clean, the health club obviously had seen better days. Barren of furnishings, its foyer echoed at the sound of Lara's footsteps on the tiles. She could hear voices coming from the weight-training room. Pushing open the door, she got the surprise of her life.

Zack was nude—lying on his stomach across a sheet-draped table, receiving a massage. The burly masseur might have been an ex-boxer. Though he glanced at her briefly, he didn't miss a stroke.

Coppery smooth and gleaming with oil as his muscles rippled in the sheen of an overhead lamp, the man she'd come to see regarded her lazily. "Pardon the informality but I'm interviewing masseurs and I've found this is the most effective way to do it," he said. "Pull up a chair."

Lara flushed scarlet at the thought of bargaining with him while he lay naked in front of her, every inch of his exquisitely formed buttocks and thighs exposed. She wanted to turn tail and run.

"Couldn't we—" she paused "—er, wait until after your massage?"

Zack's lips curled. "What's the difference? Surely you've seen your share of naked men."

As a matter of fact she hadn't—just a few illustrations in her college anatomy book and a glimpse or two in one mildly naughty movie she'd rented with her college roommates. Despite her experience with Zack in the hot tub, she'd never dreamed a man's naked body could be so visually erotic.

If he'd arranged to talk with her during a massage for the express purpose of embarrassing her, he'd certainly achieved his aim. Just looking at him was enough to render her speechless. I wonder why he's doing this? she thought. He walked out on *me*. Yet it's as if he wants to punish me for something.

"Well . . ." she said, then hesitated. "All right."

Feeling like the klutz of the century, Lara walked over to the former receptionist's desk and somewhat awkwardly appropriated its chair. It was all she could do not to focus on the multiple views of Zack's nakedness that looked back at her from the room's mirrored walls as she took up the least compromising position that would allow them to talk.

"Well?" Zack asked, clearly enjoying her discomfort. "What brings you all the way out to the foothills of the Sierra Estralla tonight?"

Lara shrugged, willing herself not to appear prudish or naive. "Haven't you guessed?"

"My blood profile matches Woody's."

After having his little joke, maybe he'd make it easy for her. She could only hope. "As a matter of fact it does," she acknowledged, "despite some pretty formidable odds."

Something flickered in his gaze. But all he said was "I'm not surprised."

Mustering her courage, Lara made her opening bid. "I know you don't feel any obligation to help Woody," she said. "And, in a way, I can understand that. So I thought...maybe we could strike a deal of some sort. You do what I want and I see to it you're compensated. That way it won't be like you're doing it for me. Or him."

She hadn't lectured him about duty. Or tried to shame him into helping his stricken father now that the test results had come back positive. He had to admit she was far more perceptive than he'd given her credit for.

Firmly he squelched the notion that, if he capitulated, he and Woody might reconcile. Even if he wanted such a thing—which he didn't—his Anglo father would refuse.

He gave Lara a calculating look.

"I have all the money I want," he answered. "Far more than I'm ever likely to spend. What did you have in mind?"

To her, seated just a few feet away as the hulking, impassive masseur hacked and kneaded his muscles, Zack was like a great, copper-colored panther, ready to spring. She found herself blushing again.

"I was just going to ask you that."

"What about part of the Bar-S? The whole shooting match should have been mine someday, by inheritance."

Lara blanched. The remark made her feel like an interloper—greedy and undeserving of the only home she could remember. Apparently that was how Zack viewed her.

"For myself, I wouldn't care," she said after a moment. "But the ranch is Woody's home. He owns it...I don't. I couldn't agree to anything like that without asking him first. And, as I said, he doesn't know I've approached you."

If Woody did know, he'd probably choose to die before accepting my help, Zack thought. *I* would, rather than take charity from him.

The shock value of greeting her nude from the massage table had worn thin and he motioned to the masseur that their session was at an end. "Thanks for coming out," he said. "I plan to interview one other person before making a decision. I'll give you a call."

Lara should have guessed what was coming next. But she didn't. She was caught unawares when Zack rose unselfconsciously and reached for a white terry cloth robe. For a moment she could see everything! The man was just too much!

Averting her face, she got up and headed for the door.

"*Lara...*" Zack's voice resonated with amusement at what he wanted to believe was a very convincing act. "If you'll wait a moment, I'm willing to discuss this further. I've asked that dinner for two be sent to my office."

Though the work space where Kevin had drawn Zack's blood was strictly makeshift, once again he was the perfect host. Settling her in the room's only comfortable chair, which had been occupied by the tribal elder from Gila Bend a few days earlier, he phone the kitchen.

"We're ready now, Jacques."

She had to give Zack high marks for thinking on his feet. After considering it for a moment, she'd have bet money that neither the massage nor the fancy meal that arrived on a white-napped trolley had been in the works before her call. They'd obviously taken some doing, particularly the meal, since the kitchen had likely closed for the day after his work crews had gone home. No doubt the chef was being paid overtime.

The food was French, cooked to perfection and imaginatively presented. Unfortunately for Lara's peace of mind, Zack continued to wear his white terry cloth robe—and nothing else. She wasn't able to forget that fact or the serious nature of their talk as she explained the bone-marrow donation process in detail.

"So," she said at last, taking a bite from the entrée she'd barely touched. "That's it in a nutshell. It's not a particularly pleasant process. But not too difficult, either. What do you think? Would you care to state what you'd consider adequate compensation?"

Since her phone call earlier, Zack had been thinking of little else. If he donated his marrow to Woody without getting something back, he'd feel he was being used. Yet, in the final analysis, he couldn't square it with his conscience to refuse. Staring compulsively at the snapshots Lara had given him and mulling over the gossip he'd read in the *Monitor,* he felt an unreasoning desire to put her in her place in addition to revenging himself on his father.

It hadn't been until he was lying on the massage table, awaiting her arrival, that the rest of his idea had fallen into place. So what if it was a complete about-face from the position he'd taken in Oregon? The situation had changed. And so had he. Belatedly he'd come to his senses.

If Lara agreed to his plan, he'd be able to cooperate in Woody's transplant while exacting poetic justice for the thrashing he'd received. Their bargain would have the added benefit of allowing him to scratch an itch that had been troubling him since they'd met.

"Actually I do have something in mind," he said, pushing back his plate.

She waited, suddenly apprehensive.

"I'll help Woody, if you'll spend a night in my bed."

At first Lara couldn't believe she'd heard him right. Had he actually said...?

The look on his face told her she wasn't imagining things. Shocked and horrified, she leaped to her feet. "You can't be serious!" she exclaimed. "That would make me a...a..."

She couldn't bring herself to say the word.

Turning a deaf ear to his scruples, Zack didn't react to her distress. "I don't see why," he said reasonably. "It wouldn't be for money. Besides, we almost became lovers in Oregon. In my opinion, we *would* have...if I hadn't backed out first."

Lara burned at his frank description of what had taken place. But she couldn't deny it was accurate. At a loss for words, she started toward the door for the second time that evening.

"Think it over," Zack warned. "You won't get another chance."

Her hand on the knob, she hesitated. She didn't want Woody to die. Yet the price she'd be forced to pay in order to save him would be devastating. Bit by bit, Zack had worn down her resistance until she'd all but fallen in love with him. Now, by forcing her to barter over what she'd have given him freely at Spirit Mask, he'd savaged tremulous, never-before-experienced feelings.

"It's retribution, isn't it?" she asked, her tone bleak as she turned back to face him. "You're trying to get at Woody through me. Tell me the truth!"

Zack's composure didn't falter. "You might have a point."

For several seconds they simply stared at each other. Then Lara said coldly, "I'll need time to think about this," unwilling to slam the door on what she believed was Woody's only chance.

Scenting victory, Zack drove his advantage home. "Take all the time you want," he said, "until 8:00 a.m. tomorrow morning, that is. Since I'm flying back to Los Angeles an hour later, that's when my offer expires."

Walking out of Zack's office without another word, Lara drove straight to the hospital. Though he seemed glad to see her, Woody was in a pensive mood. "Thought you'd gone for the day, gal," he said, giving her a searching look. "What was so all-fired important you had to tear out of here like that? Is anything the matter?"

Lara didn't doubt her shock and vexation were showing in her face. Though she disliked the need to lie, she forced herself to fabricate a plausible excuse. "One of my friends had car trouble," she said. "I had to pick her up at the garage. She was upset and we had dinner together."

Sighing, Woody looked at the night sky through his hospital room window. "There's something I've been meanin' to talk to you about," he said. "I know you don't want to accept it, sweetheart. But it doesn't look like they're gonna find a match for me. I ought to update my will..."

Putting on his reading glasses, which always made him look older and a little more vulnerable, Woody produced a handwritten list of special bequests for longtime employees like Hank Suger and Emma Tarbush, his housekeeper for more than thirty years.

"I'd appreciate it if you'd ask Cal French to put this in his safe until we get the revisions done," he said.

Heartbroken at seeing him so resigned to what he believed was the inevitable, Lara decided she didn't have any choice. She'd have to accept Zack's proposal. She phoned him that night from the Wickham before going to bed.

"Have you come to a decision?" he asked.

She paused, imagining the triumph her answer would afford. "Yes," she answered as calmly as possible. "If you agree to donate the bone marrow to Woody, I'll have sex with you."

The line hummed empty for a moment.

"Don't forget...I said 'spend the night,'" he cautioned. "I wasn't talking about a single encounter."

Hot chills washed over her at the thought that he planned to make love to her again and again. "I haven't forgotten," she said in a tight little voice.

There was another pause. "Okay," Zack replied, suddenly all business. "I can arrange to put off my California meeting for a day or two. See you tomorrow night at eight. I don't suppose I need to remind you to bring a toothbrush."

The following day Lara was so moody and withdrawn Woody finally remarked on it. "I hope it isn't anything I said or did, sugar," he told her contritely, squeezing her hand.

Reassuring him it was just a headache, she continued to watch the clock. Around 5:00 p.m. she told him she had to leave and get ready for a date.

Woody responded with his first genuine smile of the afternoon. "Must be a heavy one, darlin'," he said, innocent of the step she was about to take. "You have fun tonight, you hear?"

How do you dress for an assignation with a man you could so easily have loved? Lara asked herself as, back at the Wickham, she toweled off after her bath. In scarlet? She didn't *own* anything disreputable enough to do Zack justice!

She did have her pride. And a sexy-but-modest red dress he might remember for a while when she was once more beyond his reach.

Her body shrinking from the all-consuming pleasures it had been aching to experience just a week before, she put on her laciest underwear. Ironically it was white. Mere wisps of silk and reembroidered lace, the skimpy strapless bra and V-shaped bikini were new. And perfect for a bride. What a travesty this is of the wedding night I've been saving myself for, Lara thought. I can't believe that after this I'll ever want to marry anyone.

Zipping up her red dress, a sleek faille number with a curving, off-the-shoulder bodice and demure, bracelet-length sleeves, she studied the effect in the mirror. It would do, both as a statement of her self-worth and a mute protest. Taking a last look around her room and knowing she'd be something tarnished in body if not in spirit when she returned to it, Lara picked up her purse and car keys from the dresser.

When she arrived at Club Cochise, the gatekeeper was expecting her. He waved her through with a little salute. At quarter to eight the grounds were deserted. From Lara's viewpoint that was all for the good. Though her virginity would be forfeit, she didn't want to sacrifice her reputation. With no one around, there'd be no witnesses to spread rumors about them.

Scowling in the dinner jacket and trousers he'd worn to the Burneys' party, Zack stood in his office window and surveyed the floodlit pool area below. Am I making the biggest mistake of my life by doing this? he wondered. Maybe if I'd courted her as a man usually courts a woman, Lara would want me for myself and not just as a means to an end.

But he didn't believe it for a moment. If the gossip column he'd read was any indication, Lara had numerous playmates. Pliant and warm when he'd held her in his arms, she might be physically attracted to him. But she probably didn't think he was anything special. Considering the enmity between him and Woody, they'd never be able to forge a lasting relationship, anyway.

Having committed himself to help the father he hadn't seen for twenty years, Zack couldn't think of any justification except the one he'd insisted on. Maybe he was despicable for wanting to exact revenge from a sick man and forcing Lara to pay the price. But he'd taken one hell of a beating from Woody and not just physically. The mental image was just too graphic to forget.

He felt appropriately chastened when he remembered he'd get his comeuppance, too. His craving for Lara was so intense it had shaken most of his assumptions about who he was and what he wanted in the world. He hadn't been able to sleep, to work, even to think since the day she'd stormed into his office with her captive lab technician in tow. For him, he knew, a single night with her would never be enough. Yet once he'd completed his part of the bargain, she wouldn't want anything further to do with Woody Stone's misbegotten half-breed.

There was a step in the doorway. She'd arrived. With a hidden tremor of anticipation, Zack turned to face her. She was exquisitely dressed—and furious with him.

Though her anger would make things easier, it only caused him to want her more.

"One of the *casitas* has been refurbished," he said shortly. "We'll have our dinner there."

He didn't touch her as they walked out of his office and down the stairs.

Having examined the Club Cochise property in detail when she was negotiating to buy it for Woody, Lara knew what the *casitas* were—detached adobe guest cottages complete with living area, kitchenette and bath. They were situated some distance from the main building, on a wooded knoll that ran alongside the golf course. With only one of them occupied, the spot he'd chosen was perfect for a lovers' tryst.

But we *aren't* lovers, Lara thought as they crossed the perfectly manicured green toward the one cottage that had light in its windows. Ironic as it might seem considering the way he behaved toward me at Spirit Mask, we've become predator and victim.

She planned to make the distinction painfully clear to Zack—just shy of the point at which he'd be justified in crying foul and backing out of their arrangement. No matter how soiled and bedraggled she felt, he'd have the full use of her body until morning came. But not one inch of the free and independent person she really was.

The front door of the *casita* was unlocked. In its living area, soft music was playing. A small, round table had been set with a floor-length cloth and the finest silver, china and crystal. There was even candlelight. Silently, though his dark gaze was heated, Zack pulled out her chair.

Their hands brushed. Lara could feel the tension mount as a waiter uncorked their wine and served the meal.

"Can I get you anything else, Mr. Silverheels?" the young man asked, careful not to glance too boldly in Lara's direction.

Zack's tone was clipped. "No, this'll do. Please see to it we're not disturbed."

The meal was nouvelle cuisine, Southwestern style—picture perfect. But though she tried to eat, Lara couldn't taste a bite. All she could think of was the moment when Zack would remove her dress and run his hands over her body. Despite her fury at him for putting her in such an untenable position, she was tingling all over at the prospect.

Predictably, conversation was strained. Seemingly determined to maintain the fiction that she was a willing participant in what they were about to do, Zack talked of his work as well as a new piece of Aztec art he'd acquired for his inn near Mexico City, and relayed greetings from Don Larson, his Spirit Mask contractor. Lara replied in monosyllables. Taking only a few sips of her wine, she turned down an after-dinner brandy. Though she might be sorry later, she refused to be anesthetized.

At last Zack put down his brandy glass. "I think it's time we got down to business, don't you?" he said, helping her to her feet.

The pupils in Lara's gray eyes widened until they were fathomless pools. She felt hyperalert, defenseless, like a doe caught in the hunter's sights. But she didn't protest. She was too proud for that. Without a word, she let him lead her into the next room.

A single lamp had been left burning beside its king-size bed. They'd barely crossed the threshold when Zack took her in his arms. On her mouth, his was rough with hunger as he parted her lips with his tongue. She could feel the monolith of her anger begin to melt.

Dear God, she thought. Don't let me enjoy it! Giddy with panic, she tried to wrench free of his grasp. "No, *please*..." she whispered.

Zack wouldn't let her get away with it. "Don't you mean *yes?*" he asked mercilessly, his fingers biting into her shoulders. "Admit it, Lara... you want this as much as I do."

Anguished, she knew he was right. She only prayed she wasn't in love with him. It would be the ultimate disgrace.

Zack seemed to recognize he'd regained her cooperation. Pressing his advantage, he put his hands on her breasts with studied deliberation as he kissed her again. Arrows of desire pierced her to the quick. Though she still felt used, trapped, a thousand times regretful that a night of unadulterated sex was all he wanted, she didn't try to stop him when he unzipped her dress.

Within seconds, the gown she'd worn to shame him was a glowing ruby heap at her feet. His tawny fingers manifestly experienced at that sort of task, Zack unhooked her bra and removed her panties, causing shivers of anticipation to race over her skin.

"You'll never know how much I've longed to see you this way," he murmured, lightly stroking her nipples so that they stood up like miniature volcanic peaks. "No doubt you've been told this more times than you can count. But you're exquisite. Say you'll indulge me by letting me look at you while I take off my things."

Lara watched Zack disrobe with bated breath. He's the exquisite one, she thought despite herself. A man too beautifully and powerfully made to walk the earth. Why, oh why couldn't things be different between us?

Moments later they were in each other's arms, their skin a dramatic contrast in copper and ivory. Lara could feel the hard column of Zack's desire pressing against her thigh. Drugged with his kisses and half wild at the supremely erotic way he was touching her, she didn't understand at first when he asked her about birth control.

"Are you prepared?" he repeated, his voice blurred with need. "Or shall I..."

Lara blinked. "If by that you mean 'do I use anything?' the answer's no," she admitted. "I've never needed to."

"Because your partners have always taken care of you."

He'd made a statement of it, not a question. Slowly she shook her head. "I haven't had any other partners. You'll be the first."

Zack felt as if he'd been kicked in the softest part of his stomach. "That's ridiculous," he countered, dismay tightening in his gut. "You'll never get me to believe it."

Lara's lower lip quivered. She wanted to weep. But she didn't hesitate to meet his eyes. "Maybe so," she said so softly he had trouble catching the words. "But it happens to be the truth."

He couldn't hide from the simple honesty of her gaze. Incredibly Lily Stone's sexy, elegant daughter was a virgin. It was probably safe to say she'd never known the tug of another man's mouth at her breast. Valid beyond any doubt was that the moist, hidden sheath where he longed to bury himself was inviolate.

His assumptions about her in a shambles, Zack dropped his hands. "Get dressed," he ordered after a moment. "The deal's off. I don't deflower innocents."

Chapter Seven

Stunned and disbelieving, Lara snatched up a lap robe that lay folded at the foot of the bed and wrapped it around herself. "You mean..." Her lower lip quivered. "You won't help Woody after all?"

By contrast, Zack made no move to cover himself. At ease in nothing but his smooth, coppery skin, he was too confounded by Lara's revelation to feel any concern over his nakedness. Lithe and muscular as a mountain cat, he stood there glaring down at her.

"What do you expect?" he demanded angrily. "This isn't a something-for-nothing situation. Woody's not my favorite charity."

"But we had an agreement! I expect you to honor it."

Huddled in the black, tan and red woolen throw, which was woven in a classic Navajo design, Lara couldn't believe her campaign to help Woody had come to naught. "You won't reconsider?" she whispered. "M-make love to me the way we said?"

The prospect of easing the hunger that had tormented him since the Burneys' party was so alluring Zack nearly relented. But he couldn't—not if he wanted to keep his self-respect.

"Under the circumstances, it would be against my principles," he said. Though she probably wouldn't believe it, he had a few.

Huge tears rolled down Lara's cheeks. "I shouldn't have told you the truth," she said. "When you asked, I should have said I used something. You'd never have known the difference."

She was as green as a chili pepper when it came to sex. Not to mention that rare commodity among women, an untouched treasure. To think he'd planned to make love to her all night long...

"You little fool!" Zack derided in a fierce attempt to stifle his self-loathing and the desire for her he couldn't quell. "I *guarantee* I'd have figured it out, though maybe not in time to keep from getting you pregnant!"

It's true, he thought, wondering why he wasn't happier over their narrow escape. After the way I've ached for her, I wouldn't have lasted long.

Lara knew perfectly well what she'd have been risking by having sex with Zack unprotected. She just hadn't guessed that, merely by entering her, he'd have been able to detect her virginal state. Afterward, maybe. But by then, her part of their bargain would have been fulfilled.

If I'd guessed how he would react, I'd have lied to him and gone ahead—taken my chances, she thought. Woody's going to die because of my old-fashioned values. And because I told the truth.

Stricken afresh by the irony of the situation, she began to weep in earnest. She wished to God she'd slept with someone—*anyone*—before crossing swords with Zack Silverheels.

Sternly Zack fought back the urge to comfort her. If he took her in his arms, he'd end up doing something he'd be sorry for.

They seemed to have reached an impasse. With effort, Lara choked back her tears and silence filled the room. "Is there nothing I can say?" she asked at last. "Or do to change your mind?"

Were they simply to part, then? Live separately in the world without once having tasted each other? Was Woody to die unaided when the son he'd fathered as a teenager could so easily have given him a chance? Surely the emerging pattern of their fate was incomplete, the raw ends left dangling like ungrasped possibilities.

Unbidden, an idea occurred to Zack and he rejected it. No way, he told himself. Even to consider such a thing would be emotional suicide.

"What is it?" Lara asked immediately, hope reviving as she watched the play of emotions on his face.

Try as he would, he couldn't get the notion out of his head. If he'd thought he was on dangerous ground before, he hadn't known the meaning of the word. For him, getting too involved with Lara Stone equaled rejection. Closer contact with Woody. The reopening of all his wounds.

He'd never wanted to be tied to anyone. Yet radical as it was, he couldn't deny the solution he'd come up with appealed to him. He tried to tell himself that was because it offered the most fitting revenge of all.

"There's only one way I can go ahead with the bone-marrow donation to Woody," he said at last. "You'll have to marry me. Short of wedlock, I don't take virgins to bed."

Lara rocketed from self-pity to outrage in the sliver of time consumed by a heartbeat. "Is my whole life to be sacrificed to your pride, then?" she asked.

He shrugged. "Take it or leave it."

In her fury, she couldn't or wouldn't admit she was trembling at the prospect of having Zack for her husband. Absolutely nothing about their relationship was that simple anyway. At some point, while she'd napped dreaming on his couch at Spirit Mask, the wry, almost cherishing man she'd begun to know and like had disappeared.

In his place was a harsh opportunist. Though she still quivered like a bowstring at his touch, he'd become more adversary than lover. He planned to use her to punish Woody. Destroy her relationship with him, if possible. Maybe even take over the Bar-S someday.

He also wanted to have sex with her. In her opinion his obsession about that had everything to do with the memory of Lily and the pain Woody would feel, knowing the son he'd disowned was sharing his adopted daughter's bed, and nothing to do with affection.

By now Lara had begun to question whether Zack was guilty of the crime he'd been accused of so long ago. Despite some aspects of his behavior toward her, she had the strong feeling he wasn't. He might be a maverick or worse, but he had a moral code, unique though it was. Perhaps there'd been some misunderstanding. She could see how Lily might have taken his caustic brand of humor seriously, or felt intimidated by him.

Profoundly attracted to Zack, Lara knew marriage to him would be risky business. With all his old hatreds and resentments so close to the surface, there was a good chance she'd be hurt. Yet with Woody's life hanging in the balance and the specter of grief breathing down her neck, she couldn't afford to turn him down.

Without intending it, she let her gaze flicker over his hard midsection, dart lower. He was so utterly desirable, so neatly and beautifully made. Though revenge, not love, was his motive, he could be hers if she said the word. Already a little of her shyness, her indignation at his effrontery had faded.

"For me to spend a lifetime repaying a single act of so-called generosity on your part seems...a little excessive," she countered, facing him from firmer ground. "Isn't there some way we can compromise?"

Zack couldn't think of one. He'd never imagined himself marrying anyone. Yet perhaps because his mother had given birth to him without benefit of matrimony, he respected the institution. At gut level he didn't believe it should be taken lightly. Or that its vows should be spoken on a temporary basis.

Deliberately he blinded himself to what his offer meant when examined in that light. "What did you have in mind?" he asked.

She hesitated. "Something less."

The horns of their dilemma were pricking his flesh. "Give me a year," he said recklessly, acting out of deepest instinct. "No declarations of undying love. No children. And no further commitment, unless we both choose to extend the terms of our agreement. Surely Woody's life is worth that much."

Maybe, just maybe, he thought bitterly, twelve months of making love to her will be enough. If she refused him, they wouldn't see each other again. Someday soon he'd read about Woody's death in the newspaper.

To Lara the thought of becoming Zack's wife only to give him up later was unthinkable. He didn't love her and he probably never would. But she'd find it far too easy to care for him, despite his unfeeling attitude. Laying herself open to the repeated assault of his lovemaking on her senses was just begging for a broken heart.

There were other arguments against accepting his proposal, too. Foremost among them was the fact that, unlike a night of passion in Zack's bed, spending a year as his wife wouldn't be possible to keep from Woody. She could almost imagine them parting ways over it. Yet she couldn't return to the hospital in the morning knowing she could have saved him and chose to save herself.

There was only one possible decision she could make. "All right," she said, coming to terms with it. "I'll marry you whenever you say. But Woody can't know about it until his transplant is over and he's out of the woods."

Zack felt a wave of relief all out of proportion to the motivation he'd claimed. I've won, he thought, choosing not to delve too deeply into his emotions. After all these years, Woody's finally going to pay. Lara will be mine for the taking.

He'd worship her with all his strength.

"Done," he agreed, paving over the sudden, aberrant thought and the vulnerability it betrayed. "You realize eventually he'll have to know."

Standing there barefoot in her Navajo blanket, Lara summoned every scrap of dignity she possessed. "Of course, I do," she answered. "I'm well aware that's what this is all about."

Maybe it was partly about wishing she cared for him, too—Woody and his ill feelings be damned. If so, Zack refused to admit it. He wouldn't even let himself think about the possibility Lara might choose him over Woody someday if he pushed her to that point.

"I imagine Woody's doctors will want to do the transplant right away," he said, his proud Anglo features impassive as he put on his trousers. "If you agree, we'll be married quietly on the reservation just as soon as we can get a license."

Murmuring her assent, Lara didn't move as he picked up the rest of his clothes. Their eyes met and held. For a moment desire linked them, unextinguished by the emotional pitfalls they faced.

He didn't brush her mouth with the mockery of a goodnight kiss, though for several seconds she thought he might. "Call you tomorrow, then," he said evenly, as if they were making arrangements for a business conference. A moment later he was walking out the door.

Too shaken to drive back to the Wickham that night, Lara crawled into the bed they'd almost shared. As she did, it occurred to her Zack had probably slept in it the night before. In the interim, she felt certain, the bed linens had been changed. They didn't carry his distinctive scent.

The following morning, an old cardigan sweater she'd dug out of the trunk of the Mercedes shielding her off-the-shoulder bodice from curious stares, Lara left Club Cochise without confronting Zack again. For all she knew, he was aboard his private jet, winging his way to California. Since they'd be married on his turf, she presumed he'd take care of arrangements.

Showering and changing at the Wickham, she went straight to the hospital. Woody was in a somber mood.

"I been thinkin', gal," he greeted her, as if interrupted in the midst of a conversation with himself. "The situation being what it is, maybe it's time I put some of the property in your name—you know, to avoid probate."

"Don't you think that's a little premature?" Though Lara still felt emotionally bruised from her encounter with Zack the night before, she managed a smile for Woody's sake. For once, she had good news to impart.

Woody frowned. "I don't get it. Without a transplant..."

Sitting on the edge of his bed, which was against the rules, Lara took his gnarled bony hands in hers. "Listen up, Daddy Bear," she said. "The latest word is that you *do* get it. We've found a donor."

For perhaps a split second, the message didn't register. Then Woody's tired blue eyes lit up like a Christmas tree.

"You're kidding," he said. "Aren't you?"

Lara shook her head. "Apparently there are still a few miracles left lying around."

Woody hugged her so hard she thought her ribs would break. Then, elated, he insisted on celebrating with coffee and doughnuts in the hospital coffee shop. It wasn't until she'd wheeled him downstairs in his robe and slippers and bought them each a steaming mug of java and a chocolate doughnut that he started asking questions. The first thing he wanted to know was the donor's identity, of course.

"I'm afraid I can't help you there," she answered, hoping there weren't any dead giveaways in her voice. "The donor has insisted on remaining anonymous."

Predictably, Woody didn't understand. "I want to *thank* him," he explained, adding in deference to Lara's mildly feminist sentiments, "or her. You know... invite 'em out to the ranch, fill up their larder with steaks and things. My God, gal... it's *life* they're giving me!"

This time Lara's smile was real, though she felt a strong twinge of irony at his words. "That's probably what he or she is afraid of," she said with care. "Being overwhelmed with your two-fisted generosity. If it'll ease your conscience any, Stone Enterprises is picking up the donor's hospital tab."

Praying Woody wouldn't hate her when he found out she had married Zack in order to give him a chance, Lara did her best to be enthusiastic as he whipped up a flurry of future plans. He wasn't out of danger yet. As Dr. Gooding had warned her repeatedly, any number of things could go wrong during the regrafting procedure.

Before he could receive his transplant, Woody had to undergo megadose chemotherapy and total body radiation to kill the old, cancerous bone marrow cells. If everything went according to plan, in another week, he'd be as sick as a dog.

In less time than that, Lara thought, I'll be Zack's wife. My friends will be talking about me behind my back, wondering how I could hurt Woody that way.

"What's wrong, sugar?" he asked, pausing in his exuberant monologue to note the frown on Lara's face.

"Nothing," she insisted. "It's just a headache."

He gave her a skeptical look, and she braced herself for an outpouring of his usual fence-post wisdom.

"You been havin' a lot of them lately," he observed, going easy on her for once. "Wearin' yourself out, I guess, watchin' over things. Any sensible gal would take a little time for herself."

The remark gave Lara all the encouragement she needed to invent a minivacation. Woody accepted her absence without a murmur when, three days later, she and Zack traveled north to the reservation to be wed.

Zack was behind the wheel of Lara's convertible at her request. It hadn't made sense to rent a car. Or hire a limousine, which would have been viewed with distaste by his

Native American relatives. She'd been too shaky and tense to do the honors herself.

He was an excellent driver, and it felt good just letting him take care of her. If he was going to be her husband, she might as well enjoy some of the perks.

Now and then she glanced at him as they drove, taking care not to do it when she thought he was looking. Occasionally she guessed wrong and their gazes connected. Each time she could read intensity in his eyes. Plus a multitude of questions. If he was having second thoughts, he didn't share them with her. Or even hint at their existence. Most of the time he just watched the road while she scanned the high desert chapparal with its scattered junipers and piñon pines and kept company with her thoughts.

The wedding ceremony, which was to take place outside the hogan of Zack's great-uncle, medicine man Henry Littlehorse, would be an informal one. At Zack's request, Lara had worn riding clothes—a trim split skirt and vest of indigo suede, together with a loose, striped shirt of Guatemalan cotton and boots. A lined sheepskin jacket was slung lightly over her shoulders.

Zack was lean, handsome and distinctly Navajo in the denims and turquoise-silver jewelry he'd worn the day she and Kevin Deering had stormed into his office. His jacket and boots were similar to hers.

Several pickup trucks were parked outside the Littlehorse hogan when they arrived. A resident of Arizona for most of her life, Lara didn't find the roughly oval structure of wood and tar paper extraordinary or impoverished looking, though she guessed the family that lived there wasn't overly endowed with material goods.

Zack's relatives and friends responded to his introductions with dignity and quiet appraisal. Lara shook hands with Henry, a man in his early seventies, his plump, gracious wife, Mary, Zack's cousins, Jimmy and Buck and the representatives of several neighboring families, who'd come to see the late Margaret Tsosie's thirty-seven-year-old son wed at last.

Jimmy was fairly short and dark for a Navajo. By contrast, Buck was tall, with lean hips, a heavy torso and light complexion. His graying dark hair was pulled back in a ponytail fastened with silver wire.

Lara was startled when Buck produced a heavy squash-blossom necklace crafted in solid silver and placed it around her neck. Clearly he intended it to be a wedding present.

"Oh, please..." she said, painfully conscious her marriage to Zack wasn't meant to be a lasting one. "The necklace is exquisite. But it's so valuable. You mustn't..."

Buck's expression didn't change. "Say thank you," Zack whispered. "Buck's a silversmith. He made the necklace for you himself."

In addition to performing curing ceremonies and other rites for the community at large, Henry was a certified justice of the peace. The wedding he performed for them was both legal and the essence of simplicity. Only one part of it was influenced by Navajo tradition. For Lara it was also the most emotional one. When she and Zack were called on to eat cornmeal mush from a ceremonial wedding basket, she had the strong feeling of being connected to the centuries, part of all the men and women who'd pledged their troth according to the rituals laid down by the Indian gods.

She trembled when Zack slipped a plain silver band on her wedding finger. I *love* him, she thought, startled into awareness by the image of his capable bronze-skinned hands holding hers. Just as he is, with all his faults and emotional baggage. We belong together. How can I get him to see that, too?

In retrospect she realized she'd probably committed to him when they'd played like children, chasing their kite over the rocks at Spirit Mask. He might not be hers forever, and that thought wove sadness through the shining strands of her joy. Ditto the pain of his estrangement from Woody. All the more reason, she thought stubbornly, to seize this moment and store it away in my heart.

Seconds later Henry was pronouncing them man and wife. He nodded that Zack was free to kiss his bride. Expecting a perfunctory display of affection in front of his relatives and friends, Lara found herself melting at the bold invasion of his tongue. His strong arms crushed her as if to assert possession.

When he released her, his eyes asserted it, too. *You're mine,* he seemed to be saying, *if only for a little while. There'll be no turning back the next time we're alone together.*

Henry's wife and some of the other women had put together a modest spread of barbecued lamb shanks, corn and pinto beans, piñon cakes and a fruited honey flavored with Canyon de Chelly peach preserves. Seated beside Zack, Lara ate very little. She had the satisfaction of knowing Woody would get the help he so desperately needed. Foremost in her mind now was her relationship with the man who'd come to mean so much to her.

In Oregon I felt secure enough to give myself to him without promises of any kind, she thought, maybe because he seemed so different then. But she didn't really believe that was the only reason. Since they'd butted heads at Club Cochise, her sense of security had vanished. And she loved him still, every bit as much.

They were saying goodbye to everyone, when Zack's cousin Jimmy led forward two horses, a bay and a paint.

"The Mercedes will be fine here at Henry's place," Zack said as he gave Lara a leg up into the paint's saddle. "I thought we'd spend the night at the hogan I still own and use sometimes, at Short Mesa. It's fairly isolated. The roads being what they are, we'll find it easier to travel there on horseback."

He hadn't mentioned their destination earlier. But she didn't object. Though they'd barely touched since she'd picked him up at the airport in Phoenix that morning, except for the wedding ceremony, she allowed her hand to rest a moment longer than necessary on his shoulder.

Zack picked up the subtle change at once. What is it? he asked her silently. Are you ready to admit you want me, too? Or are you saying something more than that—something unlikely and precious I don't even dare to dream about? For a moment neither of them moved, reluctant to disturb the fragile possibilities both could sense. Then he was mounting to the bay's saddle with the easy grace she'd always known he possessed.

Thanks to him I don't have to be ashamed of my equestrian skills, Lara thought as they rode along a rutted dirt track that wound from the Littlehorse settlement toward the adjacent Hopi reservation and its lived-in fossil village of Third Mesa, high on a craggy elevation in the far distance. Beginning with my first lesson on Ringo, the pony Zack taught me to ride, I've had a lot of practice over the years.

In her eyes the high-desert landscape and the spirited bay Zack was riding provided the perfect foil for him. Seeing him here is like being given the chance to appreciate a spectacular gem in its most appropriate setting, she thought. In his erect, multitalented person, the strong-willed, unforgiving man she'd married embodied the best of two races, Anglo and Native American. She shivered with pride and fascination at the thought he'd soon be hers.

The hogan, sheep pens and rusting water tank Zack owned, which had once belonged to his mother, were situated beside a dry wash at the foot of a rough red butte. Only a few parched willows testified to the intermittent presence of moisture on the place. They were just a few miles from the Hopi "hole" in the much larger "doughnut" of the Navajo reservation.

Tying up their horses and helping her dismount, Zack unbuckled the blankets and packs that had been fastened behind each animal's saddle. "It's going to be a beautiful evening," he said. "We'll be able to sleep in the brush arbor."

For the Navajo, Lara knew, the brush arbor, with its open sides and "roof" of sticks and branches, functioned as an outdoor living room. How different this is from the hothouse atmosphere of the adobe cottage at Club Cochise, she thought as Zack watered the horses and spread out a bale of straw covered with blankets for their bed.

This time she didn't feel as if she were about to be despoiled. Her anger at Zack for forcing her to pay Woody's debts and turning their budding relationship into a trade-off based on revenge had vanished like a puff of smoke.

He chose that moment to give her one of his narrow, dark-eyed looks. "Cold feet?" he asked in the challenging tone she'd come to know so well.

She shook her head. You can't let him guess how much you care, she warned herself. The way he feels, he'd just take advantage of it. The only thing you can do at the moment is love him. And hope things will turn out all right.

Gathering up an armload of dead branches and twigs, Zack built a fire. Once the popping, crackling blaze was well established, he reached into his saddlebag and produced a bottle of wine. He'd also brought some carefully wrapped Indian corn bread.

"Dessert," he advised, sitting cross-legged on the blanket and inviting her to do the same. "You didn't eat enough of Mary Littlehorse's spread to keep a corn beetle alive."

As they sipped their wine and watched the sun sink beneath Short Mesa, they talked a little about the families that had attended their wedding. Or rather Zack did. Lara didn't say much. To her surprise her new husband seemed in no hurry to make his move. She wondered if he was waiting for some sign from her.

Stealing closer like the night, the desert loneliness surrounded them, making them feel as if they were the only two people left on earth. Their silences had lengthened and stars were beginning to appear overhead when he broke the spell at last by placing one hand on her knee.

"I'm going to get ready for bed now," he said lightly. "Care to join me?"

Though she was shaking inside, partly as a result of her inexperience and partly from her discovery of how much she cared for him, Lara rose and allowed him to lift the heavy squash-blossom necklace Buck had given her over her head. The gesture was a possessive one, yet somehow endearing, as if she were once again dealing with her lover of the Oregon coast.

They disrobed slowly in the half-light. With sunset the temperature had dropped, and despite the fire, it was getting cold. Though she didn't shiver, Lara's soft, pink nipples hardened until they were like small, protruding pebbles. She could feel Zack's gaze devouring the curves and hollows of her body.

When they were completely undressed, he reached out to lift her silky curtain of hair away from her face. "Have I ever told you," he said, letting it fall of its own weight, "how very lovely you are?"

The compliment gave her permission to soar. Freed of hesitation and tingling with her need for him, she let Zack draw her down to their rough blankets and take her in his arms.

He'd trailed kisses over her body before, in his hot tub at Spirit Mask and again at Club Cochise. She'd responded by jettisoning some of her most cherished principles—or so she'd thought. Now she realized she hadn't turned her back on them at all.

Instead she'd known with the deep knowing of the cell that the time had come to give herself to the man she loved. As he kissed her mouth and then turned his attention to her breasts, she gloried in the way it touched off brush fires in her blood. His determination to savor her was like a goad.

Her nipples damp from his mouth against the night chill and her thighs opening naturally to cradle him, Lara was astonished when Zack's kisses ventured lower. Overwhelmed by the depth of intimacy he required, she started to pull away.

"No," he insisted gently, teaching her. "This is part of it."

Lost in a wilderness of arousal, she decided to trust him. Within seconds she was scaling the footholds to paradise.

Chapter Eight

Cold and dusted with stars, the desert night absorbed Lara's cries of release and amazement as Zack led her past the brink. Resting his cheek against her stomach, he waited for the flutters and heat flush of her culmination to subside. How beautiful she was, how abandoned in her discovery! Yet how innocent. To think he'd be the first...

He was bursting with need. At the thought of entering her, he felt like a cannon primed for shot. Yet by now the depth of her inexperience was fully apparent. He was afraid of hurting her. How could he have doubted she was what she seemed? Or compared her with Lily, when the essential goodness of her nature was so shiningly clear?

The delicate being his hands caressed, the precious woman his blood sang to mate with, was a treasure he didn't deserve. Yet conversely she had a right to him. He'd pledged to worship her with his body. If she wanted it, she was entitled to all the passion and adoration he could give.

Beneath Zack's partial weight, Lara stirred. Though she still glowed like the fire that warmed their nakedness, the roses of ecstasy were fading from her cheeks. "Zack, you haven't..." she said in a soft whisper, sensing his hesitation.

He shook his head. "I was wrong to insist on this."

"No. You're my husband."

Her slender fingers meshed in the coarse silk of his hair, she'd just begun to sense the latent power of her femininity. Age-old instincts whispered of a deeper consummation to come.

"Take me," she insisted when he didn't answer. "I want to bring you pleasure, too."

With a flash of pain that was quickly over, her virginity was lost. Groaning inwardly at a discomfort he could only experience in his imagination, Zack was determined to make it up to her. If he could manage it, he'd take her back to the heights.

He couldn't guarantee how long he'd last. Or how gentle he'd be once need drove him like the piston on a locomotive. Lured by the hot, wet promise of her womanliness, he'd already begun to move.

That night, guarded by the moon's bright shield and watched only by the owl, Zack took Lara twice at her own soft urging. The second time they joined, he achieved his aim. Moving beneath him in a frantic quest for attainment, she was suddenly swallowed up by deep, implosive tremors. Exultant at the helpless sounds she made, he followed in seconds.

She was *his* now. He'd made her a part of him. For the first time Zack felt fusion, the bonding of his soul to that of another person.

"In beauty it's finished," he said reverently, quoting the traditional ending to every Navajo chant when at last they'd settled back to earth.

And in beauty just begun.

Lara fell asleep under a light blanket with Zack's hand on her breast. Somewhere in the fiery crucible of their lovemaking, she'd stepped through a one-way door. She was a woman now, in every sense of the word. One who shared a secret, amorous life with her husband.

Stirring at first light, she was disoriented for several seconds. Then she realized nothing of what she remembered was a dream. Zack was still beside her, the strong contours of his face relaxed in sleep. Against the hard copper of his cheeks, his lashes were black silk fringe. Though the fire was out, he radiated heat. She wanted to gather him close.

Her own body felt deliciously used. Every unfamiliar ache was an erotic reminder of the intimacies that had united them. Though he'd doubtless think her a wanton, she yearned to sample them again.

A slight movement, perhaps, or the changed rhythm of her breathing, prodded Zack to wakefulness. At first he didn't open his eyes, preferring to drift in remembered sensation and enjoy the feeling of what it was like for them to share a bed. Lara was there, awake. After the inevitable greed with which he'd taken her, she hadn't run from him. Would she think him perverted when she realized he'd never get enough?

Listening to the indistinct yet familiar sounds of morning at Short Mesa, he wondered what she was thinking about. Was she noticing the chiaroscuro of his dark hair and her own sun-kissed tresses? Contemplating the symphonic interplay of ivory and copper skin?

Soon, if she hadn't already, Lara would become necessary to him. And he'd begin to pay the price.

"Zack," she whispered. "I know you're awake."

Opening his eyes, he turned to face her. "Are you all right?" he asked, keeping his uncertainties to himself.

"Yes. I'm fine. It's just..."

"You're hurting from having me inside you."

"Oh, no...*no*..."

As naturally if they'd been married for years, she came into his arms. She hadn't been going to say anything. Now she thought it might be all right, if only to reassure him.

"Maybe I shouldn't ask," she confessed softly against his shoulder, "but I was wondering if you planned to make love to me again."

It was light. They'd be able to see every nuance. Every exquisite goose bump. With a groan that was less controlled than any that had passed his lips in years, Zack fitted himself to her. They were one again—man-and-woman—transcending their separateness. Cradled between her thighs, with her arms wrapped sweetly around his neck, he was master of the earth. She could feel her female power expand until it filled the universe.

Beyond spending a night at Short Mesa, Zack hadn't made any plans. It struck him Lara would want him to donate on Woody's behalf as soon as possible. Oddly enough, in light of the ecstasy they'd shared, he wanted that, too. Once his part of their bargain was finished, he'd take her on a real wedding trip. Show her how much he wanted to make a success of things.

Meanwhile they were in northern Arizona, and the Bar-S was just down the road as distances were measured in the West. He'd avoided it for years. Now, suddenly, he wanted to see it again. It was there he'd first laid eyes on the woman who so obsessed his thoughts. His mouth curved as he remembered her—a chubby, towheaded little girl enchanting grown-up men and boys alike with her glancing smiles and grubby kisses.

"What would you say to showing me around the ranch before we head south to the hospital?" he asked as they broke camp. "As I'm sure you know, I haven't seen the place since I was seventeen. It's a part of my life I won't soon forget."

A thousand thoughts competed in Lara's head. She felt close to Zack—so close that a sigh couldn't come between them. Yet she couldn't guess what his motivation might be for making such a request. Did he hope to lay his demons to rest? Or burn to infuse them with new meaning? Look over an empire he expected to command someday?

The latter thought wasn't worthy of her feelings for him. But she didn't kid herself that his feelings about Woody had changed. Maybe this is just another aspect of the revenge he plans, she thought. He probably knows as well as I do that Woody would hit the ceiling if he knew Zack was roving his personal territory as my guest.

Something about the way he'd phrased his question, linking a trip to the ranch with their subsequent journey to Phoenix and the operating room where his bone marrow would be harvested, made her feel his proposed visit to the Bar-S was a command performance. Loving Zack won't be easy, she realized, despite the rapture he leads us to. I won't always agree with the way he conducts himself.

"I suppose it would be all right if I warned Emma we were coming and explained that Woody can't know about it right now," she said. "I hope you understand. But, with the chemotherapy he faces, not to mention the problems associated with a transplant, I can't afford to let him get upset."

Zack shrugged. "Okay by me."

They stopped at a gas station in Winslow so she could phone. Lara tapped her toe nervously as she waited for someone to answer.

"Hello, Em?" she said when Woody's housekeeper picked up on the third ring. "I've, um, got a fairly major surprise for you. I'm bringing a guest by the ranch in a little while, one you might possibly remember. I don't want Woody to know about it, all right? Under the circumstances, he might get upset."

Lara knew the housekeeper, a longtime confidante of her father's, had already been told they'd found a donor. She'd stood by, listening, while Woody had explained to Em on the telephone what a transplant meant.

"Of course we won't say anything, Miss Lara, if you don't want us to," the older woman promised, her curiosity an almost palpable thing. "Hank was just about to go up to Forked Wash after some strays. Do you think maybe... he should wait?"

Answering that she would appreciate it very much, Lara speculated they'd arrive in forty-five minutes or so. It's going to be awkward, she thought as she said goodbye and replaced the receiver. But there's no help for it. Zack and I have to go public sometime. I just hope we can keep Woody in the dark long enough.

Emma Tarbush, Hank Suger and Hank's wife, Marcy, were all waiting on the front porch of the main house when Lara's Mercedes roared up the drive in a cloud of dust. They didn't appear to recognize the darkly handsome man behind the wheel, not even when he and Lara got out and started up the front steps.

Then Emma's weathered face creased in a smile. "Well, *Zack!*" she exclaimed, throwing her arms around him and giving him a delighted hug. "You're all growed up."

He grinned. "I should hope so, Em."

Though they'd once had their differences, Hank stepped forward to offer his hand. "If you want," he said, "I'd be glad to show you around."

Her brash good looks faded by the years but with an appreciative gleam in her eye for the magnificent man Zack had become, Marcy prompted Emma with a look.

"Maybe they'd like a glass of iced tea first," the woman Zack had once left stranded in her underwear suggested. "I don't know about you and Hank, but I've got lots of questions."

Despite her determination to tough things out, Lara went weak in the knees. What on earth would Marcy ask? She wasn't known for her delicate turn of phrase. Agreeing that yes, they actually *were* a little thirsty, she made a beeline for the security of the porch swing, a fixture of the Bar-S for as long as she could remember.

As if it was the most natural thing in the world, Zack took a seat beside her. He didn't rest his arm across the back of the swing. Or reach for her hand. But their knees touched. So much for circumspection, she thought. The fact that we're lovers is probably written all over our foreheads.

Unless they figured out the significance of the plain silver band she was being so careful to keep out of sight, Em and the Sugers probably wouldn't guess that she and Zack were married. If somehow they did, she'd just have to deal with it. More unlikely weddings had taken place.

There was always a big pitcher of tea chilling in Em's well-stocked refrigerator. She returned a moment later with tall glasses for everyone. Marcy was quizzing Zack about his life after he'd left the ranch, and focusing on his career.

"I hear you're a millionaire now, with a bunch of fancy resorts to your name," she teased, still a coquette despite her sun-ravaged skin and prominent veins. "*I* always thought you'd end up in the movies. Or traveling with a rodeo."

Lara could tell Zack was enjoying himself. Marcy had just told him he was gorgeous. And quite a cowboy.

"I passed the million mark quite some time ago," he answered matter-of-factly, never one to be burdened with false modesty. "You know what they say... follow your bliss and the money will follow you."

"I bet money's not the only thing hot on your tail," Marcy laughed.

Entertained despite herself, Lara couldn't help suffering the pangs of wishful thinking. If only Zack and Woody would meet and talk that way, she'd be the happiest woman on earth.

Aware everyone was dying to hear how Zack had happened to turn up at the ranch in her company, Lara took advantage of a lull in the conversation to explain that they'd met at a party in Phoenix. "At my urging, Zack was tested and his bone marrow matches Woody's," she revealed. "He's agreed to donate."

The three old friends were obviously impressed. Yet in view of the bad blood that existed between Woody and his remarkable son, Lara could tell they all had the same question.

"Like you, I'm very grateful to Zack for helping us," she said, surprising her new husband by squeezing his hand. "But you know how Woody is. We're not sure he could handle it. So we haven't told him. That's why I'm asking you to keep our friendship under wraps... at least until the transplant's complete."

Hank answered for everyone. "We sure will, Miss Lara," he promised. "You can count on us."

Draining the last of his tea, Woody's foreman got to his feet. "How about that tour now?" he asked Zack, giving the former "bad boy," who'd once caught his wife's eye, one of his rare, approving smiles. "I got to go up to Forked Wash after a bit."

Zack was more than ready to look around. And there was a lot to see. As his wealth had increased, Woody had made quite a few improvements to the Bar-S.

Meanwhile, Lara's use of the word *friendship* had stuck in Zack's mind. "If you don't tell them we're married, what are they going to think when I make love to you in your girlhood room?" he whispered in her ear as Hank pointed out the new corrals.

Startled, she searched his face.

"I'm only half joking," he assured her, guiding her with a light touch as they entered the tack barn. "But I have to admit the idea has a certain appeal."

Briefly Lara was silent, considering. It *is* awkward they don't know, she conceded. And they're bound to find out. The license will be published in the paper.

She'd just have to trust them. Probably a lot of other people, as well. "You're right. I'm going to tell Em about us," she announced when they were out of Hank's earshot. "I don't know if I'd be comfortable making love with her in the house. But we *could* shower and change."

Memories Zack would have preferred to forget came flooding back when they went inside and Lara showed him around, particularly when she pointed out Emma's sewing room. A look of strain came over his face.

"This is where..." he began, letting his voice trail off.

"You slept?" Lara finished, knowing his confrontation with Woody had taken place in his room.

He nodded. After twenty years, he supposed, it wasn't surprising his presence had been erased. Unfortunately, though the physical scars had long since healed, the beating Woody had given him would never be eradicated from his thoughts.

Maybe that was because of the mistrust and rejection that had accompanied it. Whatever the case, Zack was thinking of anything but sex by the time Lara showed him where she laid her head when she was home at the Bar-S. Her room was all ruffles and chintz, more appropriate for a young girl than the striking woman she'd become. He was about to tell her so when the housekeeper intervened.

"I put the coffee on," Emma said. "You want a sandwich or something? It's no trouble."

They'd breakfasted on coffee and leftover corn bread. Yet by now Zack was in the mood to depart. Glancing at Lara, he shook his head. "Thanks, Em," he answered. "But we have business in Phoenix this afternoon. Maybe a quick shower and change..."

As Lara had expected, the somewhat unusual request raised questions. Where—and with whom—had they slept the previous night? What kind of relationship did they have if he felt comfortable asking to bathe at her house?

While Zack went out to the car for their overnight bags, she told Emma they'd been married the day before and spent their wedding night camping on the reservation. A parade of emotions—shock, delight and apprehension—swept across the older woman's face.

"We're hoping Woody will accept it, once he's been through his ordeal and he's feeling better," Lara added, giving Zack more credit than he deserved. "It's long past time he put the bad feelings of twenty years ago behind him."

Tears fogging her glasses, Emma gave her a fierce hug. "Oh, yes," she blurted with obvious conviction. "I think so, too!"

By the time Zack returned to the house with their bags in hand, Emma was wiping her eyes on one corner of her apron. "You rascal," she laughed, holding out her work-roughened hand to him. "You haven't changed a bit! Imagine your comin' back after all these years just to steal Miss Lara away from us!"

During their trip south from Flagstaff, both Zack and Lara mulled over the amazing truth that their hastily contrived marriage had taken on some of the mutuality of a real union. Yet, despite their new closeness and the catharsis of telling Emma Tarbush they were man and wife, they didn't share their thoughts.

I never expected to feel this way, Zack mused, switching the Mercedes into cruise control and slipping one arm about Lara's shoulders. But I'm actually contented. I like being a married man.

It wasn't just that they'd become lovers, deeply satisfying and liberating though that had turned out to be. Incredibly, she was his *wife.* That simple fact eased the knot of loneliness he'd always carried inside him, no matter how pleased with his life he'd seemed.

Smoothly the Mercedes ate up the concrete ribbon of Interstate 17. And, though his concentration seemed effortless, Zack drove faster than Lara usually did. They arrived at the hospital with plenty of time to catch Dr. Gooding before he began his evening rounds.

"This is Zack Silverheels, Woody's son... and my husband," Lara said, taking the plunge as she introduced them. "Since he and Woody haven't seen each other for twenty years and they didn't part friends, I hope you'll keep our relationship confidential until he's in better shape."

Though the busy hematologist's brows went up a notch, he agreed readily enough. "Good to meet you," he said, shaking Zack's hand. "As I'm sure Lara has told you, time's of the essence here. We're already seeing a few signs Woody's current remission might break down. Could I interest you in checking in this evening? It's not too late to put your procedure on tomorrow's schedule."

Lara and Zack looked at each other. They'd been married just twenty-four hours, and things were working out better than they'd had any right to hope. Neither of them had planned on being separated that night.

Worried as she was about Woody, and eager for him to get well as soon as possible, Lara was bereft at the thought of sleeping alone. All too quickly she'd gotten used to the idea of waking up to find Zack beside her.

He was thinking similar thoughts. Still, he reasoned, maybe he should follow the hematologist's suggestion. In forty-eight hours, according to what Lara had told him, his part in the transplant process would be over. He could take her home with him, to Los Angeles.

Imagining how that would feel made his heart expand in his chest. For the first time since he was seventeen, he wasn't essentially alone in the world. Like Lara he'd forgotten that their marriage was to be a temporary affair.

"I guess so," he said with a little shrug that hid his ingrained Navajo uneasiness at placing himself in the hands of conventional medicine. "Might as well get it over with."

* * *

Solitary that night in her bed at the Wickham, Lara missed Zack terribly. As the luminous hands on her bedside clock crept slowly toward morning, she went over and over their lovemaking in her mind. Just thinking of the way Zack's mouth had tugged at her breast and the deep fulfillment of him thrusting inside her caused her to toss and turn, restless with longing.

So this is what love is like, she thought. A tingling, ache-all-over need to mate with someone who's as much a part of you as you, yourself. The willingness to shield that person from the bad opinion of others—even if he's earned it. A gut-deep yearning to heal his every hurt.

With every ounce of willpower she possessed, she kept herself from jumping out of bed, getting dressed and driving over to the hospital to see her handsome, dark-haired husband. They'd probably given him a sleeping pill. And it was the middle of the night.

In the morning Lara got tangled up in traffic. Running late, she hurried to Zack's room without stopping to check on Woody first. Used to seeing Zack up, around and full of vinegar, she was more distressed than she could say to find him wearing a pale blue hospital gown, sedated and in the process of being transferred to a gurney for his trip into the operating room.

What if something goes wrong? she thought. I'd never be able to forgive myself. Impulsively she seized his hand and walked alongside as a pretty female aide pushed him out of his room and down the hall.

Groggy as he was, Zack gave her a wicked grin. "Doin' my best to be faithful," he said, slurring his words a little. "But I'm irresistible, y'know. These nurses . . . can't seem to keep their hands off me . . ."

Lara tried to laugh. But her ambivalence was clear.

"Don't worry, Mrs. Silverheels," the aide soothed as they reached the double swinging doors that led into the operating suite. "We'll take good care of him. He's just a little nervous because this is his first time in a hospital."

Lara hadn't known. Halting the gurney, she bent to kiss Zack's forehead. He winked. "Stay out of trouble. I promise... I will if you will."

Left behind, Lara waited out his procedure in a lounge for the families of surgical patients rather than in Woody's room. Sharp as a tack, the man newspaper articles referred to as a kingmaker in Arizona politics would pick up on her mood, maybe even guess the donation process was under way. He wasn't above using his superb connections to find out who the donor was.

Two hours later Zack was in the recovery room. Still under the lingering influence of a general anesthetic, he was obviously in some pain. Allowed to spend a moment or two beside his bed, Lara longed to put her arms around him. But she didn't want to cause him any additional discomfort.

The following morning, though he was a little stiff and sore, Zack was his usual self. Lara found him in a hospital-issue bathrobe, roaming the halls.

"Are you all right?" she asked worriedly. "When I left last night, you still weren't feeling too well."

Putting one arm around her, he kissed her on the cheek. "Believe it or not," he said, sounding slightly surprised, "I'm a little the worse for wear. But I must be okay. They're letting me out of here this afternoon."

Meanwhile, immediately following its extraction, Zack's bone marrow had been tested for compatibility. As expected, the match was a good one. The transplant process had been given the green light.

Lara wondered what the next step in her relationship with Zack would be. Loving him as she did, she wanted to be with him—live with him in Los Angeles if that's what he wished. But she couldn't leave Woody in the lurch.

"They started Woody's chemotherapy this morning and he's pretty sick," she responded. "Fortunately they gave him something to make him sleep a little while ago."

It seemed bone-marrow transplants could be fairly rugged on the recipient. About to ask if Lara could be ready to leave that afternoon, Zack realized she'd probably want to remain at Woody's side.

Used to thinking only of himself, he was astonished at how protective of her he suddenly felt. Though it wouldn't be easy, he could afford to be magnanimous. He'd fly to L.A., get the meetings he'd postponed off his calendar and come back for her. They'd only be apart for a couple of days.

"Is Woody's room around here?" he asked. "If he's asleep, I'd like to look in on him."

Lara got cold chills at the thought. Was Zack willing to reconcile with his father? She didn't dare to hope too much. His bone marrow was involved. Maybe he was just curious about the process.

"He's upstairs in B wing," she answered. "I'll need to make sure he's sleeping before you go in."

They rode up together in the elevator. Used to seeing her, the nurses on the hematology floor didn't pay much attention when Lara passed the desk with a tall, black-haired man in a bathrobe. He could have been a millionaire, a movie star or a cowboy—maybe all three—and/or an Indian who hailed from one of the nearby reservations. If he was with her, he was fine in their book.

"This is it," she said. "Room 515. Would you mind waiting a moment?"

From the hall Zack could see the IV stand, so full of plastic fluid packs it looked like a Christmas tree. The electronic heart-monitoring equipment, which he'd heard was sometimes necessary because chemotherapy weakened the heart muscle, displayed several rows of jagged green lines. In the middle of everything, prone and gray looking beneath a thin hospital blanket, was a man he knew to be fifty-four—one whom illness had aged to look at least a dozen years older.

Woody.

Lara motioned him to come in.

If Zack thought he'd been assailed by memories at the ranch, seeing Woody brought them back a thousandfold. Woody at the corral, leaning over the bars of the fence watching him. Posing for the picture Zack carried in his billfold. Woody coming to the reservation to claim him after his mother died.

For some reason he didn't want to think of a horsewhip in the gnarled, bony hands that lay so limp on the coverlet. Or remember the harsh words, the mistrust. He didn't feel the anger he'd expected to feel, but rather something close to sympathy. How could life have brought such a proud spirit so low?

Even as he struggled with the urge to reach out and smooth back the thinning, sweaty gray hair, he was pierced with jealousy. Lara loved Woody so much she'd agreed to sacrifice her virginity for his sake—even marry a man she didn't love. I know she wants me, Zack thought. But that's all it is. I haven't earned anything more from her. And I don't know how. He wondered what it would take to deserve that kind of commitment.

Several hours later Lara drove him to the airport. His corporate jet, the *Rainbow Dancer,* was waiting. They kissed on the runway, uncertainty to uncertainty and mouth to mouth.

Just as Zack expected, she'd taken it for granted she'd remain at Woody's side until the worst was over. He couldn't blame her. He even admired her for it. He just wished she cared for him as much.

For her part she wished he wouldn't leave. Unwilling to divulge the depth of her feelings without some assurance they'd be reciprocated, she didn't tell him that.

"See you in a few days," Zack said, kissing her again and letting her go.

Chapter Nine

Thanks to the chemotherapy and radiation that were killing off his faulty immune system, Woody continued to be very sick. Seated beside his bed, unable to do very much but hold his hand and wipe the sweat from his brow, Lara had plenty of time to think. She spent most of it feeling—yearning for Woody to get better and missing Zack. If only they could stop carrying a grudge after twenty years.

Her new husband called her every evening from Los Angeles. Though their conversations were brief, devoted mostly to Woody's progress and Zack's frustration with the problems that were keeping him on the West Coast longer than he'd expected, it felt good just to hear his voice.

I don't know what we have together, she thought as Woody dozed fitfully one bright afternoon. Not the *quid pro quo* arrangement we started out with. And not quite a full-fledged marriage yet. We're still on uncertain ground. She only knew how much she loved him and longed to feel his arms around her again. Sometimes it was hard to believe the sexy stranger who'd approached her at the Burneys' party was really hers.

News of their marriage was getting around. And the reaction wasn't an entirely positive one. While Zack was away in Los Angeles, Lara ran into two women about her age whom she'd played opposite in tennis doubles at the Fairfield Country Club in Flagstaff. The women, who happened to be sisters, were in town to shop. They'd stopped off at the hospital to visit an elderly aunt. The older of the two, whose name was Sharon Ross, hailed Lara in the gift shop when she walked in to buy a candy bar.

"Lara...Lara Stone!" she exclaimed. "It *is* you." There was a slight pause. "I guess I should say Lara Silverheels."

Lara wasn't used to the new name yet. So far only the surgical-wing nurses who'd handled Zack's bone-marrow donation had addressed her that way. And she was highly conscious of the need to keep things from Woody for a while.

"Hello, Sharon...Diane," she said a bit awkwardly. "Um, yes. You're right. Zack and I were married almost a week ago."

The sisters exchanged a look. Sharon's face wore a triumphant "I told you so" expression.

"I understand you were married on the reservation," she said to Lara. "He's half Navajo, isn't he? And your father's natural son? The word is they haven't spoken for years."

Diane, who had a sunnier personality than her sister's, was looking uncomfortable. "Supposedly he's very handsome," she chimed in. "And rich. He used to live at the ranch, didn't he? In my opinion it's very romantic, your meeting again that way."

Lara managed to keep her mounting annoyance at Sharon under control. "The answer's yes," she said smoothly. "To all of the above."

"Well, it certainly was a surprise to everyone." Idly Sharon fingered a rack of hand-crafted earrings. "I must say I thought you and Scott Thackery were a thing. But I guess you never know. How's your father taking it?"

By now, Diane was clearly embarrassed. "Sharon, I don't think..." she began.

Lara patted her arm. "It's okay." She turned to Sharon. "Since you're up on all the latest gossip, I'm sure you know Woody's in the hospital and very sick. We haven't told him yet. And we hope *nobody else will.* Since Zack donated the bone marrow that may save his life, we're keeping our fingers crossed for a reconciliation."

It was the second time that day she'd ascribed sentiments to Zack he almost certainly didn't feel, in essence to defend their relationship. The first had come about during a conversation with Dean Kitanga, Woody's accountant.

"Is it true?" Dean had asked.

"Is *what* true?" Lara had answered, knowing full well what was on his mind.

"That you married Zack Silverheels."

"Yes. A week ago."

Dean's mouth had closed in a firm, disapproving line. Go ahead, Lara had challenged him silently. Say what you think.

"Woody isn't going to be pleased. I hope you know what you're doing," he'd said obligingly.

The opposition had only intensified her loyalty to Zack—and exacerbated her anxiety about how Woody would react. "Zack and I are hoping he and Woody will get back together," she'd said, keeping her tone businesslike and unruffled. "About that monthly report . . . I have one or two questions."

By the end of the week Zack had cleared his calendar sufficiently to leave his California base of operations for twenty-four hours. Throwing a few things into an overnight bag, he ordered the *Rainbow Dancer* readied for takeoff. I won't phone Lara until I get to Phoenix, he thought as he fastened his seat belt. The surprise will add spice to our reunion.

They were already on the runway at their destination, taxiing toward the terminal, when he decided not to go directly to the hospital. Instinct warned that if he did, he'd just be in the way. With Woody so sick, Lara would be distracted. It was better to wait until she had time for him.

In the meantime he wouldn't be at loose ends. Several pressing matters at Club Cochise demanded his attention. He'd go there first and rattle a few cages. Lara had to take a break sometime. Maybe he could talk her into driving out to spend the night with him. He'd like nothing better than to help relieve her weariness and stress.

Beneath the special laminar flow hood at the head of his bed, which was designed to clean the air and keep the likelihood of infection to a minimum, Woody was having a bad afternoon. When the phone rang, Lara was helping him take a sip of water. She didn't answer it right away.

"Hello?" she responded at last, her tone a trifle short.

There was a slight pause.

"It's me," Zack said. "Can you talk?"

She glanced at Woody. His eyes shut and his face gray from nausea, he didn't seem to be paying much attention. "For a minute," she answered. It struck her that Zack didn't make a habit of phoning during the day. Usually he caught up with her at the Wickham, late. "Where are you calling from?" she asked.

"Club Cochise. My office, not the weight-training room." Zack grinned, enjoying a memory with the potential to become a private joke.

He was back in town! A tremor of excitement raced through her. Perverse as always, he'd chosen to inform her of his whereabouts by reminding her how he looked in nothing but his coppery skin.

She didn't *need* reminding. "For how long?"

"Just this evening, I'm afraid. I thought maybe you'd be willing to drive out here."

He wasn't demanding she leave Woody's side and fly back to California with him, just asking that they sleep together—something she very much wanted herself. Knowing how high-handed and difficult he could be, Lara was grateful for his forbearance. Yet she hesitated. Club Cochise was at least forty-five minutes from the hospital. And Woody was running a fever. If it got worse during the night...

"If you say no," Zack added, teasing her in an effort to hide the sudden unsettled feeling that had come over him, "you might find yourself making love to me in a broom closet on the hematology floor."

The mental image of them dodging mops and cleaning supplies as they ravaged each other was both funny and erotic. "Maybe I'd better not," she said with regret. "Things haven't gone terribly well today. Could you... come to the Wickham instead?"

It was Zack's turn to feel some reluctance. For symbolic reasons, perhaps, he'd wanted Lara to come to him. Yet he couldn't deny he was turned on at the prospect of spending the night in her bed.

"All right," he said. "What time?"

"I can probably make it by 7:00 p.m."

It was dark by the time she stepped out of the private elevator that served the Stone family suite. Admitted by the desk clerk per her instructions, Zack was waiting, an enigmatic silhouette by the windows in the unlighted living area. She felt an overwhelming sense of déjà vu.

We're husband and wife, she thought. Yet in some ways, we're strangers.

Zack was wondering if the tentative rapport they'd achieved had disintegrated in his absence. It had been hard to tell on the phone. From where he stood she looked a lot like the young woman who'd first caught his eye: blond, cool, in perfect control. He didn't have an inkling of what she felt.

Maybe she'd thought things over and decided she didn't want to be tied to him. If so, they'd be back to unwilling compliance on her part and an outrageous bargain he wasn't sure he wanted to enforce. With the memory of what they'd shared at Short Mesa still fresh in his mind, the possibility wasn't a very attractive one.

He all but held his breath as Lara stepped out of her shoes and crossed the room, her footfalls silent against the deep pile of the carpet. Seconds later she was in his arms. Her hair silky and perfumed against his cheek, she caressed the powerful muscles of his back and shoulders.

Overwhelmed, Zack was hot in seconds. Gripping her bottom through the soft fabric of her narrow skirt, he positioned her against his arousal. With all the manliness he possessed, he wanted her to feel it, to know how ready for her he was. Simultaneously kissing her mouth from every conceivable angle, he parted her lips with his tongue.

As she had in the brush arbor at Short Mesa, Lara felt her separateness give way. Zack might be dangerous, a risky emotional proposition. But it was too late to count the cost. Forces beyond her control had drawn them together. Those same forces were sweeping her away.

"You'll never know how much I've wanted you," he confessed, removing her jacket and beginning to undo the buttons of her blouse. "Since we were last together, I haven't been able to think of anything else."

Her fingers tangling with his, she tried to help. She ached to feel Zack's body next to hers. On top of hers. Inside it. Each night, as she'd returned to Wickham and her lonely bed, she'd yearned for him to hold her, enter her and burrow deep.

"It's what I've wanted, too..."

The affirmation a husky whisper, she helped him free her arms of the blouse's confining sleeves. Moments later the front clasp of her bra yielded, spilling her breasts into his hands.

To think such pleasures existed in the world! Against her nipples, his thumbs were bold, insistent, and she welcomed them, glorying in the way her rosy peaks stood up in tight buds of ecstasy at his touch. Rank initiate though she was, her body had become greedy beyond belief. She longed to feel Zack's mouth there, and *there*—especially in that other, very private place where his attentions had so shocked and delighted her.

"You, too," she prompted breathlessly. "Shouldn't you take off your clothes?"

Stunned that she would ask, Zack almost lost his head. He had to force himself to take things slow. "You first," he insisted. "I want to stroke those pretty thighs of yours... kiss your stomach..."

Lara's delight at his hunger blazed fierce and free as he tugged her skirt down over her hips and unfastened the garters that held up her stockings. Zack might not love her as she loved him. But it was plain he couldn't get enough of the sweet madness they made together. She thrilled as his lean, tan fingers invaded her panties and began sliding them down her legs.

Removing his shirt and trousers without a single wasted motion, Zack vowed to satisfy an unacted desire. The night he'd brought her home from the Burneys' party, he'd wanted to take her with the city as a backdrop. Now he would. Just thinking about how she'd move beneath him, gathering purchase against the carpet, made him grow heavy with desire.

They were naked except for her lacy garter belt.

"You forgot to take this off," Lara said.

He shook his head. "I like the way it looks on you... especially when you're wearing nothing else."

Holding her, body to body, he kissed her again, his engorged need pressing against her. "Say you'll lie down here with me here at the edge of the world," he urged. "It's where I've wanted to make love to you since the first time we stood here together."

As Zack had imagined it, they burned out of control in each other's arms with the lights of Phoenix sprawled at their feet and the night sky almost within their grasp. Afterward, their longing only partly eased, they made love again in Lara's bed. Slowly. Luxuriously. Working up to the point of no return with little love bites and snippets of suggestive conversation.

For Lara the contrast between Zack's hard male physique and her lace-trimmed sheets was a powerful aphrodisiac. Her second release was the most soul-shattering yet. They fell asleep afterward as if they'd always fitted together, bronze body to ivory in her antique wicker bed.

Unfortunately Zack hadn't been able to do away with a meeting scheduled for the following day involving expansion at Dancing God Retreat. He'd have to get an early start. Opening his eyes before it was light to find Lara snuggled beside him, he toyed with the idea of a last-minute departure that would allow them several more hours in bed.

Reluctantly he decided against it, though he was more than ready to love her again. When she awoke, her first thought would be for Woody. She'd be anxious to get dressed and head for the hospital—find out for herself how his night had gone. Even if she hung around in the sack to please him, he guessed that's what she'd be thinking of.

There'd be other mornings, an unlimited number of them if he had his way. She'd come to him willingly the night before, made him feel like some kind of king or potentate. He didn't want to spoil things. It was better just to leave. Dressing quietly so he wouldn't wake her, Zack rode down in the elevator alone.

At first Woody's infusion of new bone marrow went smoothly enough. Then disaster struck. To Lara's horror, he came down with "graft-versus-host disease," a severe reaction to those few antigens in Zack's marrow that didn't match his. In addition to a lingering feeling of malaise and continued weakness from his chemotherapy, he broke out in a skin rash.

He also developed jaundice and a persistent infection in his lower digestive tract. Massive quantities of antibiotics were administered to counteract it, as his embryonic immune system wouldn't be fully operational for quite a while.

Lara was terrified the graft was failing. Though Dr. Gooding assured her it wasn't—that in the long run Woody's complications might actually prove beneficial by giving his new immunity a workout—she continued to worry.

Since their rendezvous at the Wickham, she hadn't seen Zack for nearly two weeks. Instead of returning to Phoenix as planned, he'd had to fly to Mexico. Now, despite her promise on the phone that she'd join him for a weekend in Los Angeles, she felt she couldn't leave Woody's side.

Zack hadn't returned to home base yet by the time she phoned. She had to leave a message with his secretary.

"Mr. Silverheels probably won't be getting in from Mexico City much before 6:00 p.m.," the woman said. "Since he expects you to be here, once he makes it across town through the rush-hour traffic he'll probably head straight for the apartment without stopping in the office first. I'll put your message there."

Did she detect a note of censure in the woman's pleasant voice? Lara couldn't be sure. She only knew that Woody needed her. Backing out of her promise to Zack was justified. Still, she couldn't help feeling awful for disappointing him. And terribly lonely on her own behalf.

By now she'd ceased to think of her marriage as a form of barter. She loved Zack, after all. Even so, she found herself toying with the idea that she was violating their agreement. She'd promised Zack marriage and that meant living with him. She was cheating him out of his rightful due.

At the airport Zack kept his driver waiting while he bought two dozen yellow roses—the closest he could come to the spun-gold color of Lara's hair. We're going to have a whole weekend together, he thought. No flights to God-knows-where. No phones to answer. No Woody. Just the two of us, making love on the Gray Hills rug by the fire and talking quietly afterward.

In the morning he'd have Giorgio serve them breakfast in bed, then take the rest of the day off so they could roll around uninhibitedly among the crumbs.

The folded sheet of white paper his secretary had brought over was propped on the so-called sleeping shelf above his adobe fireplace. Frowning, he flung his garment bag and the roses on the couch and walked over to pick it up.

The writing was Lynn Gray Owl's, the message Lara's. She wasn't coming. She was very sorry, but Woody needed her. She hoped he understood.

Giorgio had built a fire at Zack's request before leaving for the night. Swearing, Zack crumpled Lara's note and chucked it into the flames. Woody was sick. Woody needed her. It was always Woody. And no doubt it would always be. He, Zack, might be the man she'd married. But Lara's loyalty to his nemesis came first.

His muscles knotting with anger and frustration, Zack fixed himself a Scotch and took a healthy swallow. How could she do this to him when he needed her so much? Restlessly he took to pacing back and forth on the rug where he'd hoped to strengthen his marriage bond.

He didn't want to jump down Lara's throat. And lose her.

Go easy, he cautioned himself. This graft-versus-host thing can't last forever. Besides, you should have known there'd be problems. It was a sure bet Woody wouldn't tolerate your bone marrow easily. You're permanently allergic to each other.

In Zack's opinion, if Woodrow Wilson Stone knew whose marrow had been pumped into him, he'd jump out of his hospital room window.

Making a joke of things didn't seem to help. He wanted her, dammit. *Missed* her. And not just for the sex, utterly gratifying though it was. He wanted to talk to her. Get to know her. Find out what her dreams where. Her ambitions and secret cravings. Since their wedding night, extracting revenge via the former Lara Stone hadn't been a consideration.

Several hours and two drinks later, the fire had been reduced to embers. Conversely, Zack's anger was regaining the upper hand. What if Woody's situation wasn't as serious as she claimed? Maybe she was exaggerating it to avoid spending time with him.

He didn't doubt he pleased Lara when they made love. He knew when a woman was faking. And she definitely wasn't. The helpless way she'd cried out in her rapture the last time they'd been together still echoed in his head.

But she hadn't shown any inclination to have a real marriage with him, the kind that included an everyday life. And it was probably his own fault. He'd forced her into a ceremony so he could bed her without guilt and she'd capitulated for Woody's sake. Now she'd become important to him and he was getting what he deserved.

Well, he might not settle for it! Digging the number she'd given him out of his billfold, Zack phoned the hospital. For once, he'd find out what was going on firsthand.

Since it was after visiting hours, he knew the call would ring through to the nursing station. Identifying himself to the charge nurse as Woody's son-in-law, he asked for a condition report. He felt a little foolish when the woman's answer confirmed Lara hadn't been blowing smoke. The fifty-four-year-old rancher, hotel owner and political kingmaker who'd sired him at seventeen was still on the critical list.

As strong-willed as his son, Woody Stone was a fighter. He'd started to improve by the time the charge nurse mentioned everyone was pulling for him, including his "son-in-law." Puzzled, he asked Lara if she knew what the woman was talking about.

Aware she should tell him the truth, Lara couldn't bring herself to do it yet. She was afraid the emotional trauma might interfere with his recovery.

"I'm sorry, I don't," she prevaricated. "There seems to have been some mistake."

That weekend she was once again scheduled to meet Zack in Los Angeles. Waiting until the afternoon of her departure, she mentioned to Woody she might be gone for a few days. It was obvious the idea upset him.

Typically he didn't try to stop her. "You go ahead, sugar," he said morosely, turning his face away from her on the pillow. "I'll be fine. Just don't stay gone too long."

Torn, Lara considered her options. Woody was better physically. Even Dr. Gooding said so. Maybe all the medication he had to take was making him depressed. Aware his state of mind could affect his progress, she decided she couldn't leave him yet.

Apparently Zack's secretary had gone home early. When Lara phoned his office, the call switched through to the apartment, where it was picked up by Giorgio. She kept her message brief and apologetic.

Plagued by second thoughts, she half expected Zack to call her that night at the Wickham and complain. But the phone didn't ring. He's doing a slow burn, she thought apprehensively. I wonder where it's all going to lead.

She was about to enter Woody's hospital room the following afternoon when a pair of strong hands settled on her shoulders. She jumped a mile. Their grip tightened.

"You're coming back with me...*now,*" Zack said, turning her around to face him.

He was wearing his purple power tie and the charcoal Italian suit she liked so much, along with a white shirt that brought out his bronze complexion. In her view he was the best-looking man on earth. A moment later she realized he was also one of the angriest. His black eyes had gone hard as onyx. And just as cold.

"Wh...what are you doing here?" she stammered, her guilt at putting him off written all over her face.

"Moving you to Los Angeles."

He wasn't just simmering over a ruined weekend. He was demanding she abandon Woody for him. In effect he was reinstating their odious bargain! Glaring up at him, Lara fought ice with fire.

It seemed Zack was impervious to outraged looks. "Tell your father you're going out of town," he said. "That you need a break. Or tell him you've married his bastard son to save him. I don't care which. Just make it snappy. Before we can leave for L.A., we have to drive over to the Wickham and pack your things."

Chapter Ten

Zack asked his chauffeur to accompany them upstairs when they reached the Wickham. With deadpan efficiency the middle-aged Hispanic who was his regular driver in Phoenix helped Lara remove a wide assortment of clothing and personal items from the closets and drawers of her room and stash it in her matching Vuitton luggage. He didn't appear to notice that she and Zack were looking daggers at each other.

Though she was furious at the man she'd married for trashing what might have become a real union someday, ethically she realized he had a point. He'd saved Woody's life and she owed him something. Now he'd get it—provided she could fly home to visit her adoptive father whenever Zack was away on business trips. But that was all. Upset by Zack's high-handedness, she'd decided anything more than minimum compliance was out of the question. She might love him to the extent that she'd never care for anyone else. But she'd cut out her tongue before she told him so.

Needless to say the atmosphere during their flight to California wasn't a very friendly one. Ignoring her, now that she was at his beck and call, Zack sat across the aisle from her, immersed in paperwork. Lara smoldered, refusing to look at him. Instead she propped a pillow beneath her head and stared out the window. Saving Woody had been worth it. She would do it again. Just the same, it didn't make her feel very good to realize that, for the next twelve months, her life wouldn't be her own.

They arrived in Los Angeles without incident. Depositing her bags in Zack's bedroom, his regular chauffeur wished them a polite good afternoon. As soon as they were alone together, Zack pulled her into his arms.

Lara flinched. At the moment she viewed any lovemaking they might share as punishment. "I'm tired," she protested, evading his mouth. "If you don't mind, I'd rather just..."

"Go to bed? I'm all for that."

"I don't want to have sex with you tonight."

Zack's only response was to press his claim. His mouth warm and insistent as he nuzzled her neck, he felt for her bra clasp beneath her lightweight cotton sweater.

He planned to take what was his, with or without her cooperation! To her shame she knew force probably wouldn't enter into it. Just being kissed by him was enough to make her betray herself.

His bed was a shambles by the time they were sated with each other. Feeling thoroughly disgraced by the intensity of her response, Lara lay naked against the rumpled sheets, staring up at the ceiling fan's slow-moving blades. Zack's head was pillowed against her stomach. She lowered her gaze to find him looking directly at her.

Spent passion still lazy in his eyes, he launched a sudden foray against the weakest part of her defenses. "Tell me again that you didn't want to make love tonight and see if I believe you," he taunted, his mockery clearly aimed at both of them.

During the ensuing weeks, their lives fell into an uncomfortable but increasingly familiar pattern: hostility and estrangement alternating with fevered lovemaking. Lara began to believe herself capable of loving and hating the same person. She'd never thought she could be so contrary, so vulnerable, particularly since each coupling was another nail in the coffin of her self-respect.

Her only relief from the almost unbearable tension of their relationship came when Zack had to travel and she could spend a few days at Woody's side. Naturally Woody demanded an explanation for her lengthy absences.

"I'm in love," she confessed reluctantly. "The man I... care for lives on the West Coast. He wants me to be there with him as much as possible. Now that you're feeling so much better..."

Based on the charge nurse's "son-in-law" remark, she steeled herself for a marriage-related question. But Woody didn't make the connection.

"Guess I always knew this would happen someday," he said with a grin, his depression lifting now that he'd begun to believe he was going to make it. "Who's the lucky fella, sugar? Anybody I know?"

Determined to keep the truth from him until he left the hospital, Lara played it cool. "I don't think so," she said, convinced that part of her answer, at least, wasn't far from accurate. "Instead of telling you about him in advance, I'd rather have you meet him in person... as soon as you're allowed to have additional visitors, of course. That way, you can form your own opinion."

She was able to handle most of her responsibilities vis-à-vis Stone Enterprises from the extension phone in Zack's guest room, which she'd adopted as an office. Though Woody seemed pleased about her new relationship, she knew he felt a little left out of her life.

Then one day Zack received the party invitation that would bring matters to a head. Issued by a wealthy conservationist with whom he'd served on several environmental committees, it requested the honor of their presence at a Sunday afternoon reception. The festive occasion, set for a week before Christmas, was to take place at the conservationist's home in Sherman Oaks, a suburb outside of Los Angeles.

They'd just been battling over where Lara would spend the holidays. A muscle quirking alongside his jaw as if he expected her to refuse, Zack asked Lara to accompany him.

Since her arrival in Los Angeles, they'd hardly gone anywhere. On the day of the event, as she chose a sapphire silk dress that buttoned down the front, she thought, it's going to seem strange, decorating Zack's arm in public and pretending we're an ordinary couple instead of sworn adversaries in a war of pride versus the senses.

No one at the party seemed to notice anything was amiss between them. Beginning to enjoy herself after Zack got trapped in a lengthy conversation with several business associates, Lara ran across an old friend from her high school days in Flagstaff. The rangy, attractive blond scion of a wealthy Arizona family was currently living in Marina del Rey. He took great pleasure in telling her about his fiancée and reminiscing about the good old days.

To Zack, who was watching them from across the room, their conversation appeared private and somewhat intense. Already obsessed with Lara's devotion to Woody, he was all too ready to let jealousy of a new rival—particularly a confident, good-looking Anglo—take root.

Abruptly she felt his hand on her arm. "C'mon...we're leaving," he said, his voice tight with displeasure.

"But we've only just arrived!"

Obviously sensing trouble, Lara's friend bid her a hasty farewell. "Nice running into you," he said with a placating nod in Zack's direction. "Give Woody my best. And say hello to everyone."

"How could you be so rude?" she exclaimed when he was out of earshot. "If you'd given me half a chance, I'd have introduced you to Tom Saavedra. He's a former high school classmate of mine. We used to work on the school newspaper together."

Without pausing to say goodbye to their host, Zack hustled her out the door. "Sure that's all you did?" he inquired in a sarcastic tone.

The implication made Lara see red. "What do *you* think?" she asked, almost twisting her ankle in an effort to keep up with him. "You know what the extent of my experience was... better than anyone!"

Steadying her, Zack slowed his pace as they walked the remaining distance to his limousine. But he was still every bit as furious as she was. Maybe Lara's friend hadn't been flirting with her. But she'd definitely been interested in him. She hadn't smiled at Zack like that in weeks.

They barely spoke as he helped her into the limo's back seat. Ordering his driver to take them home via Mulholland Drive, he punched a button to raise the soundproof, smoke-glass window which sealed off the rear compartment. They started arguing immediately, almost without taking a breath.

"You were flirting," he accused, as if stating an unarguable truth.

Lara edged into the far corner of the seat. "No," she insisted. "I just happen to like Tom. He's a very nice guy, with a fiancée he's crazy about. You might have picked up on that under more pleasant circumstances if you didn't have such a suspicious mind."

It was as if she hadn't spoken.

"The terms of our agreement are simple," Zack lectured her, opening the bar compartment in front of him and pouring himself a soda water. "I donated my bone marrow to Woody and you gave me a year. Of *marriage,* not your services as an escort. That means you don't flirt. Or play around."

Having learned to love him for himself and not for what he could do to help Woody, Lara felt deeply insulted. She regarded being compared to an escort as a slap in the face.

"I've more than satisfied our bargain," she shot back. "We've made love on the floor, in the shower, even under the dining room table... whenever and wherever you wanted to. I advise you to stop complaining and take advantage of what you've got because, when your year is up, you're going to lose it!"

Zack's soda splashed on the upholstery as he reached for the chauffeur call button. "Max," he ordered in a voice unlike any she'd heard from him, "pull into the next overlook and take a walk."

Within moments they were making a sharp right and parking at the edge of a turnaround that offered a spectacular view of the surrounding hills. Switching off the engine, the chauffeur got out and lit a cigarette. As they watched, he strolled casually away from the car and sat down on a low stone balustrade.

Like the "curtain" that closed off the back seat, the exterior passenger windows of Zack's pearl-gray Cadillac were made of one-way smoked glass. Its owner gave Lara a slanting look. "We haven't done it in the back seat of the limo yet."

"No. Please..." She vowed she'd never forgive him if he used her that way.

Lara planned to divorce him as soon as her obligation was fulfilled. Boot Woody's unwanted half-breed son out of her life with the ease that she showered off his scent. Her words cutting deep into the essence of who and what he was, Zack reached for her top button.

It came loose and rolled to the floor in her efforts to evade him. "You want me...you know you do," he swore as he parted the blue silk of her dress to reveal her underwear. "And I'm going to make you admit it."

Her resistance intensified as, half-kneeling, he moved between her gartered and stockinged thighs. Opening her bra with little regard for her attempts to stop him, Zack cupped one breast and took its nipple into his mouth.

Abruptly Lara's struggles ceased. In just seconds she was aching to receive him. Desire coursed through her like a lava flow.

Turning his attention to her other breast, Zack looked up at her with hooded eyes. "Say it," he muttered against her flesh. "I won't continue without your permission."

Lara shut her eyes, impaled on the choice she must make. She was quivering all over with her need for him.

Unfastening her garters, he hooked his fingers inside her panties. "Say you want me. Or we stop right here..."

God help her, she couldn't bear it if he did. "You're right," she moaned in a strangled voice, threading her hands through his coarse, dark hair. "I do want you. *Go ahead.*"

Though the bone-deep repose that had followed her first release in Zack's arms was absent, the climax she reached was all encompassing. It was only afterward, when they were making themselves presentable so he could summon their driver that she realized what had taken place. In the heat of the moment, they'd made love without protection.

Wondering if Zack was aware of it, too, she didn't say anything. I don't want to have his child, she thought fiercely. *Do I?* Unbidden, a little flame of longing for that ultimate connection with him curled to life inside her. She doubted anything of the sort would happen, though. Surely the odds were against it.

The moment they returned to the apartment, Lara shut herself in the bathroom and locked the door. Peeling off her ruined dress, she realized to her dismay that she must have left her panties in the limousine. No doubt at some point during the furor of their lovemaking, the scrap of silk and lace had gotten wedged under the seat. By now, Zack's chauffeur had probably found it. The knowledge only added to her humiliation over what they'd done and her strong feeling that she'd had enough.

Getting into the shower, she remained there for almost twenty minutes. If I *am* pregnant, soap and water won't wash it away, she thought. Nor would I really want it to. But maybe it'll help me get rid of the anger and shame I'm directing at myself.

She appeared in the living area a short time later, wrapped in a white terry cloth robe with her damp hair combed back from her face. Zack was lounging on his chocolate-brown leather couch, watching basketball on television. She knew he didn't even care for the game.

After the way he'd acted, he didn't deserve her sympathy. "I need to talk to you," she said.

Obligingly he switched off the sound with the remote control. "All right. I'm listening."

Face to face with him, it was a little more difficult to say what she felt she must. She loved him, dammit. But she couldn't take any more. "After what happened in the car," she announced after a moment. "I don't plan to sleep with you again."

Zack didn't betray how much the edict hurt. Or let her see the extent to which it bothered him that she wanted to wash away every trace of their lovemaking. Like Woody's treatment of him, the latter action made him feel beneath contempt.

"I'm sorry about that," he admitted quietly. "I lost my head. It wasn't until we were putting on our clothes that I realized I hadn't protected you."

Lara's cheeks flushed as if they shared a guilty secret. Did he think that was her only reason for being upset with him? Under the right circumstances, she might have welcomed a slip-up of that sort. What she couldn't tolerate was the element of coercion that seemed to permeate every aspect of their life together.

"I mean it," she insisted, resting one hand on her hip. "What you get from now on is a *year of marriage.* That's all. Not every married couple has sexual relations."

When it was time for bed, Lara made good on her threat, opting to sleep alone in the guest room. Though he was seething inside, Zack didn't object. In the morning he had to fly to Mexico City to sign some papers related to his Rancho Santa Ana resort. She'd be free to visit Woody if she wished.

Maybe when they were both home again things would improve. They'd have a decent holiday. He promised himself he'd soften his demands, stop being so possessive of her. Hell, maybe he'd even court her. Win her over with moonlight and roses. If he gave her enough latitude, maybe she wouldn't want their marriage to end.

Lara made a point of ignoring him at the breakfast table. Stung by her distant air, Zack felt himself slipping back into an angry posture. Ultimately he couldn't curb his acerbic tongue.

"Be back by Christmas," he warned instead of saying goodbye as he walked out the door. "That is, if you don't want me to come after you again."

Not all married couples live under the same roof, either, Lara thought, going over the previous evening's discussion in her mind as she threw several changes of clothes into an overnight case. The urge to make a break for it had been there since Zack had insisted she leave Woody's side and accompany him to California. Now she listened to it. On impulse she decided to pack up everything.

Not only would she spend Christmas with Woody, she'd be with him when he came home from the hospital. Zack can go fly a kite—with someone else, she thought savagely, remembering the idyllic time they'd spent on the Oregon coast. He'd spoiled its magic by walking out on her, just as he'd ruined the wonder of their lovemaking by forcing her to view it as an obligation.

Well on the road to recovery, Woody was delighted to have Lara with him for the holidays. He was positively overjoyed when she told him she was back in Phoenix on a full-time basis.

"I'm sorry your big *ro*-mance didn't work out," he said with an engaging grin from the easy chair beside his hospital bed as she decorated a miniature artificial tree for him. "But selfishly, I'm glad you're back. Maybe next time you can arrange to fall for somebody closer to home."

When she didn't return as scheduled on Christmas Eve, she got the inevitable phone call from Zack at the Wickham. "Mind explaining why you're still in Phoenix?" he asked, his voice dangerously quiet in her ear. "You're supposed to be here in Los Angeles, with me. Is this another attempt to welsh on our agreement?"

Even then she might have relented if he'd told her he loved and needed her. Or that it wasn't just sex and revenge he wanted. But he didn't. Hurting more over the words he didn't say than those he did, she hung up on him.

With only a brief pause to regain her composure, Lara phoned the hotel's front desk to say she wouldn't accept any further calls from Mr. Silverheels. "He's no longer welcome in the penthouse, either," she added in a tone that forbade gossip or questions.

She went to bed that night wondering what direction Zack's anger would take. By now she knew him well enough to guess he wouldn't accept her defection without a fight. Probably he'd stew for a while, then show up at the hospital and try to force her into coming back with him. She expected to have at least a day's respite over Christmas before she had to deal with it.

Christmas Day dawned very cold for Phoenix—thirty-seven degrees. Lara put on her cranberry wool suit and a mock beaver coat with a sprig of holly attached to its lapel to drive over to the hospital. About to stop at the front desk to see if Zack had called again, she decided against it. You deserve a day off from your problems, she thought, heading outside with a pile of foil-wrapped, beribboned presents in her arms. You'll have to deal with them soon enough.

Handsome and urbane-looking in a dark topcoat, suit and leather gloves, Zack took hold of her sleeve the moment she appeared on the sidewalk. The garage attendant had just brought her car around.

"You won't be needing the Mercedes," he said, his breath smoking in the chilly air. "You're coming back to California with me."

He hadn't wasted a moment.

"No," Lara answered, shaking off his grip. "I've made up my mind... that's finished."

Watching them, George McMichael, the Wickham's longtime doorman, intervened. "Would you like me to call security, Miss Stone?" he asked, giving Zack a disapproving look.

Lara didn't answer him right away. She gazed at Zack, too, raising one brow as if to say, "Well?"

In Phoenix, apparently, Lara still used her maiden name. She'd probably never intended to change it. The thought that she'd go so far as to have him arrested or detained by hotel security hit him where it hurt the most.

Something closed in his face. "That won't be necessary," he said after a moment. "I hereby absolve Miss Stone of any further obligation."

A month later Lara had used up most of her tears. Though it was still wounded to a degree, her pride was healing. She'd have been fine—comfortably immersed in her former life—if only she could stop aching for Zack and reliving every moment they'd spent together. Unfortunately it seemed she couldn't. She still loved him with all her heart. Unable to sleep and generally miserable without him, she yearned for the caresses she'd insisted she no longer wanted.

To her surprise he hadn't tried to phone. Or come looking for her again. Heartsick that if she'd taken the risk of communicating her true feelings to him, things might have worked out differently, she was beginning to take him at his word. He really *had* released her from her commitment.

To make matters worse, in contrast to Woody's growing sense of well-being, she was feeling ill. Twice she'd even lost her breakfast. Maybe I ought to see someone for counseling, she thought one morning a week before Woody was due to be released from the hospital. I'm getting positively psychosomatic about this.

A moment later, she was staring at herself in the mirror. You're not sick—in mind *or* body, she realized with dawning certainty. You're going to have Zack's baby!

She'd all but stopped thinking about the possibility. They'd only slipped once. The odds in favor of conception hadn't seemed very great. Awed at the splendor and irony of her situation, Lara stood there hugging herself. She felt as if she were hugging a part of the man she loved.

Several days later an obstetrician confirmed her speculation. She was indeed pregnant—slightly more than a month along. Should I tell Zack? she wondered as she left the doctor's office. Or would he just laugh in my face?

In a way he'd never expected to, Zack had achieved his revenge. He'd impregnated her with their child in much the same manner that Woody had sired him in the back seat of a "broken-down Chevy." The only difference was that Zack had staged his contribution in a limousine.

Unlike Margaret Tsosie, Lara had a marriage license to legitimize the baby she carried. And financial security. But unless she went crawling to Zack and begged him for a reconciliation, the loneliness of her position would greatly resemble his mother's. The news was going to break Woody's heart.

Lara arranged to fly Woody home to the Bar-S in a chartered helicopter with a medic on board. After greeting his assembled ranch hands and other employees, he expressed his strong desire for a nap in his own bed. We have to talk, Lara thought as she tucked him in. This is one secret I can't keep forever. Maybe we'll have an opportunity tonight.

At her request, Hank Suger built a cheerful blaze in the brick fireplace that dominated one end of the living room. After they'd finished supper, she and Woody took their usual places in the plaid wing chairs that stood on either side of the hearth. Regular heart-to-heart talks had been conducted in them since she was a little girl.

Moodily Lara stared into the flames. Now was the time. She wouldn't have a better chance. Still, she hesitated. What would Woody say if she told him she loved the son he despised?

"You wanna tell me about it, gal?"

Startled, she met his faded blue eyes. They were full of love and concern for her.

"I know something's goin' on," he added. "I can read it in your face. It's that fella out on the Coast, ain't it? You're still in love with him."

It was as if Woody had peered into her soul. "Yes . . . yes, I am," she whispered.

"So...what's keepin' you apart? He walk out on you?"

Hot tears pricking her eyelids, she shook her head.

"Then I don't get it, sweetheart."

The tears spilled. "Maybe you would if you knew who he was," she confessed in a little rush. "If you knew he was Zack . . . Zack Silverheels."

Woody's expression froze. "You mean . . . *my* Zack?" he croaked.

There couldn't be two such arrogant, impossibly special men in all the world. "I'm going to have his baby," she said. "He doesn't know."

Still a little weak after his long hospitalization, Woody gripped the arms of his chair. The veins stood out at his temples. "I'll kill that boy for what he's done to you!" he thundered.

Lara longed to rest her head against his knee and weep. "You almost did, once," she responded, slipping out of her chair to sit on a low hassock at his feet. "He walks around like those wounds were fresh."

For the first time Woody's deep remorse for the beating he gave Zack was evident. He shoulders sagged. "If you know how many times I've regretted that . . ." he said, his voice sinking to a whisper.

"Then . . . Zack wasn't guilty of trying to seduce my mother?"

"Who knows what part he played in it? He wouldn't say. But one thing's certain. In light of what happened afterward, she wasn't blameless. I never wanted to have to tell you this, gal, but your mama wasn't the faithful kind."

Stunned, Lara didn't know what to say.

"She was foolin' around with some barroom cowpoke a month after Zack left," he added. "The two of 'em was drunk one night when he smashed up his car with her in it and killed 'em both."

The sweet, good-intentioned mother Lara had tried so hard to create in her imagination had never existed. As for Zack...

"I'd better tell you the whole story," she said.

Haltingly, because the tale was so personal and contained so many elements that would hurt the only parent she'd ever known, she told Woody how she and Zack had met and of her campaign to get him to donate his bone marrow. She didn't leave out the trip to Oregon, or Zack's initial demand that she spend the night in his bed as compensation, though she skipped the erotic details.

Woody's expression ran the gamut of astonishment, outrage and sorrow as she described how Zack had insisted on marriage when he'd learned of her virginity, ultimately settling for a twelve-month arrangement, and told him of the fragile, too-easily shattered rapport they'd achieved.

"From the beginning, his motive was revenge," Lara finished. "He didn't try to hide it. There were times when I thought he might learn to love me someday. But I don't feel that way anymore. Our relationship quickly deteriorated into resistance on my part, obsession and jealousy on Zack's. He wanted me to forsake you for him."

Woody passed one hand over his eyes. "I guess maybe we better call Cal French," he said regretfully, "and have him get started on a divorce."

Lara's refusal was instantaneous. "No... not yet."

Though he didn't put it into so many words, Woody's face held a question.

"I want my baby's parents to be married when he or she is born," she explained. "Besides, I promised Zack a year. I can afford to wait that long."

"Sure you don't want to tell him?"

Lara shook her head. "I'm too proud to settle for his pity. Or be used by him again. But that doesn't stop me from loving him, every bit as much. I suppose that's difficult for you to understand."

"The hell it is." For a moment, Woody's devastation over the way things had turned out was painfully evident. "I *always* loved that boy," he added in a tired voice. "And wanted him with me...even when I told him to get out of my sight."

Chapter Eleven

Lara and Woody returned to the Bar-S from Ulupalakua Ranch on the island of Maui when her son J.J. was two months old. Three days later, on the fifteenth of November, she strapped her beautiful, sweet-natured child into his car seat and placed him in one of the Bar-S pickup trucks for a trip to the reservation. Though J.J. might not have a father to watch over him and help him learn all the things a little boy should know, she was determined he'd get acquainted with his Navajo relatives.

Kissing the baby's rosy cheek and smoothing his silky, dark hair, she recalled the quiet months she and Woody had spent at the somewhat isolated, oceanfront property of friends. As she'd strolled beneath coconut palms and gazed out at pineapple-planted fields, she'd felt an overwhelming gratitude for the tiny, precious being growing inside her. Whatever happened, their child would always connect her to the man she loved.

At the same time she'd been heartbroken that Zack wasn't there to rest his palm against her stomach and feel the flutter of the new life he'd helped create. She prayed she'd never again be as lonely as when she'd given birth without him at her side.

During their lengthy stay on Maui, she and Woody had kept in close touch by phone with the Bar-S crew and the various operations that made up Stone Enterprises, including the Wickham. Zack hadn't written or called, though she was fairly certain the news of her pregnancy had circulated. Apparently it didn't interest him.

She hadn't filed divorce papers and, so far, Zack hadn't, either. Their standoff could go on forever; that was the pattern, after all. His estrangement from Woody was now in its twenty-first year. She had no idea whether there was anything she could do to rectify the situation. Maybe seeing his relatives would provide a clue.

Despite the uncertainty that clouded their future, it was a beautiful winter day—the air cool, the sun bright. Patches of snow were melting in the cedar-and-piñon scrub. After the verdant beauty of the islands, the reservation's dry scrabble earth and rough buttes resembled the surface of the moon. Seeing them again made her feel good inside. Their stark beauty was interwoven with some of her happiest memories.

Buck's ancient pickup was among the half dozen vehicles parked outside the Littlehorse hogan when Lara pulled up in a cloud of dust. She waited a moment, as Navajo manners dictated, and he came out to greet her, gray haired, wise looking, serene.

"Lara," he said. "It's been a long time. We're getting ready for a ceremony...initiation chant. Also a one-night cure."

Fond of the necklace he'd made for her and still appreciative of the good wishes she knew had accompanied it, she smiled up at him. "I've brought someone along to meet you," she said.

She caught a flicker of surprise as Buck looked past her to J.J., who'd just awakened from a nap. "Zack's child," he said after a moment, with certainty and approval in his voice.

"His name's J.J."

"He's beautiful. Come, the others will want to see him, too. Henry and Jimmy haven't left for the arroyo yet."

Lara beamed as Henry and Mary Littlehorse, Zack's cousin Jimmy Tsosie and, to a lesser degree, the other adults present, exclaimed over the baby. Several of the second- and third-graders who would be initiated into the tribe the following day were on hand, too, and they made the biggest fuss of all.

Within minutes Lara's beloved son wore a colorful beaded bracelet on his wrist, the gift of an admiring girl with tightly braided hair and huge, dark eyes. Sociable from birth, J.J. cooed and punched vigorously at the air with his sturdy little legs as he grasped a succession of slim, dusky fingers.

Though Henry was plainly delighted to see them, Lara could tell he was preoccupied with the upcoming ceremony. She guessed Jimmy would be helping him. Meanwhile Mary, Jimmy's wife, Inez, and several women who lived nearby had paused in their preparation of large quantities of food.

"It seems I've come at a fairly busy time," she whispered to Buck. "Maybe we could talk more easily if I came back another day?"

"I'm not involved in any of this, except as a bystander," he answered. "Why don't we pay a visit to my workshop? It's just a short distance from here. We can talk there undisturbed."

Lara and J.J. rode to Buck's bachelor digs in the passenger seat of his ancient Ford. His place was situated about a mile and a half from Henry's, up a weed-choked wash that made for a rough ride. The workshop where her necklace had been fashioned was a small lean-to built of scrap lumber beside a traditional hogan. A wall of mismatched windows let in the northern light.

"Sit," Buck said, indicating a pillow-strewn mattress as he parked his rangy, jean-clad frame on a stool in front of his workbench and picked up one of the tools of his trade.

It was feeding time. Cuddling J.J., Lara offered him her breast. For several minutes, as the baby nursed and Buck frowned over the bracelet he was making, silence reigned.

Finally, "Zack has visited here twice since the two of you were married," Lara's host said, taking the initiative. "Each time he's been alone. He doesn't speak of you. Or his child. Anyone can see he's not happy. Now you're here, without him. It's not seemly."

The concept of seemliness was an old-fashioned one, consistent with what Lara knew of tribal views on harmony and family relations. Though Buck had been very direct, she wasn't offended. On the contrary, she agreed with him. Things just weren't as simple as they might seem.

"Except for one occasion, which didn't go well, Zack hasn't made an effort to contact me since I left Los Angeles," she answered. "Apparently being a father isn't very important to him."

Buck gave her a thoughtful look. "I'm not sure he knows."

The hope that coursed through Lara was short-lived. He *must* know, she thought, if he spends any time in Phoenix.

"It's none of my business," Buck added. "But why did you leave him?" His unspoken message was clear: married people should live together.

She couldn't tell him about the encounter in Zack's limousine. Or the alternating hostility and desire that had formed the unhappy pattern of their life together.

"I love Zack," she confessed reluctantly. "But he never wanted me. He wanted revenge against my father. For him, that's what our marriage was all about."

Again Buck was silent. "I think you're wrong," he said at last. "From what I know of Zack, I'd say he cares a great deal about you. If he didn't, he wouldn't have asked you to speak marriage vows. I think you should get in touch with him."

Lara simply looked at him. She longed to contact Zack—so much that, just since returning from Hawaii, she'd come close to dialing his number a half dozen times. But she wasn't willing to risk dashing her heart against the rocks of his difficult nature again without something more concrete to go on than Buck's hunch that's what she ought to do.

Continuing to concentrate on his work, Buck examined the irregular oval of matrix-veined, greenish turquoise that would be his bracelet's centerpiece. "At least stay over for tomorrow's ceremony," he invited, changing the subject. "I can bunk here, in the shop. You and the baby are welcome to sleep in my hogan. You'll have ample privacy there."

Feeling closer to Zack on the reservation than she had in months, Lara accepted. After she and Buck had talked a while longer, mostly about Zack's childhood, he suggested they return to the Littlehorse encampment for a while. More participants in tomorrow's ceremony would be arriving throughout the afternoon. There might be practice sessions. Besides, she must be hungry. The women would be serving a lunch.

Thanks to him, Lara felt more optimistic about the future, though she couldn't say exactly why. With J.J. snuggled in a warm bunting in his canvas baby carrier, she was soon caught up in the excitement of the upcoming festivities. She didn't notice when Buck got into his pickup and drove off in the direction of the nearest trading post.

In his Los Angeles office Zack was thinking of her. Resting his eyes from the fine-print legalese of an offer to take Club Cochise off his hands for several million more than he'd paid for it, he thought how sorry he was he didn't have a picture of her—just the snapshot he carried in his wallet that had been taken when she was five years old.

But he didn't really need a photograph to remember how she looked. Or how soft and womanly she felt. Without his consciously allowing it to happen, she'd managed to imprint herself on his imagination. As he sleepwalked through the nights and days, his mouth hungered for the taste of hers. His fingertips were barren of delight without her satiny skin to touch. Now and then a whiff of her perfume seemed to hover just out of reach, tantalizing him to discover its source.

For the first time in his life, Zack wanted one woman and one woman only. In the eleven months since Lara had left him, he hadn't had the slightest interest in asking anyone else out to dinner, let alone taking another woman to bed.

If by love they mean you can't sleep at night unless the person who matters most to you in the world is there beside you, then I love her, he admitted to himself. I'd give everything I own just to watch her move. See the sunlight on her hair. Hear her laughter.

There'd been times when he'd thought she might learn to care for him. Now he was convinced they'd been moments of self-delusion. Any affection he'd imagined on her part had been little more than a mirage based on the physical response his experience had wrung from her.

To make matters worse, he couldn't kid himself—he'd been largely to blame for losing her. By now, though his "year" would have been up, they might still have been living together as man and wife if he hadn't done everything possible to drive her from his door.

Whenever he thought about his behavior at the party in Sherman Oaks and his performance in the limo afterward, he yearned to put his fist through a wall. Lara wasn't Lily and she hadn't deserved to be treated that way. She'd never given him cause for jealousy. Or been the sort to sleep around. He'd learned that the night she'd offered up her virginity for Woody's sake.

He thought now that his lack of trust in her had probably originated somewhere inside himself. In retrospect it seemed likely his conflict with Woody had left him with a deep-seated feeling of rejection, one all the success and money in the world couldn't eradicate. When Woody had accused him of disloyalty and tossed him out on his ear, he'd begun to expect everyone to treat him that way.

It wouldn't do to chafe too vigorously at the wounds he'd sustained so many years ago—not without the balm he needed to heal them close at hand. I wonder if Lara's returned from Hawaii yet, he thought, leaning back in his chair and shutting his eyes. Or if she plans to stay there until we're both old and gray.

After the triumph of buying Club Cochise out from under the father who'd made him feel like such an outcast, he hadn't set foot on the property in months. Instead he'd installed a particularly competent manager to keep an eye on things for him.

At first he'd thought he might run into Lara if he visited Phoenix, and decided it would hurt too much. Later, when someone had mentioned Woody was recuperating on far-off Maui and she was with him, he still hadn't been able to make himself go near the place. The memories that lingered there—in the massage room, the *casita* where he slept when he was on the premises, even his office—had too much potential to cut him to the quick.

Maybe I should sell, get out of Arizona altogether and turn my face in a new direction, Zack thought. But he knew he couldn't make himself do that, either, for the same reason he couldn't spend time there. With regard to Club Cochise, his feelings for Lara had left him in a permanently ambivalent state.

Just then the phone rang, disturbing his reverie. It was his secretary, Lynn Gray Owl. "Your cousin Buck's on the line," she announced.

The lean, gray-haired silversmith who was twelve years Zack's senior had functioned as a sort of guide figure during his boyhood. Since he didn't have a phone, he hardly ever called.

Zack punched the lighted button on his console. "Buck... this is an unexpected pleasure," he began.

"Listen, don't talk," his cousin replied. "There's something on the reservation I think you should see. I suggest you get your butt out here. Now."

Buck didn't issue marching orders for no reason and Zack knew it. Without the slightest hesitation, he canceled his remaining appointments and phoned the hangar where the *Rainbow Dancer* was kept. With a private jet at his disposal, he was able to leave Los Angeles without delay.

Unfortunately the isolated area of the reservation where his relatives lived was a fair distance from the nearest airstrip. He had to land near Winslow and rent a car. It was going on 4:00 p.m. by the time he parked beside the motley collection of cars and trucks that had gathered near Henry's hogan. Apparently there was going to be a ceremony of some sort.

About to go looking for Buck, Zack paused, his heart in his throat. One of the pickups bore a Bar-S insignia. Could it be that *Lara* was there? Or was he becoming an emotional basket case? Distinctly light-headed in his eagerness to find out, he approached.

He hadn't really expected to find her inside. But there she was, sitting in the passenger seat. Beneath the open Serpa jacket she wore, her blouse was hitched up so she could nurse an infant at her breast. The contrast between her white bosom and the child's silky dark hair, together with the astonishment and vulnerability in her eyes, shook Zack to his foundation. He felt as if a freight train had slammed into his gut.

"Lara," he entreated hoarsely, gripping the door handle.

"Get in," she whispered.

He complied, sliding behind the steering wheel. They looked at each other, neither of them quite believing they were actually face to face.

She was so beautiful. So precious. Incredibly, she'd had his baby!

Zack didn't doubt for a moment that the child was his, though it could have been conceived on only one occasion. Everything proclaimed it. The baby's age and coloring established paternity beyond question. But the wellspring of Zack's certainty went far deeper than that. During the long, lonely time they'd been apart, he'd learned to trust Lara. This is my *wife,* he thought dazedly, close to tears. My *child.* God, how I love them so.

Like him, Lara was ready to weep. For once, the depth of what Zack was feeling was visible on his face. Though she couldn't interpret everything that was written there, she realized her pregnancy and their baby's birth had come as a complete surprise to him. He hadn't deliberately turned his back on her in her hour of need.

So like his, the baby's dark eyes fluttered open. Staring placidly at his father, he continued to nurse. Wonderingly Zack reached out to smooth his cheek. As he did, his fingers brushed against Lara's fullness. The thrill of having him touch her again was almost too much to bear.

"J.J., meet your daddy," she said, radiating the profound love she felt for them both. "Zack, this is our little boy."

He had a son. A single tear spilled and Zack dabbed at it awkwardly with the back of his hand. "Come home to me," he begged. "I need you. And our baby."

She didn't answer and he suppressed a little wave of panic. Had he found her again, found this miracle only to lose her?

"I love you," he added urgently, the edifice of his pride crumbling almost without his knowing it. "I think I've always loved you, from the moment you walked into that party, so calm and perfect and self-confident, as if you owned the place. I don't ask that you return my feelings... just that you give me another chance."

He loved her! It was what Lara had been longing to hear. "Oh, Zack," she exclaimed, gripping his hand and squeezing it until her knuckles went white though she knew their problems weren't solved by any means. "Don't you know I love you, too?"

Undeserving though he was, he'd been handed the moon. The stars. Most especially the earth. Yet she hadn't agreed to be his wife again.

Zack knew why. The problem of Woody still stood in the way. To him it looked insurmountable. We have to talk, he thought. Come to some sort of compromise. Yet, he'd learned. Oh, how he'd learned. He knew better than to insist they hash things out right away. First they needed to bond, to touch. With a little shudder at how lucky he was to be granted that privilege, he drew Lara and J.J. into his arms.

Zack loved her. He wanted her and their baby. Feathering a sigh of contentment against his throat, Lara nestled closer. What heaven it was to luxuriate in his warmth again. Inhale his crisp, clean man-scent. Feel his heart beating. Miles from nowhere, in a pickup truck on the reservation as dusk fell over the distant buttes, she was exactly where she belonged.

For quite a while Zack was too choked up to do anything more than rest his cheek against her hair as their baby continued to suckle contentedly. "Tell me his name again," he said at last.

Her mouth curved. "We call him J.J. I wanted to name him after you...and Woody. But Zachary Woodrow seemed a bit much to hang on such a little guy. So I gave him a name all his own...John Jesse Silverheels."

That night, Lara, Zack and their son joined the circle of families camped near Henry's hogan around a piñon fire for a communal meal of mutton stew and corn bread. Their shoulders touching and their hands meeting occasionally over the precious bundle of their son, who was sleeping peacefully in his mother's lap, they both knew they had difficulties to face. Neither wanted to disturb the wonder of being together again by doing it—at least not yet.

The firelight flickering over his aristocratic, generously sculpted features, Buck looked on with obvious satisfaction. "You're staying the night in my hogan, too," he told Zack, not making a question of it.

Zack looked at Lara. "If she'll have me."

Traditionally Navajos frowned on public gestures of affection. Knowing that, Lara didn't reach across their sleeping child to kiss him on the mouth. "Of course I will," she replied.

When it was time for bed, Zack drove them up the wash in the Bar-S pickup, leaving the rental car at Henry's place. The interior of Buck's hogan, which had no openings except for a door and a smoke-hole in the roof, was very dark. Inevitably the night was turning cold.

While Lara fed their son and settled him in a nest of blankets she'd brought from the ranch, Zack built a fire. Its warmth pushed back the chill as it illuminated rough walls that were unadorned except for some clothing and a few simple cooking utensils hung from pegs.

I'd be content to live right here forever with Zack as my mate, Lara thought. I wouldn't need fancy cars or penthouse apartments to be afloat on a sea of happiness. But she did need a cohesive family.

Lying down on Buck's blanket-covered mattress fully clothed, she held out her arms.

Zack came into them, pausing to pull a ragged quilt and several blankets over them. "Do you want to talk now?" he asked. "Or shall we just hold each other?"

Chapter Twelve

Lara didn't fool herself that dealing with the issue of Woody would be easy, even though she and Zack had admitted their love for each other. She knew that coupled with what he almost certainly viewed as his mother's abandonment, Zack's hurt over being turned out to fend for himself at the age of seventeen went deep. She also realized Woody hadn't been blameless. Yet stubbornly she wanted it all: husband, child and that child's grandfather in the same family circle. Redemption and harmony among the generations.

She wasn't sure Zack could handle that. Despite his feelings for her, it might prove too difficult. "I suppose we could talk a little," she said.

Zack planted a little kiss on her forehead. He still had trouble believing they were together again. As for being the parents of a two-month-old baby...

"In that case, I'd like to apologize for my behavior toward you in the limo," he replied. "No...please. I insist. Since I found out about J.J. this afternoon, I've felt even worse about the way I acted. Never in a million years would I have wanted our precious child to be conceived in anger..."

Lara felt so sheltered, so secure. Maybe everything *would* work out. "He seems pretty satisfied with life to me," she answered. "I don't think he minds."

"Maybe not. But I do. I want you to know...my anger wasn't really directed at you...more at the prospect of losing you."

With a pang of remorse, she remembered taunting him with the promise that she'd be gone the moment his year was up. "The explosion between us was as much my fault as yours," she confessed. "I was angry, too, over the way we left the party."

Zack's arms tightened possessively around her. "Seeing you with that guy made me jealous."

"I've never been able to figure that out. What on earth made you think I'd be interested in Tom Saavedra when I had *you?*"

She could feel his faint shrug, though she couldn't see it in the uneven light. "I don't know...the way you were smiling at him, I guess. Or the fact that he was a good-looking Anglo, not some half-breed born out of wedlock."

For the first time Zack was letting her see the battle scars that etched his soul. Though she understood and sympathized with his hurt and rejection, it boggled her mind that such a confident man should ever feel second best where women were concerned. With his looks and build, the strong sex appeal he exuded, he'd been catnip since he was a teenager.

"You're crazy!" she replied. "Don't you know you're everything a woman could want? Smart, successful, gorgeous . . . *and* a fabulous lover, though of course I don't have any point of reference. As for your Navajo heritage, you know as well as I do that it adds a great deal to your special resonance."

If I don't watch out, tears are going to become a habit with me, Zack thought as he luxuriated in the perfumed texture of her hair. He was still bowled over that she could care for him the way she did. No doubt he'd played the outcast role too long. Though a lot of people would have characterized him as proud, the wry, self-deprecating stance he'd adopted as part of that role had become an integral part of the way he thought.

He just hoped his inner man wasn't waiting for Woody to sanction his self-worth in order to be happy. In his opinion the needed blessing would be a long time in coming. He was more thankful than he could say that Lara didn't feel the need for Woody's approval. If she had, she wouldn't be snuggled in his arms at that very moment.

Without having to be told, Zack knew she wanted him and Woody to get back together. Regrettably, from his perspective, the chances of that happening were slim. He wasn't sure yet what he was willing to do about improving them.

"Concerning Woody," she said, as if their renewed closeness included the lightning-quick transfer of thoughts, "Almost from the beginning I've understood you didn't do the terrible things he accused you of. I'm pretty sure he guesses that, too, though he might not be ready to say so. He admitted to me last year that my mother was a tramp. According to him, she was chasing after another man before you'd been gone a month."

So she knows, Zack thought. Even before Woody told her about Lily, she gave me credit without my having to ask. "I didn't want to tell you about that," he answered.

"But it doesn't seem to make much difference anymore. Simply put, Lily propositioned me and I refused her. I have a feeling that when she went to Woody with her story, she wanted to make me pay for what she considered her humiliation."

"Why didn't you tell Woody your side of things?"

There was a long silence. "Two reasons," Zack said at last. "First, I thought he should trust me. I was his son, after all. And, though I hated him sometimes, I'd never have done anything like that to him."

Lara cuddled closer, hungry for his touch. "What was the other?" she asked.

Zack hesitated. "I'm not sure I feel comfortable telling you. But, hell, we've taken it this far. I might as well. At the time Lily went after me, I was just a young buck, crazy for anything in skirts. Your mother was quite a dish and I lusted after her, as they say, though I wouldn't have dreamed of actually touching her. I suppose I felt guilty for my lecherous thoughts... as if I deserved some of the beating I received."

Lara didn't say anything for a moment, and Zack began to worry his frankness had been misunderstood. "She couldn't hold a candle to you," he added hastily. "And that's a fact."

With a little surge of fondness that he should feel the need to placate her, Lara pulled his chin down to hers and kissed him on the mouth.

She hadn't misunderstood at all. Zack wanted to shout for joy. Or better yet, make love to her. But he realized sex hadn't solved anything in the past. This time he'd take things slow. Give her all the gentling she deserved.

"There's really only one problem we have to face, isn't there?" he asked, deciding to meet it head-on.

Lara sighed. "Of course, you're right."

"And that's Woody."

He could feel her agreement in his bones.

"Now that J.J.'s in the picture," she said after a moment, "I want us to be a family in the larger sense of the word. And Woody's our baby's grandfather no matter how you look at it. I feel very strongly that he should be a part of our lives."

Zack didn't comment, and they were silent for quite some time as the fire burned lower, filling the hogan with its distinctive piñon odor, and J.J. made faint baby sounds in his sleep. Zack thought Lara had fallen asleep, too. But she hadn't.

"This afternoon I could tell right away you had no idea of J.J.'s existence," she said, stirring against him. "I just don't understand how you managed to stay in the dark so long. Lots of people in Phoenix knew."

He didn't ask why she hadn't seen fit to come to him with the news. It was enough that they were together again. "I haven't been to Phoenix for almost a year," he replied.

"But Club Cochise..."

"I have somebody managing it for me. Thanks to all the memories you left behind, I couldn't make myself go there. I hope you realize...if I'd known about your pregnancy, there wouldn't have been any stopping me. I'd have come after you wherever you chose to take refuge, whether it had been Hawaii or the mountains of the moon."

When Lara awoke the next morning to her son's hungry whimpering, Zack was gone. For a moment she panicked. Then, calming herself, she picked up the baby and unbuttoned her blouse. Zack could be absent for a number of reasons. He could have gone down to the Littlehorse encampment to talk with Henry, for example. Or he could have decided the prospect of reconciling with Woody was just too much for him and started back to California without them.

There was a third possibility she almost didn't dare think about. He could be on his way to the Bar-S. When she emerged from the hogan a short time later with the baby in her arms, Buck was waiting for her, his tall frame propped against the side of his pickup truck.

"Zack asked me to take you down to Henry's place this morning," the gray-haired silversmith told her. "He said to tell you he'd be back in a while."

As they started down the wash toward Henry's hogan, Zack was parking his rental car next to Hank Suger's dusty pickup by the Bar-S corral. "Is Woody around?" he asked the foreman pleasantly.

Hank stared at him in astonishment, then pointed toward the house without a word.

Less than a minute later it was Woody's turn to stare as Zack walked into his pine-paneled study without knocking. The tall, broad-shouldered man in faded denim with coppery skin and coal-black hair, Woody's own arrogant nose and mouth, could be only one person—the boy he'd ostracized so many years before.

"Son..." he croaked, starting to get up from the comfortable lounger where he always sat to read the morning papers.

Zack waved him back to his seat. "I don't know what the state of your health is these days," he said, carefully avoiding any particular form of address. "Just that Lara will have my hide if I do anything to upset it. Do you think we can talk without that happening?"

Momentarily Woody shut his eyes. "God, I hope so," he answered, "after all these years."

Though he felt awkward and tense, on the verge of changing his mind, Zack took a chair.

"I can't begin to thank you for what you did," Woody began. "Lara told me..."

Zack shook his head. "No thanks are necessary. You gave me life. And I returned the favor...for a price. We're quits. Whatever your feelings about me, or mine about you, I propose we put them aside for Lara's and J.J.'s sake.

"The circumstances of my marriage to her don't make me proud. But it seems we grew to love each other in spite of them. I want to make a home for her and our baby now. She wants you to feel welcome there."

It was as close to a plea for understanding as he could bring himself to make.

Shakily Woody lifted a hand and then let it fall. "Don't you have some questions?" he asked. "Back when you were livin' here, there used to be a bunch of 'em in your eyes."

Zack was astonished his father had observed him as closely as that. In his opinion he'd been brought to the Bar-S in an attempt on Woody's part to ease his conscience. And promptly ignored.

"Sure I've got some," he said, a touch of the old asperity creeping into his tone. "Like why you didn't marry my mother when I was on the way. And what made you bring your half-breed brat here to live after she died."

A look of pain crossed Woody's face. "Not why did I whip you like that without askin' for your side of things? Or fail to come after you, once my temper had a chance to cool?"

Zack swallowed, aware his uncaring facade was about to crack. He nodded, half afraid of what he might hear. It seemed that, weakened though he was by all the illness he'd endured, Woody still had the power to hurt him.

"Okay. I'll tell you." For a moment Woody's faded blue eyes seemed to be staring into the past. Then, "Your grandpa, my daddy, was a heller, just like me," he related. "When I got your ma in trouble, I was just a kid myself. And I got a far worse beating than any I ever laid on your back. Double, after I told him I wanted to marry her."

Zack was astounded. But he had to admit the older man's words had the ring of truth.

"As for bringin' you here, it was because I loved you, dammit. Not that I didn't envy you your good looks. Or wish you wasn't so all-fired good at everything you did. When you were fifteen, I was only thirty-two...in the prime of manhood, or so I thought. You came along and showed me up. With horses. And women. Damn near everything you touched.

"Two years later I got married for the first time. I was crazy over my new wife, and when she took a shine to you my pride was hurt. I looked the other way. As for why I didn't come after you? That was pride, too, I guess. I was sorry as hell about what I did. I *wanted* to go after you, but my pride wouldn't let me."

It was the apology Zack had been waiting twenty-one years to hear. "Pride be damned," he said, on impulse holding out his hand. "I've choked on mine too long."

Tears streaming down his leathery face, Woody took it. The two men gripped each other tightly, in an embrace of kinship.

"Lara's out on the reservation with my other family," Zack suggested after a bit, retreating to the safety of words. "If you're feeling up to it, what do you say we pile into my car and take a little ride?"

Woody grinned. "Let's do it. With your bone marrow in me, boy, I feel like a million bucks!"

Lara was toting J.J. in his canvas carrier, watching Henry and Jimmy put several young dancers through a last-minute rehearsal when Zack returned. At first she didn't see his rental car churning up dust in the parking area.

When she spotted it, she started forward only to stop dead in her tracks. Incredibly Zack was extending his hand to Woody and helping him out of the passenger seat. It seemed Emma Tarbush had come along for the ride.

The housekeeper was beaming. "Well watcha waitin' for, Miss Lara?" she demanded tartly, her hands on her hips. "If I was you, I'd take charge of these good-lookin' men before some other woman gets her hooks into them."

With a little whoop of joy, Lara ran to Zack and flung her arms around his neck. "I never dreamed you'd pull off anything so marvelous!" she cried. "Oh, I do love you so!"

In response, Zack kissed her full on the mouth. Traditional Navajo reticence notwithstanding, he took his time about it, as if to stake his claim for everyone to see.

"Wedding present," he said with a grin, letting her go. "Admittedly a little late. Don't expect this kind of service every day."

Lara embraced Woody next. His gaunt features wreathed in smiles, he returned her hug with interest. Reminiscence, fraught with nostalgia instead of regret, was the order of the day as they hung out, waiting for the pageantry to start.

Coming over to greet Woody and Emma, Henry prevailed on Zack to demonstrate for the beginning dancers how a particular step was done. With a little shrug of modesty, Zack complied. Though it had been a long time since he'd danced at any of the ceremonials, his finesse and natural grace were exceptional.

Watching him, Lara glowed with pride. When J.J. grows up, will he surpass his father the way Zack surpassed Woody? she wondered. Her mouth curving, she doubted it. Even her precious child couldn't do the impossible. She felt profoundly blessed as she imagined *two* such men alive in the world, both of whom belonged to her.

"That step...it's part of the *Yei,* who are sometimes represented as rainbow dancers," Buck explained. "In my opinion Zack has always performed it best. He was so good, even as a child, that 'Dancer' became one of his nicknames."

Lara glanced at him in sudden understanding. "Then..."

"You're right...that's where he got the name for his company."

Woody decided not to go up to the arroyo chosen as the site for the initiation ceremony. And it was probably best. According to Henry the journey of a few miles was exceptionally rough. Opting to stay at the Littlehorse encampment with him, Emma offered to babysit J.J. so Lara could accompany Zack. They drove up with Buck and stood holding hands as they watched two masked male dancers, costumed to impersonate the god and goddess Hastse-yalti and Hastse-baad, administer sacred meal and simulated strokes of a yucca whip to the initiates.

The curing ceremony, commissioned by a man afflicted with abdominal troubles, was to be held that night around a large bonfire. All afternoon the men and children gathered wood and gradually the pile became enormous. Once dusk had set in and the evening meal was finished, everyone gathered around it in a circle, with the patient taking his prescribed place.

Suddenly, masked and costumed musicians appeared, playing a variety of primitive, odd-sounding instruments. With a *whoosh,* one of them ignited the huge mound of sticks and dry branches. Flames shot up, casting an eerie orange glow over everything.

Although weary from such a full day, Woody stayed on for some of the dances. Watching them with obvious interest, he seemed right at home with his son's Navajo relatives. The half-breed issue, apparently, had never been one for him.

Lara thought of the one-eighth or one-sixteenth Navajo blood Woody possessed. Dr. Gooding had said it might have helped save him. She'd have to remember to tell Zack about it.

At last Woody admitted all the activity had been a little wearing. Putting their heads together, Zack and Emma agreed she would drive Woody back to the Bar-S in Zack's rental car.

"If you don't mind... Lara, J.J. and I will spend another night at Buck's place and bring the truck back in the morning," Zack said.

"No problem," Emma replied. "I'd take the baby, too, but I expect he'd rather stay close to his next meal."

Lara knew they wouldn't remain at the bonfire site very long after Emma and Woody drove away. Though they hadn't spoken of it, every touch, every glance they'd exchanged had conveyed the message that, like her, Zack was keenly aware the only barrier to their renewed intimacy had fallen. A young boy with chalky, artificially whitened skin was about to perform what Zack called the yucca trick, when they looked at each other, the same thought visible on both their faces.

"Let's go," Zack said.

The bonfire was a distant glow against the night sky a short time later as he led her into the dark interior of Buck's hogan. Quickly and efficiently he built a fire while she fed their son. As overextended as Woody, J.J. fell asleep at her breast. His nest of blankets was waiting. Lara kissed him and tucked him in as Zack started to remove his shirt.

Facing him so there could be no doubt about how much she wanted him, Lara did the same. That morning she hadn't bothered with a bra, and her breasts swung free, larger and more lush than Zack remembered.

He could feel himself grow heavy with desire. "You're so beautiful," he said hoarsely, his eyes devouring her white skin and rosy nipples. "Even more of a woman. When I watch you nurse J.J., and think I helped make him..."

It was the age-old mystery, but new to them.

"I want to see you, too," Lara prompted, unzipping her jeans.

His proud, firmly chiseled features betraying the passion he felt, Zack finished undressing in the firelight. Naked, the exquisitely made body that had so disturbed and excited Lara when she'd seen him on the massage table at Club Cochise gleamed like polished redwood. She wanted to kiss him everywhere.

"Zack...make love to me," she begged.

Briefly his old confusion about good women and sexy ones got in the way. "After seeing you with the baby, I'm almost afraid to touch you," he admitted. "You're like some kind of Madonna to me."

almost afraid to touch you," he admitted. "You're like some kind of Madonna to me."

"Oh, please . . . don't put me on that pedestal!"

Seconds later, she was in his arms, her fullness crushed against his chest, her hands kneading the strong muscles of his shoulders. She could feel his need, abruptly big and ready for her, against her thigh.

Zack awakened from clouded perception as if from a dream. This was Lara—the mother of his son and his sweet wife. The loving, appreciative companion of his bed. Thanks to Buck and the beneficence of the universe, they'd have a lifetime to pleasure each other.

With their baby fast asleep beside them and the *hu-hu-hu* chant of the curing ceremony a faint echo on the wind, Zack and Lara set Buck's small, sparsely furnished hogan ablaze with their lovemaking. As if the thin mattress on which they rolled with abandon in each others' arms were some kind of crucible, they forged a bond so strong that, this time, nothing could break it.

Afterward, as Lara drifted peacefully back to earth, Zack unveiled a plan.

"I was thinking about it this afternoon, while we were at the initiation, and I'd like to get your opinion," he said softly, nipping at her ear. "I don't want to give up the Los Angeles office because it's handy for business purposes. But I think we need a new home base, closer to the reservation and the Bar-S...one with corrals and a barn where a little boy can ride his pony to his heart's content."

At the thought that Zack would place J.J. in the saddle for the first time, just as he'd placed her there so many years earlier, Lara felt as if her heart would burst with pride and love. How lucky she was that when she'd grown up and become a woman, Zack had been waiting for her.

"What about a little girl?" she asked, importuning his much-loved mouth with several blunt and tender kisses. "Girls like ponies, too. When J.J. reaches his second birthday, I want you to make me another baby."

* * * * *

WORD SEARCH CONTEST

You can win a year's supply of Silhouette romances ABSOLUTELY FREE! All you have to do is complete the word puzzle below and send it to us so we receive it by April 30, 1992. The first 10 properly completed entries chosen by random draw will win a year's supply of Silhouette romances (four books every month, two from the Special Edition® and two from the Intimate Moments® series—worth over $160.00). What could be easier?

K	L	E	B	R	O	K	N	E	E	L	H	T	A	K	M	C	E
V	A	R	P	V	A	E	D	F	G	E	L	S	F	O	R	M	G
R	N	O	O	S	I	R	E	M	L	A	P	A	N	A	I	D	S
O	O	X	M	G	R	V	F	S	E	O	N	S	E	L	T	I	T
M	C	J	P	R	Y	E	E	D	O	V	B	Y	I	J	A	O	N
A	E	B	A	D	T	G	V	W	I	G	O	E	C	S	R	O	E
N	D	T	Q	M	A	N	P	O	L	F	R	L	E	T	A	F	M
C	R	G	T	P	N	I	V	L	C	I	U	R	A	R	I	N	O
E	A	E	R	E	T	N	R	U	C	Q	I	U	W	E	N	Y	M
K	W	Z	E	G	U	W	A	H	L	S	H	H	D	B	V	W	E
F	O	L	N	T	E	O	A	K	E	L	P	O	R	O	I	L	T
Z	H	G	I	D	U	R	H	D	O	A	N	E	P	R	L	V	A
B	A	O	P	A	D	B	C	L	O	G	B	H	O	A	L	I	M
E	D	N	S	S	V	E	T	Y	I	M	A	T	X	R	E	D	I
A	N	F	A	E	Z	I	W	X	A	S	L	E	E	O	C	A	T
Y	I	U	S	N	A	X	E	T	L	L	A	T	G	N	O	L	N
S	L	E	K	D	F	I	U	R	M	J	E	A	N	L	H	O	I
W	N	O	I	T	I	D	E	L	A	I	C	E	P	S	E	D	F

LOVE
NORA ROBERTS
COVERS
SILHOUETTE
DIXIE BROWNING
ROMANCE
LINDA HOWARD
TITLES
ANN MAJOR
THE O'HURLEYS
RITA RAINVILLE
INTIMATE MOMENTS
SPINE
SPECIAL EDITION
EMILIE RICHARDS
DESIRE
PAGES
LONG TALL TEXANS
DIANA PALMER
KATHLEEN KORBEL

S2MAR1

Please turn over for entry details

HOW TO ENTER

All the words listed are hidden in the word puzzle grid. You can find them by reading the letters forward, backward, up and down, or diagonally. When you find a word, circle it or put a line through it. Don't forget to fill in your name and address in the space provided, put this page in an envelope, and mail it today to:

Silhouette Word Puzzle Contest
Silhouette Reader Service™
P.O. Box 9071
Buffalo, NY 14269-9071

NAME ______________________________

ADDRESS ______________________________

____

CITY ______________ STATE ______________ ZIP CODE ______________

Rules

1. All eligible contest entries must be recieved by April 30, 1992.
2. Ten (10) winners will be selected from properly completed entries in a random drawing from all entries on or about July 1, 1992. Odds of winning are dependent upon the number of entries received. Winners will be notified by mail. Decisions of the judges are final. Winners consent to the use of their name, photograph or likeness for advertising and publicity in conjunction with this and similar promotions without additional compensation.
3. Winners will receive four (4) Silhouette romance novels (two (2) from the Special Edition® and two (2) from the Intimate Moments® series) per month for one (1) year, with a total retail value of $162.72.
4. Open to all residents of the U.S., 18 years or older, except employees and families of Torstar Corporation, its affiliates and subsidiaries.

S2MAR2

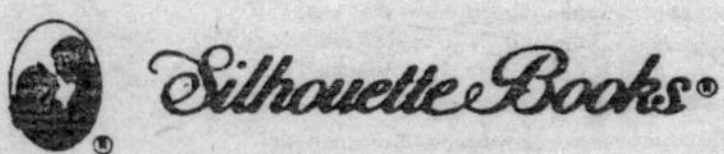
Silhouette Books